Secrets and Lies

A JAMESTOWN NOVEL

SECRETS AND LIES

MARILYN J. CLAY

FIVE STAR
A part of Gale, Cengage Learning

GALE
CENGAGE Learning®

Detroit • New York • San Francisco • New Haven, Conn • Waterville, Maine • London

GALE
CENGAGE Learning

Five Star Publishing, a part of Gale, Cengage Learning.

Set in 11 pt. Plantin.

LIBRARY OF CONGRESS CATALOGING-IN-PUBLICATION DATA

Clay, Marilyn.
Secrets and lies : a Jamestown novel / Marilyn J. Clay. — 1st ed.
p. cm.
Includes bibliographical references.
ISBN 978-1-4328-2583-6 (hardcover) — ISBN 1-4328-2583-6 (hardcover) 1. Virginia—History—Colonial period, ca. 1600-1775—Fiction. 2. Jamestown (Va.)—History—17th century—Fiction. I. Title.
PS3603.L3877S43 2012
813'.6—dc23 2011049913

First Edition. First Printing: May 2012.
Published in 2012 in conjunction with Tekno Books and Ed Gorman.

Printed in Mexico
1 2 3 4 5 6 7 16 15 14 13 12

PREFACE

History tells us that ships carrying young ladies meant to become wives to men who had already settled in the New World colony of Jamestown, Virginia, sailed from England around 1619—1620. In January 1620, Sir Edwin Sandys of the New Virginia Company in London commissioned images from a woodcut to be printed onto large pieces of paper called broadsheets. The margins surrounding the bold lettering were to be illustrated with drawings of thatched-roofed cottages with thriving gardens depicting vegetables and colorful flowers. Also shown were sturdy Englishmen and dark-skinned men and women wearing buckskin garments and feathers dangling from their straight black hair.

Sandys ordered the colorful placard to be prominently displayed in public squares in villages all over England, handed to customers who frequented local shops and tacked onto meetinghouse doors. The following excerpt from an actual letter sent from the New Virginia Company in 1619 to the governor of Virginia tells the colonists how to handle the ladies.

"We send you in this ship one widow and eleven maids meant as wives for the men of Virginia. There hath been especial care had in the choice of them, for there hath not any one of them been received but upon good commendation. We pray you all therefore to take them into your care . . . that at their first landing they may be housed, lodged and provided for till they be married. In case they cannot be presently married, we desire they may be put to several householders that have wives till they can be provided of husbands. Nearly fifty more are shortly to come, being sent by our Lord and Treasurer the Earl of Southampton and certain other worthy gentlemen, who taking into consideration that the Plantation can never flourish till . . . wives and children fix the people on the soil. For the reimbursing of those charges it is ordered that every man that marries one [of these women] give 120 pound(s) of the best leaf tobacco [as payment for the passage of his new wife]. And though we are desirous that marriage be free according to the law of nature . . . we would not have these maids be deceived and married to servants, but only to freemen or tenants as have means to maintain them."

Historians differ as to the actual number of ships that sailed from England in those early days and the exact number of young ladies aboard each ship. The exact dates of the ships' arrivals on these shores and the number of pounds of tobacco required to pay for the women's passage also differs. That many Englishmen still consulted the old-style Julian calendar at this time may account for the differing dates.

Most historians agree that the first Bride Ship carrying ninety young ladies reached Jamestown in August 1619 and that a colonist was required to pay 120 pounds of tobacco leaves for his new bride's passage. Other accounts declare that the first Bride Ship arrived in Jamestown in 1620. Another source claimed that in 1621 *three* vessels arrived simultaneously in the port of James Cittie [sic] and that although the New Virginia Company sold shares of stock in England to finance the venture, subscription sales raised only enough money to send seventy women (although they had advertised for one hundred) and in the end, only fifty-seven ladies actually made the voyage. This same source states that the amount of tobacco required for a girl's passage increased from 120 to 150 pounds. Records show that girls as young as fourteen and others as old as twenty-five, among them a few widows, traveled to the Jamestown colony.

In actuality, the ages of the young ladies and exactly *when* these first ships reached the New World is neither here nor there. We all know that women *did* come to these shores, they *did* marry men who had already settled here, and they *did* start families. Sadly, history also points out that the majority of the adventurous young women who journeyed to the New World in those early days, breathless with excitement and the hope of a new life, did not survive the horrific Powhatan massacre of 1622, when hundreds of colonists—men, women and children—were brutally slaughtered.

What history does *not* tell us is that not every young lady who made the crossing on a Bride Ship did so for the intended purpose: to find a husband and start a family. Some saw the voyage to the New World as a means to escape an unbearable life in England. Some, whose lives had become prodigiously dull, merely sought excitement and adventure. And some, such as those whose stories you are about to read, were running away, a secret tucked in a pocket, seeking in the New World a fresh start on a new, untarnished life, although woefully unprepared for the pitfalls that would plague them.

Chapter 1

February 1620

"What does the broadsheet say?" Miss Diana Falstaff asked her father, Squire Falstaff, a proud member of that lesser nobility in England known as the landed gentry. Diana and her mother and father were gathered around the fire in the great room as was their custom every evening following prayers.

That morning the squire had ridden into the nearby hamlet of Chemfordshire and arrived home carrying a colorful broadsheet given him by a shopkeeper. Also tucked under his arm was a copy of the Surrey County weekly news pages.

The squire settled back on the worn tapestry cushion that buffered the hard seat of his high-backed claw-foot chair. Clearing his throat, he prepared to oblige his daughter's request. "To serve God and Country," he read aloud, "ninety maidens shall be chosen to join the first Bride Ship to sail to the New World from these shores for the express purpose of becoming wives to those Englishmen who have already established thriving plantations across the sea. Hundreds of strong, handsome men now desire to share their good fortune with a loving wife. Maids between the ages of six and ten and three and twenty must be comely, chaste, modest and pure with no blight upon her character. Special consideration will be accorded those young ladies who can read and write. Permission from a parent or guardian and a superior recommendation from the girl's vicar, priest, or local squire is mandatory."

"Oh, my," Diana exclaimed with interest. "May I look at the pictures on the placard, Father?"

The squire handed the broadsheet to his daughter, a pretty girl of seven and ten years with smooth chestnut hair and hazel eyes.

Diana's mother, Mistress Falstaff, glanced up from her needlework. "I daresay a goodly number of young ladies will vie with one another to be chosen to make the crossing."

"Appears to be additional information about the venture in the news pages," her husband remarked. His bespectacled eyes scanned the Surrey County news pages. "Ah, yes, here it is. The young ladies chosen to make the crossing shall be presented with a number of useful items, amongst them two pairs of boots, two pairs of warm stockings, an apron, a cap and . . . various and sundry household implements."

"Things a girl will no doubt need in order to set up a home," Mistress Falstaff said quietly. Snipping a thread with her scissors, she punctuated her remark.

"In addition," the squire read on, "each young lady will receive a new petticoat and pair of lambskin gloves."

"A petticoat and lambskin gloves?" Diana looked up from the placard she'd been perusing. "My, the young ladies will feel nicely fitted out with all that new finery!"

"When is the Bride Ship set to sail?" inquired her mother.

"Departure is scheduled for mid-March, or as soon as sufficient funds can be raised to finance the voyage. The actual day of departure will, of course, be determined by the weather. I would consider purchasing a share of stock myself," the squire added, albeit beneath his breath, as it was considered unseemly for a gentleman to discuss financial matters before his wife and child, "were I able."

"Subscribers will no doubt receive a tidy return from their

investment," his wife offered.

"What else do the news pages say about the Bride Ship, Father?"

With a sudden flash of anger, the squire flung the paper aside. "You are displaying far too much interest in this sojourn, Diana! You shall not think of applying!"

"Indeed not!" chimed in her mother, her tone also alarmed. "Your duty is to marry well, right here at home in England."

"I do not seek to leave England!" Diana cried defensively. Of late, she had been reminded, and quite often enough, that the financial security for her small family rested squarely upon her small shoulders, meaning it was imperative she wed a gentleman whose station was well beyond the middling sort, that he possessed considerable wealth, or at the very least, lived comfortably on the expectation of same. Although lowering for the entire family, it was well known thereabouts that the Falstaff Manor Home, where Diana had lived all her life, had lately fallen into disrepair due to the rapidly dwindling Falstaff fortune. In the past twelvemonth Squire Falstaff had been unable to make so much as a dent in, let alone settle, his mounting debts.

"Your father and I have fastened all our hopes on you becoming affianced to a well-put young man whilst we are in London next month. There is no saying what will become of this family if you do not marry well, daughter."

Despite her resolve to remain strong in the face of such a horror, Diana managed to swallow past the huge lump of resentment that arose in her throat every time her parents mentioned the family's upcoming sojourn to London, and the primary reason for it. To feign interest in another young man was the last thing in the world Diana wished to do.

"You are young, Diana," her mother went on. "Your feelings for Hamilton Prescott will dissolve. I agree it is unfortunate you cannot wed the man you've set your heart upon, but, as you know, the Prescotts' straits are now as dire as our own."

"Wife!" the squire scolded, apparently thinking that enough had been said on the matter of the family's reduced circumstances. "It is time we all retired for the night."

Diana did not think again on the notice regarding the Bride Ship until some days later when her dear friend, Sara Wakefield, paid her an afternoon call. Though the girls had been friends since childhood, Sara's father's consequence had recently been elevated due to his appointment as churchwarden. When the girls were small, Squire Falstaff had actually invited his impoverished neighbor's child to take lessons alongside his own daughter at the Falstaff manor home on the hill. On this blustery March afternoon Sara Wakefield arrived wearing a look of supreme pleasure upon her pretty face.

Once Sara reached the upper-storey retiring chamber, which Diana favored, as the fire in the hearth made the room feel especially cozy, Sara greeted her friend, seated alone on the window seat staring fixedly into the flickering flames of the fire. "I have wonderful news to impart, Diana. I came at once to tell you!"

Despite the morose look on her face, Diana managed a tight smile. "I am glad you came, Sara." She motioned for her friend to join her on the frayed Turkish rug covering the sill beneath the mullioned window. "I confess I am in especial need of cheering today. I have spent the bulk of the afternoon sequestered here alone."

"The aspect from here is quite pleasing," Sara remarked, taking a seat beside Diana. She gazed from the window upon the somewhat overgrown knot garden below.

"Without sufficient servants to care for anything, the aspect is not as pleasing as it once was." Diana sighed.

"Do tell me what the trouble is, Diana. Have you taken ill?"

"I despair of ever feeling well again," Diana murmured. "I received a . . . lowering missive from my cousin this morning."

"The gentleman in London?"

Diana nodded. "What I have greatly feared is, indeed, to come about."

Sara reached to squeeze her friend's hand. "I am so very sorry."

Diana sniffed back a tear. "Hamilton will soon be married. What is worse is that I shall be obliged to witness him"—her chin trembled—"exchange his vows with . . . *her.* Oh!" She covered her face with both hands. "How shall I bear it?"

Sara remained silent, giving her companion sufficient time in which to compose herself. "Is it imperative you be present?" she asked softly.

"Father has declared we are all to attend the ceremony whilst in London. Afterward, we shall remain a lengthy spell in the hope that I will soon become affianced. Of course, I do *not* wish to attend the nuptials," Diana scoffed, "but there is no one here with whom I could linger." Suddenly, her hazel eyes brightened. "Perhaps I might stay with you, Sara! We could—"

Sara's blond curls shook. "No, Diana. Your father paid a call at the vicarage some days past." From the pocket of her cape, she withdrew a packet of papers. Unfolding a page, she handed it to her friend. "This is the news I came to impart."

Diana glanced at the page, but after reading the words, did not grasp the meaning. "I . . . do not understand, Sara."

"I have been chosen! This is my Letter of Acceptance . . . to join the Bride Ship! Since Papa is merely churchwarden, I needed your father's recommendation and his signature. Your father did not apprise you of my plans?"

"No, he said not a word. Perhaps because he feared I would wish to join you."

"That would be splendid!" Sara cried.

"I would not be allowed to go. I must . . . perform my duty and marry well. And, there is also the unfortunate matter of my mother's kinsman. I have not been made privy to the entire story; my mother vowed never to speak of it again."

"Regarding the young man accused of . . . killing another? You mentioned it happened long before your mother wed your father."

"I do not even know my half-brother's name, but after he was convicted of the crime, I learned he was sentenced to transportation and now resides somewhere across the sea . . . in a land called Henricus." Diana's eyes became a question. "That is not where you are bound, is it, Sara?"

"I am to travel to a place called James Cittie, named after our good King James."

"When Mother received the letter from her first-born, it quite overset her. I was but a child then. I had never seen my mother cry, and tears also filled my eyes. She and father insisted the matter had nothing to do with me."

"Surely that is the truth of it."

"Perhaps, but the unconscionable actions of my father's three sons, my Falstaff step-brothers, do indeed concern me." Anger rose within Diana. "Wastrels, the lot of them. Were it not for their wasteful spending, it would not have fallen to me to save my parents from ruin."

"Where are your step-brothers now?"

"In London perhaps, or . . . touring the continent with one of their courtier friends. However, the debt collectors know exactly where the *father* of the three Falstaff brothers resides." After a pause, Diana said, "What am I to do, Sara? I shall never be happy wed to any man save Hamilton."

Retrieving the letter she'd handed to her friend, Sara slipped it back inside the pocket of her cape. "I fear I should not be so happy whilst you remain so sad."

"I cannot expect you to share in my gloom, Sara." Diana forced the semblance of a smile to her lips. "Do tell me more about your sojourn. I promise to be as breathless with excitement as you are."

In short order, Sara said that her father had written to the New Virginia Company on her behalf in response to a broadsheet tacked to the church house door. As a result, she would soon be on her way across the sea.

"And you wish to go?" Diana asked incredulously. "But it is so very far away."

"M-my father wishes me to go." A whit of Sara's excitement faltered.

"But . . . why?"

"Papa says I shall never again be presented with such a splendid opportunity to witness for our dear Lord. Papa says the savages in the New World worship pagan gods. Their souls are in dire need of saving."

"Oh. But will not he and your mother miss you terribly? Do they not fear you will never return? I do not understand, Sara. *I* will miss you terribly even if your own parents will not!" Tears pooled in Diana's hazel eyes. "I have lost my beloved Hamilton, and now I am also losing *you!*"

Sara's tone softened. "Do not weep for me, Diana. I do wish to go, truly I do. Papa says . . ."

But Diana did not hear the rest of Sara's tale. Losing the man she had loved since childhood, coupled with the devastating loss of her dearest friend in the world, filled her heart to overflowing with grief. "I cannot bear such a loss!" She sobbed into a tattered linen handkerchief. "I cannot bear it!"

"We must make the best of our remaining time together, Diana. We shall have an agreeable time on our journey up to London. I have never stayed the night at an inn before. Your father is pleased that I am to come along. He thought it quite opportune that my need to travel to London coincided perfectly with your journey up to Town. Perhaps he is more aware of your sorrow than you think. I heard him tell my father he was pleased I would be along to cheer you."

But despite all the reasons Sara presented to lift her spirits, Diana's heart remained full of grief.

Chapter 2

One morning the following week, Squire Falstaff rode again into the hamlet of Chemfordshire, this time to hire a drover to act as coachman on the family's trip up to London.

During the squire's absence, Miss Sara Wakefield's father escorted his daughter up the hill to the Falstaff manor home. Setting her portmanteau on the cobbled drive, the shabbily dressed man turned sad eyes upon his only child.

"Yer ma and I'll miss ye fierce-like, Sara. But, make no mistake, it be the good Lord's will that ye go."

"Yes, Papa."

"At journey's end, ye must write words in a letter tellin' us yer safe like." Swiping at a tear that threatened to cloud his vision, the bewhiskered man reached to gather his pretty daughter close.

"God will see me safely across the sea, Papa. Tell Mama I love her dearly."

With a decisive nod, her father turned to go. Sara watched his backside disappear from view before turning toward Diana and her mother. All three women stood patiently whilst Squire Falstaff assisted the drover harness a pair of sway-backed horses to a rickety old carriage.

In less than a quarter-hour all was in readiness, and the four travelers climbed aboard. With a slap of the reins across the horses' rumps, the creaking carriage lurched forward. They planned to spend two nights along the way at a roadside inn.

All went swimmingly until the final day of their journey when a violent storm kicked up. Still a good half-day away from London, Mistress Falstaff pleaded with her husband to allow them to seek shelter for a third night. Squire Falstaff, citing the added expense of provisions and another night at an inn, held fast to his decision to press on.

" 'Tis only a bit of rain. We shall outrun it in no time."

"Perhaps we shall miss the wedding ceremony after all," Diana whispered to Sara, seated beside her on the hard wooden bench.

"But I shouldn't wish for the Bride Ship to sail without me!"

"I had not thought of that. Do forgive me, Sara."

Soon the heavy coach, shuddering beneath the onslaught of high winds and driving rain, became hopelessly bogged down in the muddy trenches of the rain-soaked road. The driver and Diana's father scrambled from the coach into the pouring rain, slogging through the sludge in order to press their shoulders against the backside of the vehicle and push with all their might. Despite their efforts, it soon began apparent that to unloose the coach from the tenacious grip of sticky earth was an impossible task.

Though Diana did not wish to cause her friend undue grief, she could not help hoping the coach would remain stuck in the mud forever, or at least until her beloved Hamilton had repeated his vows.

Chapter 3

Six-and-ten-year-old Sallie Mae Pigee knew for a certainty that if the action she was taking tonight did not kill her, the plan churning in her mind very well might. On the other hand, she thought, running as fast as she could down the dusty path away from her parents' hovel in the middle of that moonless night, tomorrow could mark the dawn of a grand new adventure in her otherwise shameful little life.

Sallie Mae had breathlessly counted the long, dull hours of that day, hoping against hope that nothing would go awry; that her father would come home after only two mugs of ale at the village pub that night instead of downing the eight or ten mugs he oftimes did; that her parents both fell asleep the minute their heads hit the mat and that the rain clouds she'd fretfully watched gather on the horizon that afternoon did not unleash their fury until she was long gone from home. If luck were on her side, Sallie Mae thought, she might even garner a lift on the back of some farmer's wagon on his way up to market in Lunnon.

Hoping she hadn't been seen by one or another of her three sisters who slept crowded together on the floor of the filthy hovel they called home, Sallie Mae flung another anxious gaze over her shoulder before flinging herself to the ground beneath the gnarled old oak beside the lane.

One thing would definitely change after tonight, Sallie Mae declared whilst tugging at a heavy rock beneath the tree. She would never again be known as Sallie Mae *Pigee!* Having dislodged the rock, she snatched up the bundle she'd secreted there in the pre-dawn hours of that very morn.

Muttering beneath her breath, Sallie Mae hurriedly stepped from the tattered homespun skirt she'd crawled into bed wearing and from the bundle yanked a pair of faded gray britches she'd snitched from the basket of freshly laundered garments her mother told her yesterday to take to the loft where her brothers slept. After working the trousers up over her hips, she shrugged into the wind-freshened boy's shirt she'd also nabbed from the basket. A pair of heavily darned socks, an old cap, and a jacket—for now a size in between the two youngest boys—completed her costume.

Earlier that night, Sallie Mae had hidden her mother's scissors in the folds of her skirt, and after everyone else had fallen asleep, she'd quietly snipped off her long golden curls in the darkness. Her mother would have a fit when she discovered that all that remained of her eldest daughter were limp strands of yellow hair stuffed beneath the feather pillow on the straw mat where Sallie Mae had napped every single night of her life.

Now, pulling her brother's cap down over her cropped curls, she scurried across the meadow to the rutted drove road, generally used only by farmers drivin' their cattle to market or the county fair. Sallie Mae knew the road eventually led to London. Feeling energized that she was at last on her way, each hurried step added to the distance between herself and the rest of the Pigee clan, not a one of whom Sallie Mae expected to ever see again.

As she walked and at times ran, she mulled over the fix she'd got herself into. Not to put too fine a point on it, Sallie Mae half blamed the whole beastly mess on her mother. What loving mama would pin a name as ridiculous as Sallie Mae in front of "Pigee" on a poor innocent babe fresh born? She'd been teased about her name her entire life. If she'd been given a proper name like Mary or Betsy or simply Ann, the gang of ruffians would never have chased her into the hay meadow that wretched day. They wouldn't have tormented her with jeers and jibes, and what's more—white hot anger rose within Sallie Mae—they wouldn't have each taken a turn at her.

"Sallie Mae Pigee! Sallie Mae Pigee! Let's see if she can rut as good as she struts!"

The boys, each bigger than Sallie Mae—who was not a robust, country girl, but rather a delicate sort of lass—had cornered her behind a haystack, picking at her until she screamed for mercy. Then whilst two of them held her down, the third one yanked her skirt over her head and jerked her legs apart. When he was done, another took a turn. One was ready to mount her when old Mr. Wilson appeared and chased them away with a pitchfork, Sallie Mae included.

Nine months later to the day, she gave birth to a pitiful little babe. Thank God the mite was born dead. Sallie Mae had hidden her shameful condition for nigh on eight of those nine long months . . . and might have hid it the entire time if the weather hadn't changed.

"Sallie Mae, what 'ave ye gone an' done?" her mama cried the day they left off wearing heavy woolens and donned homespun skirts and muslin blouses tied at the neck with a string. "Gel, you're as big as a cow! How are we goin' feed another mouth?"

"It weren't my fault, Mama!" Sallie Mae burst into tears. She'd been a'dreadin' this day for months.

"I shoulda' knowed ye'd go an' ruin y'self! Too darn proud of that yella' hair, ye are!" Both fists parked on her hips, the older woman assessed her daughter's misshapen form. "Here I thought ye'd a'finally growed tits!"

Sallie Mae hung her head. "It weren't my fault, Mama. Honest, it weren't."

"Ye sayin' ye weren't *there?* That ye dinna' know what ye was a'doin'?"

Scalding hot tears snaked down Sallie Mae's cheeks. "I couldna' stop 'em, Mama. There was four of 'em. They was a'chasin' me . . . and—"

"Looks like they done caught ya!"

The day Sallie Mae's babe was born dead, she wrapped its limp little body in a rag and took it to the churchyard cemetery. She knew full well Vicar Stephens wouldn't let her bury her bastard boy there; still she left the lifeless bundle on the stoop, hopin' his pretty little wife would take pity on the moppet and give it a proper burial.

Then . . . just as Sallie Mae turned to go, she spotted the broadsheet tacked to the meetin' house door. Though she couldna' make out all the words, her readin' skills not bein' what they ought, she did see "Bride Ship." Which brought to mind a bit o' talk she'd overheard between her sister Paulette and two o' her mates. The girls, only fourteen, was lamentin' the fact they was too young to become wives to the settlers in the New World colony 'cross the sea.

Sallie Mae stood there, her mouth agape. A'course she knew that the recent "Blight Upon Her Character" would render her unfit. But the ship would need sailors, wouldn't it? A smart fella' who could cook up enough victuals to satisfy an army shouldn't have a bit o' trouble hiring on to help out the cook. Sallie Mae vowed right then and there to make her way up to Lunnon and join the Bride Ship crew.

Now, scurryin' away from home, Sallie Mae decided that if she was to spend the next several months paradin' as a boy, she'd best practice talkin' like one. Lowering her voice, she repeated some of the rougher language she'd heard her brothers use. She also reminded herself to *act* like a boy, not squeamish o'er things like rats or snakes or spiders. Her eldest brother, James, the one who'd run off to sea when he was a lad of thirteen, said sailors slept in their clothes. If she stayed out of trouble—in other words, was never ordered to strip to the waist for a lashin'—her secret should be safe. Now that her breasts had returned to normal size, her shape was more akin to a twelve-year-old boy than a grown-up girl of six and ten. Her plan, she reasoned, was indeed foolproof.

The night being cool, Sallie Mae pulled her jacket closer about her. Casting fearful glances to either side of the road, she hastened her step. She'd heard tales of foot-travelers being waylaid by menacing characters on these roads at night. Not that she had anything to steal. Not a single coin jingled in her pockets. Yet the sounds she did hear—animals rootin' around in the bushes, big-eyed owls hootin' from the treetops—were enough to jangle her nerves. Nevertheless, she thought, nothing was a'gonna stop her from hirin' on that ship headed for the New World. Once there, o' course, she'd abandon her disguise and find herself a decent man who'd treat her proper-like.

Hours later when the pink light of day began to dawn on the horizon, Sallie Mae inhaled a small breath of relief, which became a gnawin' in her mid-section. Coming upon a roadside inn, Sallie Mae slowed her step. Perhaps she'd rest her heels a bit, not *inside* of course, but beneath the shade of that old oak in the yard. She might even summon the courage to go 'round back and beg a crust of bread.

Seated cross-legged on the ground, Sallie Mae watched the commotion in the inn yard. A farmer's cart drawn by a pair of oxen lumbered up. The farmer hopped down, leaving the cart and his boy across the road. Sallie Mae turned next to stare at a pair of sleek mounts tied to the rail. Fine riggin' told her the horses belonged to well-heeled gen'lemen.

A quarter hour later, she watched a stable boy drive a shiny black coach and team to the front yard, the spirited horses stampin' their hooves and tossin' their manes. Sallie Mae watched folks pour outta' the inn and climb aboard. Off they went in a cloud of dust. Sallie Mae wondered if perhaps she'd stumbled onto the crossroad that linked up with the main highway into Town, which meant she was closer to London than she thought.

Some moments later, a swift maroon coach flew into the yard amid a shower of pebbles and debris. Driver hopped to the ground, tellin' his passengers that at the sound of his horn, the coach would depart straightaway.

"There, you, lad! Quit yer lollygaggin' and tend to m' horses! I need fast mounts, no half-dead nags, y' hear? *You* lad! Hop to it, I say!"

Wonderin' who the man was a'shoutin' at, Sallie Mae glanced about. Seeing no other lads in the yard, she stood up and although still uncertain whom the driver was addressin', cautiously approached the man.

"Ain't got all day!" The coachman tossed the reins to Sallie Mae, then hurried after his passengers into the inn, presumably to break their fast. Thoughts of food set Sallie Mae's stomach to growlin' again.

Suddenly a larger boy came from behind the inn and angrily snatched the ribbons from her. "I'll unbridle 'em. You fetch the nags from the shed."

"But he don't want nag—"

"Fetch the bays, boy!"

The pungent stench of dung led Sallie Mae to the mews behind the inn, and in moments she returned leading a pair of feisty-looking bays, which she handed off to the older boy. He expertly hitched the horses to the maroon coach, then tossed the reins of the tired animals he'd unhitched to Sallie Mae.

"Well, whad-er-ye await'en fer? Git 'em to the stable. Tie on the feedbags and get yer arsh back out 'ere. Sun's up and there's plenty o' work to be done."

After she'd carried out the boy's orders, she returned to the inn yard and was astonished when the driver of the maroon coach tossed her a coin! The next several coaches that rumbled into the inn yard found Sallie Mae at the ready. To unhitch a horse was a task she'd performed hundreds of times, and she certainly knew how to tie on a feedbag and brush a mare's coat till it shone.

By noontime, Sallie Mae had earned more money than she'd seen in her entire life. She discovered fine gentlemen on horseback paid the most. In no time, she was hailin' them with friendly greetings like: "A fine day to ye, sir!" or, "Very handsome mare, sir; be glad to take care o' her for ye!"

Mid-afternoon, Sallie Mae was allowed to eat her fill of what was left of the victuals cooked up for the morning travelers. She washed the barley porridge down with a mug of small ale she paid for from her earnin's. Soon afterwards, the boy who'd been ordering her about declared it was time to muck out the stables, and since she was the new "boy" in the yard, that dubious honor fell to her.

Time to move on, thought Sallie Mae. Fearing the bossy youth might attempt to confiscate her earnings, she tied the coins into the hem of the chemise she still wore beneath her brother's shirt, fetched the bundle she'd arrived with, tied it to the rope holding up her britches and . . . ducked out. Didn't matter to her that the sky had darkened and storm clouds now hung low overhead. She intended to reach Lunnon a'fore nightfall, and a few drops of rain weren't a'gunna' stop her. Quickenin' her step, she attempted to stay dry beneath the canopy of branches overhangin' the road; nonetheless, in minutes the heavy downpour drenched her plum through.

Although the drivin' rain made it difficult to see what lay

ahead, Sallie Mae soon detected the sounds of men's voices up ahead. Clearly, someone's coach was stuck in the mud. She soon came upon the farmer whose wagon and oxen she'd spotted earlier at the inn. Now, he was hitchin' his oxen before a team of horses tethered to the rickety old coach she'd also spotted lumberin' past the inn. The four men—coachman, a tall finely turned-out gentleman, the farmer and his boy—were assembled at the rear tryin' to heft the heavy vehicle out of the muddy ruts.

As Sallie Mae approached, the finer-dressed gentleman glanced up. "Lend a hand, boy!"

"What would ye have me do, sir?" Sallie Mae shouted over the howling wind.

"Hop onto the platform and slap the reins!"

Sallie Mae scrambled to do as the man bade. Perhaps there'd be another groat in it for her.

In minutes, the oxen dragged the tired horses and mud-splattered coach from the sludge.

"Whoa, there," Sallie Mae shouted as the coach wheels, slingin' mud right and left, rolled onto a graveled surface. Indeed, this was the main road that led straight into London. From her high perch, she held the reins taut as the men unhitched the oxen and returned them to the farmer's wagon.

When the coach driver clambered up beside her onto the platform, he asked, "Where 'ye headed, lad?"

"Lunnon, sir."

"Yer welcome to ride a-ways with us."

"Thank 'ye, sir. Right kind o' ye."

Although the rain eventually let up, the sky remained cloudy, diminishing what little light was left of the day. When dusk fell, Sallie Mae was unable to detect much of what lay ahead, or on either side of the road.

"Are we near Town yet, sir?" she inquired of the driver, whose name she'd not been made privy to.

"Traffic's snarlin' up. 'Spect we're drawin' near. Where ye aim to light, boy?"

"Quayside."

"As it happens, I'm to deliver one o' the young ladies inside the coach to the East End. Set to board a ship bound for the New World, she is."

Sallie Mae's head jerked up. "The Bride Ship?"

Driver directed a quizzical gaze her way.

"M'brother's a seaman," Sallie Mae explained. "I heard him tell of a ship set to carry young ladies 'cross the sea. I'm off to sea m'self, sir," she added proudly.

"You ain't runnin' away from home are ye, lad?"

"No, sir! I-I been . . . workin' at a inn yard; mean now to join m' brother at sea."

"Hmmm."

What a stroke of fine luck! Sallie Mae'd had no idea where to start lookin' for the wharf. Her original plan had been to follow along the banks of the Thames till she spotted a sea of masts pointin' skywards, then ask someone which bark was the Bride Ship . . . or she might have spotted it on her own, if'n they was a steady stream of girls headed that direction.

Today's storm had no doubt delayed many of those en route to London, meanin' the ship had likely not sailed, nor would it do so tomorrow. Wind was still blowin' the wrong direction. Accordin' to her brother, wind had to be just so. A vessel could languish in the harbor for days, even weeks, a-waitin' favorable wind. A flutter of excitement coursed through Sallie Mae. The fact she was to be delivered straightaway to quayside meant she'd be on board ship and settled in long before the ship put out to sea.

Sallie Mae turned her attention to the sights on the busy

thoroughfare they'd just entered—that is, those she could see in the dim light. Rain had freshened the air a bit, but it had also slickened the cobbles, making it difficult for heavy coaches and carts to maneuver around one another. Hundreds of people bustled about on foot—men totin' kegs on their shoulders, fishmonger's wives balancing baskets with the day's catch on their heads. Dogs barkin', street vendors cryin', carters shoutin', and street urchins duckin' 'tween carts and horses' hooves. Noise was deafenin'!

"Never seen the like," Sallie Mae muttered. Then, between narrow wooden structures, she began to catch glimpses of the river. "The Thames?" she asked, sitting up straighter, a long gaze directed that way.

Far too occupied steering the horses through the maze on the street, the driver made no reply.

Passing by taverns, lights flickering from within and delicious smells emanating forth, caused Sallie Mae to think again about eatin'.

"Ye 'spose his lordship means to pause soon for a bite to eat, sir?" she asked a bit louder.

The driver snorted. "If'n he do, he won't be a-payin' to fill *yer* belly!"

"I've blunt to buy me own supper!" Sallie Mae insisted.

"Master's bent on reachin' his kinsfolk 'afore we stops to rest. This here's only Southwark. We've not yet crossed London Bridge."

With a sigh, Sallie Mae turned again to surveyin' the surroundings. Not yet in the heart of London, and this was the busiest place she had seen in her life. The thickening snarl of traffic caused everything to move at a snail's pace. Fewer wooden structures now obscured the river, so she was afforded a clearer view of it. However, the pungent stench that arose from the brackish water caused her to pinch her nostrils together.

When all vestiges of daylight disappeared, the most she could make out of the river were curls of wispy fog hangin' low over the water like a tattered shroud. She noted the slimy embankment leading down to the water appeared quite high and steep. It was now too dark to tell where land left off and water began.

Suddenly sheer pandemonium broke loose. A thump against the side of the coach apparently caused one of the rear wheels to give way. Hitting the slick cobbles, it crumbled to pieces when the rear of the heavy vehicle slammed to the ground. From within the coach, Sallie Mae heard the women's screams. The carriage teetered precariously, then toppled completely over, tumbling like an empty barrel down the steep embankment toward the river.

Sallie Mae lunged for the arm of the coach driver, but he'd already been flung from his perch high into the air. She screamed when her small body followed suit. Once the rickety carriage dashed again to the ground, it splintered completely apart, sending stunned passengers, bags and valises flying helter-skelter into the turgid black waters of the River Thames.

Chapter 4

Earlier that same morning, north of London . . .

"You are not old enough," Prudence Plumleigh declared to her younger sister, Faith, seated opposite her in a tidy conveyance tooling toward London this cloudy March morn. "The notice specifically stated that only girls between sixteen and twenty-three would be chosen to go."

"I am aware that I am not yet six and ten," Faith replied saucily. "But, I soon shall be." More than anything, Faith wished to accompany her older sister on this adventure of a lifetime. In fact, by all rights, *she* should be the one going. Of the three Plumleigh sisters, she was by far the most adventurous, and certainly the prettiest. They favored one another, of course. Both Faith and Prudence had their mother's coloring, fair skin, auburn hair. But Pru wore her hair in a tight knot at the nape of her neck, whereas Faith's long auburn tresses hung in thick waves down her back.

"In addition to not being old enough," Prudence added, "it is too late for you to obtain the proper recommendation. Therefore, once we reach London, you shall proceed straightaway to Aunt Elsa's home and there's an end to it."

Faith's chin shot up. "Perhaps I will, and . . . perhaps I will not."

"I cannot think why I attempt to talk sense to you. Without a proper Letter of Acceptance you will not be allowed to board the ship."

"We shall see."

"Faith, you do not have a Letter of Acceptance. The ship will depart before week's end, and you haven't our parents' approval or Vicar Crowley's recommendation." Huffing with exasperation, the older girl turned to gaze from the coach window at the English countryside they were swiftly flying past.

"Well, since you are the elder of us, I shall simply tell the captain I gave my Letter of Acceptance to you for safekeeping and you . . . lost it."

"You will say nothing of the sort. Mother is coming up to Town to fetch Hope, and she will expect to find you at Aunt Elsa's."

"Mother might be disappointed."

"Oh!" The toe of Prudence's half-boot tapped irritably on the straw-strewn floor of the small coach. "You are incorrigible, Faith Plumleigh! You would never have been chosen to go. You do not meet a single one of the stringent requirements to join the Bride Ship."

Faith pinned her sister with a cool gaze. "And you meet all of them?"

Prudence squirmed. "Apparently I . . . satisfied enough of them."

Faith began to toy with the folds of her green serge skirt. "Mama will not know I have gone with you until it is too late. Once the ship has sailed, she cannot very well stand on shore and demand it turn around and bring me back."

Her sister's lips thinned with annoyance. "You will *not* be allowed to board the ship, Faith."

Moments later, both girls felt the swift pace of their conveyance begin to diminish.

"Whoa, there, easy now." The driver directed the cattle before him into the busy yard of a roadside inn. When the coach shuddered to a standstill, he hopped to the ground and addressed the girls through the opened window.

"Need to change horses. Thought you young ladies might want for a bite to eat."

"Thank you for your thoughtfulness, John," Prudence replied primly. "Come along, Faith. I, for one, am not hungry, but I do feel a need to use the necessary."

Faith's green eyes cut round. Was her sister feeling ill . . . *again?*

Moments later, both young ladies were settled across from one another at a rough-hewn table in the common room of the inn, Faith enjoying a dish of shepherd's pie and a mug of watered whey.

"This is quite tasty, Pru. You should have some."

Prudence pulled a face. "The stench here makes my stomach feel queasy."

Faith made no reply. After she'd eaten, both girls climbed back inside the dusty coach. John let down the leather curtains covering the windows on both sides of the vehicle.

"Must we let down the curtains the entire way, John? With no fresh air inside, I fear I shall fall ill."

"Stable boy said they's a storm cuttin' up nasty down the road a piece. Curtain'll keep you ladies dry."

Sure enough, in less than a quarter hour, drops of rain began to pelt the cloth top of the coach. Gusty wind snapping the thin leather curtains sent the girls scooting to the center of the bench, their knees knocking together as the light vehicle buffeted from side to side.

"I expect this is very like a storm at sea," Faith remarked.

"A storm at sea is something you will never experience."

Just then, another blast of wind sent the coach listing that direction. Clinging to the leather strap dangling from the roof,

Faith said, "Perchance a few young ladies will change face about embarking upon such a treacherous voyage. Very likely the captain would welcome a replacement. Would mean he'd not lose his passage money. The Bride Ship will sail whether or not there are ninety young ladies aboard," she declared.

"Mother needs your help at home. The boys are difficult to handle and with Hope returning home from school . . ."

"Mama will not miss me. Hope is Mama's favorite. I will not be missed."

"Mama favors Hope because Hope is not incorrigible. She will, indeed, be of help. But that does not mean they will not also require *your* assistance."

Remaining calm in the face of her sister's protests, Faith said, "No one can stop me from boarding that ship if it is what I wish to do."

"If Papa were here, he would have none of it."

"Papa is at home minding the farm and the boys."

"Faith!" Prudence fairly shouted. "You are *not* going to the New World, and there's an end to it!"

For the space of a few seconds, Faith said nothing; then, when the wind seemed to wane, she took up the subject again. "I confess I am a bit confused by a few things, Pru."

"You are confused by more than a *few* things."

Faith ignored her sister's retort. "Since you are the only one of us who declares she cannot sleep unless she is tucked snugly in her own bed, and since you are always the first to come down with the sniffles when cold weather sets in, why would *you* volunteer to spend upwards of eight weeks aboard a drafty ship in order to travel to a land Vicar Crowley declares is known for harsh winters? Why is it that out of all the young ladies in our parish, you were the *first* to volunteer?"

Not meeting her sister's gaze, Prudence pulled a handkerchief from her pocket to dab at her nose.

"There, you see. Already this bit of rain has given you the sniffles."

"I am *not* sniffling. I-I volunteered to travel to the New World because I was moved by Vicar Crowley's admonition that it was our Christian duty to bring the Lord's Word to—"

"*Piffle!* I know exactly why you volunteered, Prudence Plumleigh, and spreading the Lord's Word hasn't a thing to do with it."

Prudence's eyes narrowed. "You know nothing, little sister."

Faith's accusing gaze did not falter.

Prudence's lashes fluttered against her flushed cheeks while her fingers twisted a corner of her handkerchief.

"I suggest, Prudence, that you pray harder than you have ever prayed in your life"—Faith's tone was firm—"that we—yes, I said *we*—reach our destination as quickly as possible and that once there, *you* find a husband straightaway, one who is desperate for a wife and . . . more importantly, one who cannot count."

Prudence stared aghast at her younger sister. "I cannot think what you mean."

Faith's green eyes softened. "I know the fix you are in, Pru. I know you would never have given in if . . . if you had not been . . . sorely tempted."

"You know nothing." Prudence squirmed on the hard bench.

"I know you are carrying a secret," Faith said softly, "in your belly."

"Oh-h!" The older girl's brown eyes grew round. She covered her face with both hands. "I am so ashamed, Faith. I did not know what to do or where to turn. Please do not hate me."

Faith reached to comfort her sister, but a spray of cold rain blowing through the window prevented her. Wiping the mist from her cheeks, she said, "I could never hate you, Pru. The truth is I am jealous that despite everything, you managed to convince Vicar Crowley to recommend you for the Bride Ship. Especially when it was his son who—"

"How do you know *that?*" Prudence cried.

Faith looked contrite. "I . . . followed you one night. I saw you and Isaac in the meadow and—"

"You *watched?*"

"No! But it is not as if I do not know . . . how it is done. After all, we have lived all our lives on a farm."

Prudence worked to compose herself. "The . . . the storm appears to be letting up."

"Did you reveal to Isaac that you are—?"

"I cannot see where that is any of your concern." She looked away. "I . . . I suppose you mean to tell Mama."

Faith made no reply.

"So, you *do* mean to tell her."

"I am not cruel, Prudence. To tell Mama or Vicar Crowley would serve no purpose. Isaac wishes to take holy orders. A scandal would ruin his chances to obtain a living. I would never deliberately hurt anyone."

"You are hurting me."

"To hurt you was never my intent. I merely wish to accompany you on the journey so that I may be on hand to help you. And . . . I, too, wish to marry. There is no one for me in our little hamlet. Vicar Crowley said that in James Cittie there are a dozen men for every woman. It would be lovely to have a choice."

"I believe you mean to tell Mama."

"Well, I can hardly tell her if I am *not* here. You need my help Pru, more than our mother does. I may be younger than you, but I am far stronger. If Mama knew of your plight, she would understand. You need me, Pru, and *I* need your help getting aboard that ship."

"So, that is the way of it. W-what do you wish me to do?"

"Tell the captain you lost my Letter of Acceptance."

"I do not wish to tell a lie."

Faith's lips pursed. "What difference will one more lie make?"

The older girl smiled shakily. Since the driving rain was no longer blowing into the coach, she reached to fold the curtain back from the window. Faith helped to secure it.

"To be truthful," Prudence began once the girls were resettled and inhaling deep breaths of rain-freshened air. "I am frightened to death of what lies ahead. And I am not speaking only about the . . . babe. The voyage frightens me. I would not wish to . . . perish at sea, or die alone in a foreign land."

Faith reached to squeeze her sister's hand. "You will not perish at sea, Pru. I will not allow it."

"If it is the Lord's will . . ."

"I am convinced it is His will that I come along to help you." Faith's head tilted. "Else why did He make me privy to your secret?"

A resigned sigh escaped Prudence. "I am carrying a secret. And now I must lie in order to protect it."

"Secrets *and* lies," Faith murmured. "We must pray the Lord will forgive our abominations."

London, later that day . . .

"Only eighty young ladies will be allowed to board the Bride Ship, miss."

"But the advertisement said *ninety* young ladies would be chosen," Faith argued. She and Prudence had reached London near dusk and headed straight for quayside, where even at this hour, longboats were ferrying young ladies toward one of two gaily painted vessels bobbing in the Thames.

"I only got eighty names on m' list," the man guarding the jetty steps said. "If'n yer name ain't on m' list, ye ain't a'gittin' on the boat."

"My name *should* be on that list, sir. My sister and I received our Letters of Acceptance the exact same day."

"But ye only handed me *one* letter, miss. And they's only *one* Plumleigh on m' list."

"I demand to see the person in charge," Faith declared.

"Faith, please. You are—"

"Do be still, Prudence. Sir, I wish to speak with your superior officer."

"Won't do ye' no good, miss. Yer name ain't on m'list, which means you ain't gittin'—"

"Then I shall simply reapply."

"Time's run out for that, miss. Credentials must be checked—"

"My credentials, sir, are impeccable. My sister's name is on that list, and my credentials are identical to hers. Now, where is the man in charge?"

"There a problem here, Macintosh?" A gentleman wearing an impressive-looking nautical uniform bounded up the jetty steps two at a time.

Five or six other young ladies, whose names had already been checked off the list, rushed toward the empty longboat and after handing in their belongings, began to excitedly climb aboard.

"What seems to be the trouble here?" the uniformed officer asked.

"This young lady insists that her sister *misplaced* her Letter of Acceptance."

The higher-ranking officer smiled pleasantly at the girls. "Which of you is . . . ?"

"I am Faith Plumleigh, sir, and my name *should* be on that list." Faith's gloved forefinger tapped the rather soiled piece of paper clutched tightly in a grubby hand.

The officer turned toward Prudence. "And you must be the

sister who . . . ?"

Prudence nodded tightly, "I-Indeed, sir, I did, indeed, m-misplace my sister's letter. I am terribly sorry, sir."

Her chin elevated, Faith sniffed piously. "Which is exactly what I just said. By the by, why it is that only *eighty* young ladies are to board the ship when the advertisement clearly stated that *ninety* would be selected?"

The officer cleared his throat. "The New Virginia Company was successful only in raising sufficient funds to send eighty young ladies to the New World."

"But I thought the men we married were to pay our passage."

"It will be some time before those funds can be collected, miss. In the meantime, provisions to fit out two ships must be paid for." A curt nod told Faith the discussion had drawn to an end. He motioned for the man with the list to step aside. In hushed tones, the men conferred.

Prudence whispered, "I fear I am a dreadful liar, Faith."

"Hush!" Faith hissed.

"But what if they turn us *both* away?"

"They will not turn us away. Now do be still." Watching the men, Faith experienced some alarm when the uniformed officer walked away, but her staunch demeanor remained firm.

"M' commandin' officer says you may indeed board a ship, miss, but only after *all* the other young ladies has arrived and only *if* there is a vacancy; in other words—"

"I understand perfectly, sir," Faith interrupted. "I will be allowed to board a ship if some young lady does not appear within the allotted time."

"In the meantime, ye shall *not* be allowed on board."

"But where is my sister to pass the night?" Prudence asked. "Darkness will soon be upon us. She cannot simply wait here on the wharf!"

"I can sleep in the carriage, Pru. Unlike you, *I* can sleep anywhere. John will stand guard, or rather, *sit* guard. I will be perfectly safe inside the coach until morning." Faith turned again to the man. "Exactly *when* shall we know if there is a vacan—"

"The ladies must check in by four of the clock tomorrow afternoon. Instructions was clearly outlined in the packet o' papers ye received."

As the girls moved away, Prudence offered to pass the night in the carriage with Faith, but they decided that, given her condition, she would be more comfortable on board ship.

"Fret not," Faith said cheerfully as the sisters embraced. "You know of my knack for making things turn out the way I wish. For a certainty, I shall sup with you tomorrow evening."

Faith watched her sister climb into the longboat and saw it disappear into the thick fog swirling above the water. Turning, she dispatched John to a nearby tavern to fetch them both a bite to eat, then she settled in for the night. However, it was not long before the goings-on up and down the wharf kept sleep at bay. Randy seamen, loud and boisterous from the Thames-water beer they consumed, caroused the north bank of the river, rife with taverns, brothels and boardinghouses. Curled up on the hard carriage bench, Faith eventually dozed off, but only after stuffing the fingers of her gloves into her ears to shut out the noise.

That same night on the south bank of the Thames . . .

Plunged beneath the pitch-black waters of the river, Diana Falstaff couldn't see a thing. The weight of her soaked garments pulled her down, down, down; then suddenly her descent shuddered to a halt. Desperately fighting the water that held her captive, Diana surmised her skirt had fixed on . . . *something.*

Grabbing one fistful of cloth after another, she managed to right herself, then suddenly her head shot out of the water. Gasping for air, she fought the waves rushing onto shore as she groped for something, *anything,* to cling onto. What she found felt prickly and slick with slime, but it wasn't going anywhere, so she wrapped both arms around it and held on tight.

Gasping for air, she finally found her voice. *"Help! He-e-l-p me, please!"*

A furious splashing nearby claimed her attention.

In moments the splashing ceased, and she felt movement beneath the water. Of a sudden, she knew her skirt was free, for it billowed up around her. Then a cold wet hand grasped her arm. Loosening her grip from what she suspected was a tree root, she let her rescuer drag her onto the muddy embankment where she lay for a time coughing and sputtering.

Without a word, Sallie Mae dove back into the foul-smelling water. Beneath the surface it was dark as pitch, but she knew other souls were floundering, and she meant to do what she could to save them.

She and her siblings had spent many summer afternoons in the pond in the meadow, but this was the first time she'd ever saved a human from drowning. She'd once saved a kitten, but her brothers insisted that kittens could swim, so perhaps that didn't count. But most humans couldn't swim, and on this tragic night, apparently she was the only one who could.

After several plunges into the river, Sallie Mae never once caught sight of another soul. Apparently, the Thames had carried all but two of them to the very bottom.

Her chest tight, Sallie Mae finally dragged herself onto shore. "I fear they's all g-gone, miss." Exhausted, her teeth began to chatter from the cold.

Pulling herself upright, Diana gazed toward the waterlogged lad, his small body shuddering. "The wherrymen have come.

Perhaps they'll find . . . someone." A sob escaped her. "I-If only we had stopped when the storm began."

For what seemed like hours, the pair sat huddled together, their eyes blanched from the wind as they tried to see through the dense fog that all but obscured the river. Suddenly an enormous apparition burst onto shore and headed straight toward them. Both girls sprang to their feet. Diana screamed.

Sallie Mae, possessing a bit more presence of mind than her grieving companion, realized the apparition was one of the horses, apparently also flung into the river along with the others.

"Whoa, there!"

As the animal galloped past, she managed to snatch the leather strap trailing behind it in the mud. The frightened horse whinnied, but with a shake of its dripping mane, obeyed her command. Calmed, Sallie Mae led the animal to a nearby tree and wrapped the wet leather strap around the trunk. With the horse tethered, she worked to extricate the dangling scraps of wood tangled up in its harness.

Later, a wherryman from one of the boats came ashore. The man spoke a few words to Diana, then left again to resume his search. Anxiously watching, she sat on the muddy embankment praying that any minute her parents and Sara would come straggling out of the water. Sometime later, the lad who'd rescued Diana left with the wherryman. She'd heard them talking in hushed tones. She hadn't learned the boy's name, or where the two were headed.

Eventually the night watchman, a wizened old man carrying a lantern, bells and a pikestaff, appeared. Diana had earlier heard him calling out the hour, "Eight o' the clock; rain 'as ceased! Nine o' the clock . . ." and so on.

He soon approached Diana. "Ye'd best be moving along, miss. Petty Constable'll think yer a vagrant and lock ye up in the high cage."

"But I cannot leave, sir! My family . . . they are all . . . surely someone will . . ."

Just then, another of the wherrymen approached. "Ye'd best accept the fact yer loved ones is a-restin' at the bottom of the river, miss."

"*No!* You must keep looking!"

He shook his head. "If'n a body don't surface in the first quarter hour, they's not likely to."

"Bodies'll likely wash up at Dead Man's Stairs," the night watchman said matter-of-factly.

"Dead Man's Stairs?"

The wherryman nodded. "Down river, miss; near Wappin'."

"But . . . cannot *something* be done?"

"Nothing left to do, miss. Watchman here, he knows they's a carriage tumbled into the river. Folks drowned."

"Thames swallows up hundreds o' folks ever' year. No need to send for the 'zaminer since they's no bodies to 'zamine."

"But . . . shouldn't someone . . . know their names?"

A look passed between the men.

"Names don't matter none, miss. Watchman, he'll report the accident to the Constable on the morrow. Four souls perished, ye say? Two men, two women."

In the darkness, the horse neighed.

"That yer horse, miss?" the watchman asked.

"It was one of the carriage horses. The other one . . . seems to have disappeared."

"Drowned or run off, most like," the wherryman said.

"Or fell lame when the coach tumbled into the river," the watchman added. "If'n it was lame, no doubt already been slaughtered for its flesh. Ye'd best make use of this one, miss, and be movin' on."

Shocked, Diana cried, "I cannot simply go away and . . . and leave my family *here!*"

"Ye can write yer loved ones' names down in yer parish Death Registry," the wherryman said, "if'n it'll make ye feel better. Watch is right. Ye'd best move along now. Not safe here for a pretty young thing all alone."

"But . . . *where* am I to go?"

Both men shrugged before they wandered off.

Chapter 5

Dawn found Diana Falstaff still sitting anxiously on the wet riverbank, her knees drawn to her chest, her clothing sodden. Nothing could persuade her to leave the site where her parents and dear friend Sara Wakefield had . . . disappeared. The rain had ceased hours ago; now a swirling greenish-gray fog hung low over the black water, making it impossible to see anything. Exhausted from her all-night vigil, Diana's head fell forward onto her knees. In seconds, her eyes fluttered shut.

A half hour later, noises coming from somewhere jolted her awake. The sky had lightened and the low-hanging fog lifted; in places, even dissipated. Hoping she might now be able to see farther out over the water, Diana sprang to her feet and, grabbing handfuls of water-logged skirt, she trudged through the muddy sludge to the water's edge. Her eyes scanned the river as far as she could see, hoping for a glimpse of her father or mother or Sara, clinging to a piece of wreckage or other debris in the water. But she saw no one. On the far north bank of the river, she spotted a few torches flickering near a jetty and from the windows of one or two great houses, light shone from a window. Smoke curled lazily from chimneys.

Becoming aware now of noises above her on the cobbled street—a cock crowing, gulls calling as they swooped low over the water, the clatter of a farmer's cart—Diana surmised the huge city was coming awake. Still, she stood dejectedly staring out over the placid water that only hours ago had claimed the lives of everyone in the world she held dear.

What was she to do now?

At length, she turned and spotted the horse that came charging up out of the river in the darkness, still tethered to the tree. With a heavy heart, she headed that direction, her anxious gaze now searching the riverbank for something, *any*thing, that might have belonged to her family. She stepped over splintered pieces of the carriage and assorted debris, then, spying an object, she hastened toward it. Drawing nearer, her eyes filled with tears when she saw that the object was the end of Sara's brown leather valise jutting up from the muddy shore.

Giving a smart tug, she released the bag and sank to the ground, one finger tracing the gold *SW* stamped beneath the clasp. Although covered with grit, the leather still felt smooth and cool. Tears pooled in her eyes when she recalled Sara telling her that her father had oiled the bag to render it waterproof.

Blinking through her tears, Diana undid the clasp. She and Sara were close on the same size; perhaps she might borrow a dry garment from her friend. She choked back a sob. Sara would no longer need her things. Not caring who might be watching, Diana stepped out of her sodden skirt and dropped it behind her in a crumpled heap. From inside Sara's bag, she drew out a clean, dry plaid woolen skirt. She hurriedly pulled it on over her damp petticoat and stockings. Snapping the clasp, she picked up the valise and, with a resigned sigh, trudged toward the horse.

"Come along, Horse. It appears we have no choice but . . . to leave." Loosening its tether, she turned her back on the river and, leading the large animal behind her, began an upward climb to the street above. Already it was teeming with carters, porters, farmers herding knots of bleating goats and sleepy-eyed cattle toward London Bridge.

Feeling set adrift in a world full of strangers, Diana managed to scramble onto the horse's back, sans saddle. In front of her, she tightly clutched all that was left of her former life, Sara's grimy valise. Uncertain where she was headed, she and the horse joined the thickening throng on the cobbled street. All she knew now was that the world she had known and loved all her life was gone forever . . . and she had no clue where to turn.

Quayside that same morning . . .

With the dawn came even more disruption as the wharf filled up with seamen and journeymen scurrying thither and yon. The river soon became clogged with vessels. Tilt-boats sporting colorful canopies, slow-going barges and heavy merchant ships heading for jetties to unload their cargoes, competed for water space with dozens of wherrymen who, with their longboats, daily plied a trade on the Thames.

Mid-morning, Faith Plumleigh climbed atop the platform of the coach to watch the goings-on as she whiled away the long hours of the day seated beside John.

"The Thames is far wider than I expected," she mused. "The river seems a virtual forest of masts. I never knew there were so many boats in all the world."

"Do seem quite a lot o' 'em," John agreed.

Afternoon, more and more people converged on the already teeming wharf. Faith anxiously watched as scores of young ladies gathered on the jetty, most accompanied by one or more family members, who remained by their sides until it was time to present their Letters of Acceptance to the man holding the list.

"Oh, dear, so many have come," Faith moaned. From her perch beside John, she watched emotional farewell scenes unfold on the wharf. Heartbroken mothers held onto their daughters as long as possible, siblings embraced, fathers merely nodded a curt goodbye. Faith, who had earlier asked John to drive the small coach as close to the jetty steps as possible, overheard one woman ask the man if letters could be delivered home to England from across the sea. He assured her that missives were indeed carried back and forth, although delivery was often a hit-or-miss proposition.

When at last the shadows of the long day began to lengthen and the busy throng thinned, Faith decided to approach the man at the jetty steps to ask how many, if any, berths on the Bride Ship remained unfilled. When he told her that only two young ladies had yet to check in, her stomach tightened. She was about to resume her post atop the platform when her attention was diverted by the sounds of weeping. Spotting a girl clinging to an older woman clutching a tattered old valise and an elderly man hovering close by, Faith drew nearer the distraught family.

"But I do not *wish* to go, Mama! I am afraid!"

"You must go, child. We've ten other mouths to feed. This likely be yer only hope to find a man. Tell her, husband."

The girl's father seemed dismayed. "If'n she don't want to go, Mother, I don't 'spect we outta' force 'er—"

"Oh, shut yer mouth, you old fool! Ye're a-goin' gel and there's an end to it. Stop yer frettin' and git on that boat!"

"No-o-o! I won't go! *I won't!*"

That same day on the streets of London . . .

Finding herself alone in the city that morning after both her parents and dear friend Sara Wakefield had been swallowed up by the Thames, Diana Falstaff rode aimlessly for hours. She knew she should attempt to locate her kinsmen in London, but she had no idea where the Prescotts lived. Given the enormous size of the city, she could look for days, perhaps weeks, and never find them. More than once, she'd turned onto a narrow side street, which seemed only to meander around and around and eventually lead nowhere. London's wider thoroughfares teemed with horse-drawn carts and wagons piled high with goods. Walkways were crowded with shabbily dressed people and knots of hungry-looking waifs, some crying for mamas that were nowhere in sight, others trying to keep up with mischievous urchins darting here and there, stealing an orange or apple from a distracted vendor's cart. As the long hours of the day dragged on, the oppressive sights and noise and stench of the city further repelled Diana.

Tears filled her eyes, and she'd slump onto the horse's long neck, crying uncontrollably; then, regaining control, she'd sniff back her tears and try to think what to do. It occurred to her that she might attempt to locate her stepbrothers, but . . . she did not wish to see them. Truth to tell, she also did not wish to see the Prescotts, or attend her beloved cousin Hamilton's wedding ceremony. The absence of her parents would, no doubt, throw a pall over the festivities, but it would not delay them. To locate her kinsmen now would throw her at the mercy of the Prescotts for the remainder of her life. But how was she to go on now without her parents, or Sara, by her side? If she did not locate her kinsmen's home, how long would it be before *they* learned of the accident, or would they ever? Perhaps Hamilton would inherit her father's lands and the small income from the tenants who still farmed it. Perhaps, if she could find the Prescotts' home *before* Hamilton said his vows, there might still be a chance for the two of them to be together. But no. Hamilton would never cry off. He was too much the gentleman. He would marry the girl his parents chose for him. And in all likelihood, the creditors would claim the Falstaff lands and everything else of value in the house, which meant that she now had . . . no worth. Despite her deep love for her family's lovely manor home in the country, with no money, how would she manage? *What was she to do now?*

She began to ask if someone could direct her to Wapping and the Dead Man's Stairs. Perhaps she would find the bodies of her parents, or Sara, washed up there, which would at least confirm . . . their deaths.

Much later that afternoon, Diana's diligence finally brought her to the jetty known as Dead Man's Stairs, but seeing no swollen bodies floating on the foul-smelling water, she hurriedly moved on.

"Come, Bug-a-Boo"—which is what she'd begun to call the horse because the mare had given her and the lad who pulled her from the river such a fright—"I haven't a clue where I am going, but I suppose I'd best get there before nightfall."

The aroma of food wafting toward the cobbled street from the taverns lining the north side of the river reminded Diana that she'd eaten nothing all day. But she had no money with which to purchase anything. Sliding off the horse's back again, she wandered toward another steep staircase that led down to the river. Perched on the top step, she listlessly gazed out over the water. But here the overpowering stench of rotting fish and dank and dark and forgotten things soon repelled her.

Tears filled her eyes. Could she *ever* accept that both her parents and dear friend Sara were now a part of this foul-smelling river now lapping innocently against the bottom step of the jetty? Because the accident had happened so quickly there had not been time even for a quick goodbye. One minute they were jouncing along inside the carriage, the next, they were flying through the cold night air, never to lay eyes upon one another again. It was a cruel, unjust fate.

Suddenly her reverie was broken by the voice of a wherryman who'd silently rowed up to the jetty. Grasping an oar in one hand, the other end immersed in the water, he asked if she wished to be ferried somewhere. Diana shook her head and continued to sit, chin cupped in her hands as she contemplated her uncertain future. At length, her growling stomach again urged her to seek out sustenance. Returning to her patient companion, she retrieved Sara's valise and searched inside for a few coins with which to purchase a crust of bread or meat. Instead, she drew out a packet of papers. Examining them, she realized that one of the pages was the important missive Sara had excitedly shown her the afternoon she told her of her plans.

Suddenly an idea sprang to Diana's mind. In her hands she held Miss Sara Wakefield's Letter of Acceptance from the New Virginia Company inviting her to join the Bride Ship. She was also in possession of Sara's valise, which contained all her belongings. But Sara was gone. What if Diana *became* Sara Wakefield? To travel to the New World and make a new life for herself was far and away more appealing than any other option open to her.

Her eyes quickly scanned the letter. It said the young ladies must present themselves by four of the clock on this very day . . . or be turned away. Glancing skyward, Diana determined from the lengthening shadows that it must be near four of the clock now.

"Sir," she called to the waterman, "where might I find a ship called the *King's Embassy*?"

"Be glad to take ye there, miss." The man's tone conveyed his eagerness to earn a few coins.

"Thank you, sir. I shall ride. Just, please . . . point me in the right direction."

A bit farther down the wharf . . .

The sound of horses' hooves ringing upon the cobblestones drew Faith Plumleigh's attention from the sobbing girl pleading with her parents. Instead, Faith turned to watch a dark-haired girl, curiously attired in a mud-splattered bodice and blouse over an impeccably clean plaid skirt, hurriedly dismount and lead her horse—from whose neck a muddy brown leather valise dangled—toward the man at the jetty steps.

Worrying her lower lip, Faith felt compelled to follow the girl with the horse. She reached the stairs just as the man standing there wearily asked the late arrival her name.

"I am Miss Sara Wakefield, sir." The girl handed the man a folded-up piece of parchment. "Here is my Letter of Acceptance."

Faith's breath caught in her throat as she watched the girl *and* the horse climb into a longboat and slowly head for one of the pair of Bride Ships anchored some distance away in the harbor. She had only just dejectedly turned away from the jetty when she spotted the girl who had been pleading with her parents thrust her chin up and flounce past her mother.

"Miss!" Faith called, thinking that if the girl had changed her mind about going, she might obtain *her* berth on the ship. When neither the girl nor her parents took notice, Faith broke into a run. She simply *had* to know if the girl had indeed changed her mind about going. Just then, she saw the girl's father—trailing a few feet behind his overset wife and daughter—toss a crumpled piece of paper to the ground.

"Won't be a-needin' this," he muttered.

Faith snatched up the fluttering page and a second later cried, "Fetch my bag, John!"

Reaching the jetty steps, Faith handed the soiled piece of paper to the man, now seated on the top step resting his weary limbs.

"I found my Letter, sir," she announced smartly. "It had slipped between the cushions inside the coach."

An eyebrow lifted. "That so, Miss."

Not until the longboat had nearly reached the ship did it occur to Faith that the man had not examined the Letter or demanded to know her name so he might check it off his list. Which was fortunate, since she'd been so excited to finally be in possession of the coveted Letter of Acceptance that she hadn't bothered to read the name of the girl to whom it was addressed. But, then, perhaps the precise name on the letter no longer mattered. She was at last on her way to Prudence and the New World!

CHAPTER 6

The first time Sallie Mae climbed into the hammock slung between two posts in the cramped space below deck she shared with the cook, she fell right back out and landed with a thud on the damp wooden floor.

"A fine sailor ye'll make, lad!" The *King's Embassy* cook laughed. "Now git ye'self some sleep. We'll have a passel of hungry ladies to feed on the morrow."

After Sallie Mae's valiant attempt the previous night to save those poor souls who'd drowned, one of the wherrymen had asked if she'd like a lift somewhere. When Sallie Mae told him her plan was to go to sea, he'd offered to carry her to the quay. This morning long before the sun burned through the mist, she'd found her way aboard one of the two barks bound for the New World. She'd felt dreadful leaving the young lady she'd pulled from the river alone on shore last night, but didn't feel she could pass up the offer to get herself where she needed to be.

Boarding the ship early that morning, she quickly learned that nearly any healthy man wearing a shirt, shoes and trousers who stepped up and volunteered to go to sea was willingly given the opportunity to do so. A volunteer saved the captain the trouble of pressing an unwilling man into service. All that was required of a new recruit was to state his name and age. Since apparently *any* name would do, Sallie Mae promptly shortened hers to "Sal" and changed Pigee to "Peters," then watched with satisfaction when her new name, Sal Peters, was set down in the ship's muster. The officer even promised to pay her wages!

"How old are ye, lad?" He'd asked without looking up.

Borrowing from her brother James's experience, Sallie Mae replied, "Thirteen, sir."

"Shoulda' knowed," the man muttered, "yer voice still sounds like a girl." Still, he didn't look up. "Ye say ye can cook?"

"That's rot, sir. I kin cook anythin'!"

"Cook's pantry's up them steps; in the forecastle."

Inquiring the precise way from a fellow sailor, Sallie Mae soon found the cook's pantry, and later the ship's store, located in the bowels of the ship, where dozens of hogsheads of salted fish and beef, barley, oats, ale, and kegs of water were stowed. On the way, she'd learned where the rest of the crew bunked, a cramped space squeezed beneath the forecastle under the bow. To sleep near only the cook at night, fully clothed, would mean she'd have less trouble keeping her secret safe.

Once she met the cook, a wiry fellow called One-Eye, named for obvious reasons—he wore a black patch over his blind eye, but claimed he could see as well as ten men out of the other—the pair set at once to work. Though the heavy hogsheads were cumbersome to push around, tilt, then return again to an upright position, she did her best to do all her new employer asked of her.

"Hogsheads gets lighter as we go," One-Eye assured her, then left her to line up the casks according to their contents: dried peas next to the corn, barley and oats to the fore, the ones marked fish and beef aft. Only once did she come upon a pair of barrels far too heavy to scoot aside and had to ask One-Eye for assistance.

"Don't mind yeself about these two, lad," One-Eye declared, puffing even as he shoved both heavy hogsheads up against a far wall. "We'll not be getting' into these on this voyage." He leveled a one-eyed gaze at her. "Ye dinna' open 'em, did ya?"

Sallie Mae shook her head. "No, sir. Look to be nailed shut."

"You jes leave 'em be. Now, get y'self up on deck and stir that pot so the gruel don't git lumpy," One-Eye said gruffly.

Actual cooking on-board ship, Sallie Mae learned, was done over an open hearth constructed of bricks. Pots and kettles hung over an iron tripod affair. The "cook room," or galley, was situated near a hatchway that opened onto the hold, strategically placed so that flying sparks and smoke would be less apt to ignite a deadly fire on deck. Once a meal was prepared, One-Eye told her, the heavy pots of food were carried down a steep flight of steps to an enclosed cabin on the 'tween deck where the ladies assembled to eat. Additional food was carried to the round house, located in the stern above the quarterdeck, where the ship's officers, chirurgeon and, at times, the minister and his wife took their meals. The rest of the twenty-five or so crewmen ate standing up, or resting their rumps on piles of hemp or rigging, anywhere they could find on the main deck.

After cooking up enough victuals of a morning to feed everyone on board, Sallie Mae found it took several hours to sand the wooden trenchers and spoons clean. Almost immediately it was time to begin preparing the next meal. For Sallie Mae, the grueling work proved both hot and tiresome—hefting shovels full of coal, stoking the fire and carrying heavy kettles from here to there took nearly all the energy she had in her small body.

But she soon realized that staying busy the majority of the day might prove a blessing in disguise, for by noon of that first day, she realized her plan to masquerade as a lad was not entirely foolproof. Apart from the trouble she encountered staying put in a hammock long enough to actually sleep at night, there was another matter of import she had not considered. A private matter. Generally speaking, when a sailor needed to relieve himself, he simply did so off the side of the ship, taking into account the direction of the wind, of course. If it happened to be raining, as she was told it did nigh on every morning, and a sailor was on deck, he didn't bother stepping to the side of the bark; he simply did his business right where he stood. Since that was not something Sallie Mae could do, finding a slop bucket when she needed one, and the privacy to use it, became an ongoing problem.

"You plagued with the flux, lad?" asked One-Eye when she'd come hurrying back to her post by evening that first day, stuffing her shirt into her trousers after she'd ducked 'round a corner where she'd earlier spotted a slop bucket.

Blushing, Sallie Mae did not reply, just quickly returned to work. Because she had also begun to fear that her feminine voice might give away her gender, she'd taken to rarely speaking, thus perpetuating the notion that she, or rather *he,* was a timid young fellow, not given to useless chatter. When she did speak, her replies were so meek and mild that when asked her name, some mistook Sal for Saul. Rather than correct the mistake, she answered to either moniker, telling herself that all she really had to do was successfully complete this one journey across the sea, then all her troubles would be over. She also made a special point of remembering to keep her jacket tightly buttoned across her chest, something she realized she had not worried about last night when she plunged into the river. But it had been dark as pitch then and the poor girl on shore was far too distraught to notice anything amiss.

Sallie Mae did recall the coach driver telling her he was to deliver one of the young ladies inside the coach to the Bride Ship. So, that first night at supper, when Sallie Mae recognized the very girl she'd pulled from the river, she was not taken aback.

"You," said the dark-haired young lady, raising sad hazel eyes to gaze full at Sallie Mae when she handed the girl a trencher of steaming hot victuals. "It is you, isn't it?"

Sallie Mae nodded, her meek reply a mere lop-sided grin.

"You disappeared before I could properly thank you." The girl spoke softly. "You were very kind to help. I am indebted to you for pulling me from the river."

Sallie Mae shrugged. "T'weren't nothin', miss."

"You were very brave." The girl murmured before she moved on.

Although Diana Falstaff feared her heart might break in two from the heavy burden of grief she carried, that she actually had somewhere to go gave her reason to rejoice. Upon her arrival late that afternoon, Diana had learned that half the young ladies had boarded the *King's Embassy,* the other half the *Queen Anne.* The final young lady to board the *King's Embassy* did so soon after Diana. Both were assigned to the same cabin.

Four groups of ten girls each were to occupy one of four narrow enclosures lining opposite sides of the ship in the hold below the 'tween deck. The berths they slept in were merely wooden troughs on the floor, each space lined with a straw-filled mat, each girl's individual sleeping space separated by a length of board. Although there was barely room to walk between the end of the row of troughs and the wooden bench hugging the inside of the ship's wall, a space beneath the seat of the bench was where the girls were to store their personal belongings.

Upon entering the cabin for the first time, Diana had spotted the small "Welcome" bundle awaiting her on an empty berth. Pulling apart the strings, her eyes filled with tears when she saw that the bundle contained the promised new petticoat, made of coarse, unbleached white muslin, and a pair of warm lambskin gloves. Fingering the gloves, she recalled again her friend Sara excitedly telling her about the finery to be given each girl who made the journey to the New World. Laying the gloves aside, she attempted to shove aside the painful memories that rose up every time she thought about Sara or her parents. She drew out a crisp white linen cap and apron, and two pairs of sturdy brown leather boots, similar to the ankle-high brogues she'd seen the Irish girls who used to serve her family wear. There were also two pairs of warm, knitted stockings. Folded up beneath the welcome bundle was a coarse woolen bed rug, which Diana hoped would also be hers to keep. Already she could tell the creaky old ship was drafty, and bobbing about as it was now in the freezing waters of the Thames made the air below deck feel especially cold.

Perched on the bench, Diana replaced her ruined kid slippers with the new leather boots, all the while fighting against the horrendous memories of the night before. With tears swimming in her eyes, she silently thanked Sara for wishing to travel to the New World and having the courage to make her dream come true, for it now meant that *she* would be taken far, far away from England and the terrible loss she'd suffered. Of a sudden, rage filled her heart, and she vowed never again to return to London, or to England. And she hated the Thames River for snatching from her everything she held dear. All that was left now were precious memories of the safe and secure life she'd had with her parents—memories that now must remain hidden away in her heart and never spoken of again.

Although Diana kept primarily to herself that first night, early the next morning mere moments before the ship was set to sail—for the wind had indeed picked up, rendering the weather favorable for sailing—complaints from two young ladies in the dining chamber claimed everyone's attention.

"The conditions aboard this vessel are intolerable!" one young lady declared to the captain moments after all the girls had crowded into the small cabin to break their fast.

"I have never before slept on the floor and I do not intend to do so again!" chimed in a second girl.

"Captain," the first girl spoke up louder, "Miss Templeton and I have decided *not* to make the journey. We insist you return us to shore at once!"

"Very well," the captain replied. "I shall dispatch a man to row ye to shore at once. Be quick about it, ladies. We sail within the hour."

There was a good bit of scurrying about as the two unhappy young ladies, one of whom had slept in Diana's cabin, gathered their belongings and hurried up on deck. The longboat, which had already been tied down for the voyage, was lowered and the ladies promptly rowed ashore.

The empty berth left by the departing girl in Diana's cabin was quickly filled.

"Gather your things, Prudence. The captain says you may switch cabins. We shall travel together after all!"

"Are you certain, Faith?"

"Of course I am certain! I would not say so otherwise!"

Chapter 7

That night, Prudence Plumleigh snuggled closer to the thin board separating her sleeping trough from the one where her younger sister lay. "I feel so much safer here beside you, Faith."

"I confess I was relieved when the captain agreed to let you switch cabins," Faith whispered in the darkness. "I shall be better able to look after you here."

"I am truly glad you insisted upon coming, Faith. I wonder how our mother took the news when John told her you'd also boarded the ship."

"I'll wager it came as no surprise."

Prudence grinned. "I expect not. She knows how headstrong you can be when you've set your mind to something. We shall write to her once we reach land. She will be pleased to know we are together and both safe."

Following the mid-day meal the day after the ship reached open waters, the ship's minister, Mr. Douglass, addressed the young ladies, squeezed in beside one another on backless benches in the cabin where they assembled for meals.

"Order, please," said the spindly, bespectacled man. Gazing over his audience of chattering females, he cleared his throat, apparently believing that to be sufficient notice that he wished now to speak.

When the weak gesture failed to elicit silence, his wife, a plumpish woman whose tidy white cap covered a mass of wiry gray hair, rose to her feet and barked, "Cease your nattering at once, ladies! Mr. Douglass has important matters to impart!"

Order reigned instantly. Mr. Douglass cleared his throat again and offered up yet another prayer of thanksgiving for the simple fare they'd just consumed. He then commenced to praise the young ladies for their courage and bravery in embarking on this important voyage across the sea in the name of England and their king.

"Fulfilling the purpose of this mission, ladies, which is for each of you to enter into the state of holy matrimony and . . . ahem, bring blessed children into the world, will ensure the growth and prosperity of the crown's newest colony, James Cittie, or, as it is now called, Jamestown."

Light applause followed the minister's remarks, but when the girls' excited chatter again rose up, Mrs. Douglass sprang to her feet. Her glare alone brought the ladies' exuberance to a halt.

In a droning tone, Mr. Douglass recited rules drawn up by the ship's captain. The one most heartily emphasized was that, for the duration of the voyage, the ladies were to remain below deck *at all times,* in or near their respective cabins.

"We are not allowed to stroll about on the main deck?" one young lady indignantly objected.

Mrs. Douglass responded to the girl's question. "Ye are to stay below deck out of harm's way. As surely ye noticed when ye came aboard, the main deck is a labyrinth of riggin' and ropes and tethered sails. For safety's sake, we must *all* stay below deck . . . at *all* times."

"But what are we to do every day?" asked several girls in unison.

"Our cabins are quite small, ma'am." Faith Plumleigh, unable to restrain herself, actually rose to her feet to speak out. "Are you saying we are allowed to leave our cabins *only* to gather here for meals?"

Mrs. Douglass edged aside her mild-mannered husband. "Those of you young ladies accustomed to a daily walk-about will find sufficient space between yer cabins for a promenade. The remainder of yer time should be spent a'readin' yer Bibles."

"We are to spend all day, every day, reading our Bibles?" Faith exclaimed.

"Ye are to make wise use of yer time, and I can think of no better way than readin' the Lord's word. Eight weeks is not such a long stretch. The voyage will be over afore ye know it. I will, of course, be addressin' ye regarding what to expect in the New World . . . yer homes, the men, and such like."

Faith resumed her seat on the crowded bench near the back of the room beside her sister. "I, for one, do not intend to spend every day reading my Bible."

"Faith, please," her sister whispered, "you mustn't draw attention to yourself."

"You may, of course, linger here for as long as ye wish after meals," Mrs. Douglass added. "However, ye mustn't cause a ruckus such as would alarm the crew. Remember, under *no* circumstances are ye to speak with the seamen. The men have been instructed *never* to address ye young ladies. If one of ye was to fall ill, send a message straightaway to either m'self, Mr. Douglass, or the ship's chirurgeon, Mr. Emerson."

Faith popped again to her feet. "If we are not allowed to address a member of the crew, precisely by whom are we to send a message?"

Mrs. Douglass's lips pursed. "Any one of you may scratch on *my* cabin door. Remember, if a girl is observed speakin' to or behavin' in an untoward manner with a seaman, she will be confined to her cabin for the duration of the voyage. Understood, ladies?"

There were nods all around, but when Faith popped up again to speak, even her sister's eyes rolled skyward. "Are we allowed to speak to the cook, madam? This morning, I discovered I did not have a spoon at my place and I—"

Mrs. Douglass huffed with exasperation. "You are allowed to speak with the cook, young lady, and to the cook's helper, but only whilst in this room." She paused, a stern gaze seeming to dare the impertinent miss to speak out again. Resuming her seat, her husband rose once more.

He told the girls that when they reached Jamestown, they would not be required at once to settle on a man and marry, but that when they did take a husband, the gentleman would be required to repay, in tobacco, the New Virginia Company for the girl's passage to the New World. Until such time as they married, they were *never* to be treated as servants and that *any* impropriety on the part of any man in Jamestown must be reported at once to Governor Yeardley.

"Sir," a young lady inquired, "many of us are wondering where we are to live in Jamestown, before we marry and have our own homes?"

"An excellent question, miss. Upon arrival, each of you will be assigned to a family with whom ye'll reside. The Jamestown colonists are even now aware that a pair of Bride Ships is en route to their shores. You will be assigned to a family who will provide shelter and sustenance."

The minister then rather timidly veered toward the matter of modesty in a girl's demeanor and dress, but after speaking only a few tentative words, a tug at his sleeve by his outspoken wife interrupted him. "I will address that intimate topic with the ladies in one of my lectures. I daresay the girls have heard quite enough for one day."

"Very well, madam." Mr. Douglass favored his wife with a relieved smile and hastily gathered up his strewn papers.

Diana Falstaff was among the first of the young ladies to quit the room and at once headed toward the steep stairs that led to the main deck, seemingly in direct opposition to the rule forbidding such excursions.

Moments earlier, One-Eye had sent Sallie Mae up on deck. When she spotted the girl she'd pulled from the river hurriedly walking toward the enclosed area where the animals—pigs, goats, half a dozen cows, and one lone horse—were penned and tethered, she turned full around to watch the pretty girl, her dark head primly covered by a tidy white cap, her eyes lowered demurely as she walked. When Sallie Mae saw the girl pause to stroke the chestnut mare's nose, she hastened that way.

" 'Cuse me, miss. Is that the same horse what come chargin' up on shore that night?"

The girl nodded.

"Wha' do ye call 'er?"

"Bug-a-Boo."

Sallie Mae grinned. " 'Cuz she near frightened us silly comin' outta' the water like she done?"

The girl smiled tightly.

Sallie Mae stroked the horse's nose. After a pause, the dark-haired girl again spoke softly. "I-I am glad you are here. What is your name?"

Sallie Mae blanched. She hated tellin' fibs. "Crew calls me Sal."

"Thank you again for your kindness, Sal."

Without revealing her name, the solemn young lady hurried away. As Sallie Mae returned to work, sweepin' ashes from the outdoor hearth, her heart ached for the grief-stricken young girl. Were she not so caught up maintainin' her own perfidy, she'd befriend the sad miss who'd lost her loved ones that terrible night. Though Sallie Mae's family was alive and well, the pleasant memories of her former life still sometimes tugged at the edges of her mind before she fell into an exhausted slumber at night.

She wished now she had thought out her plan a bit more carefully. Scarcely into the voyage, and already she'd ripped a hole in her jacket, the part that covered the swell of a breast. Every day she lived in fear that the small tear would become a large rent. Every time she bent to grasp the edges of one of the heavy barrels to shift the hogshead to one side or another, the coarse fabric of her jacket caught on the rough edges of the barrel's metal binding. What would happen when her jacket became ripped to shreds? The shirt beneath her jacket was made from an even thinner fabric. When *it* ripped apart . . . then what?

"Girls!" Mrs. Douglass's commanding voice caused the girls to look up from their trenchers one afternoon that week.

Seated in the rear of the cramped quarters, Faith Plumleigh groaned.

"Today I shall address a topic of supreme importance." She opened her Bible, and after thumbing through it, read aloud the verse likening the value of a good woman to rubies, and several other passages of a similar ilk.

"I admonish ye girls to cease yer babblin' and chatterin'. Otherwise, the young men ye meet in Jamestown will think ye are loose-minded and frivolous. There will be no time for frivolity in the New World, ladies. Yer new lives will consist of *hard* work, harder and rougher than any ye have ever known."

Several girls exchanged alarmed glances.

"I expect some of ye have been accustomed to servants waitin' upon ye; like as not in the New World, ye will not be afforded that luxury. Not unless yer man is possessed of a great deal of property and has bondsmen to serve him. In yer new lives, ladies, ye will likely do yer own chores and care for yer own families without help."

Diana Falstaff chewed on her lower lip. It had never occurred to her that she would not have one or more servants to assist with running her household. Even in her parents' reduced circumstances, they retained the services of a housekeeper and cook. And her father kept a stable hand. How would she manage with no one to help? She knew nothing about running a household.

"Ye will be required to plant and tend yer own corn," Mrs. Douglass added, "and in the autumn, yer man might even call upon ye to help him harvest his tobacco leaves."

Diana's hazel eyes widened. *Harvest tobacco leaves?* She had never performed any sort of physical labor in her life, and most certainly nothing . . . in a field!

"Tobacco is money in the New World, girls, and when yer husband needs tools or such like, he will no doubt pay for them and any other household items ye might be a-needin' with tobacco leaves."

One young lady spoke up. "Are you saying we shall *not* be given an allowance by our husbands?"

Diana eagerly awaited the answer to that question.

Mrs. Douglass's lips pursed. "Whether or not ye receive money from yer husband, my dear, will be his affair." She shuffled through her papers. "Now, then, where was I? Ah, yes. You girls would not have been chosen for this sojourn if ye did not know how to conduct yerselves properly, but seein' as how ye have every last one left yer parents behind, parents who would ordinarily be a-preparin' ye for marriage, in their absence, I will impart the Godly advice they would 'ave give ye.

"When ye go a-lookin' for a man, I am telling ye true now, ladies . . ." She shook her index finger at her captive audience. "Don't go a'lookin' for somethin' as frivolous as . . . *love!*"

The collective intake of breath was audible. Several girls exchanged surprised glances.

"This is not a romantical adventure, ladies! Ye are not on a journey to find love. Make no mistake, love is a *foul* vice; it blindeth the wit and causeth silly girls to fall into groanin' and complainin'. There is no time for blushin' or weepin' in the New World, ladies."

Faith Plumleigh's eyes narrowed.

"Romantical love is a vile and corrupt thing. It may seem at the outset to be sweet and pleasurable, but in the end it causeth reason to flee. A chaste maiden should pay no more heed to her feelin's of love than she would to the devil. When ye meet a man, ladies, it will be his hatred of all things pure, and *not* his affection, that driveth him to praise yer beauty and yer wit. When he declareth that he shall die if ye do not welcome his attentions or return his love, ye would do well to ask him how many amongst the thousands and thousands of lovers in the world hath died of love? Bah!

"To overcome the temptation of frivolous love, girls, ye must keep the ardent one from yer sight, and instead, turn to prayer in yer hearts."

Faith could restrain herself no longer. "But, madam, how are we to know if we wish to marry a man if we keep him from our sight?"

"Listen well, my dears," admonished the minister's wife. "If the man ye have set yer cap for hath a fault, think on *that* rather than the fanciful phrase he so easily tosseth about. A man who wishes only to draw ye into his embrace is a man to be despised! It is yer *virginity,* ladies, that must be regarded with reverence, for to lose it afore ye marry will rain down all manner of sorrow upon yer heads. So graceless a creature as the unchaste young lady will only bring sorrow to her kinfolk and mockin' amongst those who once loved her. All who knew her will shun her lest she contaminate them!"

Beside Faith, Prudence Plumleigh's brown eyes were round with fear. Faith reached to squeeze her older sister's hand. "Take no heed of her, Pru," she whispered.

"A man will not wed a woman who can so easily be drawn in by loose and vulgar talk, for once sated with his own pleasure, that man will despise and desert her. Ye must be pure in yer thoughts, ladies, holy, and unspoilt by lust . . . or lust's evil twin, *love!*"

Fearful that the woman's diatribe was having a detrimental effect upon her sister's fragile state of mind, Faith whispered, "Shall I tell her you are ill, so that we may leave?"

With tears now pooled in her eyes, Prudence squeezed them shut and shook her head. "We mustn't draw attention to ourselves."

"Away from the watchful eye of yer parents, girls, in a strange and foreign land, ye will find yerselves surrounded by uncivilized men, many who have not seen or touched a woman in many months, years, even decades."

"Are the men in Jamestown as old as all that?" cried one young lady.

"A good many of them are."

"But, I thought we was meant to marry *young* men!" Her reply elicited a ripple of agreement.

"Girls, girls! What have I just said about chatterin' and babblin'?"

"That we mustn't," came a meek response.

"Indeed." Mrs. Douglass jerked on the pointed ends of her laced bodice. "You girls will soon be tempted by many a man's loose talk but, remember, a man will take to wife a *chaste* woman. Do not think that to snare a man ye must resort to feminine wiles or cunning. It is yer Godly purity and virtue, yes, yer *virtue,* that will win him in the end."

She snapped her Bible shut. "Let us pray."

Following a lengthy prayer that set many of her listeners to fidgeting, Mrs. Douglass cheerfully said, "Tomorrow I will impart the counsel of a wise man who hath writ a book upon the duty of marriage. Now return to yer cabins, ladies, and think on these things."

Faith turned to Prudence. "You needn't think on anything the old shrew says."

Once in the privacy of their cabin, Prudence wailed, "Oh, Faith, Mrs. Douglass is right!"

The sisters sat huddled together on the narrow bench that ran the length of the room along the ship's outer wall. They kept their voices low lest they be overheard by other girls milling about in the close confines of their cabin.

"No decent man will have me now. And if I do marry, he will surely thrust me aside once he learns I am . . . n-not pure."

"You mustn't take on so." Faith attempted to console her sister. "You are pretty enough to snare a man the minute we arrive in Jamestown. Many a babe is born before the allotted time has elapsed. All will turn out well in the end. I am certain of it. Don't fret, Pru; you risk injuring the babe."

"I cannot help myself. I should never have allowed Isaac to . . . t-touch me."

"I do own Isaac is a good-looking chap."

"Oh-h-h-h," Prudence wailed. "It was so *horrible,* I cannot bear to think on it."

Faith looked bewildered. "W-what was horrible? Surely, you do not mean . . . ?"

"I mean . . . *it.* It was horrible."

"But I thought . . ."

"I thought I must be doing something wrong. Isaac seemed to find it . . . pleasurable. Oh, Faith, I never wish to do it again, *ever!*"

Faith's brow puckered. "Well, that may pose a problem. I rather expect you shall be obliged to do it again at least once. Your husband must believe the babe you're carrying is his."

"Oh-h-h-h!" Prudence's head fell to her sister's shoulder.

Faith drew her close. After a pause, she said, "Pru, did you and Isaac commit the act . . . just the one time? Perhaps you are *not* with child!"

Prudence sniffed. "W-we did it . . . several times. I am so ashamed, Faith. Do you despise me for my sin? I despise myself."

"I love you, Prudence. If no man wishes to marry you, we shall simply put forth a . . . small falsehood."

Prudence swiped at her eyes. "Oh, Faith, we have already told so many lies. God will never forgive us another."

Faith tapped a forefinger to her chin. "We shall say that . . . your husband was killed; that when you volunteered for the Bride Ship, you did not yet know you were with child." She smiled with satisfaction. "Now, cease your silly frettin', Prudence Plumleigh. It will all come out right in the end, you'll see."

Although Faith managed to persuade her sister to dry her eyes, she was not certain she had put all of Pru's fears to rest. The following afternoon before Mrs. Douglass rose to address the girls, Faith wisely led her sister to their cabin and insisted she lie down whilst she returned to the 'tween deck to listen obediently to the afternoon lecture. Prudence, she decided, had heard quite enough from the pious Mrs. Douglass.

Chapter 8

Sallie Mae knew that Mrs. Douglass was addressing the young ladies every afternoon. Before she left the dining chamber balancing stacks of soiled trenchers, the woman had generally already commenced to speak. Sallie Mae began to slow her steps so she might hear a bit of what the minister's wife had to say. After all, once they reached Jamestown and she abandoned her disguise, she would also need to know what to expect.

Although they were not yet a fortnight out to sea, already Sallie Mae longed to join in the feminine chatter and laughter. The lewd-talking crewmen repelled her. The only time she felt free to speak was when she stood behind the table dishing up a girl's victuals and handing across the filled trencher. Each day she looked forward to seeing the pretty dark-haired girl she'd pulled from the river. She always made a point to address her. It occurred to her, however, that garbed as she was in tattered boy's clothing, perhaps she quite likely repelled the ladies. But considering her numerous dips in the Thames and the long hours she spent working every day, it was no wonder her shirt and trousers were soiled to the point of stinkin'.

"As promised, girls," Mrs. Douglass began that afternoon, "today I shall speak on yer duties in marriage. I will also address what ye may and may not expect afore ye marries."

Relieved that her sister was tucked snugly in their cabin in the hold, Faith settled back to ignore every single thing the woman said.

"Jamestown is not London, ladies, nor is it Bristol or Brighton. Ye cannot stroll into a shop for a new bonnet. Ye'll find no costly silks from which to fashion yer weddin' gowns. In short, there are no gewgaws to be had in Jamestown."

This remark elicited gasps of surprise from a number of the girls.

"Moreover, yer actual weddin' ceremony will not be akin to anythin' ye've witnessed at home. Most like, ye will simply stand afore the minister a'wearin' one of the frocks ye brung with ye. There'll likely be no music as there are no musical instruments in Jamestown, although I expect there might be singin'. Dependin' on the time o' year, there may or may not be a weddin' feast. Food in Jamestown is plentiful at harvest. Rest of the year ye must be frugal with yer foodstuffs."

"But we will have plenty to eat, won't we?" cried a rather plumpish young lady, who appeared not to have yet suffered from a lack of foodstuffs.

"Ye'll have plenty to eat. Now, as to yer homes. At the outset, it may be nothin' more'n a simple bark hut, or . . ."

"But we was tol' the men had thriving' plantations!"

Exclaimed another, "If'n we wished to remain poor as church mice, we'd 'a stayed in England!"

As several more girls loudly protested, Faith listened with perverse pleasure.

"Order, ladies! I insist upon order! Ye'll overset the crew."

Just then, the door of the cabin flew open and the ship's captain stepped in. "Mutiny, Mrs. Douglass?"

"On the contrary, sir. The girls were . . . cheering. All is well, sir."

"Ah." The captain gazed toward the now hushed gathering. "Very well, then. Carry on."

After the uniformed man had exited the chamber, Mrs.

Douglass glared at her charges. "I trust in future ye will kindly restrain yer'selves." She cleared her throat. "Now then, I shall address the matter of maintainin' domestic harmony in yer marriages. As ye know, God hath designated the husband as head of the household, meanin' yer man will be the absolute authority in yer life. In all ways, ladies, ye must submit to him."

At the back of the room, Faith folded her arms across her chest and turned to study her companions. About half the girls were near her and Pru's age; many appeared older. A few looked as if they had lied the other way, about how many years they had in their dish. Perhaps the men who'd organized the mission had not found it as easy as they thought to sign up young girls, or perhaps the organizers were less vigilant regarding the requirements than the man guarding the jetty steps had been.

It occurred to her that during the past fortnight, no one had ever read off the names on the revered list. It seemed now that they were out to sea, no one cared who was here. Each girl had been assigned to a particular cabin when she came aboard, but since then, friendships had formed, and many girls had traded places with one another. Because the task of looking after her sister weighed so heavily upon her mind, Faith had not formed a close friendship with any of the girls. Still, she thought it odd that no one came 'round at night to check on them.

Her cogitations turned to Prudence. Unfortunately, her sister was not faring well. She felt sick to her stomach nearly every morning now and tossed and turned throughout every long night. Faith wondered how the girl would last the entire voyage with little to no sleep and next to nothing in her stomach.

Sometime later, she was relieved to hear Mrs. Douglass say, "Now, return to yer cabins, my little doves, and think on these things."

Exhaling a breath of relief, Faith popped to her feet. "I dare-say this little dove could do with a breath of fresh air."

Most all the girls hurriedly streamed from the close confines of the cabin into the small patch of sunshine that filtered through the open hatch onto the 'tween deck. Faith gazed with longing toward the main deck. Due to the mass of sails flapping overhead, the glorious sunshine never reached the nether regions of the ship where the girls bunked, and it rarely reached the 'tween deck where they ate. Suddenly, from the corner of her eye, Faith spotted one girl halfway up the steep stairs leading to the upper deck.

In an instant, she decided to follow the errant miss. Once they both stepped onto the main deck, Faith recognized the girl as the one who'd boarded the ship directly ahead of her, the one who arrived at the jetty steps on horseback.

"Wait up," Faith called to the girl, who was walking quite swiftly and was already several yards ahead of her. Catching up, she said, "I see you are not cowed by the old lioness."

Diana's eyes cut 'round, but she said nothing. Nearly running now, Faith marveled at how expert the girl was at dodging ropes dangling from the flapping sails and stepping around coils of hemp scattered thither and yon. Her eyes forward, her chin elevated, the girl skirted past busy crewmen as if the men weren't even there.

"I believe we share a cabin. My name is Faith Plumleigh. Must we promenade so swiftly? The air here is so very pleasant, it would be delightful to slow down a bit and enjoy it."

The girl did not reply, nor did she slow her gait.

"Perhaps you are walking swiftly so as not to be caught disobeying the captain."

Diana glanced at the pretty auburn-haired girl scurrying to keep apace. "I have special permission from the captain to sojourn here."

It was then Faith noticed the girl was carrying a brush . . . a *hair* brush. She quickly put two and two together. "Ah. You are allowed to come here to tend your horse."

"I was unaware anyone knew I had brought along my horse."

Faith grinned. "I was near the jetty steps when you arrived that afternoon. I watched you and your horse climb into the longboat."

"I see." Diana did not recall seeing her companion on the jetty steps, but she did recognize her as the one who persistently asked impertinent questions of Mrs. Douglass.

Upon reaching the corner of the main deck where the animals were housed, Diana set to work brushing the mare's flank whilst Faith stroked the horse's soft nose. A pair of crewmen swabbing a nearby section of deck leered at the girls.

Faith could not help darting looks at the ruddy seamen. Both wore brightly colored breeches; but it was their muscular forearms and strong chests that claimed her attention. Inhaling a deep breath of gloriously fresh air, she reached to loosen the strings of the tidy white cap she wore. Letting it fall down her back, she shook out her long, red-gold curls. "The sunshine feels splendid on my back. You are fortunate the captain granted you permission to tend your horse. I daresay arriving in Jamestown with a horse will provide you an added advantage with the gentlemen."

"Excuse me?"

"A man will find a lady who also possesses a horse especially attractive."

Vigorously brushing the mare's flank, the flicker of a smile softened Diana's features.

"Well, I have not seen *that* before," Faith remarked dryly.

Diana glanced up.

"A smile. You appear quite glum for a young lady setting out on the adventure of a lifetime."

Diana turned back to her work. "Forgive me. I have not meant to be dour."

Faith spoke in a low tone. "With Mrs. Douglass lecturing us every day, I expect more and more of the girls will soon become too fearful to smile." She stroked the horse's smooth hide. "What do you call her?"

"Bug-a-Boo."

Faith giggled. "An apt name, to be sure. I meant, what do you call your horse?"

The corners of Diana's lips lifted. "I was referring to my horse."

"Oh." Faith laughed. "I thought you meant Mrs. Douglass. I daresay Bug-a-Boo suits her, as well. I declare I have never heard such silliness. I have decided to thwart her by falling in love the minute I step off the boat."

Just then, the pair of seamen sauntered past. One touched the brim of his grimy cap. "Hallo, ladies."

Faith eyed the men coyly. "Perhaps I shall fall in love *before* I step off the boat."

Diana followed the direction of the younger girl's gaze. "We'd best return to our cabin." Clearly the impressionable girl needed looking after far more than her horse did. She gave Bug-a-Boo a final pat on the rump and briskly headed toward the steep stairs that led to the hold.

Faith hurried to catch up. "You've not yet told me your name."

"Sar . . ." Diana began, then blurted out, "Diana." Since they'd boarded ship she'd noticed that not a single person, besides the girls themselves, called any one of them by name. Mrs. Douglass referred to them collectively as "young ladies" or her "little doves." Even the day Diana approached the captain to obtain permission to come up on deck to tend her horse, he had not asked her name. Since it was still quite painful to repeat her dear friend Sara's name, she decided that henceforth, she would remain as she'd always been: Diana. She did rather prefer the surname Wakefield to Falstaff, only because that name also evoked heart-wrenching memories. "Diana Wakefield."

"Well, Diana, perhaps I shall accompany you up on deck again . . . to help you tend Bug-a-Boo. Do you walk her about the deck?"

"Only when the sea is calm."

"Oh!" Faith exclaimed, lifting her skirt a few inches and twirling about. "I am so-o happy to be on the ship! Do come for me the very next time you mean to walk your horse. I shouldn't wish to spend every single day cooped up in our stuffy little cabin." Around and around she twirled. "The air smells so sweet and fresh! I feel as free as a bird, as if I could fly!"

Diana hurried her pace. Upon reaching their cramped quarters, she busied herself putting away the brush she used to groom her horse.

Her color heightened, Faith strolled into the cabin, eyeing her new friend with suspicion. She distinctly recalled hearing the dark-haired girl tell the man guarding the jetty steps that her name was Miss *Sara* Wakefield. Perhaps she and her sister were not the only girls on the Bride Ship hiding secrets in her pockets.

Chapter 9

One evening following supper, Mrs. Douglass surprised the girls by standing up to address them at that late hour. Because several days had elapsed with no lecture, Faith had assumed the minister's wife had said all she had to say on the matter of men and matrimony.

"I decided to break with tradition, ladies, and deliver my lecture this evening. Tonight's subject concerns your dowry."

At once a young lady exclaimed, "We was told we wasn't required to have no dowry, ma'am!"

Amidst a ripple of agreement, Mrs. Douglass smiled serenely. "Ye are all bringin' a dowry to yer marriages, my little doves; one yer husbands will value far more than gold or rubies. I am speakin' of . . . yer virginity."

Faith's green eyes squeezed shut. She reached to grasp her sister's hand and noted that already her palm felt clammy. "Shall we leave, Pru?"

"Oh, no, we mustn't," Prudence whispered

"Then you must not listen," Faith insisted.

"Make no mistake, ladies," Mrs. Douglass began, "a maid found upon her wedding night to be unchaste brings a severe impediment to her marriage. She also rains down eternal shame upon herself, and loathing from her husband. However"—she smiled—"since I know that each of you is pure and chaste, I shall not belabor the point."

A relieved sigh escaped Faith's lips.

"Instead I shall speak further upon yer duties in marriage. Ye'll find there are many, but yer *first* duty is to cause love to grow day-to-day—"

"If we do not marry for love," one of the girls pointed out, "how are we to cause it to grow?"

"One often does not *begin* the marriage with love," Mrs. Douglass replied patiently, "or base the marriage upon it. Love *followeth* marriage. And I shall tell ye how to cause it to grow. Once wed, ye must remember always to dispatch yerselves with courtesy toward yer man. Ye must refuse to carry resentment—most especially at the outset, when both of ye are likely to be vigilant in yer observances of one another, easily alarmed or jealous, perhaps even suspicious. Throughout yer marriage, ye must avoid offending one another, and never let the sun set upon yer wrath.

"Most importantly, ye must not expect yer man's reason always to be awake. Since it is not in a man's nature to subtract fuel from his flame of anger, therefore, as his wife, ye are duty-bound to endure the consequences of yer own, and perhaps his, thoughtless actions and bitter words. Remember, the Bible tells us, it is a man's right to raise a hand unto an errant wife, to strike her if that be necessary in order to bring her into submission. Although a man should believe in his wife's honesty until he has absolute proof against her, if she faileth to live up to the trust he hath placed in her . . . then woe be unto her."

Seated beside her on the backless bench, Faith could feel her sister's body trembling. Squeezing her hand tighter, she leaned into her ear. "Be not afraid, Pru. Your husband will never know!"

Mrs. Douglass's words drowned out any reply from Prudence. "A husband's authority must be conceded in all things, girls. Including the yielding of yer body. To refuse yer man in the marriage-bed is of such frustration as to cause a man to lose all reason. It is an act as grievous as desertion."

Faith did hear her sister murmur, "I am doomed."

"If ye find yerselves in a love-less, or intolerable marriage, girls, remember: God sometimes giveth thee a trial as punishment for misdeeds ye bring with thee into the marriage. Make no mistake, my little doves, yer future happiness rests squarely upon yer own shoulders. Now go; read yer Bibles, pray without ceasin' and keep yerselves pure in thought and word and deed."

Faith's heart thumped with fear as she and her sister joined the throng of girls squeezing through the doorway, and in the dim light of evening, carefully descending the steep steps into the bowels of the ship. On the way to their cabin, her sister said nothing. Even later, in the flickering candlelight, as all the girls stood facing the ship's wall to remove their clothing and modestly don their nightrails, Prudence remained silent.

Lying awake on her pallet, Faith whispered, "Pru, are you sleeping?"

"I am especially weary tonight, sister. You must fret no more about me."

Reaching across the low board that separated their berths, Faith touched her sister's shoulder. "I love you, Pru."

Sallie Mae recognized the signs. Because she had so recently experienced the happenstance herself, she knew for a certainty that one of the girls on the ship . . . had a Blight Upon Her Character.

"Some gel still retchin' ever' day?" One-Eye asked when she entered the galley one morning.

"Can't stomach yer cookin'," Sallie Mae retorted.

Perhaps the most unpleasant duty on board ship, that of tossing the contents of the slop buckets over the rail mid-morning and again the last thing at night, had fallen to the youngest seaman: Sal Peters. Each morning, the pungent odor of vomit seemed to waft about Sallie Mae's person for a good half hour after she'd completed the loathsome task.

"Poor girls' beginning to suffer from ship fever, most like," One-Eye replied absently.

"Most like," Sallie Mae agreed.

But she did not believe it for a minute. Because the particular bucket containing the retch always sat outside the same cabin soon after breakfast, she knew from which group of girls the sickly one hailed. If more than one girl was tossing her biscuits throughout the day, it would mean that several had come down with the fever. No; to Sallie Mae's way of thinkin', the condition of one of the prim and proper misses had slipped right past her clergyman's notice, and she had come aboard the ship carryin' a babe in her belly.

One-Eye said no more on the matter until a week or so later, when a bona fide outbreak of ship fever struck the entire ship. Half a dozen crewmen and at least twenty of the girls fell ill. Morning and night every slop bucket reeked of retch. It was all the healthy members of the crew could do to keep the area below deck—where the girls, the Douglasses and the ship's chirurgeon lived—swabbed with vinegar water in an effort to prevent the outbreak from spreading.

Making matters worse was that a second dreaded illness soon followed the first, one that could have been prevented if the ship's chirurgeon had been alert to his duties. The matter came to his attention only when he himself lay abed suffering from a particularly wretched case of the fever. One day when Sallie Mae entered the chirurgeon's cabin to bring him a bowl of thick pea soup, the sickly man feebly pointed to a bushel bag sitting in the corner of his cabin, the one filled to the brim with dozens of now somewhat moldy lemons and limes. "Hand 'em out to the ladies. Tell them they must eat one a day, rind and all."

Since their journey began, Sallie Mae had often seen One-

Eye sucking on a lemon and had gratefully accepted the few he'd handed her. She did recall her brother James, the one who'd run off to sea as a lad, once telling the family that lemons prevented a dreaded shipboard illness called scurvy. However, to distribute the miracle fruit amongst the ladies at this juncture rather seemed to Sallie Mae like a day after the fair. Those girls who were not retching from the fever were already afflicted with the tell-tale swollen gums and tongues, some so swollen they could barely swallow what small amount of broth another managed to spoon into their mouths. Sallie Mae knew it would not be long before their gums hardened, turned black and their teeth all fell out. Because they could not eat, most souls afflicted with scurvy died not from the illness, but from starvation.

At least twice each day now, Sallie Mae entered the girls' cabins toting a mop and bucket of seawater with which she tried to remove from the floorboards the malodorous reminders of the meal just consumed.

To see so many of the young ladies lying abed, their usually soft, glowing skin now a sickly greenish-gray, most clutching their stomachs and groaning, or openly heaving right where they lay, tugged at Sallie Mae's heart. The girls who had not yet fallen ill did what they could to relieve the suffering of their cabin-mates, cleaning their faces after they'd retched, spoon-feeding them gruel or broth. Several times when Sallie Mae was in one of the cabins, her eyes met those of the pretty girl she'd pulled from the river.

Thus far, Diana Falstaff had escaped the illness. However, her new friend Faith had not, and neither had Faith's older sister, Prudence. It had surprised Diana how quickly so many of the girls had fallen ill. One day they were all chattering and laughing as usual, the next, more than half were too sick to pull themselves up from their mats to make their way to the cramped cabin where they took their meals.

Both night and day, the sounds of groaning and retching kept those who had not yet fallen ill terrified that they would be next. Though Diana feared one or another of the horrible diseases would also strike her, a part of her wished it would. As the long, dull days aboard ship came and went, the throbbing ache in her heart had not lessened. If anything, it had grown more acute.

Keeping melancholy at bay whilst cooped up in such close quarters for days on end was difficult at best. Making matters worse was that in the past few days, the skies had darkened, and for days and nights on end, cold rain fell relentlessly, seeping through the floorboards of the main deck above and soaking everything below. There was no place to hang up one's wet clothing to dry. Not only every cabin, but every nook and cranny throughout the hold and the 'tween deck above was wet and drafty. The bench that ran along the outside wall in the girls' cabins always held at least a quarter inch of putrid rainwater. Their straw-filled mats were wet, either from vomit or rainwater dripping through the cracks of the floor of the deck above. There was no point in putting on dry clothing; in minutes a clean, dry frock became sodden and cold.

For Diana, moving through the day wearing soaked garments was a constant reminder of the long hours she'd spent sitting on the banks of the Thames, wet to her skin as she strained for a glimpse of her parents or Sara. More than once, she actually prayed the retching illness would strike her and quickly carry her away, so she might join her loved ones in Heaven.

It came as no surprise when one morning two of the girls in Diana's cabin and three more from cabins across the way did not awaken. Before the ladies had gathered to break their fast that morning, those five girls' limp, lifeless bodies, wrapped in tattered pieces of an old sail, were unceremoniously slipped into the dark waters of the sea; their burials quickly followed by the two crewmen whose souls had also departed their bodies during the night.

It was a subdued group of young ladies who gathered to break their fasts that morning.

"Yer lookin' kindly pale, miss," Sallie Mae said to the sad-eyed miss she'd pulled from the river when she handed the girl a trencher full of lukewarm gruel. "You been eatin' the lemons like I tol' ye?"

"Indeed." Diana nodded. "Thank you, Sal."

Sallie Mae bent to retrieve one of the last of the fruit from the basket on the floor. "Ain't many left. Best eat this one 'afore it goes bad."

"Thank you." Diana smiled. "I will."

"Here, take another. Don't want to take no chances, miss."

"Oh, no, I shouldn't take another," Diana protested when the lad tried to press a second fruit into her hand.

"This one's a mite fuzzy. Best eat it right away."

"I'll give it to one of the girls still lying abed ill."

"A capital plan to be sure, miss."

Sliding onto the bench beside the only girl whose name she knew, Faith Plumleigh, Diana asked, "How is your sister feeling this morning?"

"Quite poorly. Though I have a bit of hope she will soon recover. When I left a moment ago, she was sitting up."

"Splendid. You appear to be much improved." Diana delicately dipped her spoon into the lumpy mixture before her.

"One of us must endeavor to stay well," Faith murmured. "Prudence is not nearly so strong as I."

Diana could tell that her friend was deeply concerned for her sister's welfare. "The cook's helper insisted I take a second lemon." She placed the fruit before Faith's trencher. "Perhaps you should eat it. Or persuade Prudence to do so."

"Thank you." Faith scooped up the second fruit and dropped it into her pocket, along with the one she'd been given, which she intended to deliver straightaway to Prudence. Since the day her sister had contracted ship fever, Prudence's spirits had sunk even lower than her health. Faith feared if the sickness did not soon claim her life, melancholy would.

"Prudence, please eat the lemon." Faith pressed the somewhat moldy fruit into her sister's cool hand when she returned to their dank cabin that morning.

"They are too sour. You eat it." The sound of hard rain pounding the deck overhead all but drowned out her weak reply.

All the girls were crowded into the cabin, some lying vacant-eyed on their mats, others attempting to brush rainwater from the narrow bench along the wall in order that they might sit and talk quietly to one another or read from their Bibles.

"The lemon will prevent your teeth from falling out," Faith insisted.

Prudence pulled her damp cloak closer about her thin shoulders. "What does it matter if my teeth fall out?"

"Prudence, please."

"I wish we had never got on this wretched boat. I could have contrived a way to . . . to destroy the babe, with no one the wiser."

"Prudence, you mustn't speak of such things!"

"I have never felt so cold and wet, or so ill in the whole of my life." She slumped down onto the damp mat and closed her eyes. "If you wish to help me now, Faith . . . I beg you, pray for my demise. I am beyond caring."

"I will do nothing of the sort!" Faith lay down beside her sister. So long as there was breath in her own body, she would not let her sister die! She would not!

Chapter 10

As each day passed, the choppy waters of the sea grew more boisterous. One night the bank of dark clouds unleashed a torrent of especially hard rain. The ship's constant roiling caused many of the girls who were not already suffering from ship fever to be struck with violent cases of seasickness. Despite the crew's efforts to pump water up from the bilge and onto the main deck so that it might roll back into the sea, rainwater continued to pour through the floorboards to the 'tween deck and on down into the girls' cabins.

Faith again fell ill, lying beside her sister, her eyes closed, unable to eat a bite of what was brought back to the girls who lay too sick to move.

At the storm's onset, Diana suffered a touch of seasickness, but by the third day of torrential rain, she was amongst the handful of girls who navigated their way through the rain-soaked passage and up the steep steps to the cramped enclosure where they took their meals. From inside that cabin, the shriek of the wind howling through the ship's sails sounded especially loud. Suddenly she heard the men shouting, *"Go hull! Go hull!"*

Minutes later, the captain hurried into the cabin. "Eat yer fill quickly, ladies; there'll be no more victuals today."

The girls exchanged frightened looks.

"Crew is furling the sails and securin' the riggin'; helm will be secured leeward. Ship will soon resemble an empty bowl. Easier to resist the strong wind."

Cries of alarm followed the pronouncement.

"Stay calm, ladies. As I said, there'll be no more victuals today. Galley's been locked up tight. Hatch to the upper decks will soon be battened down. When ye've finished eatin', return to yer cabins and stay put. No one will be allowed to leave the hold until the storm passes, which, I'll not lie to ye, could be quite a spell."

At that moment, a furious gust of wind slammed against the vessel, nearly knocking the captain off his feet. The ear-splitting creak of the hull caused several of the ladies to cry out. Hanging onto the podium, which thankfully was nailed to the floor, as were the tables and benches, the captain declared, "The ship will not break apart, ladies. Now, get to yer cabins at once. Pray the Lord will keep us safe!"

Their eyes wide with fright, the girls sprang to their feet, each holding onto the edges of the tables in their struggle to stay upright as they hastened to the exit.

Because only a bit of light flickered through the battened-down hatch and through cracks in the overhead deck, the corridor was partial lit. Inside the girl's cabins it was very nearly dark. To lie down in their berths on the floor seemed the safest choice, so most of the girls did just that. For those poor girls already lying ill, the wind and thunderous pounding of waves against the side of the ship added to their discomfort. Amidst the pitiful moaning and retching sounds, Diana heard her cabin-mates' frightened pleas.

"Dear God, I don't wish to die!"

"Save us from thy wrath, Lord!"

"Call me home, Lord; please, take me now."

As the long hours of the afternoon dragged on, the fear in Diana's heart turned to resolve. Perhaps the Lord was, indeed, answering her prayers. Perhaps she, too, was meant to perish, as had her parents and Sara, at the bottom of the sea. If her demise were imminent, she would not resist. God knew what was best for each of His children and she would accept His will, whatever it might be.

Some hours later, Diana pulled herself to her feet in order to make her way to the corner of the room, where, behind the cabin door, sat one of several chamber pots. It was nestled inside a larger holding pot anchored to the floor in order to keep the whole affair from tipping over. Afterward, as she was settling back down again onto her sleeping mat, she offered up a small prayer of thanks that she had managed to complete her mission without a sudden lurch of the ship pitching her against the wall, or flinging her forward onto the girl whose berth lay nearest the door. Just then, from the corner of her eye, she noticed the shadowy form of another girl rising from her mat. Thinking that she, too, was headed for the necessary, Diana pulled her damp bed rug to her chin. But, just as she began to relax, she heard the familiar creak of the outer door open.

Diana sat bolt upright. The girls had been instructed not to leave the cabin. Thinking that perhaps this was one of the girls who so frightfully ill she did not know what she was about, Diana sprang to her feet to bring the sick girl safely back to bed. Although the pitching and roiling of the ship threatened every step, Diana managed again to reach the fore of the cabin. To her horror, in the dim flicker of light, she could see that the girl ahead of her was Prudence.

"Prudence!" Diana called as she made her way through the cabin door and it slammed shut behind her. "Come back." The slick planked flooring made each step Diana took arduous. "You will fall, Prudence! Come back!"

But Prudence, as if sleepwalking, had already gained the stairs. Suddenly, a mighty gust of wind literally flung the vessel onto its side. An instant later, a river of water gushed through the hatch that the wind had flung asunder. Water flooding the stairwell rushed like a river down into the hold. The current knocked Diana off her feet, pressing her against the wall at the bottom of the steep stairs leading upward. Ahead of her, by sheer force of determination, she saw Prudence make her way up the tilting stairwell, both hands clinging to the rail as she doggedly put one foot in front of the other.

Working to right herself as the ship teetered to one side, Diana managed to slog through the ankle-deep water and also fight her way to the top. The hatch that gave onto the main deck now stood wide open. Thrusting her head through it into the driving rain, Diana at last spotted Prudence moving away from her like a ghostly apparition, the folds of her long cape billowing about her body like a sail. Stumbling only slightly, she, too, climbed through the narrow hatch. Horrified, Diana could scarcely believe her eyes when, in a flash of lightning, she caught a glimpse of Prudence walking upright on the *sidewall* of the ship! Its shoulder to the sea, the main mast now lay virtually prone upon the water, the hull riding the mighty waves, perilously high up, then crashing back down again.

"Prudence! Come back!" Diana shouted, although the instant the words left her mouth, she knew they would not be heard above the deafening roar of the wind and the pounding rain upon the deck.

"Stay right there, miss! I'll get her!" came a shout from nearby.

Blinking through the downpour, Diana recognized the lad who had pulled her from the river. Clinging for dear life to the outer rim of the hatch, her body pressed against it to prevent the flapping lid from knocking her back down the stairs, Diana watched, her heart in her throat, as the boy nimbly scrambled up the ship's wall in a valiant effort to reach the girl who seemed determined to walk straight into the sea.

"No-o-o!" Diana screamed when suddenly she saw Prudence

take one final step forward and disappear off the side of the ship.

"No-o-o!" She cried again when, without hesitation, the boy flung himself into the raging water after her. "Dear God," Diana pleaded. *"Help them!"*

For the span of several seconds, Diana spotted no sign of either Prudence or the lad. Other seamen hurried past, shouting to one another as they rushed about in the driving rain, scurrying to retighten rigging and secure the furled sails, which the treacherous wind seemed determined to unfurl.

"Get back to yer cabin!" one shouted at Diana as he ran past.

She ignored the order and stood rooted in place, her anxious gaze trained on the spot where she'd last seen Prudence and the boy disappear into the raging sea.

Suddenly, another mountainous wave crashed onto the deck. Tugging at the hatch, Diana backed a few steps down the stairs in an effort to prevent the bank of high water from flooding the hold. A moment later, she risked a peek up from the hatch at the exact same instant a jagged bolt of lightning lit up the sky. Diana blinked. Coming straight toward her was a . . . *girl!* She wore no cap. Her wet blond hair lay plastered to her head. She was dressed oddly, in a pair of loose-fitting britches and cumbersome boots. What was left of her jacket hung in tatters from her shoulders, but beneath it, the thin wet fabric of her shirt clinging to her slight body did nothing to hide the unmistakable evidence of her gender. When the girl stumbled, her small breasts jiggled. Over one arm, she carried a cape. *Prudence's cape!*

Shivering from the cold and gasping for air from her plunge into the ocean, the girl appeared grief-stricken. "I couldna' save her, miss! It was too dark beneath the water and I—"

"Put the cape on!"

" 'cuse me?"

"The cape! Put it on!"

Asking no questions, the girl did as instructed. And none too soon, for at that instant another crewman angrily shouted, "Ye ladies get below deck where ye belong!"

Diana reached to grasp Sallie Mae's wrist. "Come with me."

Sallie Mae did not protest. Above them, both girls heard the hatch bang into place and something heavy being dragged over it to secure it.

Reaching the cabin door, Diana pulled Sallie Mae inside, where nearly all the girls now lay awake, their alarmed cries blending with the thunderous roar of wind and waves battering the ship.

"We shall all die!"

"Save us, Lord! Save us!"

"Hail Mary, Mother of God . . ."

Sallie Mae wasn't at all certain what to do, so . . . she did exactly as the girl, the one she'd only weeks ago pulled from the River Thames, told her to.

Through the noise and chaos inside the cabin, Diana led the girl to the far end where her berth was located. Flinging back the lid to the bench that covered the area where her things were stored, Diana rummaged around and produced a semi-dry skirt. "Put this on. Then lie down here, on my mat. You can explain in the morning."

Sallie Mae did not protest. And minutes later she had to admit, simply to lie on something flat, even if it was being buffeted by high wind and tempest-tossed waves, felt . . . glorious. In minutes, despite the ruckus the frightened girls were making and the nasty storm outside, Sallie Mae slept. Like a babe.

Diana did not know if Faith Plumleigh was awake or not, and if she were awake, whether or not she was alert enough to know that her sister Prudence was no longer lying beside her. In order to be on hand to comfort the younger girl when she awoke, she decided it best if she waited out the remainder of the storm in Prudence's berth, next to Faith. It distressed her when the mere act of crawling into the trough to lie down beside Faith caused the slumbering girl to stir.

Jerking upright, Faith groggily muttered, "Prudence, are you all right?" A sudden lurch of the ship sent her toppling toward Diana. "You are soaked to the skin! Here—" in the darkness, she began to tug at her own bed rug, "—take my bed rug. Go back to sleep, sweetie." With that, Faith fell back onto her own mat and into a fitful slumber.

Diana did not sleep the entire night. At dawn, the gale winds and hard rain were still pounding the surprisingly sea-worthy vessel, although intermittent lulls made Diana think the worst of the storm might be over. Later that morning, she began to drowse, and eventually sleep claimed her own weary body.

"Where is Prudence? What have you done with my sister?" Alarmed cries awoke Diana with a start.

Although Faith was not yet fully recovered from her own illness, terror gave her the strength to haul herself up from the floor in a frenzy. *"Prudence! Where are you?"*

Diana scrambled to her feet. Grasping Faith's shoulders, she pulled her down onto the bench along the wall. "Faith, I've something to tell you."

"Where has Prudence got to? Where is my sister?"

Diana wrapped her arms about the overset girl and held fast. "Faith, listen to me. Your sister grew delirious in the night. During the storm, she arose from her bed and . . . wandered up on deck. I and . . . and the cook's helper chased after her. The . . . lad dove into the water to try to save—"

"No-o! *No!* Prudence cannot be gone; she is *not!*"

"We did all we could to save her, Faith. Truly we did."

"No-o-o! No!" Beginning to weep, Faith's auburn head slumped onto Diana's shoulder.

Diana's arms tightened about the distraught girl. "I am so sorry, Faith. She did not know what she was doing. I am convinced she did not suffer."

"I meant to look after her."

"But you have been ill."

"She was frightened and . . . and . . ."

"We were *all* frightened."

"Y-you do not understand."

"I understand that you are ill, Faith. Come, you must lie down." Diana urged Faith to her feet and led her the few steps to her mat on the floor. "Please lie down. I will sit here beside you until you fall asleep."

After Diana had settled Faith's bed rug about her, she too lay back. When she could tell from her companion's even breathing that she had fallen asleep, Diana quietly arose and made her way to the end of the room where, to her surprise, the little blond also lay sound asleep. The poor child must be weary to her bones, Diana thought. She sat down on the bench and reached to open her Bible. She could only guess what horrors the delicate girl had endured since their voyage began. What, she wondered, could have possibly caused this girl-child to pass herself off as a lad and join the crew on a sea voyage fraught with danger? If she wished to travel to the New World, why had she not simply applied to be chosen for the Bride Ship the same as the other girls had done?

Watching the wisp of a girl sleep, a surge of emotion welled up within Diana. Suddenly she realized how closely she and the little blond were linked. This brave child had risked her own life—not once, but twice—to save the lives of strangers, people unknown to her and whom she might never see again. Surely, this slight girl was the bravest person she had ever known.

An unexpected wave of guilt washed over Diana. Her life had been spared, and not once had she thanked God for the second chance she'd been given; instead, she had prayed for death. The self-loathing that filled her brought tears of remorse to her eyes. Clearly it was *not* God's will that she perish . . . else He would have taken her along with her parents and Sara when their carriage plunged into the river. She had also not fallen ill these past weeks, nor had she drowned during last night's storm. Truly, God meant for her to live.

Covering her face with both hands, Diana wept. Of a sudden, she realized that dwelling on the loss of her parents and Sara was in reality self-pity. *She* no longer had her loved ones in her life, and she sorely missed them; when the real truth was, they were even now safe and secure in the arms of God. And He had spared *her* life for a reason, perhaps because He needed her to help care for others of His children, ones who were still here and suffering.

Diana sniffed back her tears and glanced toward Faith, lying ill and heart-broken on a damp mat on the floor. In the days to come, she would need help accepting her grievous loss. Turning back toward the flaxen-haired girl, she wondered if perhaps this child, too, had not also suffered a great loss, one so horrendous it had driven her to hide her identity in an attempt to escape a life she found deplorable. Whatever her secret, she, too, needed looking after. At that moment, Diana vowed to offer help wherever she could. And no matter how bleak her own life seemed, she would never, ever again pray for death to claim her before it was God's will that she go.

Just then, the little blond's blue eyes sprang open.

Chapter 11

"What am I to do now, miss?" Sallie Mae sat up in bed, her flaxen curls askew, her eyes round. "If the captain learns I'm a'hidin' here, there's no sayin' what he will do. I've abandoned m'post. He might tie me to the mast and order me lashed till I die!"

"You mustn't fret," Diana whispered. "I shall think of something."

"I'm scared outta' m'wits, miss! I'm no better'n a thief now. I ain't paid m'passage."

"This is the Bride Ship. Once we reach the New World, the man you marry will pay your passage."

"But . . ." Sallie Mae shook her head. "I would never 'ave been chosen for the Bride Ship, miss."

"Of course, you would. You are the most selfless person I have ever known. There have been days when your friendly smile was the only ray of sunshine we saw." Emotion again welled up within Diana. "You risked your life not once, but twice, to save the lives of strangers. You are an angel."

Sallie Mae shook her head. "I ain't no angel, miss. I'm jes' a country lass what wished to travel to the New World the same as the rest o' you."

"And so you are. No matter why you chose to parade as a lad, you saved my life once, and now I shall save yours."

At that instant, Mrs. Douglass burst into the girls' cabin to tell them the cook was preparing a meal and that they could soon gather on the 'tween deck to eat. She then moved slowly down the row of berths, nodding to herself as she glanced here and there, occasionally pausing to look closer at one or another of the girls who was still lying abed ill.

From where Diana sat quietly on the bench, her Bible open on her lap, she cast a glance at her new friend, who had lain back down on Diana's mat upon the floor. Diana noted the girl's frightened gaze following Mrs. Douglass's progress. When the woman left, Diana moved to sit beside the newcomer.

"Whilst we are gone from the cabin to eat, you must move to the last berth at the end of the row." Diana's hazel eyes directed Sallie Mae's toward the empty berth. "The girl who slept there was the first to perish from ship fever. Earlier this morning, I checked her storage bin beneath the bench and her things are still there. They are now yours. Put on the white cap and if you have not already done so, slip out of the britches you were wearing and stuff them here, beneath my mat. I shall contrive a way to dispose of them."

Sallie Mae cast a furtive glance that direction. "Are you certain it'll be all right for me to take the . . . dead girl's things?"

Diana nodded. "There has been such a great deal of confusion these past weeks, and what with the chaos from the storm, I am persuaded no one will even notice you are here."

Sallie Mae worried her lower lip. "I feel awful about abandonin' One-Eye. Ship's store must be a dreadful mess, hogsheads tumbled about, sacks of grain sittin' in water."

Diana reached to clasp the girl's cold hands, which were a pale bluish color; in places, still wrinkled from her swim in the ocean. "You'll find a lovely new pair of lambskin gloves in your storage bin. They'll warm your fingers in no time."

"Oh, no, I mustn't! I should return to m'post and help One-Eye." She made as if to scramble to her feet.

"One-Eye will find another helper," Diana protested, one

hand reaching to pull her back. "You are far too slight to be doing such heavy work."

"I'm a good cook, I am!" Sallie Mae declared hotly.

Diana smiled. "Indeed, you are. I have never eaten such delicious biscuits. Hard as rocks; and the weevils were especially tasty." Her jest elicited the desired response from the pretty little blond, who grinned sheepishly.

"If'n ye raps the biscuits on the edge of the table a'fore ye eats 'em, a good many of the weevils will fall out."

Diana grinned. "I confess I had not thought of that." Though she longed to know why the affable girl had been parading as a lad, Diana refrained from asking, reasoning that if she knew nothing about her, including her name, she would not be obliged to tell a lie if questioned. She also prayed no one would question her regarding what happened during last night's storm. She did not yet know if Mrs. Douglass knew that one of the girls had drowned. Moments ago, when the older woman strode into the cabin, she said nothing about a drowning death. "Wait until the cabin is near empty, then do precisely as I said," Diana instructed before she rose to her feet and approached Faith, now lying awake in her berth, a look of sad defeat in her green eyes.

"Do you feel well enough to gather with the rest of us for a meal, or would you rather I bring something back for you?"

Exhaling a weary sigh, Faith raised up from her pallet. "I can do nothing for Prudence now. I shall come along."

"Your beautiful sister is in Heaven." Diana smiled serenely. "And I am right here beside you."

The cabin where meals were served was especially crowded that afternoon. Since the girls had eaten nothing in virtually two days, everyone was hungry. Diana noticed that One-Eye had indeed commandeered another helper, a surly-looking youth who did not look up as he dropped a dollop of something lumpy onto each trencher before he handed one to each of the girls. Diana wondered if perhaps the fellow viewed the menial task he'd been assigned as beneath his superior sailing skills.

Though the boy never met her eyes, she made a point of politely thanking him before making her way to the rear of the room and sliding onto the bench next to Faith. Before everyone commenced to eat, Mr. Douglass rose and led them all in a lengthy prayer of thanksgiving and praise to the Lord for bringing them safely through the storm.

"Not all of us were brought safely through the storm," Diana heard Faith mutter.

Before the girls concluded the tasteless meal, the ship's captain entered the room. Diana noted his dark clothing seemed especially rumpled, and his side-whiskers now more closely resembled a beard. Glancing over the sea of feminine faces, he stepped over the backless bench to sit beside the portly Mrs. Douglass. In low tones, the two began to converse. Feeling something was afoot, Diana anxiously watched the pair.

Seconds later, when the first girl rose to deposit her empty trencher into the wooden bucket at the top of the room, Mrs. Douglass spoke up.

"Do not leave the room, ladies. The captain has a matter of import to discuss with you."

Diana's cheeks grew hot. Was it possible the captain knew the cook's helper was now secreted in their cabin?

The captain rose to stand behind the podium. Unfolding a sheet of paper, he said, "I shall call out yer names as they appear on the New Virginia Company roster."

Diana's heart began to pound.

"Before ye girls was allowed to board the ship in London," the captain reminded them, "ye was required to present yer Letter of Acceptance to the gent at the jetty steps. Since we set sail . . . several of the ladies has lost their lives due to . . . illness and such like." His eyes scanned the sea of rapt faces. "It is my duty to present the New Virginia Company with a reckonin' of those young ladies who complete this journey. Therefore I shall commence keepin' a daily record of . . . uh . . . those ladies who are still with us."

Beside her, Diana became aware that Faith's breathing had become shallow. Scooting closer to her grieving friend, Diana slipped an arm about her shoulders. "I shall explain what happened to Prudence, if you like."

"M-my name is not on the list," Faith whimpered.

Diana leaned closer. "Excuse me?"

"My name is not on the list. At the last minute, I took another girl's place."

"What was *her* name?"

"I failed to ask. I just snatched up her discarded Letter and gave it to the man. You may recall I was the last girl to come aboard that day."

"Oh." Diana hadn't a clue now how the various perfidies would sort themselves out. Already the captain had begun to call out names. She listened carefully lest she miss the name she must answer to.

"Alice Thompson."

"Present, sir."

"Mary Frasier."

"Here, sir."

He moved down the list, calling out the names Betsy Howard, Susannah Elder, cousins Ann and Beth Fuller, Emma Peters, Debra Greene and sisters, Laura and Minnie Whitbeck.

When no answer was forthcoming after Minnie's name, he looked up and repeated, "Minnie Whitbeck?"

"I believe she passed away, sir," Ann Fuller said. "When all her teeth fell out, the poor thing was unable to eat. She passed away soon thereafter."

They all watched as the captain dipped a feather quill into an inkwell and scratched out the dead girl's name. In the next few minutes he scratched off several more names, and scribbled notations next to the names of those girls determined still to be ill.

Diana's anxiety grew until at last he inquired if Sara Wakefield was present.

"Here, sir," Diana replied, not unaware that beside her, Faith's head jerked up.

She said nothing by way of explanation, but when the captain called out the name Prudence Plumleigh, Diana's eyes widened when she clearly heard Faith respond, "Present, sir."

Eventually, after the captain had called out the final two names, Jane Anderson and a Miss Hester . . . he leaned down to show the list to Mrs. Douglass.

Taking the wrinkled page from him, she rose to her feet. "Neither the captain nor I can make out this young lady's surname. Are any of you acquainted with either Jane Anderson, or Hester . . . Brown-feld-ston, or Brown-bridge-ston?"

The girls exchanged puzzled glances. Seizing the moment, Diana spoke up. "I believe a girl named Hester is even now lying ill in our cabin."

A moment later, Ann Fuller said, "I am convinced there was a Hester in *our* cabin. But she was not ill."

"Yes, she was!" insisted another. "Hester passed away . . . perhaps a sen'night ago. I cannot say for certain. But it was before the storm."

"I heard a girl drowned *during* the storm!" one of the girls called out.

Alarmed, Diana wondered how such a rumor could have started. She had said nothing about Prudence's death to anyone save Faith, and in her distressed state of mind she did not believe Faith had mentioned the tragedy to anyone. Apparently one of the girls lying awake on the floor had indeed overheard her telling Faith what happened to her sister.

"The way I heard it," spoke up another girl, "one of the sick girls went berserk and jumped into the ocean."

Diana's throat constricted as beside her Faith's head dropped to her arms on the table.

"It was not one of *us* who drowned," declared Ann Fuller, "it was the cook's helper, the flaxen-haired lad who gave us the lemons."

"The boy drowned?" asked another girl. "How dreadful!"

"You didn't see him here today, did ya?" Ann exclaimed.

"Order, please, ladies!" Mrs. Douglass snapped. "Since there are not *two* Hesters on the list"—her gaze quickly scanned the names—"perhaps we are safe in concluding that Hester *'somebody'* is alive and, although not entirely well, is sequestered in one or another of yer cabins."

In quite a calm tone, Diana again spoke up, "The Hester in my cabin became ill *after* she and I ventured up on deck during the storm."

"Ah-ha!" The captain leapt to his feet. "And what do ye have to say to that, young lady?"

"E-excuse me, sir?" Diana worked to remain calm despite the fear constricting her throat.

"One of my crewmen reported seeing *two* young ladies on deck during the height of the storm. I take it you were one of them, Miss . . . uh?"

"Wakefield, sir," Diana replied, attempting without success to swallow past the huge lump of anxiety in her throat.

"Might I inquire why you and another young lady blatantly disobeyed my order not to leave yer cabins that night?"

The room became as silent as a tomb as all eyes trained on Diana. It had already been speculated that one young lady had perished during the storm; but on the other hand, Faith had just openly declared that she was Prudence Plumleigh. Therefore, to bring up the matter of Prudence's demise at this juncture would serve only to muddle matters further. Therefore, Diana simply said, "I and . . . another girl, whose name I believe to be Hester . . . grew frightened and . . . and decided to climb the steps to the hatch, which was standing wide open, sir—"

"I am aware that the hatch door blew open during the storm. Do go on."

Diana cleared her throat. "Well, you see, sir, the second I peeked through the hatch, the cook's helper appeared from out of nowhere. He shouted at us to get below. But suddenly a huge wall of water crashed onto the deck. A second later, the cook's helper was swept overboard. I screamed, which must have caught the notice of another seaman, for when he hurried past, he told both of us, Hester and myself, to get below deck at once. Which is exactly what we did, sir."

"I see. That does confirm the rumor that the lad drowned." The captain's lips thinned. "Be aware in future, Miss Wakefield, that when I issue an order, I expect it to be carried out. No exceptions."

"I apologize for disobeying you, sir."

Mrs. Douglass turned to the captain. "I apologize for both girls' actions, sir. You are quite right; we have been remiss in keepin' up with the ladies. Ye have my word, sir, the matter shall be corrected at once."

"Thank you, Mrs. Douglass." The captain inclined his head toward the older woman, then, with a nod at the ladies, he exited the cabin.

Diana exhaled a sigh of relief, and made a mental note to convey to the girl in her cabin that henceforth she would be known as Hester . . . Brownfeld, Diana decided. Since no one seemed to know exactly what Hester's surname was, Brownfeld should serve nicely.

"Now then, ladies," Mrs. Douglass said after the door closed behind the captain, "I have been instructed to appoint a girl from each cabin to serve as Monitor. The Cabin Monitor will report to me every mornin' on the welfare of her mates. I will report to the captain which girl is ill or, God forbid, if any of my little doves . . . took flight during the night."

A hubbub ensued; then the girls settled down again, chins lifted, gazes eager.

"Would any one of ye be willing to volunt—"

Diana spoke up. "I will be happy to serve from my cabin."

"Very well, Miss Wakefield." The woman consulted the list. "Sara, is it?"

"Yes, ma'am. Although I . . . prefer to be called Diana. Diana Wakefield, if you please, ma'am."

Mrs. Douglass looked up. "Well, what exactly is your Christian name, Miss Wakefield? Sara or Diana?"

"Diana, ma'am. Sara is, or rather, *was,* also my mother's name. To avoid confusion in our household, I was called by my . . . um . . . my grandmother's name, which is Diana."

"Very well, then."

"Perhaps you should make a notation on the list," Diana suggested.

"That will not be necessary, Miss Wakefield, so long as *you* know who you are."

Several girls giggled.

Diana exhaled another breath of relief, realizing with alarm that in the past few minutes she had forwarded more falsehoods than she had in her entire life. Although the final one did have the ring of truth to it: she *had* been known in her household as Diana.

Later, as Sallie Mae gobbled the food Diana brought back to

her, they agreed that although the captain had readily accepted Diana's explanation regarding the drowning death of the lad, it might be best if Sallie Mae remained hidden here in the cabin lest One-Eye, or another of the crewmen, notice a marked resemblance between her and the cook's late helper.

"For now," Diana whispered, "your name is Hester Brownfeld."

Sallie Mae nodded. "I do feel much more like meself now, wearin' a skirt and bodice, I mean. Fortunate for me, there was girls' clothes available."

"Did you also find the new petticoat?"

"I'm a'wearin' it." Sallie Mae grinned. "Never before had such a nice one, warm as hot muffins, it is."

"And the boots?"

"Put 'em on straightaway." She stuck out one foot.

Sallie Mae felt far more relaxed now than she had in weeks—months, really, all things considered. She hadn't felt truly at ease since before that terrible afternoon when the gang of boys chased her into the hay field and altered her life forever.

"I am so glad I am the one who discovered who you truly are," Diana whispered with genuine sincerity. "Since you saved my life, now I feel as if I am saving yours."

"Quite true, you are, miss."

"You must remember to address me as Diana."

Sallie Mae grinned. "I must also remember me own name, Hester Brown-feld, ye say?"

Both girls giggled.

"Make no mistake, I am a-twitter to be a girl again, Diana. Sure as I'm sittin' here, I never worked so hard in all me life. Them barrels of salted meat and grain would'a been the death of me, sure. I worked far harder on this ship than I did back home in England. There was eight of us there."

"Do not feel you must tell me who you really are or why you

wished to hide away on a ship. I would never pry."

Sallie Mae's eyes misted over. "For now, let's just say that . . . I wished to make a fresh start in the New World because"—her chin trembled—"because I-I didn't seem to fit in any corner of the old."

Diana reached to squeeze the girl's hand. "That is sufficient explanation for me."

"I hope we stay friends forever, miss." Sallie Mae sniffed back her tears.

"I am persuaded we shall."

"Must I also be Hester Brownfeld once we reach the New World? Oh . . . my!" Suddenly, Sallie Mae's blue eyes grew round as Mrs. Douglass and the ship's chirurgeon, Mr. Emerson, stepped into the dimly lit cabin. Carrying a flickering candle, Mrs. Douglass strode in wearing a determined expression on her face. Mr. Emerson, wearing the long robe and flat cap denoting his profession, carried a small black bag. He set the bag on the floor as he knelt beside the first girl who lay prone upon her mat.

"You'd best lie down," Diana whispered. "Remember, you are unwell."

It was a few minutes before Mrs. Douglass and the chirurgeon approached the last of the ailing girls. Sallie Mae.

"Hester, dear," Diana said, rising from the bench where she was seated, piously reading her Bible. "This is Mrs. Douglass. You recall, she is the nice lady who delivered the edifying lectures to us."

Sallie Mae turned blank stares on first one, then all the faces peering down upon her.

"She is a bit confused," Diana said. "Several of the girls have suffered delirium."

"Clearly, her humors are unbalanced." Mr. Emerson declared. "I must bleed her."

A squeak of alarm escaped Sallie Mae. Frightened round eyes appealed to Diana for help.

Unable to think of anything to say, Diana shrugged.

"Mustn't fret, dear." Mrs. Douglass knelt beside the patient as the doctor rummaged around inside his bag, now resting upon the bench. "Mr. Emerson has bled a number o' my little doves."

"Have ye not been bled before, miss?" the doctor asked as he uncorked a jar filled with slimy black creatures.

Sallie Mae vigorously shook her head.

"I understand it to be quite painless," Mrs. Douglass said. "Make no mistake, it will aid in yer healin'." She reached to press the backside of her hand to Sallie Mae's brow. "Why, I do believe her fever has broke. She feels quite cool to me."

"Not feverish, eh?" the doctor mused. "Well then, what seems to ail ye, lass?"

Before Diana could assist by supplying a list of believable symptoms, Sallie Mae clutched her middle. "Aew-h-h-h!"

"Ah, stomach cramping, is it?"

To Sallie Mae's immense relief, the doctor set aside the jar of leeches.

"I've just the thing," he said. Turning back to his bag, he withdrew a small green flask, which he handed to Diana.

"See she eats nothing save broth and give her four drops of this three times a day." He glanced back at Sallie Mae, who by now had rolled to her side, still clutching her middle. For good measure, she let out a few more pitiful-sounding wails.

Just then, Faith strolled up. "She'll not last the night."

"Faith!" Diana scolded. "Hester will recover the same as you have." She turned to Mrs. Douglass. "A few days ago, Miss Plumleigh was quite ill, but as you can see, she is right as rain now."

Already the chirurgeon had packed up his bag and turned to go.

Mrs. Douglass rose also to her feet. “Minister unto her as best ye can, girls. The Lord will reward ye for yer kindness.”

Sallie Mae opened one eye to peek at the pair as they departed. That the man had not attached blood-sucking leeches to her backside meant the Lord had already rewarded her. Truth to tell, she’d come *this* close to yankin’ off her skirt and grabbin’ those britches again.

CHAPTER 12

The day the dark clouds drifted away and the sky brightened, Mrs. Douglass announced at the mid-day meal that the captain had granted the girls permission to promenade on the upper deck. When their excited chatter died away, the minister's wife added, "In small groups, I could not keep a watchful eye on all of ye at once."

"Mrs. Douglass said we may take our dampest garment to the upper deck to dry!" Diana excitedly told Sallie Mae when she and the other girls returned to the cabin. The cramped enclosure was abuzz with activity as the girls rifled through their damp clothing in order to determine which garment to spread over the longboats in the hope that it might dry quickly.

"I shall also check on Bug-a-Boo again whilst I am there." She had hastened up on deck soon after the storm let up to check on her mare and was relieved to discover that the animal had suffered only minor scratches during the gale winds. Apparently its narrow enclosure, and additional tethers provided by a kind-hearted seaman, had kept the horse safely confined. Not all the animals housed on deck had weathered the storm so well.

Sallie Mae, hungrily consuming the trencher of food Diana had brought back to her, lifted an imploring gaze. "Do ye think it safe for me to go up on deck?" she asked in a low tone.

"You have been tucked away here for nigh on a sen'night. I

daresay to show your pretty face now shan't draw undue attention." Nothing more had been said about the lad who drowned, and everyone seemed to have accepted that this girl was indeed Hester Brownfeld. Perhaps all danger of recognition had passed.

Sallie Mae's face lit up. Though she did not miss parading as a lad, or all the disagreeable things her masquerade entailed, she did sorely miss spending several hours a day in the open air on deck; even those days that were cold and wet were more to her liking than the close confines of a cramped cabin. Although most of the girls had recovered from their debilitating illnesses, the air in the hold was still deplorably stale. It still reeked of vomit, the unmistakable stench of unwashed bodies and other malodors associated with too many people squeezed into a space far too small to accommodate them.

Long before Mrs. Douglass appeared at the cabin door to escort the girls to the upper deck, they were, every one, ready and waiting.

Except Faith.

"I cannot go." She sat down on the bench next to Diana.

"Why ever not?" Diana asked.

Faith looked at her as if she'd gone daft. "The upper deck is the last place Prudence was alive. Besides, I find I cannot forgive Mrs. Douglass. It is *her* fault my sister is . . . no longer with us."

"Whatever can you mean?"

"Her lectures were far and away too severe." Faith's green eyes flashed angrily. "It was Mrs. Douglass's harsh words that led my sister down the path to melancholia. Prudence sobbed her eyes out following every discourse. I refuse to spend a single moment in close company with that dreadful woman."

"Faith, you mustn't judge Mrs. Douglass harshly." Diana's head shook sadly. "I have come to know her quite well now that I am Cabin Monitor. She is a caring person and her advice to us was well meant."

"She is not at all kind!" Faith cried.

"It is God's decision who lives and who dies."

Faith folded her arms across her chest. "Whatever my sister's faults, she did not deserve to die."

Seated to Diana's other side, Sallie Mae was making every effort not to overhear the heated words between the two girls.

Of a sudden, Faith leaned around Diana to glare at Sallie Mae. "You were there, and yet *you* did nothing to help her!"

Diana gasped with horror. She had not revealed to Faith, or to anyone, that the flaxen-haired girl was in truth the cook's helper and that it was she who had bravely plunged into the ocean in an attempt to save the drowning girl. Now, she declared, "Hester and I lagged too far behind Prudence to be of any help. When I saw your sister leave the cabin, I called out to her. Whilst Hester and I were up on deck, she also called to Prudence. We both did all we could to halt your sister from her path of destruction. I myself watched the cook's lad jump into the ocean in an attempt to save your sister. If you recall, he, too, lost his life. Hester and I both tried to help Prudence."

"She was given no proper burial. No sweet words were spoken over her."

"That was your doing," Diana quietly reminded her friend. "When the captain read off the names of the girls, you claimed to be Prudence . . ."

Faith sprang to her feet. "I wish I had never come on this voyage! Nothing is progressing as it should." She flounced away. And remained in the cabin whilst the rest of the girls enjoyed a refreshing stroll in the sunshine on the upper deck.

Today Diana's chestnut mare neighed with recognition when both she and Sallie Mae stepped away from the other girls to approach the animal.

"She seems to be faring well enough," Sallie Mae said.

"Indeed." Diana smiled.

Both girls rubbed the mare's soft nose.

"I am sorry yer friend Faith is so distressed," Sallie Mae said with genuine feeling.

"I shall tell her the truth one day. About you, I mean. There is no saying what she would do if I told her now. I cannot risk placing you in jeopardy with the captain."

"Don't ye wonder why she claimed to be her sister Prudence?"

Diana shrugged. "It appears not a one of the three of us is truly who we claim to be."

At that moment, they both heard Mrs. Douglass loudly declaring it was time to go below. With a final pat on Bug-a-Boo's rump, Diana and Sallie Mae hurried away. Seconds before they reached the hatch and began their downward descent, Sallie Mae caught a glimpse of One-Eye. When she noted the cook's one *very* sharp eye aimed straight at her, her heart plunged to her feet.

Chapter 13

On the eightieth day of the ladies' voyage to the New World, a cloudless sky dawned over the two ships slicing through the water on their way across the sea. For most of the journey the second Bride Ship had appeared as a mere pinprick on the horizon. As it had not been sighted since the storm, everyone aboard the *King's Embassy* wondered if its sister ship had blown off course. All prayed that a more dreadful fate had not befallen the smaller bark. Today its white sails billowing, the *Queen Anne* was sighted. Late in the afternoon, however, the beautiful weather and sighting of the *Queen Anne* was eclipsed by something far more exciting.

"Land ahoy!" cried a sailor from his lookout point high atop the poop deck. Rowdy cheers from the seamen followed the proclamation.

In the hold, a girl seated on a cabin bench murmured with little interest, "What do you suppose the crew is cheering about?"

"I heard nothing," said another girl flatly.

When a second, more exuberant cheer arose, wide-eyed girls began to spill from their cabins into the narrow passage toward the steep steps leading to the hatch, the round door of which was standing wide open today, allowing a steady stream of sunlight and much-needed fresh air to filter down below.

Mrs. Douglass and her husband also appeared in the corridor. "Girls! *Girls!* Ye are not allowed up on the main de—"

But the woman's words were lost over the squeals of thirty-plus girls excitedly pushing and shoving to be the first to climb the steps to the main deck for a glimpse of the land they would all soon call home.

It was two days before the wind picked up sufficiently to successfully push both barks up the James River and into the blue-green waters surrounding the triangular fort built by the early colonists in oh-seven. The twelve-foot-high walls of the fort, constructed of rough-hewn timbers lashed together with hemp, appeared still to be in good repair. Since those early days, the fledging fort had prospered, and the township of Jamestown now extended a good distance inland from the riverbank.

As the *King's Embassy* drew nearer the fort, the girls again disregarded captain's orders and all crowded up on deck, craning their necks to see over both rigging and railing and the heads of the crew, busily trimming sails and securing dozens of dangling ropes.

As numerous soundings were taken and depth determinations made, Diana and Sallie Mae stayed close by one another. So excited was Sallie Mae to have finally reached the end of her long voyage, she didn't care now if One-Eye spotted her or not. She hadn't told Diana about the day the cook eyed her, as she hadn't wanted to worry her new friend. Both girls excitedly watched now as the first longboat was untied, flipped over and a dozen girls handed, one by one, into it.

"Faith, do come with us!" Diana called to the only girl that day who was not a-twitter with excitement.

"I am not certain I wish to go ashore." With that, the disgruntled Faith turned and threaded her way back through the crowd of girls pushing and shoving in their haste to leave the ship.

Diana made no effort to further coax her friend, for already the longboat she and Sallie Mae had climbed into was slowly, cautiously being lowered down the side of the ship. At last, it settled with a splash onto the sparkling surface of the sea.

"I can scarcely believe we are here!" cried Sallie Mae.

"I wonder where we shall live." Diana's long gaze scanned the shore for a glimpse of the village. "I hope we remain near one another."

Awaiting them on shore, Governor Sir George Yeardley and all seven of his esteemed council members were elegantly turned out this afternoon in brightly colored doublets and matching galligaskins, gleaming white hose and black leather shoes adorned with silver buckles.

Catching sight of the men, Diana suddenly became aware how unkempt and bedraggled she and the other girls must appear after their eight long weeks on board a filthy ship. Glancing about, she noted that nearly every girl's blouse and bodice was stained and dirty. Every girl's skirt was rent, a few even hung in tatters about their legs. No one's hair was clean or brushed; most of the girl's faces were blotched with dirt, and their arms and hands were brown with grime. Glancing down at her own hands, she grimaced. At home, she was careful always to keep her hands clean and her nails trimmed and buffed.

"We look a fright," she muttered to no one in particular.

"We look as if we've been on board a filthy ship for nigh on three months," said Ann Fuller, crushed next to Diana as they waited to disembark from the longboat.

When it was finally dragged ashore, elated colonists cheered and applauded the girls' safe arrival.

"Gor! My legs feel too wobbly to hold me!" Sallie Mae exclaimed when her first tentative steps sent her colliding into Diana, who had also stumbled in the soft sand.

"They will think we've consumed too much ale!" Diana laughed.

"I own I am drunk with happiness!" exclaimed Ann Fuller, whose plain face was so joyful, she looked almost pretty. "M'brother John don't know me or our cousin Beth have come to join him!"

"Welcome to Jamestown, ladies!" hailed the governor after all the ladies had arrived. A bulky man of some forty years, he wore the small pointed beard of an aristocrat and a wide-brimmed plumed hat over his shoulder-length periwig.

"Thank you, sir," Diana politely responded. "We are very happy to be here."

Moments after the governor turned to lead the chattering girls and beaming colonists into the fort, Sallie Mae again caught sight of One-Eye. This time the man was not looking at her, but was instead hurrying the opposite direction, around the outside perimeter of the fort. She grinned smugly. She had now safely arrived in Jamestown, and there was nothing he or anyone else could say about it. Plain and simple, she was just one of the girls who'd journeyed to the New World on the Bride Ship.

She leaned to whisper into Diana's ear. "I feel it's safe now to tell ye my given name."

Diana gazed at the apple-cheeked girl whose blue eyes sparkled mischievously. A breeze ruffled the golden curls peeking from beneath her tidy white cap. A surge of emotion filled Diana's heart. Once again she realized she owed her very life to this slip of a girl and once again, she vowed to do all in her power to protect her new friend from harm. "By what name do you wish to be known in Jamestown?"

"Sallie Mae."

Diana grinned. "It suits you."

"I have decided to keep Brownfeld as me surname. Though I'm thinkin' of shortenin' it to Brown. What do ye think?"

"I think Sallie Mae Brown is a splendid name."

Smiling happily, both girls turned their attention to surveying their surroundings. A row of tidy houses with thatched roofs overhanging wattle-and-daub exteriors backed up to two walls of the triangular-shaped fort. Curls of smoke wafted from every chimney and disappeared into the tall treetops. Here and there a dog lay asleep in the sun, although the parade of colonists streaming into the fort awoke many, who promptly sprang awake, barking and yelping as they ran in circles at the feet of the excited settlers. On each of the three corners of the fort, imposing iron cannons rested on raised dirt platforms. Today, the pillory at the far end of the fort stood empty. Diana saw that Jamestown's meetinghouse, situated in the center of a spacious greensward and shaded by a stand of tall oaks, was the largest structure inside the fort.

"Do ye suppose this be the whole of the village?" Sallie Mae asked with wonder.

"Surely there is more," Diana replied, noting that there appeared to be less than two-dozen small houses here inside the fort. The sight of the pillory had not alarmed her, but the cannons gave her pause. What, she wondered, were the colonists obliged to fight off?

Upon reaching the meetinghouse, also constructed in the customary wattle-and-daub fashion, although it rested on a sturdy foundation of cobblestones, the governor led the girls into the cool, dank interior of the building. They filed into and soon filled up the first several rows of polished wooden pews.

"Smells nice in here," Sallie Mae declared.

"The pews are made of cedar," Diana replied. "It does smell pleasant." Laughing, she added, "But, then, anything would smell better than the ship."

At that moment, Diana spotted Faith squeeze onto the end of the row where she and Sallie Mae sat. Catching the eye of the auburn-haired miss, she smiled, but was dismayed when Faith's lips merely thinned and she ducked her head. Faith was the only young lady there with no look of wonder or excitement in her eyes. Diana sighed. Perhaps once they'd settled into their new lives, her friend would be able to shake off the depression that had overtaken her since her beloved sister's death.

Jamestown's minister, Reverend Martin, opened the proceedings with a lengthy prayer of thanksgiving for the ladies' safe arrival, for the beautiful weather they were enjoying and for everyone's good health and welfare. Governor Yeardley then stepped to the podium and began to educate the girls regarding the settlement's history. A half hour into the program, many of the girl's bright smiles had begun to dim as the governor seemed to drone on and on about how the new country had been named nearly forty years earlier by the adventurer Sir Walter Raleigh, who had dubbed the land Virginia in honor of Queen Elizabeth, then known as the Virgin Queen.

He told them of the hardships suffered by the first colonists and the deadly year they now called the "starving time," when hundreds of colonists perished from lack of food.

"Ye must not think to search out the gravesites of any of yer kin, ladies, for the graves of those brave souls went unmarked. The naturals thought we English were gods who'd magically appeared on these shores on floating islands. They fear both our cannons and our 'firesticks,' which is what they call our muskets. Because we did not want the naturals to think us mortal, or to know how fast we were dying off, we smoothed over the graves of our forefathers in the hope they'd go unnoticed."

He told them that despite their cunning ways, the Indians, collectively called Powhatans, although there were many different tribes with many different names, had shown the colonists how to grow the food they now ate—corn, squash, pumpkins, onions, apples, grapes, and berries.

"Jamestown's communal storehouse is now nearly full of grain," the governor said, beaming, "which is freely given to new settlers whilst they wait for their first crop to come in."

He told them that when the first settlers discovered that the gold, which they'd expected to find here, was, in fact, not here, Jamestown's most precious commodity quickly became tobacco. While the first tobacco crop grown by Goodman John Rolfe had yielded only a few barrels of leaves, the colony recently shipped over fifty thousand pounds of rich golden tobacco leaves back home to England.

Following that pronouncement, a mighty cheer arose from the colony's proud planters.

Diana thought it strange that the governor used the phrase "back home" to England. Did the colonists not now think of Jamestown as their home? She certainly meant to, as she had no intention of ever returning to England. She cast a glance about at the pleasant faces gathered inside this fine building. All of these brave souls were now her family.

She returned her attention to the governor. He was now expounding upon the inroads the settlers had made in dealing with the naturals. During the first House of Burgesses meeting held the previous July, a ruling had been adopted that prohibited a colonist from selling or giving the Indians strong drink, or firewater, as the Indians called it. A new law also limited the number of naturals who could gather at any one place to no more than five at a time.

"Overall, the Indians are friendly," he declared, "still, one never knows what might set one off, and when angered, one never knows what an Indian will do. So, ladies, please remember to watch ye'selves. Most Indians do not speak English, but many have learned a goodly number of our words even though they feign ignorance. Keep in mind the savages have keen senses . . ."

"Savages?" murmured Sallie Mae with some alarm. "Jamestown has . . . savages?"

Diana turned her palms upward. As the governor spoke, she was beginning to realize that she, in fact, knew precious little about the land she had decided to adopt as her new home. She thrust her chin up. She would not let the mere mention of some sort of savage living somewhere thereabouts dim her spirits.

The governor launched into talk of other rules the Burgesses had adopted concerning the imbibing of strong drink, card playing and the proper manner of dress, when suddenly a commotion arose. One of the girls it appeared had fainted dead away. Her limp body now lay sprawled across the aisle. Several men from the rear of the building rushed forward. Between them, they carried the ashen-faced girl from the building into the sunlight.

Mrs. Douglass rose to her feet and boldly addressed the governor. "If you please, sir, all the girls are weary to their bones; many have been ill and are still quite weak. I beg ye, sir, let us get the girls settled in straightaway."

Without a word of protest, the governor withdrew from his doublet pocket two rather tattered pieces of paper given him by the ships' captains. The pages, Diana surmised, contained the names of those girls who had completed the voyage. Yeardley handed both lists to his council secretary, an elderly man he introduced as Mister John Pory. Pory began the lengthy task of matching up the girls with the various families who'd volunteered to provide them shelter and sustenance. Unfortunately, a good many of the girls were obliged to climb back into a shallop, as their sponsors resided in the burroughs of Kiccowtan—located a good distance away on the back side of the peninsula—or in a township called Henricus, located farther upriver.

At the mention of Henricus, Diana's ears perked up. She recalled it as the city where her half-brother, her mother's son from her previous marriage, resided. Although Diana had never met the man and, in fact, did not even know his name, she wondered if perhaps she did, indeed, have a blood relative living nearby.

At length, Diana was assigned to the home of Mister and Mistress William Larsen. Larsen was an esteemed member of the governor's council and lived in a fine—by Jamestown standards—four-room house located some distance outside the fort.

Sallie Mae, who had again answered to the name Hester Brownfeld, went to live with a couple named Weston. As she walked with the Westons along the dirt road toward their home, she promptly told them that while Hester was, indeed, her given name, she had gone by Sallie Mae her entire life. "I've also decided to shorten my surname to Brown," she announced breezily.

Goodman Weston, a scruffy-looking sort not unlike the peasant farmers who lived in the tiny hamlet Sallie Mae hailed from, appeared confused but said nothing. His wife, a thin woman with straggly brown hair, agreed to honor her guest's wishes, and thereafter referred to their houseguest as Miss Brown, a surname that pleased Sallie Mae, as it did not begin with the letter P or, in any way, sound like Pigee.

Faith, along with two girls named Annabeth and Robin, who had both made the crossing on the *Queen Anne,* left the fort with Mister John Evans and his wife. Evans, also a councilman, lived in a very fine two-storey house built of clapboards that had been painted white. Their lovely home, Mistress Evans was quick to point out, had actual glass-paned windows, a fact that seemed to impress Annabeth and Robin, who made admiring comments. Faith said nothing as both her family home near Stamford Heath in England and her Aunt Elsa's town home in London all had glass-paned windows.

"Some homes' windows merely have wooden panels that slide back and forth," Mistress Evans added. "And some bark houses have only oiled cloth to ward off the chill. Some houses have no windows at all."

"How . . . primitive," Faith muttered.

The wattle-and-daub home that Sallie Mae entered was, indeed, primitive, consisting of only two rooms on the ground floor and a cramped loft above. Still, it was finer than the crude hovel she had lived in all her life in England.

Goodman Weston set Sallie Mae's small bundle of belongings down on the earthen floor inside the home's only door. Glancing about, Sallie Mae wondered upon which corner of the floor she would sleep. She had barely framed the thought in her mind when Goodwife Weston pointed toward a rickety set of stairs that led upward.

"We've made a bed for ye in the loft, Miss Brown. Would ye like me to show ye?"

"In the loft, ye say?" Sallie Mae followed the pale woman with tired gray eyes up the steep steps. Both Goodman Weston and his wife were so thin and wan, Sallie Mae wondered if they had enough food between them to share with a stranger. When the women emerged onto a platform composed of loose floorboards, which contained half a dozen hogsheads, both ducked so as to avoid hitting their heads on the low-hanging rafters.

"It smells pleasant up here," Sallie Mae observed with a smile.

"They's dried apples an' pears in them two hogsheads."

"Ah."

Tucked in behind the barrels, Goodwife Weston led Sallie Mae toward a corner where a narrow cot, complete with a thin mattress and even a pillow, stood.

"Oh, my! I am to sleep *here?* On a real bed?"

"Indeed. Yer cot is just above the hearth. Nice warm air should drift yer way in winter." She paused. "But, then, as pretty as you are, Miss Brown, I 'spect ye'll be wed long 'fore winter sets in."

Sallie Mae felt her cheeks grow warm. Diana had more than once told her she was pretty, and now this nice woman had also mentioned her looks. Despite feeling proud, *too* proud, her mother said, of her flaxen hair, she had never thought of herself as comely. Luckily, her cropped hair was growing out fairly quickly. Perhaps some nice Jamestown fellow would notice her yellow hair and also think her pretty.

A few streets over, Diana Wakefield was getting settled into her new home with Mister and Mistress Larsen. The Larsens, she had learned as they walked through the settlement toward the house, had two children, a four-year-old boy named Edward and a baby girl named Ellen. While the children's parents were away, Mistress Larsen left the children in the care of their servant, an Indian woman.

Soon after entering the tidy four-room house, little Edward came bounding into the room to fling himself into his mother's arms. Though she was a robust sort, nonetheless she staggered a bit beneath the healthy boy's weight.

"Do take him, Will." She handed the child off to her husband, a large man with black hair and a full beard. "You have grown far too heavy for me to lift, Edward," she said as the boy's father carried him from the room.

Diana then noticed the Indian woman standing silently near the hearth. It was her first glimpse of a dark-skinned natural. The woman, whose long black braids lay over each shoulder, wore a knee-length buff-colored garment with tattered fringe along the bottom. On her feet were soft suede boots. Holding a straw broom, the Indian woman was apparently sweeping stray ashes back into the fire. The hearth, Diana noted, was every bit as wide as the one in the great room of her family's manor home. Inside was a raised oven constructed of large round stones. The oven featured not only a spit, but two shelves for baking. A pig was now roasting on the spit. On the oven shelves several pans sizzled with something that . . . smelled delicious!

"Our dinner will soon be ready," Mistress Larsen said, hanging up her shawl on a peg near the door.

"It smells wonderful," Diana enthused. Suddenly she was quite looking forward to eating a tasty meal again. All the girls had grown weary of living on lumpy gruel and weevil-filled biscuits.

"Our Indian servant's name is Cheiwoga," Mary Larsen said, crossing the room toward the hearth. Holding the Indian woman's gaze, Mistress Larsen said slowly, "This is Miss Wakefield. Can you say Wake-field?"

Her expression solemn, the young woman repeated, "Wakefield."

"Sara, is it?" Mary Larsen inquired.

"I prefer Diana."

"Very well, then. Diana." She turned back to the Indian woman. "You will address our guest as Miss Wake-field."

Returning to the common room without his son, Mister Larsen headed toward the entrance to retrieve Diana's brown leather valise. "I'll put this in Miss Wakefield's room."

"This way, Diana," Mary Larsen said. "You do not mind if I call you by your given name?"

"Please do."

"You are welcome to address me as Mary." She lowered her voice. "The majority of the men here in Jamestown, especially those of my husband's rank, prefer to be addressed as Mister, followed by their surname. Those of a lesser rank are generally called Goodman, and then their surname."

"And your servant? Am I to address her by her given name?"

Mary chuckled. "I do not believe Indians have two names."

They entered a small room at the back of the house. Diana

glanced about at the sparse furnishings, a low truckle bed topped by a plump mattress and pillow, a faded bed rug across the foot, a small washstand and a two-shelf open cupboard. The floor in this room, she noted, was not composed of wooden planks as was the common room, but was instead, merely hard-packed earth. On the floor before the bed lay a round rug made from pieces of braided fabric. The room had one narrow window with a wooden covering, which looked to Diana as if it swung open on a pair of hinges.

Larsen placed Diana's bag on the floor near the bed. "I understand you brought along a horse, Miss Wakefield?"

"Indeed. Mine was the only horse on board ship, although there may have also been one on the *Queen Anne.* Mine is a chestnut mare. I . . . rather doubt she will respond to her name."

"Which is . . . ?"

"Bug-a-Boo." Diana grinned.

"Ah. Well, nonetheless, I shall go and fetch her." Turning, he flung over his shoulder, "I shan't be long away, Mary."

"Edward will be overjoyed when he learns you brought a horse."

"Are there not many horses in Jamestown?"

"Oh, my, no. Very few, indeed." A hand swept the room. "I expect it is far smaller than you were accustomed to in England. It will one day be Edward's or Ellen's room, but for now, it is yours. Although"—she smiled good-naturedly—"you might not be with us for long. All the unmarried men in Jamestown have been a-tremor awaiting you ladies' arrival."

Diana's hand touched her unwashed hair, which in places was matted with mud. She hadn't properly bathed in weeks, not since her unexpected dunk in the Thames. "I fear our unkempt appearance today merely repelled them."

Mary Larsen smiled. "We look past outer appearances here, Diana. What is in a woman's heart matters a great deal more than her looks. Make no mistake, a good many men, those who are most anxious to select a bride, did not notice you girls' dirty faces or disheveled clothing. We every last one of us endured an arduous shipboard journey, and not one of us arrived here fresh, or sweet-smelling."

Diana blushed. "I suppose not." Still, she hoped to soon be offered a tub, or even a bucket, of warm water with which to wash herself.

"For weeks now," Mary went on, "the men have been sprucing up their homes, adding indoor ovens, enlarging rooms, enclosing sheds and whatnot, all in the hopes of enticing a young lady to become his bride."

Diana glanced again at the sparse little room. It was far smaller than any chamber in the spacious Falstaff manor home, but it was tidy and seemed clean enough. Except for the floor. How did one "clean" a dirt floor? She had never beheld such a thing, not even their stillroom or servants' quarters had dirt floors.

Mary Larsen moved toward the doorway. "I will send Cheiwoga in to help you put away your things, if you like."

"Thank you, but I brought so little I am certain I can manage. Does Cheiwoga also live here?"

"On the contrary. She leaves Jamestown at the end of each day, after she clears away the supper things and washes up."

"Where . . . does she go?"

"Why, home to her village, I expect."

Diana blanched. "The Indian village is nearby?"

The older woman smiled. "There are *many* Indian villages, Diana, and quite a few are, indeed, nearby. Perhaps a hundred or more are scattered here and there throughout the forest."

"Oh, my."

Mistress Larsen sighed. "We often spot Indians lurking behind our buildings or hiding in the treetops. Many truly are savages, and unfortunately think nothing of their savagery. We often hear of fighting and conflicts between the tribes. The Indians' ways do quite mystify us. But there appears to be no taming them."

"Does it not frighten you to allow one of them to care for your children?"

"Some Indians are gentle and kind. Cheiwoga has always been good to my little ones."

Diana digested the information. She did so wish to like her new home, but some aspects might take a bit of getting used to.

Mary Larsen smiled. "I hope my talk of Indians does not frighten you. Everything must seem new and different to you now. Make no mistake, it will not be long before you come to love this land as much as the rest of us do."

"I am certain I shall."

"In the interim, a bit of caution would serve. Especially if you venture into the forest. One never knows when one might stumble upon an Indian village." She laughed. "To be sure, you will recognize one when you see it; tee-pees, bark-covered hovels, little naked children running about. I confess, the Indian children's nudity even puts me to the blush."

"Oh." Diana's eyes widened.

"You will find a good many things here in Jamestown that are different from what you were accustomed to in England. But, the plain truth is, I would not trade my life here for anything I left behind. Not for all the tobacco in Virginia."

Diana smiled a bit shakily. Already, her new life had succeeded in diverting her thoughts from the terrible tragedy she'd suffered. For that alone, she felt exceedingly grateful. Still, for the nonce, she decided to put a wide berth between herself and the forest where tribes of warring savages lived.

At the far end of town, Faith Plumleigh faced her own vexation.

"We are all three to sleep in the same bed?" she cried.

"The bed is quite wide," Robin said cheerfully.

"I take it you came from . . . means, dear," Mistress Evans said quietly. "Our home is one of the finest in Jamestown, Miss Plumleigh, but compared to the grand houses in London, or any one of England's fine country homes, we . . . simply cannot measure up. I apologize for inconveniencing you."

Annabeth and Robin were quick to express their approval of the accommodations. "We are none of us large girls," Annabeth said with a merry laugh. "The bed is plenty wide enough."

"Well, I do not intend to be here too very long," Faith loftily declared. "I intend to marry the first man who asks, or perhaps I shall not marry at all. Perhaps I shall return home to England."

"Return to England?" Robin, a pretty girl with long, dark hair, pulled a face. "I would not get on that horrid ship again for anything."

"Nor would I," exclaimed Annabeth. She pinched her nostrils together, which caused Robin to laugh merrily.

"I shall leave you girls to settle in," Mistress Evans said. An older woman with graying hair, she made no further attempt to alter Faith's opinion of her lovely home.

Faith sat down on the edge of the bed. Three grown girls in this tiny bed would mean they must each sleep straight as a board. She'd had more room in her narrow compartment on the floor of the ship.

"Well, I think our little room is quite nice." Robin said. "Look, there are two chests with pull-out drawers."

"Which means one of us will not get one," Faith countered.

"There are plenty of drawers," Annabeth pointed out. "I am convinced there will be sufficient space for all our things. I, for one, did not bring a great deal with me."

"I did not have a great deal to bring!" Robin exclaimed with another merry laugh.

The jolly little Robin was fast getting on Faith's nerves. She sprang to her feet. "The two of you may put your things wherever you wish. I will use whatever space is left over. For now, I am in need of fresh air."

"Perhaps we might all take a stroll before supper," suggested Robin.

Faith had already reached the threshold. "I prefer to be alone." With a swish of skirts, she exited the room.

"Well, get her!" said Annabeth.

"She is simply weary from the journey," Robin said sympathetically.

But Faith was not simply weary from the journey. She was weary of people being friendly and pleasant and going about life as if nothing had changed, as if they did not know how it felt to lose a beloved sister. For her to be pleasant and smile and say please and thank you and oh, how lovely, was asking far too much.

She hated herself for not doing what she'd set out to do: look after Prudence. She should have been there to save her, or at the very least assure her that all would be well once they reached Jamestown. Someone should pay for her sister's death; the question was, *who?*

CHAPTER 14

Long after sunset Faith was still walking the dusty roads of Jamestown, wondering what to do now that she was alone in this God-forsaken place. Truth was, she had not come here only to look after Pru. She had wished for adventure herself and to find herself a husband. Instead, she should have talked Prudence out of coming and helped her find a way to get rid of the babe or tell Isaac about it and insist he do right by her. Now, the worst had happened and it was up to her to make it right. But *how?*

"Prudence! Prudence, is that you?"

Before she knew it, Faith had nearly collided with a young lady walking beside a tall young man and another girl. "Forgive me," Faith muttered, "I was not looking where I was—" When she glanced up, she vaguely recognized both of the girls who were regarding her with bright smiles.

"It is I, Ann Fuller," the plain one said. "You remember my cousin Beth. We all came over on the same ship."

"Oh." Faith made as if to move on.

"This is my brother, John," Ann went on. "John, this is Prudence . . ." She paused and laughed gaily. "Suddenly, I do not recall your surname!"

Faith's lips thinned. "My name is Faith, not Prudence."

Ann looked surprised. "But I clearly recall you answering to the name Prudence. Plumleigh, yes; you said your name was Prudence Plumleigh."

"My name is Faith. The captain spoke the wrong name in error. I suppose to him all pious-sounding names—Faith, Prudence, Charity, Temerity—seem all of a kind. If you will excuse me."

"Ann," the gentleman said quietly, "Miss Plumleigh appears to be in somewhat of a hurry."

"Indeed, I am in a great hurry." Faith thrust her chin up and skirted past them.

"It was a pleasure meeting you, Miss Plumleigh." John Fuller politely touched his cap and moved aside as Faith flounced past him, his sister Ann and cousin Beth.

As Faith hurried away, she clearly heard one of the girls exclaim, "How utterly rude!"

"Think nothing of it, Ann," John said. "Jamestown is aswarm with pretty young girls now. There is ample time to play matchmaker."

That week, Sallie Mae settled into the daily routine of the family with whom she lived. Her day began early when Goodman Weston hurried outdoors to fetch a few sticks of wood for the fire while his wife began the task of preparing something with which to break their fast. To Sallie Mae fell the task of sweeping the live embers still glowing in the fire into a pile over which the kettle would be hung to boil. Most mornings the three began their day with little more than a trencher scarcely full of corn mush, which was simply corn that had been ground into a fine meal, then boiled in hot water till the mixture took on the consistency of paste. If on the previous day Goody Weston and Sallie Mae had baked bread and any still remained, they all tore off a piece and consumed it along with their mush. After breakfast, Goodman Weston put on his faded black felt hat and trekked through the woods to the small plot of ground where he and two other men were girdling the trees in preparation to plant corn, each hoping to harvest enough from their meager crop to see them through Jamestown's upcoming bleak winter.

The three men, Sallie Mae learned, had only recently worked off the seven-year indenture they owed Councilman Evans. For completing their term, each man received a suit of clothing, a few tools and one acre of land. Though the practice was frowned upon and in some cases, not allowed, Goodman Weston had married whilst serving his indenture and his young wife was again increasing. Sallie Mae guessed the slight girl to be no more than twenty, yet what with her tired eyes and wan appearance, she appeared much older. Sallie Mae also learned that this was her third pregnancy, and that she had not yet been able to carry a babe to term.

"I hope ye don't think we offered to shelter you cause we be a'needin' yer help," the young woman said to Sallie Mae one morning as the two prepared to strip the threadbare sheets from the bed and wash them, along with several pairs of soiled breeches and two of her husband's shirts.

"I do not think that a'tall," Sallie Mae replied cheerfully. "I am pleased to do whatever I can to help you and yer man."

" 'Tis more difficult than I thought to scrape out a livin' here in the New World," Goody Weston said on a sigh.

As she attempted to lift a heavy bucket of water off the ground and pour it into the sawed-off barrel in which they would rub clean the linens, Sallie Mae hastened to help. Still fresh in her mind was her own ill-fated pregnancy, during which she clearly recalled the sick-to-her-stomach feelin' that very often assailed her when she tried to perform strenuous tasks. Many mornin's she had noticed poor Goody Weston lost her breakfast when she was engaged in a chore as simple as bendin' over to slide logs into the fire. Already Sallie Mae feared the poor girl might not be able to carry this babe to term either.

One night at the Weston house, Sallie Mae was about to drop

off to sleep when she heard raised voices coming from the small chamber located beyond the hearth on the ground floor. It only took a few moments to realize what Goodman Weston and his wife were quarreling about. He was demanding she perform her wifely duty that night, and she was simply too weary to do so. Lying on her small cot in the loft, Sallie Mae pulled the pillow over her head to snuff out the couple's angry words and the unmistakable sounds that soon followed. Unfortunately, the same scene was repeated over and over again, nearly every night that week.

On the first Sabbath the girls were in Jamestown, a colony-wide picnic was held on the greensward following services. A dozen or more planked wooden tables were laden with delicious-smelling foodstuffs—baked and fried fish, roasted beef and pork, assorted vegetable compotes, corn pudding, freshly baked bread, sugared cakes, and currant and apple pies with thick fluffy crusts—all of which the ladies and the colonists greatly enjoyed.

Amidst the excited chatter and laughter, Diana and Sallie Mae sought out one another and stood exchanging stories regarding their new families and the homes where they now lived. After Sallie Mae told Diana as clearly as she could where in Jamestown she now lived, she asked, a bit absently, as she was far more intent upon gobbling up the thick wedge of apple pie on her trencher, "What did your letter say?"

"I have received no letter," Diana replied, also a bit absently. She had never tasted such delicious jelly tarts.

Setting her empty trencher aside, Sallie Mae reached into a pocket and withdrew a folded-up page. "This appeared on our doorstep early one morn." She grinned sheepishly. "Apparently I ain't the only one in the Weston household who can't read. We had the devil of a time makin' out the word Hester. See, just there. It says 'Hess-ter B,' don't it?"

Diana studied the folded-up missive. "Indeed, it does appear to be addressed to a Hesster B." She turned it over and over in her hand. "Who is it from?"

"Didn't open it. Wasn't certain it was truly meant for me." She shrugged. "If you recall, Hester B. ain't truly my name. I thought perhaps it was meant for . . . *her.* Or perhaps all the girls on the Bride Ship received letters. A welcome message, or some such. Did you not get one?"

"No." Diana shook her head. "Do you suppose we should read it?"

Sallie Mae colored. "I ain't real good at sorting out words and such. I thought if you also got a letter, yours might say the same thing as mine. Or perhaps you'd be so kind as to read the letter for me. It likely ain't meant for me," she said again.

Before Diana and Sallie Mae could break the seal and unfold the page, an incensed Ann Fuller joined them. At once she launched a tale about how she and her brother John and cousin Beth had run into one of their shipmates the first night they all arrived in Jamestown.

"She insisted her name was Faith, and not Prudence, and then she simply flounced away in the rudest manner possible! She did not even acknowledge my brother John."

"Her name *is* Faith," Diana said quietly. "And she is overset for a reason. Faith only just learned of her sister's tragic death. The two were quite close."

"But she did not even acknowledge John or speak to Beth," Ann persisted.

"Faith is quite distraught," Sallie Mae put in.

Ann lifted her chin. "Well, if you ask me, that girl has the evil eye."

Diana sucked in her breath. "Ann, what a dreadful thing to say!"

"Her eyes are as green as the sea, and I saw fire in them!"

She cast a gaze about as if expecting to see some sort of malicious mischief manifest before them right then and there.

"Ann, you are leveling a serious charge," Diana scolded. "We have not come to the New World to be unkind or spread untruths about one another. I beg you to leave off judging Faith. She is simply grieving the loss of her sister."

Ann sniffed.

"I would like to meet yer brother," Sallie Mae said quietly.

"We both would," Diana added agreeably. The letter in her hand forgotten, she slipped it into her pocket to peruse later.

Later that afternoon, Diana found herself quite enjoying the leisurely walk home. She purposely slowed her step so as to prolong the pleasant interlude. Ann Fuller had, indeed, introduced both her and Sallie Mae to her brother John, but it was Diana to whom he seemed instantly drawn.

"How long have you been in Jamestown, John?" she asked, looking up into the tall man's warm brown eyes. Diana thought he was a fine-looking man, fashionably dressed in black gathered breeches and a green doublet, his neat brown hair grazing his stand-up collar.

It had pleased her to see that today nearly all the girls looked clean and tidy. Even the colonists, who had looked almost as filthy and unkempt as the girls did the day they arrived, appeared to have bathed and donned fresh clothing before attending Sabbath services. Diana was glad she had had ample time in which to wash and dry her long hair and freshen her meager assortment of clothing. Today she had chosen to wear the rather prim gray gown with the embroidered white collar that Sara typically wore to worship.

"Come summer, it will be five years," John answered her question.

"Oh, my. Quite a long time, indeed."

"A man must be willing to work if he wishes to make a go of it here, but I've never been one to shy away from hard work."

"Do you plant tobacco?"

"I do indeed." He smiled. "Planting for this year's crop is complete. My seedlings are growing taller and sturdier every day."

"Do you not fear the Indians? I confess when Governor Yeardley and Mistress Larsen mentioned there are Indian villages nearby, I grew somewhat alarmed."

He smiled down into her upturned face. "I can understand why the notion of Indians might alarm you, Miss Wakefield. Hardly anyone in England has seen a real Indian. Certainly not a sheltered young lady like yourself."

"Nor do we know a great deal about them," Diana added.

"You need not fear the Indians, Miss Wakefield. We have lived peacefully alongside them for many years now. Nearly all the well-put families in Jamestown, and all the large plantations, have Indian servants. A few planters even employ Indian braves to work in the fields."

"Mistress Larsen's Indian woman, Cheiwoga, seems a pleasant sort." They turned a corner and headed up another shady path toward the Larsen home.

"I have an Indian woman who cleans and cooks for me," John said. "Her name is Tamiyah. She is quite trustworthy. Several freemen and I have employed the same woman for years."

"Freemen?" Diana was pleased to be learning a great deal about the New World from John. It surprised her that she so quickly felt comfortable conversing with him, almost as if they had known one another a great length of time.

"A freeman is a man who came here of his own accord, as opposed to a man indentured to another who paid his passage over, or one who committed a crime back home in England and was sentenced to transportation. We are called freemen because we are beholden to no one."

Diana smiled. "We were told we are to marry freemen." Suddenly she felt color rise to her cheeks. "I-I did not mean to suggest that . . ."

He grinned. "We were told that you young ladies are not to be treated as servants."

They both fell silent and a moment later paused before the Larsen home to wait until John's sister Ann and the young man walking beside her caught up to them.

"Thank you again for introducing me to your brother, Ann," Diana said pleasantly.

The girl sniffed with disdain. "I am glad now your friend Miss Plumleigh snubbed us the other evening. I should not wish *her* sort hanging after John."

Caught off guard by Ann's heated response, Diana rushed to her friend's defense. "I explained to you earlier, Ann, that Faith is mourning her sister. I trust you will extend Christian sympathy toward her. She is a sweet girl." Diana held Ann's cold gaze as she spoke.

Her chin at a stubborn tilt, Ann sniffed piously.

Diana could see from the look on the girl's face that she did not accept her explanation regarding Faith's behavior. For now, Diana chose to say nothing further on the matter, and instead turned toward John. "I am quite pleased to have met you, Mister Fuller."

"And I you, Miss Wakefield. I hope I will see you again."

Diana's lashes fluttered against her flushed cheeks. "Thank you for escorting me home."

"My pleasure, to be sure, Miss Wakefield."

That night, as Diana knelt beside her bed to pray, she asked the Lord to please quiet the unrest in Ann Fuller's mind regarding Faith, and to please help Faith accept His will regarding her sister's death.

Rising to her feet, she decided on the morrow she would pay a call on Faith and offer whatever comfort she could. Left unchecked, Ann's malicious gossip could have tragic consequences indeed.

It was not until the following morning that Diana remembered the letter Sallie Mae had given her to read. Alone in her chamber, she tore open the seal and unfolded the single page. But the terse message scrawled on the somewhat soiled piece of paper stunned her. "I knows who ye are. If'n ye wants to stay alive, say nothing about what ye saw."

Dear God, Diana thought, what could it mean? Was the message truly intended for Sallie Mae, or was it meant for the dead girl, Hester Brownfeld? She didn't know now which of her friends to assist first. Should she warn Faith that Ann Fuller was spreading malicious lies about her? Or pay a call on Sallie Mae and . . . what? Question the girl further. Diana realized now that she still did not know why Sallie Mae had left England under cover of disguise, or who she truly was. Could the simple country girl have committed a crime in England and be running from the authorities? Did she know something that she shouldn't? It all seemed quite forbidding and sinister. Deliberating further, she decided to check first on Faith, then decide what to do regarding Sallie Mae.

Realizing she didn't have a clue where Faith lived, she asked Mister Larsen to which family Miss Plumleigh had been assigned. When he supplied the needed information, complete with directions to the Evans' home, Diana set out on Bug-a-Boo. Upon locating the neat two-storey home, she rapped at the door. It was promptly opened by one of the Evans' Indian servants, who led her into a neat parlor where Mistress Evans sat alone, her gray head bent over her needlework.

When Diana told Mistress Evans that she wished to see Faith, the woman confided to Diana that she had experienced a great deal of concern over Miss Plumleigh. "It is clearly evident something is troubling her, and I haven't a clue what it could be. I fear she regrets her decision to come to Jamestown."

In a soft tone, Diana told her that Faith's beloved sister had recently perished and that Faith was distraught over the girl's death.

"Oh. Well, that does explain her refusal to take part in anything. She did not wish to attend the picnic on Sunday. I saw her walk away alone soon after services. I do not believe she lingered long enough to eat a single bite. She often does not come down for dinner. I fear the poor child will waste away."

"I should have come sooner."

"I am convinced she will be glad to see you, dear. As am I."

Faith declined Diana's offer to take a ride on horseback, but agreed to a short walk. The Evans' home sat a bit apart from the other homes in this far-reaching section of Jamestown. Directly behind the house lay an extensive kitchen garden. The girls paused to admire it before entering a lovely meadow that fronted the forest. Here and there clusters of tall trees provided a shady respite from the warm sun beating down upon their backs. Once they had chosen a tree beneath which to sit, Diana asked how her friend fared since arriving in Jamestown.

Faith seemed reticent to speak, her head lowered, her lips pressed tightly together.

Diana's heart went out to her. "I am sorry you are bereft, Faith. Prudence would not wish you to suffer so."

"How can you know my sister's wishes?" Faith muttered.

"If your places were reversed, would you wish Prudence to suffer as you are now?"

Faith worried her lower lip. "I am still so very angry with myself. If I had known Prudence left the cabin that night, I could have saved her."

"You are forgetting that you were also ill. You could not have managed the fierce wind and the pounding rain. I do not know how Prudence managed . . . it was as if . . . as if she were being led straight to her death. I own that seems shocking, but . . . I saw her. I called to her again and again, and she did not once look back. Your sister seemed bent upon ending her own life."

Faith had commenced to weep. Diana gathered her friend into her arms and rocked her as she had seen Mary Larsen do with her babe. "You are not the only one of us who has suffered a tragic loss, Faith."

Faith did not lift her head until near the end of the tale Diana told regarding her own parents' drowning deaths only a few months prior.

Sitting back, Faith gazed into her friend's now tear-filled eyes. "I wonder how have you borne such a loss."

"I remind myself as often as possible that my parents and my dear friend . . . Sara . . . are safe in our Heavenly Father's arms. I am convinced they are far happier where they are now than those of us still here on earth."

Faith swiped at the traces of tears still glittering on her lashes. "Your friend's name was Sara?"

Diana nodded, biting her lip even as she felt her chin begin to tremble afresh.

"Sara is the name you gave the man at the jetty steps."

Diana looked up.

"You took your friend's place on the Bride Ship," Faith stated coolly.

"I had nowhere else to go."

"I will try to remember all you have said, Diana." Faith attempted a smile. "Thank you for coming today."

"I wish I had come sooner," Diana murmured. "But now that I am here, there is something else I must ask of you. Please do not ask me to explain why. I fear the reason would only anger you."

Faith's gaze grew quizzical.

"I must ask you to apologize to Ann Fuller."

"Apologize to Ann Fuller? Whatever for?"

"Ann is of the opinion that you . . . were rude to her the night you met her and her brother and cousin Beth whilst walking."

Faith did not reply at once, then said contritely, "Perhaps I was rude. But I was . . ." She glanced up. "Ann has a brother?"

Diana grinned. "She was attempting to introduce you to him that night, but she insists you snubbed them and walked away without acknowledging him."

"I was inordinately overset that night."

"I told Ann that your sister had recently passed away. Though I supplied none of the particulars," she quickly added. "I also explained to Mistress Evans just now. She is quite concerned for your welfare."

"I have not meant to worry her."

"It will be to your advantage to seek Ann out as soon as possible, perhaps on Sabbath next, and tell her how sorry you are for . . . for . . ."

"Oh, very well. But it seems quite silly. Especially since you told her why I have been overset."

"Do be kind, Faith. An apology will smooth things over, and you will never have to think on it again."

"Oh, very well," Faith huffed. "I will seek out Ann." A moment later, she added, "You are my only friend here, Diana."

Both girls rose to their feet. "I understand there are two girls right here whom I am certain would befriend you, if you would let them."

Faith shrugged. "Perhaps I need no other friends."

Chapter 15

The following day, Diana felt compelled to seek out Sallie Mae. Trying to recall the convoluted directions the girl had given her, she was pleased when she headed Bug-a-Boo down a narrow path near the river and right away spotted Sallie Mae and her mistress outdoors on the grassy area in front of a small wattle-and-daub house. She quickly reined in her mare and dismounted.

Dismayed to discover that her friend's sponsors were a good deal less well put than hers or Faith's, she glanced over one shoulder at the tiny hovel. It seemed hardly large enough to hold two people, let alone three. But she did not allow her feelings to show. "I am so happy to know where you are," she exclaimed to Sallie Mae.

"I be right here helping Goody Weston," Sallie Mae replied cheerfully. "We laundered the bed linens a day or so ago, and today we're a'makin' soap."

"Making soap?" Diana spotted a barrel that appeared to be full of wood ashes and another that reeked of something rotten. "I would not know where to begin," she murmured.

The two other women laughed. "Puttin' up soap is a hateful task," Goody Weston said, "but one can't risk runnin' out of it, what with the menfolk a'workin' in the fields and comin' in filthy. We done set the leach, but the lye ain't yet strong enough, so we's about to pour it over fresh ashes."

"I see," Diana murmured, although she didn't. She noted

that Sallie Mae had returned to her task of building up the outdoor fire. "What are you doing?" she asked.

"Grease and lye hafta' be boilt together," Sallie Mae replied. "Fire must be plenty hot to melt the grease."

"W-where did you get the grease?"

"Refuse grease," replied Goody Weston, "saved up all winter from yer cookin' and yer butcherin'. Ye also saves yer discarded wood ash outta' the fire." She stirred the mixture she was tending. Changing the subject, she inquired, "Who ye be a'stayin' with, Miss Wakefield?"

Relieved to abandon the confusing topic of soap, Diana smiled. "Councilman and Mistress Larsen."

"Ah." Goody Weston sighed ruefully. "Mistress Larsen won't be a'needin' you ta' help make soap. I hear she has a Indian woman a'doin' all her heavy work."

Diana nodded, suddenly assailed by a pang of guilt as she watched Sallie Mae work so hard when nothing of the sort was required of her or Faith. "P-perhaps I could help the two of you now," she offered, although a trifle weakly. "If you wouldn't mind showing me what to do."

"That be right kind of ye, Miss Wakefield. As I said, we've already set the leach, but we be a'needin' to add in more water and ash as the mixture boils. With another pair of hands helpin', we'll have a barrel of nice soft soap in no time."

Diana unpinned her sleeves and pitched in to do what she could. But a good two hours later, she experienced some regret over her quick offer to assist. She had never performed any sort of physical labor in her life. Back home in England, she had used both hard and soft soap but never once questioned where the stuff came from. Now, she assumed that her parent's lower-order servants had made the family's soap in a fashion similar to this. Heaving a weary sigh, she realized now that if the task of making soap was one required of most Jamestown wives, at least she now knew a bit about the process.

"Diana, you look a fright!" Sallie Mae laughed as they rolled the barrel of soft soap through the doorway of the small house. "Your cap is askew and ye've ash all over yer face and gown. Mistress Larsen will wonder what happened to ye."

"I expect I should be going." Diana was fairly panting from her exertion. "I wonder if I might trouble you for a mug of water before I set out, Goody Weston. I find I am quite thirsty."

"No trouble at all," exclaimed the thin woman. She hurried back inside the house to fetch the drink.

Diana quickly turned to Sallie Mae and in a low tone asked, "Do you and Goody Weston work this hard every day?"

"There's a good deal to be done every day. Goody Weston is such a frail little thing, I fear for her and the babe she's a'carryin'. I don't believe she could manage without my help."

"But she managed before you came, Sallie Mae. Mrs. Douglass said we are not to be treated as servants."

"Oh. I . . . dinna' know that."

Diana grinned. "That is because you were still parading as a lad when Mrs. Douglass spoke to the rest of us each day on the ship. You are so very kind-hearted, Sallie Mae. I do not wish to see the Westons take advantage of your selfless nature."

When Goody Weston reappeared carrying a scraped-out gourd full of fresh water, Diana politely thanked her. "I wonder if Sallie Mae and I might"—she cast a quick gaze about in search of a spot where they might talk amongst themselves—"sit across the road for a spell beneath that tree."

"Oh, I really shouldn't," Sallie Mae said. "We be a'needin' to put the kettle on and start cookin' up victuals for—"

"We really should talk, Sallie Mae," Diana said firmly.

"You go along," Goody Weston said. "I kin manage the cookin' and such like."

Seated on the ground out of earshot of anyone, Diana came

straight to the point. She hadn't brought the letter with her since Sallie Mae couldn't read. "I came today especially to tell you what the letter said."

"Oh, did you read it?" Sallie Mae's gaze was innocent.

"Indeed. And I confess I am a bit concerned. The message was quite . . . cryptic."

"Cryp-tic? I don't know what that word means, Diana."

"It means mysterious and also . . . alarming. The message warned you to 'keep silent about what you saw.' There was also a . . . threat."

Sallie Mae seemed unmoved. "Well, clearly it don't concern me. What do I know that I can't talk about?" She answered her own question with a word and shrug. "Nothin'."

Diana inhaled an exasperated breath. "I do not mean to pry, Sallie Mae, but if there is something . . . in your past, perhaps, that you may have seen that might incriminate—"

Sallie Mae huffed. "Diana, I don't know what that word means either. I told you I don't know nothing." She made as if to get up. "I'd best get back to work now. Poor little Goody Weston—"

"Can do without you a few minutes longer," Diana interrupted. "Sallie Mae, please try to think. Is there anything that you witnessed—that word means 'saw'—back home in England, or perhaps even on the ship, that . . . perhaps you shouldn't have seen?"

"I can't think of nothin', Diana. Although—" She paused. "I dinna' tell you, but I'm certain One-Eye recognized me that day on the ship when we all went up on deck. I caught him lookin' straight at me. He dinna' say nothin'. Jes' stared at me real hard like. I never saw him agin after that." She paused. "Yes, I did. Come to think on it. I saw him the day we left the ship. He didn't see me. But I saw him hurryin' around the outside of the fort." She shrugged. "Likely he has kinfolk here and was a'wantin' to see 'em afore the ship sailed."

Diana sighed. "I cannot think what that has to say to anything. If One-Eye meant to turn you over to the captain, he would have done so whilst we were still on the ship." She glanced again at her fresh-faced friend. "You've broken no law, have you, Sallie Mae?"

"Not that I know of." Sallie Mae's blond curls shook. "I think I woulda' knowed if I had, don't you?"

"Well." Diana sighed again. "I confess I cannot think what this means. Perhaps the letter was, indeed, intended for Hester Brownfeld." She paused to consider. "Perhaps it would be wise if you were to broadcast the fact that your name is Sallie Mae Brown, lest whomever believes you to be Hester continues to threaten you. Clearly, poor Hester was up to some sort of mischief."

Sallie Mae all but ceased to listen when Bug-a-Boo, munching on grass, crossed the lane and drew nearer them. Sallie Mae reached to stroke the mare's nose.

"Perhaps you could come again and we could take a ride on Bug-a-Boo," Sallie Mae suggested.

"That would be splendid." Diana rose to her feet. "I promise I will come again soon, Sallie Mae. I expect I should get home and wash up before supper. I must look a fright."

Sallie Mae laughed. "Ye look like ye been a'makin' soap."

Diana didn't know what to think. Perhaps the note was indeed meant for Hester Brownfeld. She tried to put the matter from her mind as she went about her days, generally spent in pleasant pursuits such as playing with the children or simply talking with Mary Larsen, who was still nursing her infant daughter. When done, she very often handed the baby off to Diana, who cuddled and cooed over it. Diana had never before been around young children and found she greatly enjoyed the little ones.

Young Edward was, indeed, thrilled that there was a horse in the shed and did not miss a day of accompanying Diana there to tie on a sack of oats and brush the mare's coat till it shone.

The boy begged his father to let him sit atop the horse and told Diana he meant to gallop his own pony up and down the streets of Jamestown one day.

"I am certain you will make a fine horseman," she said. "In the meantime, you may watch me ride Bug-a-Boo up and down the street. A horse requires a good bit of exercise, you know. I fear Bug-a-Boo grew quite restless confined to her narrow compartment on the ship."

"Did you not ride her up and down the deck?"

Diana laughed. "She would have had a difficult time sidestepping the ropes and rigging. On a few occasions, I carefully led her around the deck. But only in fine weather."

"D'ye suppose Father would let me lead Bug-a-Boo around our yard?"

"I fear you are too small for such a task. But we can certainly ask if he would allow you to accompany me."

John Fuller called several times that week to see Diana. One evening Mary Larsen invited him to come earlier the following evening and share the family's evening meal.

John arrived dressed in his Sabbath clothes and looking every inch the eager suitor. He even brought Diana a bouquet of wildflowers: daisies, and pink and purple coneflowers mixed with a few sprigs of late-blooming dogwood. She thanked him, and Mary put them into an empty ale jug filled with well water. That morning she and Diana had decided to serve a nice venison stew with spoon bread and butter, and to top off the meal, a special pie Cheiwoga made from treacle and a type of nut she called *pakawns.*

Following the meal, John and Diana set out for a walk, both

remarking on the balmy feel of the warm night air. The two had enjoyed several evening walks and very often ran into other young couples, also strolling the dusty streets of Jamestown. Diana continued to be fascinated by the unusual sights she beheld in the colony.

"Do people live in those loaf-shaped structures?" she asked, pointing across the way at several of the odd-looking hovels.

"Those are bark houses," John told her. "Most were built by the early settlers because they go up quickly. The frame is formed from green sapling reeds still flexible enough to bend, then the whole structure is covered over with pieces of bark stripped from trees. The bark is held in place, stitched, if you will, with lengths of hemp."

"Some appear to have an actual door and even windows," Diana marveled.

"The early colonists copied the pattern from the Indians, who live in similar structures, although"—he laughed—"the Indians' homes appear to be more neatly made."

"They are very unusual."

"But not terribly practical. Bark houses are quite cold in winter, and a strong wind can easily topple one . . . as many an unfortunate settler has learned. A newborn babe was once killed when its parents' bark house tumbled in upon it."

"Oh, how dreadful!" Diana continued to gaze about as they walked. "It appears the majority of houses in Jamestown are constructed of wood and some sort of sand or mud mixture topped with a thick thatched roof."

John nodded. "Roofs are made from cattails and reeds gathered from the marsh. Daub is, indeed, a mixture of sand and mud. A man can build a simple wattle-and-daub house without employing the services of a house-wright. Frame is held together with wooden trunnels. Iron nails are far too expensive, and there are few to be had here. I recall a couple of men once attempted to build a fair-sized clapboard house with only a few nails and the thing fell in on them. Killed them both."

"Oh!" Diana's eyes widened.

John's head wagged. "Dozens of eager settlers swooped in to sort through the rubble in order to steal the dead men's nails. Only later did they bother to uncover the dead bodies."

"How frightful!" Diana cried.

"In my estimation, that is a prime reason we sorely need women in the colony. To civilize us men."

"Unfortunately, not many women know how to build a house."

"Most men didn't either, in the beginning, and back then, Jamestown had no house-wright or cabinetmaker. Sadly, our cabinetmaker now stays busier building coffins than he does furniture."

"Oh, my," Diana murmured, becoming quite alarmed by what she was learning about Jamestown from John.

"Unfortunately, sickness is rife here both winter and summer."

"And still Englishmen come," Diana marveled.

"Fortunately, more and more tradesmen have come. We've a new ironworks factory north of here in a settlement called Falling Creek. We also have a blacksmith, who is kept plenty busy."

"But there are so few horses," Diana pointed out.

"Blacksmiths make the axes that fell the trees to build the houses. And this one brought along a screw jack."

"A what?"

"Screw jack." John chuckled. "A mechanism that lifts heavy objects. Comes in handy for repairing a ship's mast and hoisting clapboards onto a ship to send back home to England. It is also quite useful in building a house."

"I see." Diana laughed. "The settlers do appear quite industrious. Still, on the whole"—her gaze darted back and forth at the hovels on either side of the road—"everything here seems so . . . drab."

"There are only two painted clapboard houses in the entire colony, Governor Yeardley's home and that of Councilman Evans."

Diana caught herself before inquiring what sort of house John lived in. She did not wish him to think she was considering what sort of home he could offer were he to ask her to become his wife. All the same, she surmised his house boasted at least three chambers—a common room, no doubt with a fireplace, and two bedchambers, one used by John and the other now shared by his sister Ann and cousin Beth.

It startled her when John's next remark sounded as if he had been thinking in the same vein. "I understand Reverend Martin will conduct two weddings this coming Sabbath."

"Indeed. It seems a bit soon to me for couples to be pairing off. The couples' banns were only just posted."

"Convention is not followed as closely here as it is in England."

"Rachel Miller is a very pretty girl. I am not surprised a young man quickly snatched her up. And Laura Whitbeck is mad for Claude Fraser. Laura has a beautiful voice. She often sang for Sabbath services on the ship."

"I expect you sing as well, do you not? And are proficient on the virginals?"

Diana looked up. "Why would you think that?"

"You appear quite well brought up, Miss Wakefield. Although you have said little about your former life in England, I assume you received a privileged education, tutored in the feminine arts, music, dancing and the like."

Diana held back the sudden moisture that sprang to her eyes whenever she thought of her parents and the home in England she would never see again. She feared if she spoke of her former life now, tears would flow. Instead, she asked John a question.

"Why did you and your sister Ann wish to leave England?"

John considered. "I am an adventurer at heart, and I believe Ann left because she had been spurned in love. She has spoken little of it, but I gather the father of the young man she wished to marry did not think her quite good enough for his son. That a Bride Ship was leaving England proved opportune for Ann. She sought sanctuary here with me, although I believe she would have found her way here even if there had been no special ship coming."

"I am sorry to hear of Ann's disappointment in love," Diana murmured, the thought bringing up her own, still raw, heartache. "We are fortunate that here we shall not be obliged to concern ourselves with our parents' approval of a match."

"Ann remarked upon that very thing."

They walked a bit farther, neither speaking, Diana still working to push down nostalgic memories from her life in England, and instead enjoy both John's company and the warm night air. Before walking too much further, she and John met up with several other couples also out for a stroll. John paused to introduce the freemen to Diana, and if she was acquainted with the young lady, the girls exchanged pleasantries.

At one point, three men came striding toward them, all dressed in a rather unusual fashion—buckskin shirts with fringe on the sleeves and buckskin breeches tucked into high-topped leather boots. Strings of blue glass beads hung around their necks. One of the men, the nicest-looking of the three, Diana noted, wore several silver rings with brightly colored stones on his fingers. Slung over his shoulder was a large bow and a quiver full of arrows. Diana could not help noticing that John did not pause to speak with the men; in fact, he barely nodded to them. When they were out of earshot, she asked him who the oddly dressed men were.

"Jamestown's traders," he replied in a decidedly disdainful tone. "Lieutenant John Sharpe, Richard Tidwell, and . . . the fine-looking one is Noah Colton."

Diana grinned. For a man to acknowledge that another man was fine-looking seemed amusing. "I take it you mean the tall one with the broad shoulders and golden hair."

"So, you did notice."

"It appears some sort of animosity might exist between you and this particular gentleman."

John inhaled sharply and spoke plainly. "Noah Colton is no gentleman."

She stared up at him. This was the first judgment upon anyone's character she had heard from John Fuller. Though she could not help wondering what might have caused him to so heartily dislike the trader, she decided not to question him further. Having reached the end of Jamestown's longest street, which ran the length of the entire settled area, she merely said, "Perhaps it is time we turn back."

A few days later, Diana made good on her word to take Sallie Mae for a ride on Bug-a-Boo. The girls—their long blue skirts spread over the mare's flank—both sat astride the animal on a small rug supplied by Mary Larsen. As there were so few horses in the settlement, the girls received a good many stares from passersby.

"John told me that I am being referred to as 'the girl with the horse,' " Diana remarked in a lighthearted tone.

"Your horse is one of very few in the colony." With Bug-a-Boo trotting at a leisurely pace, Sallie Mae felt free to look about. "Jamestown feels so very peaceful. The cheery sound of birds chirpin' and the leafy trees swayin' in the breeze remind me of the meadow at home."

"You sound like a poet," Diana said. It pleased her to be able to offer her friend a respite from the hard work she endured every day. It also pleased her to impart the answers to some of Sallie Mae's questions regarding Jamestown's oddities, such as the loaf-shaped houses and the round stone structure that sat smack in the center of one dirt road.

"It's a communal oven," Diana explained. "Apparently the smaller hovels, such as the ones made from bark, do not have indoor ovens. Women bring their unbaked bread or pies here and slide them into the openings on long-handles griddles, then come back for them later."

"I wonder they do not get their baked goods mixed up and instead of takin' their own bread home, they leave with another's. Goody Weston doesn't have an indoor oven," she added. "We bake bread sittin' the pan on a cleared space on the floor inside the fireplace. Takes a good long while to bake, but it's quite tasty all the same."

When it was Sallie Mae who pointed out both of the town's water wells to Diana, she felt another stab of guilt over her friend's situation. Until now, she'd had no idea where Jamestown's water wells were located.

"I generally come here once a day," Sallie Mae said, "sometimes oftener, to carry water back home."

"How do you . . . *carry* water? Does it not slosh out of the bucket?"

Grinning, Sallie Mae pointed to a lad just then drawing water up from the well. "See. Just there, the boy will hook both of his buckets to the end of that yoke, which he'll balance atop his shoulders."

"The contraption must be terribly heavy. I wonder that you could lift such a thing, Sallie Mae. You are not a very large girl."

"Goody Weston is smaller than I and far more frail. I am persuaded she could not lift them."

When the girls had slowly ridden up and down most all of

Jamestown's dusty paths, Sallie Mae suggested they ride into the dense forest that lay beyond the village.

Diana faltered. "I confess I am far too fearful to venture into the woods. I should not wish to come upon a tribe of Indians."

"But you see plenty of Indians every day right here in Jamestown," Sallie Mae pointed out.

"But here, there are far more of us," Diana countered.

On another afternoon, Diana brought Sallie Mae to the Larsen home for a visit, but never once did Sallie Mae come on her own. Diana knew it was because her friend stayed far too busy helping Goodwife Weston with all manner of heavy work. A fact that continued to trouble Diana.

At the Evans home on the outskirts of town, Faith soon discovered the pastime she most enjoyed was spending afternoons alone in Mistress Evans's kitchen garden, where she busied herself pulling the weeds that threatened to choke out the new plants. The older woman had planted a fine assortment of vegetables and herbs—radishes, parsley, cabbages, leeks, red and yellow carrots, cucumbers, summer squash, purslane, and herbs such as basil, burnet, colewort, chicory, fennel and hyssop. Faith picked many herbs daily that very often found their way into the families' soup pot. She even began hanging some of the more aromatic herbs from the rafters in the girls' room, something Mistress Evans remarked upon.

"I used to do that myself when I was a girl," she said, breathing in the pleasant aroma of the scented herbs.

"I had hoped you would not mind," Faith said quietly.

"Of course, I do not mind, dear. You may hang some in the common room, if you like. I am certain my husband would also enjoy the pleasant scent."

One of the afternoons during which Faith busied herself in Mistress Evans's garden, she was surprised to come upon a small orange cat sleeping beneath an umbrella of squash leaves. Not wishing to disturb the kitten, she went quietly about her work. Sometime later, she detected the squash leaves moving. She smiled when she spotted the orange cat arching its back into an inverted U. After stretching its small body out long and lean, it noiselessly padded straight up the narrow path between the row of plants and sat down beside her. A golden stare fixed upon Faith.

She stared back. "I have nothing for you, Cat; no pan of milk, or smelly fish tail. And since I am fairly certain you do not mean to help me, you had best trot away."

The following two afternoons when Faith entered the garden, there sat the cat. "I still have nothing for you, Cat. Now run along and leave me to my work."

But the cat did not budge. Once when Faith was bending low over a bed of purslane, she was startled when the small animal jumped onto her shoulder. "Oh!" she cried. Laying aside her digging tool, she carefully reached behind her head to scoop up the soft kitten and lift it onto her lap. Its golden eyes held her gaze. "Why do you persist in following me, you silly cat?"

Burrowing into Faith's lap, the kitten began to purr. Her lips pursed, Faith picked it up and set it on the ground. "You do not wish to be my friend. No one wishes to be my friend. Now, go away."

As if it understood perfectly, the small orange cat padded away, its tail curved gracefully in the air.

That night as Faith lay in bed listening to the even breathing of her two bed-mates, Annabeth and Robin, she thought again of the little orange cat and how sweetly it purred when she held it. Suddenly, tears gathered in her eyes. Why had she turned the cat away, when the truth was, she had hoped to see it in the garden that day? The fuzzy little creature brought a smile to her lips, which was something she experienced infrequently of late.

Of a sudden, an odd thought popped into her head. Perhaps Prudence had sent the cat to comfort her. And she had turned it away. Hot, scalding tears snaked down her cheeks.

The next morning, she could hardly wait to get to the garden to look for the cat. Today she had tucked a piece of ham steak into her apron pocket. Not long after arriving in the garden, she was pleased to see the little orange kitten slithering amongst the plant rows as it wound its way to her.

"So there you are, silly cat. I've brought something special for you today. But you must come and get it."

When the cat reached her, it hopped right into her lap and began to purr. A smile on her lips, Faith spent a good quarter hour not working in the garden, but gently petting the kitten, which she decided to call Sunshine, both because of its color and because "sunshine" was what the sweet, furry creature had brought into her life.

Thereafter, Sunshine followed Faith everywhere. Though it secretly pleased her that the kitten would have nothing to do with either Annabeth or Robin, she did not mind that it did welcome the occasional caress from Mistress Evans.

On the following Sabbath, Sunshine even trotted along behind the family as they walked into the fort for services. Following his sermon, Reverend Martin did, indeed, marry two couples, and the entire congregation enjoyed Goodwife Fraser's lovely voice raised in song. Afterward, the colonists gathered on the green for the wedding feast. That afternoon, most all the young boys and even some of the men engaged in a rowdy game of quoits.

Faith made good on her word to Diana and drew Ann Fuller aside to offer a sincere apology for not pausing that first night to converse with her and her cousin Beth. "I understand my friend Diana Wakefield mentioned to you that I am mourning the loss of my sister."

"My sympathies, to be sure," Ann said, although Faith detected precious little of it in her tone.

Unable to think of anything else to say, Faith leaned down to scoop up Sunshine, who'd been following close on her heels. Cradling the kitten in her arms, she wandered off.

Standing nearby, Diana noticed Faith conversing with Ann and hoped that following her apology, Ann's injured feelings would be placated and henceforth she would refrain from maligning Faith with unjust tales. She smiled when she noticed that tucked beneath Faith's arm was a small orange kitten. Something sweet and soft to cuddle was precisely what Faith needed to lift her spirits.

Diana spent the bulk of the festive afternoon in John Fuller's company and that of a few of his friends, also freemen who were doing the pretty for young ladies who had arrived on the Bride Ship. Before the day was over, she was presented with the opportunity to introduce John to both Sallie Mae and Faith. Both of her friends were cordial to him, and she and Sallie Mae enjoyed petting Sunshine. However, Sallie Mae was obliged to leave the company of her friends before the festivities concluded when Goodman Weston fetched her, saying his wife was feeling unwell.

Later, near the time all the colonists began to disperse, Diana happened to see one of the trader men whom she and John had met up with the other evening on their walk—the handsome one; the one named Noah Colton. Today the tall blond man was not wearing his odd clothing. Today he was as finely turned out as Governor Yeardley, in a maroon-colored doublet with a froth of cream lace at the neck and sleeves, black galligaskins, white hose and black shoes with silver buckles. Today the sun-bronzed gentleman was smiling broadly as he made his way through the crowd, tipping his plumed hat to the ladies and shaking hands with the men. Diana noticed that he seemed to have caught the eye of Ann Fuller, as well as several of the other young ladies clustered around her. Smiling broadly, Ann contrived to speak with him before he moved on. Given that Ann's brother did not like the man, Diana idly wondered what John would say to that.

She continued to watch as the handsome man approached the Evans family, which now included Faith as well as Annabeth and Robin. When the charming trader leaned down to say something to Mistress Evans, his remark brought an answering smile to her lips. After greeting Mister Evans, he presented Colton to the three young ladies. All the girls, Diana noted, had been staring agog at the handsome man, as would she, if she had been fortunate enough to be amongst their party.

Diana soon noted the charming trader walking from the meetinghouse in the company of the Evans family. She experienced a mild pang of regret that she had not been engaged in conversation with Faith, so that she, too, might have met the fine-looking man.

Later that night as she lay in bed thinking over the day, she could not help wondering what could have caused John to be so disdainful of the handsome trader. John was one of the kindest and most pleasant men she had ever known. It was unlike him to shun anyone. Also apparent was that Noah Colton was very well liked by everyone in Jamestown. What could have caused animosity to fester between two such very agreeable men?

Chapter 16

A few evenings into the following week, John Fuller again called upon Diana and they again enjoyed a leisurely stroll along the dusty streets of Jamestown, conversing about one thing and another. Moments before John bade Diana good night, he introduced a fresh topic of conversation.

"I expect I should warn you. Ann has been recruiting converts to her notion that your friend Faith has the evil eye."

Diana gasped. "I plainly saw Faith speaking to Ann following services on Sunday last. I assumed, and rightly so, as Faith confirmed it, that she apologized to Ann and that all was now well between them."

John shrugged. "Apparently Ann harbors some sort of grudge against the lovely Miss Plumleigh."

Diana could scarcely believe her ears. "What is Ann saying now?"

"I do not like carrying tales, Diana, but I did overhear her telling her friends that Miss Plumleigh's housemates had said that Miss Plumleigh hung foul-smelling herbs from the rafters in the Evans' home, claiming the weeds would ward off evil spirits."

"Faith would never say such a thing!"

"Ann said Miss Plumleigh's housemates also told her the girl now has an orange cat who accompanies her everywhere. Ann declares the cat to be her . . . familiar."

"Oh!" Diana cried. Part of the charge was true; Diana herself had stroked Faith's orange cat Sunshine. The distressing thing was that everyone knew that a witch always chose an orange cat as her familiar. Both shocked and dismayed, Diana shook her head. "The world abounds with orange cats, John. I hardly think owning one is proof of the crime Ann is leveling against Faith, nor is it evidence that she is a . . . oh, I *refuse* to say the word." She wrung her hands together. "Why would your sister persist in forwarding such nonsense?"

John shook his head. "I could not say. But do not let it trouble you. I am sorry to have overset you and for no good purpose. Let us put the matter aside and speak of it no more."

"But I cannot allow Ann to continue spreading such vile accusations against Faith! Think where this could lead, John. Even today, in England, there are countless cases of innocent women being hanged merely upon the word of some zealot in their villages. Some are given no proper trial and the accuser is required to present no proof whatever of the poor woman's crime."

"I am aware of such goings-on." John sighed. "Ann and I grew up in Lancashire County, where the Pendle Witch Trials were held. Unfortunately, ten people were hanged. Perhaps that has spurred her imagination."

"King James is such a strong believer in witchcraft that he authored a book warning us against their curses. This is an abomination, John! You must speak with Ann. Promise me you will. *Please!*"

"Indeed, I will, Diana. Fret no more about it. I promise to call a halt to this nonsense straightaway."

Diana hardly slept a wink that night as images of Jamestown's pillory flashed through her mind. By morning, she still had not thought of an answer. To go the governor, who the girls had been instructed to approach if any sort of complaint or problem arose, would only add fuel to this fire. The fewer people who knew of this matter the better. It was one thing if Ann did, indeed, harbor a grudge against Faith and was speaking in a malicious vein so that she and her friends could have a laugh at Faith's expense; but if someone, *anyone,* in the colony overheard and did not know the rumor was simply idle talk amongst a few silly girls and they took it up and spread the accusations, the consequences could be dire, indeed. Diana could not allow such a thing to happen. But . . . what could she do? How was she to silence Ann when Faith's apology had been insufficient to do so?

The next afternoon she paid a call on Faith and was taken aback by the positive change in her friend's demeanor. The two retreated again to the shade beneath a thicket of trees in the meadow behind the house.

"Oh, Diana, I have met the most handsome man in all the world!" Faith gushed. "He is a trader; Jamestown's *premier* trader," she added. "Perhaps you caught a glimpse of him on Sunday last? He is acquainted with everyone in Jamestown. Everyone likes him and declares he is the most charming man in the entire New World."

"I confess I did notice a finely turned-out gentleman moving through the crowd; quite tall and with golden locks to his shoulders. He seemed very charming."

Faith sighed dreamily. "Noah Colton is a god amongst men."

"That he is," Diana sheepishly admitted. It was easy to see how the handsome man could quickly capture a girl's heart.

"He accompanied the family home and stayed to supper. Throughout the meal, I was aware that he was stealing glances at me and of course, I could not help looking at him. Neither could Robin or Annabeth. They were both giggly and silly, but not I. I conducted myself in quite a refined manner."

"I am certain he was most impressed."

"To be sure, I was impressed by him! He said he has been in Jamestown for many years and that he owns a plantation and several additional plots of land."

Diana's hazel eyes widened. "I wonder how he was able to accumulate so very much land." John had not mentioned that the trader was also a landowner.

"He is obviously quite wealthy. In addition to being a trader *and* a landowner, he also conducts a trapping business."

"What does he . . . trap?"

"Animals, silly." Faith giggled. "Fox, bear, marten, beaver. He sells the furs to other settlers and to the English. Noah said Englishmen pay a premium for fine beaver pelts. Make no mistake, Noah Colton is a *very* wealthy man. His clothes are cut from the finest cloth, and his doublet was fastened with silver buttons."

"He did, indeed, look very fine."

"I expect he also has a fine home. With glass windows." A smile played about her lips. "I was vastly amused when Mistress Evans proudly pointed out her glass window panes. Poor woman; she must think us all paupers. I expect your family home has glass windows, does it not?"

Diana nodded, somewhat tightly.

"There, you see? I expect Noah Colton's home does as well."

"But if his primary occupation is that of trader"—Diana changed the direction of their discussion—"how does he also have time to plant, and to trap?"

"He is obviously quite brilliant!" Faith exclaimed on a merry laugh.

"It is good to see you cheerful again. I was also pleased to meet your little friend Sunshine on Sunday last." She reached to pet the orange kitten, now playfully batting at a clump of daisies near their feet.

"Sunshine took to Noah at once. My kitten does not like everyone, you know. He will have nothing whatever to do with Annabeth or Robin." Just then, the orange kitten padded onto the blanket and hopped into Diana's lap. "You see? It is almost as if he likes whomever I like and no one else. My housemates were both green with envy when Noah singled me out."

"How did he single you out?" Diana asked, absently stroking the kitten's soft fur and enjoying its purrs of pleasure.

"After we supped, he and Mister Evans left the table to have a mug of ale. But later, he asked if he might be permitted to sit with me a spell. I confess I was astonished."

Diana looked up. "As I would have been!"

"You should have seen Annabeth's and Robin's faces when Mistress Evans knocked at our bedchamber door to say the gentleman had asked to see me." Faith's auburn head tilted smugly. "Of course, I came down at once. Noah and I sat together in the common room a bit, then we strolled up and down the street."

"Oh, my." Diana marveled. "What did you speak about?"

"He told me about his trading expeditions and the various treaties he has single-handedly master-minded with the Indians. Only this morning, Mister Evans said that a number of tribes would deal with no one but Noah Colton. Which I find vastly impressive. Noah is not a boy, Diana. He is a man, a *real* man, who has accomplished a great deal of import here. His looks alone are enough to turn a girl's head. Oh, Diana, do you suppose I am in love with him?" She clapped her hands together, the noise startling Sunshine, whose sideways leap made both girls laugh. Faith gathered the kitten into her arms and snuggled it to her cheek. "I am also in love with you, little fellow. Do you feel the same way about John Fuller, Diana?"

The question caught Diana off guard. "N-not exactly. John is very kind and we are . . . we converse easily, but he . . . he . . ." Abruptly, she changed the subject. "I wonder if you have seen John's sister since you delivered your apology."

"Ann called here only this morning to see Annabeth and

Robin. The three of them sat in Mistress Evans's parlor with their heads together, whispering and giggling. When I walked into the room, they ceased nattering and turned to stare at me. I knew they were talking about me, but I do not care." She sprang to her feet and, holding Sunshine, twirled about on the grass. "I am so happy, Diana! At times I feel so happy I cannot draw breath!"

"I am pleased, Faith, truly I am. But I would not want to see the handsome trader break your heart."

Faith leveled a shocked look at her friend. "Why ever would you say such a thing?" She returned to sit on the blanket in the shade. "It is true there are plenty of young ladies in Jamestown who are far prettier than I. Even Robin is prettier than I. But Noah did not ask for permission to call upon Robin. He asked if he might call upon me."

"Has he called again?"

"Not as yet, but I am certain he will. At the moment, he is away on a trading expedition. He told me he is often away for weeks at a time. He asked if such a long absence would overset me." A pleased look appeared on her face. "Why do you think he would ask such a thing if he were not thinking of *me* as his wife?"

Diana flinched. "Oh, Faith. I fear you presume too much. You have only just met the man."

"Noah leaves me breathless. He kissed me," she confided.

Diana's eyes widened. "You allowed him to . . . kiss you? So soon?" She had not yet considered such a thing with John. The only man she had ever allowed to take liberties with her was Hamilton. And she had known him all her life.

"I could not help myself. It happened so very naturally, as though it were meant to be. Oh, Diana, I will surely die if I cannot marry this man. I do *so* wish to marry him. I do not wish to marry a yeoman farmer like my father."

"Nor do I," Diana admitted.

"Mister Evans said there has been talk of Noah being named governor of Virginia. Why, to marry him would be akin to becoming queen of the New World. I would make a very fine queen, would I not?"

Diana smiled. "You would make a lovely queen."

"I would appoint you to my court; as my head lady-in-waiting." Of a sudden, she pulled a face. "But I would not include Hester Brownfe—"

"You mean Sallie Mae Brown?"

"Yes, well, whatever the girl is calling herself these days. We know nothing of her, Diana. I do not even recall her being on the ship at the outset, then suddenly there she was, and the pair of you were inseparable."

"I became acquainted with her during the time you were ill."

"All the same, I cannot think why you persist in befriending her. She is clearly not *our* sort. I daresay if she saw her name written out she would be unable to read it."

Diana's eyes widened. Did Faith harbor some sort of grudge against Sallie Mae? Had Faith sent the cryptic note? And because nothing had been said about it, the girl surmised, and correctly so, that Sallie Mae had been unable to read what the ominous message said.

"I cannot have someone of her ilk in my court," Faith concluded with disdain.

"I do not believe Governor Yeardley has a court."

"I do not believe Governor Yeardley has a wife. But he has advisors, as does the king. That you and I were assigned to reside in the households of two of his councilmen means that we are already members of New World royalty," Faith reasoned, "or at the very least, New World aristocracy."

"Perhaps," Diana murmured, although her tone sounded a trifle dubious and somewhat distracted as she was still mulling over what she might have learned regarding the threat to Sallie Mae.

At length, another dreamy sigh escaped Faith. "I do wish Prudence could know of my good fortune."

"To be sure, she would be vastly pleased," Diana agreed.

"I cannot help but be persuaded that Noah is the man for me and that my future is now set."

For her sake, Diana truly hoped so.

As she rode home that afternoon, she also hoped that this new turn of events would prove to everyone, and most especially to Ann Fuller, that Faith Plumleigh was as normal a young lady as any other in Jamestown. She wanted the exact same thing they all did: to find a man who loved her, marry him and start a family in this wonderful new land called Virginia. She prayed there would be no further threats or charges leveled at either of her friends.

Chapter 17

Late one night at the Weston hovel, long after everyone had repaired to bed, Sallie Mae was awakened from a deep sleep by creaking sounds moving across the floorboards of the loft. Earlier that night, she had experienced great difficulty shutting out the Westons' raised voices as Goodman Weston angrily insisted his pregnant wife perform her wifely duty, only this time the poor woman apparently fought off her husband's advances. Now, in the darkness as the footfalls drew nearer, Sallie Mae's heart pounded with fear.

Lying as still as a possum, in seconds the shadowy figure loomed above her in the darkness, but the split-second the man reached for her, she drew one knee to her chest and with a lunge, kicked him as hard as she could in the groin. Leaping from her bed, not pausing to snatch up shoes or clothing, she streaked past the groaning man to race down the stairs and out the door of the house into the street.

She'd gone only a few yards when of a sudden someone grabbed her from behind and a sack, or hood of some sort, was shoved down over her head clean to her shoulders. When she cried out, a hand clamped over her mouth, preventing any further sound from escaping. In an instant, the man, or men, lifted her off her feet and began running as fast as they could, carrying her prone between them. Neither her hands nor feet were bound but, with her feet not touching the ground, there was no possible means of escape. Something told her they were headed for the river, which was nearby, and that the men meant to toss her into it, but she didn't know if they intended to kill her first, or were counting upon the fact that, being a woman, she could not swim and her sudden, unexpected plunge into the deep water would be sufficient to do the job for them. Or . . . maybe they meant to hold her under until she was no longer breathing.

Suddenly, from out of nowhere, the sounds of yelping dogs startled her, and apparently also the men, for she heard one of them curse. The ruckus sounded as if three, perhaps even four, mongrels had given chase. Because the man's curse was in plain English, Sallie Mae surmised her captives were not Indians, as had crossed her mind. Apparently one yelping dog nipped the heels of one of the men, for again she heard him swear. Then he must have tripped over something, perhaps one of the dogs, for suddenly he thrust Sallie Mae at the other man, who threw her over his shoulder like a sack of oats. In seconds they did, indeed, reach the water's edge and suddenly, Sallie Mae felt herself flying through the air. Seconds later, she landed with a splash in the cold water of the James River.

Feeling certain that the river would, indeed, be her ultimate destination, she had taken the precaution of inhaling as deep a breath as possible before being dragged underwater. Sinking quickly toward the bottom, she reached at once to peel off the hood, but wisely kept her mouth shut and, holding onto every bit of air in her lungs, still did not fight to resurface. Instead, underwater, she began to move her hands back and forth and very slowly and quietly rose to the surface.

Not wanting to draw dangerous attention to herself, she fought the urge to gasp for air, to cough or sputter once her head bobbed up. Instead, beneath the water, she continued to keep herself afloat with rapid arm motions, drawing in only quick, short breaths of air. The only part of her body that was visible, if, in fact, she were visible at all in the pitch-black darkness, was the top of her head and the tip of her small nose. From shore, she could still hear the dogs barking and the sounds of a scuffle as the men fought them off. Maintaining her tenuous position in the water, she heard grunts of displeasure from the men as they latched onto sticks or rocks and began to swing at the animals. She heard the dogs' pitiful yelps as one by one they tucked tail and ran. Except for perhaps one, for soon after hearing a thud, as in rock hitting bone, she heard the man utter, "Got 'em!"

"Let's get out of here," the other one said.

She heard mixed noises then; a few grunts from the men as they tossed their weapons aside, one of which splashed into the water, the sudden noise of which gave Sallie Mae a start; then she heard one man say, "Come, on; she's dead." The final sounds she heard were the men's footfalls as they receded into the distance.

Then everything fell silent.

Now allowing herself the luxury of inhaling deep gulps of air, Sallie Mae drew in as much air as her lungs could hold while continuing the fluttery motions of both arms at her sides. But her arms were beginning to burn. Did she dare swim ashore now? Were the men still close by? And what of the dogs? Would they hear her emerging from the water and once more give chase? For the dogs to set up a ruckus would certainly alert the men, if they were still within hearing distance.

Best to stay put a spell longer. Carefully, she lay back on the surface of the water, both hands making sufficient motions to keep her body afloat. Staring up at the night sky, she silently thanked God that it was a moonless night and even the gleam of her white night rail might not be visible from shore. Besides, since the thin garment was now wringing wet and plastered against her naked body, it might no longer appear white anyhow.

Lying there atop the water, her heart still pounding like a drum, her mind skittered over the events of the past half hour. Had the men been lyin' in wait for her? Perhaps they'd meant to steal into the house and abduct her from her bed. They could accomplish that feat easily enough. The Westons had no lock on the door. She suspected few of the settlers' homes did. To enter the house and steal up the stairs to the loft in the dead of night would prove a simple task. With the sack over her head and a hand clamped o'er her mouth, two grown men could easily cart her down the stairs and whisk her away in the night. Apparently by dashin' into the road, she had merely altered their plan a whit, simplified it, as it were. They dinna' have to enter the house.

Heaving a long sigh of relief that she was still alive, Sallie Mae had to admit now that clearly, someone did, indeed, want her, or poor Hester B, dead. Someone believed that she, or Hester, knew something, something sinister and threatening to . . . someone. But who? And why? None of it made sense. She was not a threat to anyone. She knew *nothing!*

Every so often, she gently lifted her head to peer toward shore in search of . . . something, anything that might spring from the darkness and pose another threat to her life.

When at last the first, faint glimmer of light began to appear on the horizon, and Sallie Mae had heard no further sounds save those of the water gently lapping onto shore, she felt it might now be safe to swim toward shore.

Dragging herself from the water, her night rail soaking wet and clinging to her body, she came upon the dead dog where it lay. Already a woodland animal had stolen up and was tearing away at the mongrel's bloody flesh.

Realizing she was virtually naked, Sallie Mae glanced about for something with which to cover herself as she made her way through the settlement. Colonists were early risers, and it was very likely someone would see her. Something slapping against the rushes near shore caught her eye and she trudged that way to snatch the thing up then, with horror, realized it was the very bag the men had pulled over her head. She wrung the water from the sack and, smoothing out the wrinkles, held it against her front as she set out, intending to make her way to the Larsens' home and perhaps hide in the shed till Diana came out that morning to tend to Bug-a-Boo.

At the Larsens' home, with her heart still in her throat, Sallie Mae stole into the shed, a part of her fearing what sort of commotion the mare would raise if her sudden presence startled it.

But upon spotting her, the large animal merely glanced up and blinked, then, when she reached to softly stroke its muzzle, the horse shook its mane and twitched a shoulder in an attempt to shake off a fly.

"I've nowhere else to go, Bug-a-Boo. I am certain yer mistress wouldna' mind if I hid here with you for a spell."

Because the mare did not whinny or stamp its hooves, some of Sallie Mae's fears lessened. "I'll jes bed down in the corner," she said. Feeling her way along the wall inside the darkened structure, she dropped to her knees and patted a place on the scratchy straw, then gingerly lay down upon it. That she might be able to find the rug she and Diana used for a saddle occurred to her, but not knowing where in the shed it hung, she dismissed the notion and attempted to snuggle in as comfortably as possible on the prickly hay. As the nervous fluttering in her mid-section began to die away, she drifted off to sleep. She hadn't a clue what would happen on the morrow, but one thing was certain, she would never, ever, again return to the Weston home. Come to think on it, she might never, ever, set foot out-of-doors again.

★ ★ ★ ★ ★

"Sallie Mae?" Diana exclaimed when she caught sight of her friend curled up asleep in the shed a bit later that morning. Diana knelt beside the sleeping girl. "Sallie Mae?" When no answer was forthcoming, she reached to touch her friend's bare shoulder. The girl stirred. "Sallie Mae, has something happened?"

The little blond's blue eyes sprang open. "I ain't done nothin' wrong, miss!"

"Of course you haven't. But why are you here? What has happened?"

Tears welled up in Sallie Mae's eyes as she drew her knees to her chest.

Diana extended a hand toward the cowering girl. "Let us go inside. It is time we told Mister Larsen about our trouble. Surely he will know what to do."

"No!" Sallie Mae jerked away. "I canna' tell him! He'll insist I tell the governor, and I can't do that. Don't make me."

"You are in danger, Sallie Mae."

"If we tell the governor I ain't Hester B, then everyone'll know I was a'hidin' on the Bride Ship, that I ain't even supposed to be here. Then what? I don't want 'em to send me back to England. I can't go home."

"Very well, then, we shall begin by telling Mary. She will understand."

Sallie Mae chewed on her lower lip. "I canna' go in like this, I mean, a'wearin' me night shift."

"No, no, of course not." It was only then Diana noticed the girl was not fully clothed. She rose to her feet. "I shall fetch one of my gowns. Wait here. I shall return straightaway."

"I ain't a-goin' nowhere," Sallie Mae assured her friend.

Diana went straight to her bedchamber and soon returned carrying one of her own long skirts, a blouse and bodice.

In the shed, whilst Sallie Mae drew the clothing on over her damp night shift, Diana took care of feeding Bug-a-Boo. When Sallie Mae emerged into the sunshine, Diana was pleased to see that her demeanor seemed somewhat calmer. Still, she tossed furtive looks right and left before they hurried into the house.

"I am most sorry to alarm you, Diana. I was nigh on scared outta' m'wits last night. Come what may, I cannot return to the Weston home. I can't."

"I am persuaded you will not be made to return. But we must apprise Mary of the problem. She will no doubt feel obliged to tell her husband. Mister Larsen will eventually know of the trouble."

Sallie Mae nodded tightly.

Inside the Larsen home, both Mister and Mistress Larsen expressed surprise that Diana had a guest so very early that morning.

"How nice to see you, Sallie Mae," Mary Larsen said. "We were just about to break our fast. You are welcome to join us."

A nervous smile flitted across Sallie Mae's flushed face. "Thank ye, ma'am. I own I am powerful hungry."

"Do sit down, Miss Brown," Mister Larsen said. "We've enough food on our table to feed Jamestown's militia. Cheiwoga cannot seem to tell the difference between our one small family and her entire tribe. She always prepares far too much, consequently a great deal goes to waste."

"Or goes home with her," Mary added in a low tone. "Sit there beside Diana, Sallie Mae. I'll just go and fetch Edward. He insists on eating with the grown-ups now."

Sallie Mae slid onto the bench beside Diana. Whilst awaiting Mistress Larsen's return, she quickly surveyed the room. Although she'd been here once before, Diana had led her straight through to her bedchamber and she hadn't noticed that here in the common room, the planked-wooden floor was covered with a round braided rug. Or that a neat row of pegs lined one wall where the family hung their outer garments. Two ladder-backed chairs, as opposed to scooped-out tree stumps, which the Weston's used for sitting, sat before the fire. On the hearthstone, the Larsens' Indian woman was silently preparing the morning meal. Sallie Mae gazed with awe at the large oven inside the fireplace. Why, it even had handy shelves for baking and a spit for roasting meat! Her alert gaze traveled above the fireplace where a long sword and fowling piece hung. To one side of the hearth, a staircase with a nice, sturdy railing led to the loft.

Compared to the Weston hovel, the Larsen home was a virtual mansion. Sallie Mae's brow furrowed. What would she do if Mister Larsen insisted she return to the Westons?

Breakfast that morning was also a source of astonishment to Sallie Mae. There were *two* kinds of meat! The Westons hardly had meat at any meal, unless Goodman Weston had snagged a rabbit or squirrel that day. Here they had both ham steak *and* fried pork for *breakfast!* A serving of fluffy egg custard and a warm wedge of thick yeast bread smeared with butter was also laid upon her trencher.

"There's plenty of egg custard if you'd like more, dear."

"Oh, no, ma'am, I fear I've made a pig of meself . . . but I own I was frightful hungry, ma'am."

"What brings you calling so early, Miss Brown?" Mister Larsen asked, wiping his mouth on a scrap of clean linen. "Not that you are not welcome to visit anytime," he added with a chuckle.

Diana and Sallie Mae exchanged a look. But it was Diana who replied, "Sallie Mae wished to tell me something and . . . um . . . it could not wait."

"Ah, I see." Larsen grinned indulgently. "Girlish secrets, no doubt." He pushed up from the table. "If you ladies will please excuse me, I've a bit of business to attend to. I shan't be long gone, Mary." He walked toward a peg, snatched up his hat and left the house.

"Well, girls," Mary Larsen said, looking from one to the other. "I think one of you needs to tell me what is afoot, but first . . ." She signaled for Cheiwoga and told the Indian woman to take little Edward out of the room. When she turned back to the girls, a frightened look had already transformed Sallie Mae's features.

Biting her lip, she shot a fearful look at Diana.

Both women gazed expectantly at their guest.

"D-during the night, I-I was scared outta' m'wits when I heard Goodman Weston come up the steps to the loft, where . . . I sleep—"

"Oh, my dear!" Mary Larsen gasped. A hand flew to cover her mouth. "Say no more, Sallie Mae. I will tell William the minute he comes home. This is an outrage! You were right to flee, dear. William will know what to do."

"But, ma'am, I . . . I mean Goodman Weston, he dinna' actually do nothin'. But I knowed what he was a'comin' fer and . . . and when he bent to . . . touch me, that's when I kicked him, hard. Right where I knowed it would hurt. Then I run down the steps and uh . . . uh . . . I-I thought perhaps I could hide in the shed with . . . with Bug-a-Boo."

Mary Larsen reached to squeeze Sallie Mae's hand. "You were right to come here, dear."

"I-I don't want ta' cause no trouble, ma'am. I mean fer Goody Weston. She needs her man to look after her. She's . . . increasin' and she's such a frail little thing."

"Sallie Mae is so good-hearted," Diana said to Mary, "she never wishes harm to come to anyone. But clearly, Sallie Mae, the man meant to harm you."

"I expect there will be consequences, Sallie Mae. There are

laws in Jamestown regarding such behavior. The families who offered to provide for you young ladies were all instructed on how to treat you properly. Goodman Weston has clearly overstepped the bounds. He will be punished, or at the very least, reprimanded."

Sallie Mae chewed on her lip. "W-will they ship me back home to England?"

"You've done nothing wrong, dear. So far as I am concerned, you can stay right here." Mary Larsen looked across the table at Diana. "I own your little truckle bed is quite small, Diana, but perhaps you girls could manage to squeeze in together."

Diana quickly nodded assent, but Sallie Mae just as quickly said, "I could sleep on the floor in Diana's room. I've slept on the floor my whole life, ma'am."

"Well." Mary Larsen pushed up from the table. "We'll sort out something."

A half hour later, the girls had carted in several armloads of fresh straw to Diana's room, and Mary Larsen had produced a faded bed rug, which she spread over the pallet of hay. Sallie Mae declared it a capital bed. Little Edward was also taken with it.

"It's smashing, Mother! Can I have a straw bed, too, please?"

"But, dear, you have a fine little bed, just like Diana's."

"But I want a hay bed! I want *this* bed. Sallie Mae can have mine if she wants it. Can we trade, Mother, can we?"

The women laughed. Eventually Mary Larsen gave in to her son's pleas and it was decided that whilst she and Sallie Mae transferred the hay bed to Edward's room, and carted his truckle bed into Diana and Sallie Mae's room, Diana would take a ride on Bug-a-Boo . . . to the Westons to fetch Sallie Mae's things.

"I own I am not surprised to see ye, Miss Wakefield. I supposed

Miss Brown had sought refuge with you. I take it ye've come for her things?"

Diana nodded.

"They be in the loft."

Diana followed the woman up the steep steps. On the way, neither spoke. Once they'd reached the rumpled cot where Sallie Mae slept, Diana averted her eyes.

"I kin guess what happened last night," Goody Weston began, "and I feel real sorry 'bout it. M'husband, he don't mean no harm." She reached here and there, retrieving Sallie Mae's strewn things. "He's jes' a man and . . . well, men has their needs. 'Course I know what he done was wrong." She rolled Sallie Mae's clothing into a ball and handed the bundle and the girl's boots to Diana. "I jes' hope he dinna' hurt her."

Blushing, Diana did not make eye contact with the married woman, who she felt was speaking quite plainly on a delicate matter to an unwed girl. "I-I do not believe Sallie Mae was harmed. She said she . . . managed to escape before the . . . the actual deed was done," she concluded, her tone barely above a whisper.

"What's that ye say? M'husband . . . didn't . . . ?"

Diana shook her head.

"Well," Goody Weston let out a breath. "There's a relief!"

"Good day to you, ma'am."

"You tell Miss Brown, no hard feelin's. She'll fare much better with you and the Larsens."

Diana exited the house and headed toward Bug-a-Boo, who was busy munching on the patch of grass growing alongside the path in front of the house. As she flung the bundle over the mare's back, Goody Weston called to her.

"Do ye s'pose they'll bring charges?"

"I could not say," Diana replied. Standing on tiptoe, she flung herself onto the mare's back. Gathering the reins, she added, "Sallie Mae wishes you no harm, Goody Weston."

The woman nodded. "Thot's right kind o' her."

That afternoon, after Mary Larsen had relayed what she knew of the incident to her husband, he left the house to confer with Governor Yeardley. After supper that night, both girls heard the Larsens discussing the matter, the walls of the house not being thick enough to shut out voices coming from another chamber. Larsen said the governor had said that since the deed had not actually been completed, no charges would be leveled against Weston, but the man would be issued a stern warning, and in future, no other young ladies would ever be assigned to the Westons' care.

"Yeardley said this was not the first infraction. One young lady has already been raped. She, of course, has been removed from the home and the offender is even now locked in the pillory. At present, public humiliation is the extent of the law in these matters. The governor agreed that Miss Brown should remain here with us."

In the dimly lit girls' bedchamber, Sallie Mae drew in a relieved breath and moments later, turned toward Diana.

"There's something more I need to tell you," she began in a very low tone. Beginning from the minute she ran from the Westons' home into the street, she told Diana all about the horrible ordeal that followed.

Before she'd finished the tale, Diana was gasping aloud.

"We must tell Mister Larsen, Sallie Mae! The danger is far greater than I feared."

"But, I'm still alive. Can't we keep it to ourselves a bit longer? The men think I've become fish food. Perhaps that'll satisfy 'em and they'll leave me be."

"I don't know, Sallie Mae. That seems quite foolhardy to me. When the men discover you are not dead, they'll no doubt redouble their efforts to kill you." Diana thought a bit longer. "Can you not think of a single reason why someone might wish you dead?"

"I can't think of nothin'. I been wrackin' my brain all day tryin' to think what the trouble could be. I didn't do nothin' wrong 'afore I left home, except that one thing . . . but—"

"What one thing, Sallie Mae?" Diana demanded. "You must tell me everything, and leave nothing out. If I am to sort out the puzzle, I must know everything. What did you do?"

"Oh, miss." Tears welled in Sallie Mae's eyes. "I fear if I tell you the whole truth, ye'll think ill of me. Ye'll no longer wish to be my friend, and . . . and I ain't never had a real chum 'afore."

"I'll not think ill of you, Sallie Mae, I promise."

Sallie Mae fell silent for a long moment, then in a tone just above a whisper, she said, "I knowed what Goodman Weston meant to do to me last night because . . . it weren't the first time such a thing has happened."

"Oh, Sallie Mae. How perfectly dreadful! I am so sorry."

"T'other time was far worse. The boy who . . . who forced hisself on me, he got a babe on me. But the poor little mite was born dead. That's why I run away from home, miss. That's why I was pretendin' to be a lad on the ship. Same as you, I dinna' have nowhere else to go. I come all this way to Jamestown to make a fresh start."

In the darkness, Diana heard her friend's muffled sobs. She moved from her bed to Sallie Mae's. Squeezing in beside her, she gathered the younger girl into her arms. "I will always do whatever I can to help you, Sallie Mae. I love you like the sister I never had, and every bit as much as the dear friend I lost to the River Thames the night you saved my life. I will never abandon you, Sallie Mae. Never."

Sallie Mae sniffed back her tears. "I love you, too, Diana. I feel like I've found me a new sister."

Despite the fact that they had not yet sorted out their other problem, both girls slept soundly that night, unaware that before too long their lives would be altered once again.

Chapter 18

The following fortnight, Sallie Mae lay tucked in bed suffering from an onset of lung fever, brought on, no doubt, by the many hours she'd spent submerged in the river. Her voice grew hoarse, her nose red and runny and she ached all over. Diana worried, Mary fussed, Cheiwoga brewed healing tisanes, and Sallie Mae was simply grateful no one produced a jar o' slimy leeches. She and Diana conjectured that her absence from services might help forward the notion that she, or rather Hester B, had, in fact, drowned or disappeared, and that unfortunately, no one cared enough to report the girl missing.

"You would report me missin', wouldn't ye, Diana?"

"Of course I would, Sallie Mae."

By the third week, when no further frightening mishaps occurred, the girls began to relax a mite, although they both agreed to keep a sharp eye out for anyone caught staring overlong, or even casting a quizzical look at Sallie Mae. One morning as they were smoothing the cover panes on their beds, Sallie Mae shyly mentioned to Diana that on that very day seven and ten years ago, she had come into the world.

"Today is your birthday?" Diana exclaimed. A part of her wondered how Sallie Mae could be certain that this particular day was, indeed, the exact day marking her birth. Then she recalled that one evening last week, Mister Larsen had made mention of the month and day. Perhaps Sallie Mae had taken notice of the remark and begun to count off the days. "We must do something special to mark the occasion! What would you like to do?"

Sallie Mae did not hesitate. "Ride into the woods." She had mentioned a yearning to do so before, but Diana, unable to shake off her fear of the forest, had always balked.

Today, she inhaled a fortifying breath. "Very well. But, only a short way. I shouldn't wish us to get lost . . . or abducted."

"Bug-a-Boo could outrun anyone who'd wish us harm," Sallie Mae said with a laugh.

As the girls walked into the common room for breakfast that morning, Diana said, "I mean to tell Mistress Larsen where we are off to, so if we do not return in a timely fashion, she can send a search party to look for us."

"Look for you . . . where?" Mary asked, a smile playing at her lips as she set an earthen bowl full of oatmeal porridge onto the table. "What sort of mischief are you girls planning?"

"Today is Sallie Mae's birthday—"

"Why, happy birthday, Sallie Mae!" Mary cried. She paused to give the flaxen-haired girl a hug. "How many years do ye have in your dish, if I may be so bold?"

Sallie Mae blushed. "I now be seven and ten."

"So, Diana, you are no longer the eldest of our girls." Mary grinned. "Ye are both the same age now." When her husband appeared in the common room, she told him it was Sallie Mae's birthday. Diana said they were planning to take a short ride into the woods.

"Sallie Mae has been wanting to see the forest ever so long."

"Just do not venture too far away, girls," Mary warned. "I shall have Cheiwoga pack a little luncheon for you."

Soon after breakfast, the girls set out on Bug-a-Boo, Sallie Mae holding the reins, Diana sitting behind, an arm tightly clasped about her companion's middle. A small basket containing bread and cheese and two apples dangled from Bug-a-Boo's harness.

At the end of Jamestown's longest street, the dirt road funneled into a narrower path that led straight into the woods. Here, the trees and underbrush grew thick and dense. In the forest, both girls remarked upon how much cooler the air felt without the hot summer sun beating down upon their backs.

"It feels quite delightful here," Diana admitted. Loosening her grip on Sallie Mae's middle, she lifted her chin to inhale a deep breath of fresh cool air. "And it smells quite nice."

"It is so still and peaceful," Sallie Mae whispered. "I think it would be capital to have a little house right here."

"But what of the Indians? Mistress Larsen said some are quite savage, that they lurk in the treetops." She cast an anxious gaze upward. "I don't see any Indians," she murmured.

Sallie Mae giggled. "Only squirrels and birds lurk in the treetops. Listen to the birds' merry chirpin'. And the squirrels a'scoldin' us."

Diana's long gaze dropped to the forest floor, where all manner of greenery, lacy ferns and flowering vines grew. "There are so many odd plants. I wonder what they are called." She noted several trees covered with purple flowers. Others had vines encircling the trunks that were loaded with white and pink blossoms. "I did not realize the forest was so beautiful," she breathed. "If I had known, I might have come sooner."

Suddenly, a woodland creature, which neither of the girls saw, scurried across the path, causing Bug-a-Boo to throw her head up and skitter sideways on the path.

Fear lurched to Diana's throat. "What was that?" she cried.

Occupied with holding taut the reins and settling the mare, Sallie Mae did not reply.

"We must go back!" Diana declared.

But already Bug-a-Boo had calmed and was obediently trotting forward.

"Perhaps we might stop and rest," Diana suggested.

"In a bit."

"We mustn't become hopelessly lost, Sallie Mae."

"I see a fine spot up ahead where we might rest."

"And afterward, we will go back?" Diana asked hopefully.

Sallie Mae headed the mare off the path and onto an area covered with clean-smelling pine needles. Moving a bit deeper into the thicket of pine trees, she chose the perfect spot to dismount. "Smells especially lovely here, don't it?" She slipped off the animal's back and led the horse to a nearby tree around which she looped the leather strap.

Both girls walked a few feet away from Bug-a-Boo and settled onto the scented bed of pine needles. Diana pulled off the cloth covering the basket and handed a wedge of bread and cheese to Sallie Mae. As they munched, the girls talked quietly.

"I confess I feel a mite lazy since I come to live with you," Sallie Mae remarked. "Seems like I ought to be workin' 'stead a'enjoyin' meself ever' day. Don't seem right somehow."

"You have been ill, Sallie Mae. Besides, you've nothing to feel guilty about. We are both young and free now. Neither of us has a household to manage or a husband and children to care for. We should be enjoying ourselves. Once we marry, we shall have plenty of time to spend toiling—"

Sallie Mae giggled.

"What do you find amusing?"

A merry smile on her lips, Sallie Mae hopped to her feet and holding a pretend broom, began to dance about the clearing. "Look at me, Diana, I am a'toilin'!"

Enjoying her friend's carefree abandon, Diana shared in her laughter.

Returning to sit, Sallie Mae said, "Here, I thought I'd only been a'workin' all me life, when all along, I've been a'toilin'!"

"I daresay, when we are married, we shall both spend every day toiling."

Suddenly, an ear-splitting thunder of hooves startled both girls. They glanced up just as a huge white stallion streaked through the woods only a few feet beyond where they sat.

Her eyes wide, Diana leapt to her feet. "What was that?"

"I saw a' Indian sittin' on that huge white horse!"

"Come along, Sallie Mae."

The ride out of the woods did not take nearly so long as the time it took to get there.

"Have ye both seen ghosts?" Mary Larsen asked when the girls entered the house. "Your eyes are as round as moons."

Diana gulped. "We . . ." She cast a gaze at Cheiwoga, bent over her work near the hearth. "We saw an Indian on a huge white horse."

"Oh." Mary Larsen laughed. "An Indian riding a huge white stallion is a legend around here. Some say the horse can fly. Others say they've seen it streak across the midnight sky. You've nothing to fear, girls. The forest was simply playing tricks on you."

Diana and Sallie Mae exchanged dubious looks.

"Come, I've a surprise for you." Mary Larsen led the wide-eyed pair into her bedchamber, which held a good-sized bed, a low wooden crib where baby Ellen now lay asleep, and on the floor in the corner, lay Edward's smashing new straw pallet. Mary motioned toward her bed. Upon it sat a parcel wrapped in tissue paper. "I had meant to put this in your room, but you girls returned far quicker than I expected. It's a birthday gift for you, Sallie Mae."

"A gift . . . for me? I never got nothin' on me birthday a'fore."

"Well, you have now."

"Open it, Sallie Mae," Diana said, eager herself to see what was inside.

"Oh, my," Sallie Mae murmured after she'd turned back the tissue paper. "Ain't that nice. W-what is it?"

Perched on the edge of the bed, Mary laughed. "I own the fabric must appear quite plain, unbleached, instead of a pretty color, but I thought you might dye it and make yourself a new gown."

"D-dye it?"

"Indeed. We've no drapery shops in Jamestown to purchase pretty fabric." She fingered the drab muslin. "Ladies boil berries, or even bark, to make colored water. You soak the fabric in it, and when the proper shade is reached, you wring out the cloth and let it dry. Oh!" she popped to her feet. "I've also been saving this for a special occasion." She went to her cupboard and produced a rather crumpled sheet of purple paper. "This once held sugar. It comes in cones, you know. When boiled, the paper will yield a lovely violet color. A lavender gown will look very nice with your yellow hair, Sallie Mae."

Sallie Mae fingered the pretty paper then unfolded the cloth. "There seems to be a good bit here."

"Quite possibly enough to make both you girls a new gown."

"Oh!" Diana exclaimed with delight.

That night the girls lay in bed, the wooden shutters in their room thrown open to let in the cool night air. Diana thought it unwise to sleep with the window open until Sallie Mae pointed out the bramble bush beneath it and they both agreed that the opening was, in fact, not nearly large enough for a grown man to climb through. They settled down for a quiet chat.

"It was frightful kind of Mistress Larsen to give me the fabric," Sallie Mae said. "I dinna' have the heart to tell her I ain't never sewed nothin' in me life. I know how to mend, a'course, but I ain't never stitched up a new garment, from scratch, I mean."

Diana grinned. "Nor have I." Images of the many beautiful

gowns she'd left hanging in her wardrobe at home flitted through her mind. She had often wondered who might be wearing her frocks now, and who might be residing at Falstaff Manor. Had her father's kinsmen reclaimed the property? Did they ever learn what had happened to the family? She supposed Sara's parents would never know of the tragic accident that had befallen their daughter. With a sigh, she pushed the disturbing images from her mind. "I know how to embroider," she murmured. "If we left the cloth white, I could embroider a nice edge along the bottom. Although . . . we've no colored yarn."

"How shall we stitch up new gowns when neither of us knows how to sew? How do we cut the fabric into the proper pieces to fashion a frock?"

Diana thought a moment. "Perhaps Beth Fuller might help. On the crossing, Beth often sat on the bench along the wall stitching away at . . . something. She lives with my friend John."

The next afternoon, the girls paid a call upon Beth Fuller. John had pointed out his home to Diana during one of their evening strolls, but she'd never actually been inside the house. Its size, she discovered, three rooms and a loft, was similar to the Larsens' home, although John's was built in the wattle-and-daub style as opposed to clapboards. A nice rail fence set the house apart from the street and also ran down the sides of the house. However, since it appeared that he owned no cow or chickens, Diana did not know what he was fencing in. Or out.

John's cousin Beth, a pretty, soft-spoken girl with light brown hair, professed her pleasure to see the young ladies, and after they'd told her why they'd come, she agreed at once to help with the project. In addition to working on her own intricate samplers, Beth confessed that word had already got out in Jamestown that she sewed, and already she'd been commissioned to make gowns for wives of several wealthy planters.

"Oh." Diana's enthusiasm dimmed. "Neither Sallie Mae nor

I have the funds to pay you, Beth."

"I do not want your money," Beth insisted. "I am pleased to help you. But if you should receive a compliment on your new finery, I'd be obliged if you mentioned who made it."

Diana brightened. "It would be our pleasure!"

With Beth taking the lead, the girls began at once to soak the fabric and the purple paper in a kettle full of boiling water. In no time, all three girls expressed delight as a lovely lavender color emerged. When Sallie Mae exclaimed over a particular shade, Beth snatched up her scissors and trimmed off a length of the dyed cloth. Diana wished for a darker shade, so they allowed the remainder of the fabric to soak a while longer.

The following day, after the material had had ample time in which to dry, Diana and Sallie Mae returned. Beth produced an inch tape, which she used to determine the girls' measurements, then she cut the necessary shapes from the violet cloth to make two gowns. For contrast she used Sallie Mae's lighter color for the inner lining of the slashed sleeves in Diana's frock and vice versa for Sallie Mae's gown.

"Oh!" Sallie Mae's eyes widened. "We are to have slashed sleeves? I have never owned such a fashionable frock!"

The following Sabbath, both Diana and Sallie Mae wore their new finery. As usual, a wedding ceremony followed the service, with two couples repeating their vows. Afterward, the good reverend delivered yet another marriage sermon. Diana thought Reverend Martin's marriage sermons sounded very like the lectures Mrs. Douglass had delivered to the girls on the ship, concerning what to expect once wed and how to get on in a Christian manner with one's new husband.

When the sermon finally drew to a close and everyone had filed from the meetinghouse into the sunshine on the green, John Fuller sought out Diana. "You look prettier today than either of the brides," he whispered into her ear.

"Thank you, sir." She smiled up into his warm brown eyes.

The tall man cast a gaze at Diana's companion. "And you look very pretty as well, Sallie Mae. I confess I knew that my cousin has been busy for days stitching up your new gowns."

"Beth is a very talented seamstress," Diana said.

"So . . ." came a feminine voice from behind them, "where did your new dresses come from?"

Hearing Faith Plumleigh's saucy voice, both Sallie Mae and Diana turned.

"Beth Fuller made our new frocks," Sallie Mae told her.

"Hmmph. I would never wear anything made by one of those Fuller girls."

"Faith!" Diana cried. "You are speaking disparagingly of John's sister and his cousin."

Faith's chin shot up. "And John's sister continues to speak disparagingly of me."

"Oh, dear," Diana said with dismay. "I had hoped Ann had left off her slanderous remarks. John, did you speak with her as I asked?"

"Indeed, I did. I confess I was unaware that she was continuing to—"

"Hello, my pretty," came the rich sound of a male voice from behind Faith.

All three girls glanced toward the handsome gentleman who was now smiling down upon the beaming, auburn-haired Faith. Diana's heart did a funny flip-flop in her breast. Was she at last to meet the renowned Noah Colton?

Beside Diana, John coolly excused himself and hurried away.

"Pray, introduce me to your friends," the handsome man admonished Faith. The gentleman looked splendid today in a blue velvet doublet with gold buttons and matching galligaskins. The plume in his hat exactly matched the blue of his eyes.

Glowing with happiness, Faith stepped closer to him and affectionately twined her arm through his. "I am not certain I wish to."

Diana could not help noticing that the trader had fixed an intent gaze upon Sallie Mae, which despite the charming man's . . . charm, caused an alarm bell to sound in her head.

"Then I shall introduce myself. Noah Colton, at your service, miss. And you are . . . ?"

"Oh, very well," Faith conceded. "This is Miss Diana Wakefield and Miss Hester . . . I mean, Miss Sallie Mae Brown. This is my Noah," she said possessively and tightened her grip on the man's arm. "He is Jamestown's *premier* trader. He will one day be named governor of Virginia."

The handsome man shrugged. "I fear Miss Plumleigh is far overstating my consequence." Yet the confident gleam in his eye and the tone of his voice said he believed her sentiments to be true. Just then, Governor Yeardley and two of his councilmen appeared. The men drew Noah away, leaving the three young ladies standing alone together.

"Faith, he is so handsome!" Sallie Mae enthused.

"Indeed, he is," Faith returned archly. "And I intend to marry him."

Diana's eyes widened. "So, he has asked you then?"

"Not yet. But he will. I have a . . . way of making things turn out the way I wish. He called upon me nearly every night this past week. And," she added, "we spend a great deal of our time . . . gloriously alone."

"Oh, my." Diana breathed, taking her friend's words to mean that she had allowed the handsome man to kiss her again; and perhaps even again.

"What of you and John?" Faith asked. "Has he offered for you yet?"

"I have seen John rarely of late. He said he worked past sundown nearly every night this last week sweeping his plants."

Sallie Mae looked confused. "Sweepin' his plants? So John has also been a'toilin', eh?"

Both girls giggled merrily.

Seemingly confused by their mirth, Faith did not join in.

In moments, Noah returned. "It was a pleasure meeting you, Miss Wakefield and . . . *you,* Miss Brown." He reached for Sallie Mae's hand and bowing low over it, his lips grazed the backside of her hand. Then he turned to Faith. "Come along, sweetheart."

As Faith again twined her arm through his, both Sallie Mae and Diana heard her peevish remark as the pair walked away, "Why did you kiss her hand?"

Colton's explanation, if, indeed, he made one, was lost on the breeze.

Sallie Mae stood gazing with awe upon the honored hand. "No gentleman has ever kissed my hand before."

"Forgive me for speaking plainly, ladies," said John Fuller who had again stepped up beside them. "Noah Colton is no gentleman."

Later that evening, as the girls were tending Bug-a-Boo, Diana came across an item she'd never before seen in the shed. Carrying it to where Sallie Mae stood brushing the mare's flank, she asked, "What is this?"

Sallie Mae glanced up. Her expression clouded when she instantly recognized the item. "It's . . . the bag the men threw over my head the night they carried me off. It was caught in the rushes when I climbed outta' the river. I used it to cover my nakedness when I run through the settlement that mornin'. Rip it up, Diana!"

Diana was smoothing out the rough cloth. "There's a word faintly visible on one side. It says . . . Gunpowder."

"Toss it in the rubbish bin! I don't wish ever to see it again."

"But, it might be a clue, Sallie Mae."

Sallie Mae looked dubious. "Don't ye suppose every settler who owns a musket would also own such a bag? Muskets don't fire without gunpowder, ye know."

Diana sighed. "Well, perhaps I shall use it as a feed bag for Bug-a-Boo."

Sallie Mae continued brushing the mare's coat. A few minutes later, she said, "Where did you put the bag, Diana?"

"I hung it on a peg."

Sallie Mae moved that direction and returned a moment later carrying the bag. "I recall seeing one of these, a full one, on the Bride Ship."

"But the *King's Embassy* had no gun deck."

"There was a great many of these bags in the ship's store. Once, when I brought one to the cook house, thinkin' it was grain, One-Eye called me a stupid lad and boxed m'ears."

"How dreadful, Sallie Mae!"

"I couldna' read the wordin'. I jes thought it was a small bag o' barley. I remember he snatched it from me, real angry-like, and disappeared."

Diana's eyes widened. "That must be it, Sallie Mae! One-Eye had secreted bags of gunpowder onto the ship to . . . carry somewhere."

"You mean, he was *smuggling* 'em?"

Diana slowly nodded. "Exactly. But, to whom did he deliver them? It was obviously a clandestine venture—"

"A what?" Sallie Mae's face screwed up.

"A secret. One he didn't wish anyone to know about." She went on, "The note makes sense now. 'I know what you saw.' You saw the bags of gunpowder." Her tone grew excited. "What else did you see, Sallie Mae?"

Sallie Mae thought a minute. "There was somethin' else kinda' odd. At the outset, One-Eye set me to linin' up the hogsheads, barrels o' peas together, fish in a row, and so on. I come upon a coupla' barrels I couldn't budge, so I asked him to help me move 'em. He got real angry and wanted to know ifn' I'd opened one. I told him I hadn't. But, truth is, I did peek inside one cask."

"What did you see?" Diana demanded.

"Muskets. Dozens of 'em. I thought it was odd then that hogsheads full of muskets was mixed in with the provisions, but I dinna' say nothin'. Voyage wasn't yet underway. I dinna' know exactly how things was done on a ship. One-Eye pushed the heavy casks to the back and said we'd not be gettin' into 'em; said it was none o' my concern."

"I am convinced we have stumbled onto the very reason why those men want you dead, Sallie Mae. When One-eye recognized you that day on the deck, he grew fearful. Then, when we arrived here, he told the men to whom he delivered the contraband that you knew about it, at least about the gunpowder. Perhaps he didn't believe that you hadn't looked into the casks containing the muskets. I've no doubt now that One-Eye was involved in a subterfuge. It is unfortunate that you did not see the faces of the men who grabbed you."

Sallie Mae sighed. "I own I should have tried harder to get a look at 'em. But I was frightful scared hidin' in the water, and it was frightful dark that night. I couldna' see a thing. I jes knew the men wasn't Indians."

The girls cogitated further, wondering who in the colony One-Eye would have delivered muskets and gunpowder to.

"We mustn't rush to judgment," Diana said at length. "Perhaps because you were not seen for a fortnight after your abduction, the men who threw you into the river do, indeed, believe that you drowned and now they feel safe. With the ships gone from the harbor, One-Eye is no longer in Jamestown." She paused. "However, the party he brought the muskets and gunpowder to are still here. It is imperative we stay alert and continue to be watchful, Sallie Mae."

Chapter 19

"I am pleased you were able to sneak from the house again," Noah Colton said, taking the bed rug Faith carried under one arm and spreading it on the ground beneath a cluster of tall trees in the meadow where the two often secreted themselves late in the evening.

"It is a lovely night," Faith exclaimed, gazing up at the stars twinkling overhead. "I am pleased the rain let up." She dropped to her knees and snuggled close to Noah on the bed rug.

"You are certain neither Mister nor Mistress Evans heard you leave the house?"

"They are both sound sleepers, and with Annabeth now wed and gone, Robin sleeps more soundly. Not a one of them stirred as I tiptoed down the stairs."

"We must be careful never to arouse suspicion." He slipped an arm about her shoulders and drew her even closer.

Faith knew he meant to kiss her and, as always, she would let him. She'd been happier this past fortnight with Noah coming to call than she'd ever been in her life. Of late, they'd begun to meet one another later, much later, after everyone else lay abed. Any night now, Faith expected the handsome man to propose marriage.

"You intoxicate me," Noah murmured into her ear, his tongue trailing a tingling path around the perimeter of one earlobe.

"I hope I do more than intoxicate you."

"Very well, then." He cradled her to his chest. "You bewitch me."

Faith giggled. "You'd best not say that within Ann Fuller's hearing."

"Ann Fuller is a shrew merely wagging her tongue. I am persuaded nothing will come of it."

Faith gazed dreamily up at him. "Well, I hope something will come of this."

"Of what?" he murmured.

She drew back. "Of you and me."

He reached for her. "Come back here, wench. I wish to kiss your pretty neck and your—"

Faith pressed a hand to his strong chest and held fast. "I am allowing you to take liberties with me, Noah Colton, when clearly I should not. Mrs. Douglass said—"

"Who is Mrs. Douglass?"

"I told you about her. How her harsh words led to my sister's—" She paused, then, regaining herself, went on. "She is the woman on board ship who lectured us about love and marriage. According to her, I should not be allowing you to kiss me."

Grinning, Noah grasped one of her hands and opening the palm, smothered it with kisses. "You are an adorable lass and I cannot resist you."

"Nor I you." Faith sighed dreamily as she melted again into his embrace. "You are the handsomest man I have ever seen." Her eyes drifted shut. Being with Noah these last weeks had shown her exactly how Prudence must have felt when she slipped away to be with Isaac. But, of course, that was not precisely the same thing. Prudence did not love Isaac and Faith *did* love Noah. And, despite the fact that he had not yet said those magical words, she knew he loved her. He was kind and sweet and considerate of her feelings. And although all the girls in Jamestown coveted him, he had eyes only for her. Perhaps, she thought now, he simply needed a little . . . nudge. "I love you, Noah," she whispered. Tears of love welled up in her sea-green eyes. "I love you with all my heart and soul." She gazed up into his handsome face, which in the moonlight appeared even more appealing. When his chiseled features relaxed into an easy grin, she breathed a sigh of relief.

"I love you too, poppet."

"Do you, Noah? Do you really and truly love me?"

" 'Course I do. You are far and away the prettiest girl to step off either Bride Ship. I expect England is still mourning the loss of its prettiest girl."

"Noah, you are teasing me." After a pause, she said, "If you love me, does that mean . . . ?"

"It means I am mad for you." One hand touched the stiff bodice that encircled her midsection. "What do you say we remove this confining thing?" Not waiting for an answer, his fingers nimbly plucked apart the laces. When done, he tossed the stiff garment aside. "There, that feels much better, does it not?"

"I do feel . . . freer." Faith's hands nervously splayed to cover her middle. Despite her entire body being fully covered, she added, "I feel a bit . . . naked."

"You are far from naked, sweetheart." With a wicked grin, he shrugged out of his jerkin and in one smooth motion, yanked his white linen shirt clean off over his head.

"Oh-h-h, my," Faith breathed, her eyes taking in the strong mounds of his chest and shoulders. She cautiously reached to touch the bare flesh of a shoulder, which felt surprisingly soft and warm. Then, in the darkness, her fingers felt a rough patch. She sat up straighter. "What is this?"

He shrugged. "A scar."

"You have been hurt? Oh, my darling!"

"It was nothing."

Her finger gently caressed the knotted skin. "But the injury was so very near your heart. Oh, Noah, do tell me what happened. I want to know everything about you, my dearest."

"It's merely an old knife wound."

"Oh!" Faith's eyes widened. "Thank the dear Lord you were not killed." Again, she softly stroked the ugly scar that began just below his shoulder and ended perilously close to his heart.

"Who hurt you?"

"An Indian."

Faith sucked in her breath. "You fought with a savage?"

"This savage was an intruder in my home. When he burst in, we struggled. He came at me with a knife and . . . tried to kill me."

Her heart in her throat, Faith hung onto every word. "And you killed him?" she asked in a hopeful tone.

He nodded, a bit tightly. "Let us speak of it no more." He reached to draw her close.

Faith's eyelids fluttered shut. "Oh-h, Noah."

When he expertly pulled her thin muslin blouse from the waistband of her skirt, then up and off over her head, she offered no resistance whatever.

Dear God in Heaven, she prayed, *thank you for sparing this man's life and for drawing us together.*

When Noah pulled her down onto the bed rug alongside him, she snuggled closer still. When his strong fingers inched, ever so slowly, up beneath her long skirt, soft moans of pleasure escaped her. She thought she would die from sheer longing when Noah began to softly caress the bare flesh of her stomach and buttocks. Not a single word from Mrs. Douglass's well-meant lectures sprang to Faith's mind now. All she could think of was how very, *very* much she loved this man, and how thankful she was that he also loved her. He had even said the words.

He loved her!

Faith gave herself to Noah that night, and for two nights following. After their late nights of lovemaking in the meadow, she did feel a bit drowsy during the day; still, the long hours passed quickly as she thought ahead to the glorious time she'd have that night with Noah. Each morning when she awoke and stretched languidly, memories of the previous night's lovemaking still fresh in her mind, she never once experienced a moment of remorse or regret. His handsome face and the memories of his touch were all she thought about every minute of the day. Over and over again, she thanked the dear Lord for sparing his life and for bringing them together. God may have taken Prudence from her, but in His infinite wisdom, He had a wondrous plan in store for her: to become the wife of the most wonderful man in all the world. She had no doubt now that Noah would soon say those other magical words: "Will you become my wife?" and she would lovingly reply, "Yes! Yes, I will!"

One rainy night at the Larsen home, an insistent rapping at the door disrupted the family dinner. Mister Larsen rose to see who might be calling at such a late hour.

"Governor Yeardley, do come in, sir. We have concluded our evening meal. Perhaps you would like a mug of stout ale."

Flinging raindrops from his hat and cape, the bewhiskered man stepped inside. "Don't mind if I do, Larsen; but make no mistake, this is not a social call."

"Has trouble arisen, sir?"

The men headed to the table where the family was still gathered. The governor commandeered Larsen's chair at the head of the table, whereupon his host had no choice but to slide onto the backless bench beside his wife. She gestured to Cheiwoga to fetch the proffered mug of ale for their guest. On the opposite side of the table, Diana sat beside Sallie Mae, who was holding baby Ellen on her lap whilst Mary urged young Edward to eat the remainder of his creamed peas.

"I have come to speak with Miss Wakefield," the governor said without preamble.

The sound of her name startled Diana. Why did the governor wish to speak with her? Had something happened to John?

The governor swallowed a long draught of ale from the mug. "Which of you young ladies is . . . ?"

"I am Diana Wakefield, sir. This is Miss Sallie Mae Brown."

"Ah." The governor glanced toward Sallie Mae. "So, you were the young lady who . . ." He cleared his throat. "Yes, well, this matter concerns another of the young ladies who made the crossing with you, a Miss Faith Plumleigh."

Diana's heart sank.

"As you may have heard, there has been some talk regarding . . . a certain . . . uh . . . well . . . an unsavory charge has been lodged against Miss Plumleigh."

"Oh, my!" Mary Larsen cast a quizzical gaze from Diana to Sallie Mae, then to her husband.

"Sir, I can assure you," Diana boldly spoke up, "that whatever has been said against Miss Plumleigh is completely without merit."

"Be that as it may, I am duty-bound to investigate the charges. Do I understand, Miss Wakefield, that you have indisputable evidence that Miss Plumleigh is not—"

A sudden flash of anger shot through Diana. "Did Miss Fuller present any evidence to support her outrageous claim, sir? I am assuming the charge was lodged by Ann Fuller."

At that instant, another rap sounded at the door. Larsen rose to answer it. When he swung open the door, John Fuller strode in.

"Evening, John."

"Bit wet out there," John replied, brushing raindrops off his doublet as he stepped in. Catching sight of who was seated at the Larsen table, he froze. "Forgive me, sir, I did not mean to intrude."

"Come in, Fuller," the governor bellowed. "Ye may as well hear this, since it involves yer sister."

Both Larsen and John Fuller walked to the table and sat down.

Her heart still hammering in her breast, Diana asked John if he knew that his sister had spoken with the governor.

"Concerning what?"

"John." Diana's tone sounded a trifle miffed. "Concerning the untruths she has been spreading about Faith."

"Ah," John leaned forward. "Perhaps I may be of some assistance, sir. I confess I was unaware that my sister had lodged a formal complaint against Miss Plumleigh, but I can assure you, she has no grounds for such a vicious charge."

"The charges are pure fabrication, sir," Diana chimed in, quite angry now, at both the situation and at John. "Completely unfounded and . . . and ridiculous!"

"It all began one evening, sir, when my sister Ann became overset when she felt that Miss Plumleigh had snubbed her. Then when . . . uh . . ." John's lips firmed. "When it appeared that Noah Colton had set his cap for Miss Plumleigh, instead of my sister, who had also taken a fancy to him, well, sir . . ." He flung an apologetic look at Diana. "You know how the fairer sex can be."

The governor chuckled. "Yes, and I can easily see how that devil Colton could arouse jealousy amongst the ladies. A'course that little Miss Plumleigh is also a looker. So I take it, in your opinion, Fuller, this is merely a case of jealousy run amok."

"Indeed, sir. I own I am a trifle embarrassed to admit it, but there it is." John leaned back.

"Well, considering your sister was unable to present any proof of her claim; no cows or chickens keeled over dead . . . except . . ." He paused. "There was that one dog found dead down by the riverbank." With a shrug, he dismissed the oddity. "At any rate, Miss Fuller just kept referring to Miss Plumleigh's 'evil eye.' Truth to tell, I have met Miss Plumleigh and in my estimation, she has very pretty eyes!" He laughed roundly at his own jest. "Glad you stopped by, Fuller." He drained his mug, then pushed up from the table. "So far as I am concerned, this investigation is at an end." He stood up, prompting both John and his host to follow suit.

The governor tied on his cape and settled his hat onto his head. "Suppose I should have expected that with so many young ladies in the colony, sooner or later, one would begin to slander another."

"Jealousy amongst the ladies is to be expected, sir," Councilman Larsen agreed.

"Especially where that handsome devil Colton is concerned," added the governor with another chuckle. "That son-of-a-bi—" Catching himself, he darted a sheepish gaze at the ladies. "Beg pardon, ladies. Would that all my problems could be so easily solved. Good night, Larsen. Fuller, I'm counting on you to make it clear to your sister that I don't want to hear another word said against Miss Plumleigh. We've got plenty on our plates to deal with here in Jamestown; we sure as hell don't need silly females stirring up trouble a'purpose."

Diana was vastly relieved that the vexing problem had been put to rest. But she still felt a bit peeved with John for not being more forceful with his sister Ann. When she and John were left alone together in the common room, she voiced her sentiments.

"John, I trusted that you had silenced Ann. I would not have wanted to see Faith hanged simply because your sister thought her a witch."

"I did speak to Ann. But a day or so afterward, I overheard

her telling a friend how jealous she was of Faith and how she was casting about for a way to harm her."

"And you said nothing more at that juncture?"

He appeared contrite. "I can see now that I should have. I was in a rush to get to my tobacco field. Thank heaven the rain came when it did. I believe the bugs on my plants are nearly all washed off. But do let us put this ugly business behind us"—he leaned toward Diana—"and speak on a more pleasant topic."

Diana made every effort to push aside her annoyance. "Had you not turned up tonight, I shudder to think what action the governor would have taken."

"Be that as it may, Miss Plumleigh has been spared, and I expect she and Colton will soon pledge their troth to another."

"Which will make Faith very happy."

"If they do marry," John said in a considering tone, "be aware that you will be unable to persuade me to spend time with them. The four of us, I mean. Together."

Diana took no heed of that remark. Her ears had suddenly perked up at his mention of Noah Colton. Colton was a trader. Suddenly, she wondered precisely what he traded. Curious to know why John so fervently disliked the man, she decided to simply ask. "Why do you so heartily dislike Noah, John?"

His gaze grew shuttered. "Because he . . . was vastly unkind to a woman I once cared deeply for."

Not wishing to pry, Diana backed down. "I am sorry, John."

He inhaled a breath. "That Noah feels drawn to Miss Plumleigh should come as no surprise."

"Why do you say that?"

"Because she and his former wife look enough alike to be sisters. Auburn hair, green eyes. His wife was also a great beauty."

Stunned by the news that Noah had formerly been married, Diana murmured, "Noah's wife is now . . . ?"

"Gone."

"Oh." Knowing how it felt to lose a loved one, a surge of sympathy welled up inside Diana for the handsome man. Perhaps she had judged Noah harshly. Perhaps he, like Faith, was still grieving the loss of a loved one.

They turned to talking of other things, however, before too very long, Diana pleaded a megrim and rose to escort John to the door. She still felt a bit vexed with him and wished time alone to collect her thoughts.

Two evenings later, again following dinner at the Larsen home, another rap sounded at the door. Already in her bedchamber with Sallie Mae, Diana's ears perked up. She was half expecting John to call again tonight. Because it had been pouring rain the night both he and the governor called, they did not go for their customary walk.

From their bedchamber, both girls heard Mister Larsen greet this evening's caller. "Good evening, Colton."

Sallie Mae and Diana exchanged surprised looks.

"Good evening, sir," Noah Colton replied. "If I have your permission, sir, I would like a word with a young lady I've been given to understand now resides here. Miss Sallie Mae Brown."

In her bedchamber, Sallie Mae's cheeks grew hot.

"Certainly. I'll have my wife fetch Miss Brown. Would you care for mug of ale whilst you wait?"

When Mary Larsen appeared at the girl's bedchamber door, Sallie Mae was far too stunned to speak.

"A gentleman is asking to see you, Sallie Mae."

"W-why does he want to see me?" Her blue eyes were round.

"Would you like me to come along?" Diana asked. She rose to her feet, and when Sallie Mae nodded, she followed her from the room.

When Sallie Mae spotted the handsome Noah Colton seated

at the table, his hands wrapped around a mug of stout ale, she blushed to the roots of her curly blond hair. And, seemingly, lost her tongue. However, in his inimitable charming fashion, Noah Colton took charge of the situation.

"You look lovely this evening, Miss Brown." He stood. "I had hoped to persuade you to take a stroll with me. The rain has let up and the air smells quite fresh."

Standing near Sallie Mae, Diana could hardly believe her ears. She watched the pair leave the house, and although she felt a bit guilty for doing so, she peeked through the opened window near the door as they walked up the path and turned onto the street. Trying to shake off her apprehension, she returned to her bedchamber.

She could not help wondering why Noah Colton was here, as opposed to being with Faith. Had something untoward happened between them? Why had he suddenly decided to pay a call upon Sallie Mae? Not that she wasn't every bit as pretty as Faith. Since she'd come to live here and was eating well, her thin frame had filled out and her flaxen hair was now thick and curly. But, Diana recalled, she and Noah Colton had not exchanged more than two words the day they met and he kissed her hand. Was he after Sallie Mae for some other reason, perhaps a more . . . sinister one? She could hardly wait for Sallie Mae to return home and clear up the mystery.

She did not have to wait long. In less than a quarter hour Sallie Mae burst into the room telling Diana that she only walked a short way up the street with Noah Colton before she insisted they turn around and come back.

"Did he do or say something to frighten you?" Diana asked breathlessly. "Perhaps I should have come along."

"No, he was quite charmin'. I jes dinna' know what to say to him! I ain't never had no gentleman caller a'fore," she said. She yanked off her clothing to prepare for bed. "Never had time for such frivolous things at home . . . nor since I been here, for all that. I spent all m' days a'workin' at the Westons', and you know what I been doin' since." She paused to blow out the pine knot candle before crawling into bed. "What do you and John talk about when you go walkin'?"

"You seem discomfited, Sallie Mae."

"Discomfited? I swear, Diana, half the words you use I ain't never heard b'fore and can't even guess what they mean."

Diana grinned in the darkness. "I mean it appears that you were uncomfortable tonight in the company of Noah Colton."

"You can say that again!"

Diana did not reply at once. "Do you really need me to say it ag—"

"No. I knowed what ye meant this time." Sallie Mae flopped to her side on the little truckle bed. "I dinna' understand half o' what he said either. The plain truth is you . . . and him are far and away above my station."

Diana sat bolt upright. "That is untrue, Sallie Mae! We are in the New World now. One's station is of no consequence here."

"Where we live in this world don't make no difference. I *feel* as if I am beneath you and . . . most ever' one else, for all that. I wish I could talk like you."

"Talk like me?"

"Say things proper like."

"Perhaps I could teach you proper elocution."

"There you go again!" Sallie Mae huffed. "I don't know what . . . el-o-cu-tion is."

Diana could not halt the giggle that bubbled up in her throat. "We shall begin lessons tomorrow."

The next day dawned clear and bright with no clouds in the sky or anywhere on the horizon. The girls chose a shady spot in the yard for Sallie Mae's first lesson. An apt pupil, she readily agreed to practice saying "you" instead of "ye" and to clearly speak the ending of a word, rather than leave it off. By the middle of the day, the air had turned quite warm, which was typical for late summer days in Tidewater, Virginia. Following luncheon, Sallie Mae announced she would pay a call on Goody Weston, just to see how she was getting on.

"Perhaps I can fetch her a bucket o' water, or help wash the linens whilst I'm there."

"That is very kind of you, Sallie Mae," Mary Larsen said, "but do be watchful, dear. If *he* should turn up, I daresay ye'd best not tarry."

Sallie Mae cast a quizzical gaze at Diana, who ascertained that her rosy-cheeked friend did not know the meaning of the word *tarry.* "If Goodman Weston is at home, you'd best not linger."

"Oh. Well, I expect he will be *toiling* in his cornfield."

Diana smothered a grin and after Sallie Mae was gone, decided to pay a call upon Faith, to see how she was getting on.

Once there, Mistress Evans showed Diana up to Faith's bedchamber. "Faith has refused to come down for the past two days," the older woman said, a worried frown creasing her brow. "I do hope you can determine what the trouble is."

Entering the small room, Diana found Faith lying upon the bed, still wearing her night shift, though it was well into the afternoon.

"Faith, are you ill?" Diana asked.

When no answer came, Diana gently touched her friend's bare shoulder. The girl did not feel feverish. Glancing about, she saw that the glass window pane had been raised, allowing a nice breeze to waft into the room. To Diana it felt quite pleasant. Not too hot and certainly not too cool.

She knelt on the floor beside the bed. "Would you like me to get you a mug of water or ale? Mistress Evans said you have not been below stairs in a day or two. You must be famished, sweetie.

Would you like me to bring you something to eat?"

"How can I eat?" came a thin voice.

Diana heard a sniff, then the girl's shoulders began to quake as muffled sobs wracked her trim body.

"Oh, Faith. I am so very sorry."

Faith turned to gaze at her guest. "How do you know what has happened when I have not yet told you?"

The last thing Diana wanted to do was divulge to Faith that Noah had paid a call upon Sallie Mae. "Do tell me what the trouble is."

Faith began to sob. But a few moments later, her sobs waned and she sniffed. "You will know soon enough, I suppose. Noah is g-gone!"

Diana perched on the side of the bed. "Do you mean he is away on a trading expedition? Did something happen between the two of you, Faith?"

When tears again began to slide down her friend's pale cheeks, Diana produced a handkerchief and watched as Faith dabbed at her red-rimmed eyes.

"It is all Ann Fuller's fault."

"That dreadful business was resolved," Diana exclaimed. She told Faith of the events that transpired the night Governor Yeardley called at the Larsen home. "The governor declared the matter closed. What can the trouble be now?"

"The trouble is Noah. He says he cannot risk harming his reputation by marrying me, even if the charges are untrue. He believes even to associate with me will spoil his chances to be named governor. He wishes to be governor that much."

"Oh, Faith, I am so sorry."

"I hate Ann Fuller! My life is over and it is all her fault. *She* is the one with the evil eye."

Diana reached to embrace her friend. "Noah will come around. I am certain he loves you. John said you are the image of his late wife."

Faith drew back to stare at Diana. "Noah has been married? He had a . . . *wife?*"

Diana bit her tongue. "I assumed he had told you. You have spent a great deal of time together."

"Oh-h-h." Faith wailed and threw herself back onto the bed.

Diana's heat sank. Her disclosure had served only to make matters worse. She did not know what to say now, but she hated to leave her friend in distress. "He will come around," she said. "I expect a good many men in Jamestown have lost wives. There is a great deal of sickness in the colony. In the few months we have been here, an alarming number of colonists have perished due to the heat and . . . something called yellow fever."

"I wish *I* would die of it!"

"Faith, you mustn't say such a thing."

"My life is already over. No man will wish to marry me now. Not that I would marry anyone save Noah. He is the only man I will *ever* love."

Diana said nothing for a long moment, then began quietly, "Mrs. Douglass warned us against falling in love. Perhaps she knew the pitfalls and did not wish to see us hurt, as you are hurting now."

"Clearly, Mrs. Douglass knows nothing of love."

Or had never laid eyes on Noah Colton, Diana thought. She did not know many females who could resist falling in love with that handsome man. She was not certain she could resist him had he singled her out. She hoped now that he did not have evil intentions toward Sallie Mae. Unable to think of anything further to say, she rose to her feet.

"I shall ask Mistress Evans if I might bring you a wedge of that nice apple pie I smelled baking when I arrived."

On her way home that afternoon, Diana continued to mull over

Faith's heartbreak. She wondered if it was, indeed, due to Ann Fuller's spiteful tongue. Or was Noah's sudden change of heart due to another reason? Noah being fearful that to marry Faith would tarnish his reputation certainly pointed up the shallowness of his character. It also seemed odd that he had not told Faith about his late wife, or mentioned the heartache he had surely suffered following her death. It was becoming more and more apparent to Diana that Noah Colton was hiding something. But what? She fervently hoped Sallie Mae would remain vigilant when she was with him and not fall victim to the handsome man's charm.

Chapter 20

When John Fuller called at the Larsen home that evening, Diana was pleased to see him. It was a warm summer evening with hundreds of stars twinkling overhead. As they strolled along the dusty road that eventually led to the river, Diana told John about her visit with Faith and Noah's odd reaction to the charges Ann had leveled. She also told him how surprised both she and Sallie Mae were when Noah called on Sallie Mae.

"Noah's reason for no longer wishing to see Faith comes as no surprise to me," John said.

"But the charges were false. Governor Yeardley declared the matter closed. Why would Noah think that to marry Faith would besmirch his reputation?"

"Colton's actions speak quite plainly of his character. That he feels drawn to Sallie Mae is also not surprising."

"What do you mean?"

"Sallie Mae is the image of his first wife."

Diana's jaw dropped. "Noah has had *two* wives?"

"Charity was a taking little thing: blond with blue eyes the same as Sallie Mae. She was the daughter of the late Richard Benson, one of Jamestown's councilmen. She could not have been above five and ten years the day they married."

"What happened to her?"

"She died soon after giving birth to their second child."

Stunned, Diana cried, "He has *two* children?"

"One, now. The first, a son, died the night he was born."

"How terribly sad for Noah . . . to have lost a son . . . and two wives. Where is his other child now?"

"His little daughter lives with Mistress Benson, Charity's mother. Her father died this past winter. God willing, Mistress Benson's health will hold, for she is now left to raise the little girl alone."

"Perhaps when Noah remarries, his new wife will become mother to the child."

"Perhaps. Although that was not the case with his second wife."

Reeling from the startling disclosures about the handsome trader, Diana murmured, "I wonder why he chose not to tell Faith anything of his past?"

John shrugged. "I daresay your friend Faith is well rid of the scoundrel."

It suddenly occurred to Diana that she and John did see eye-to-eye on a great many things. She glanced up at the tall man walking beside her in the moonlight. That she could depend on him being truthful with her was comforting.

"It seems uncommonly warm tonight," John murmured.

Again, Diana agreed with him. Although a slight breeze was wafting inland off the river, it brought precious little cool air with it. She had untied and removed the sleeves from her gown before they set out, but even that provided little relief from the heat.

John headed down a path leading straight to the river. The sound of the water lazily lapping onto the shore soon reached Diana's ears.

"What of you, Diana? Would you wish to raise children?"

A sudden raspy quality in his tone sounded odd. She said, "I hope to have children of my own one day."

"One day . . . soon?"

Of a sudden, it dawned on Diana where John's questions

were leading. That he should bring up the subject was understandable. They had been seeing one another exclusively since they met, and now that the colony was overrun with wife-seeking men and not a single Sabbath had passed with less than two couples pledging their troth to one another, marriage and children were on everyone's mind.

When she did not answer at once, John murmured, "Perhaps I am being presumptuous."

They were now quite near the water's edge. John's tone of voice was so low, Diana had to strain to hear him over the waves. Suddenly, memories of that horrible night in London flooded her mind. "We must turn back, John!"

"But, we—" When she swept past him, he hastened to catch up to her. "You are aware of my feelings for you, Diana."

"John, I do not wish to speak of that now." She hurried up the path.

He lengthened his stride. "I had hoped the river might provide a romantical setting."

"I do not like the river." She lowered her head. She had not yet told John of the tragedy she had suffered before coming to Jamestown. For some reason, she feared that to speak of it with him might somehow bind her to him; that he would misinterpret her grief and begin to feel that she needed him, or that she wished to cling to him now that she had no family of her own. Suddenly she realized she did *not* want any of those things with John. Her pain over losing her parents and Hamilton was not yet erased. She realized she was merely marking time with John in an odd way, clinging to him because instinctively she knew there was no chance he could break her heart. The sad truth was, she did not love John and she could never, ever feel that way about him.

Apparently mystified by her actions, John grasped hold of her arm and drew her to a standstill. "Diana, what is it?" He reached to grasp her hands, then drew both to his chest. "Tell me what the trouble is, I beg you."

She did not meet his gaze.

"I think I understand, Diana. You are as overcome as I with emotion. I feel the same way about you, my darling. What I am trying to say, and making such a muddle of, is, will you marry me, Diana? Will you be my wife and bear my children?"

Her eyes squeezed shut. "Oh, John, I—"

"What is it, my dear? Surely you have no concerns regarding our living. My tobacco fields will provide quite comfortably for us. Even now, I am able to offer you a fine home. One day I will build a larger house. We get on quite well together, Diana. I see no reason why we should not—"

"I cannot marry you, John!" she blurted out. "I cannot!" With that, she jerked both hands free and ran back up the dusty road all the way to the Larsen home.

Why had he spoilt things between them by proposing marriage? Why were her feelings such a tangle? Why could she not put her concerns for Sallie Mae's safety from mind when it appeared that all danger had passed? Why did nothing make sense anymore?

The following morning at breakfast, Mister Larsen announced that the governor had called a town-wide meeting for that evening.

"Women are generally not required to attend such gatherings, but Yeardley believes it will be of benefit to our newest colonists." He directed a smile at Diana and Sallie Mae, who were enjoying a tasty morning meal of fried samp and corn bread.

"What is on the governor's agenda for this evening?" Mary Larsen asked.

"One matter of import concerns the orphans brought from

England last year whose indentures were sold. Many of the children have now run away."

"Orphans were brought from England to Jamestown?" Diana asked incredulously.

Mary said, "I believed it was a travesty when I saw the poor things being herded off the ship, but apparently the Virginia Company thought it was a good way to rid the streets of London of them, so here they came."

Appalled, Diana thought that even though a shipload of children had been removed from the filthy streets of London, plenty more remained. But she did not voice her sentiments.

"At any rate," Mary added, "I refused to purchase one of the indentures since the governor declared that if any one of us thought to adopt them, he would remove the child from the home. They were here to work and not to join our families, he declared." She shook her head sadly. "In my estimation, it was a regrettable business." She looked to her husband. "What does the governor mean to say about it?"

"That our traders, Colton and Sharpe, recently discovered a number of the runaway children living in the woods in the mixed village—"

"The mixed village," Mary interrupted to explain to Diana and Sallie Mae, "is where those white men who took Indian wives live. I can't imagine how they get on there, but because Jamestown ostracized the men, and the Indian women were shunned by their people, I expect they saw nothing for it but to band together." She turned back to her husband. "What does the governor intend doing now that the children have been found?"

Larsen's lips thinned. "I think his remedy unconscionable, but he intends that in order to brand the children as runaways, they shall be required to wear a pot hook. A lead collar," he explained to both wide-eyed girls.

"How dreadful!" all three women cried.

Larsen's head wagged. "When Yeardley sets his mind to something, there is nothing for it." He drew breath. "The majority of the governor's remarks tonight will be directed toward the men, but he feels that as future wives of settlers, the ladies need to know what sorts of mandates their men folk are faced with. Therefore, you young ladies are required to attend."

"Mark my words, William, I will not be the only woman there who will be appalled when he speaks of the runaway children."

"Be that as it may, my dear, neither the governor, nor most men, pay a whit of attention to anything a woman says."

That evening, the entire Larsen clan, excluding the Larsen children, who Mary left in the care of her trusted Indian woman Cheiwoga, set out to walk to the meetinghouse inside the old fort.

For most of the way, Diana and Sallie Mae lagged a bit behind the Larsens in order to speak quietly with one another.

"You have not been yer usual cheery self today," Sallie Mae said, a look of concern in her blue eyes. "Are you still overset about the runaway children, or did something untoward happen last evening between you and John?"

Diana sighed. "There is a good deal in Jamestown that does trouble me. But there was also a good deal in England that I found troubling. I expect the bulk of my dispirits stem from the fact that John did, indeed, ask me to marry him last night."

"But is that not what ye've been a'wanting?"

"I suppose you must think me daft for . . . for not accepting."

"Not in the least, if ye do not care for him; although he seems to care a great deal for you."

"I am still in love with . . . a man back home in England." Diana's chin began to tremble. "A man I will never see again."

"I am sorry, Diana. I did not know." Sallie Mae slipped an arm around her friend's trim waist.

Both girls fell silent. The occasional moo from a cow, the bleat of a goat, the mingled voices of other settlers flocking to the meetinghouse filled the air. Diana saw several Indian women stringing up ears of corn outside their employers' homes. In sunny days to come, the corn would dry. Another Indian woman sat on a doorstep gouging out the remnants of flesh inside a gourd, which, when cleaned out, would be used as a mug or bowl. At length, Diana said, "Do you mean to see Noah Colton again?"

"I expect I shall. He said he would call again once he returns from his tradin' . . . I mean his *trading* expedition." Sallie Mae's gaze fastened on the toes of her brown leather boots peeking from beneath her long skirt as she walked. "I own that his occupation as a trader rather interests me. I did not know till this mornin' that he also tracks down runaway children."

Diana leapt on the opportunity to divulge all she'd recently learned about the handsome trader. For some reason, she could not abandon her suspicions regarding the man and did not want to see him lure Sallie Mae down a path of destruction. "Has Noah mentioned to you that he has had not one, but two wives?"

That Sallie Mae nodded surprised Diana. "He said I reminded him of his first wife, Charity. He also told me about their little daughter."

"He did not divulge a bit of that to Faith. Perhaps he is being more forthright with you than he was with her, for . . . whatever reason."

Sallie Mae did not respond at once. As they neared the meetinghouse, she said, "To be honest, Diana, another man in Jamestown has caught my eye."

"Where did you meet him?" Diana asked excitedly. "*When* did you meet him?"

Sallie Mae grinned. "I have not yet made his acquaintance.

Therefore I cannot reveal his name, as I do not yet know it."

"Perhaps he will be present tonight."

"I was hopin' that very thing," Sallie Mae confessed with a giggle.

Diana could not help wondering if she would see John tonight and if he would demand—or rather, ask, as John seldom demanded anything—for an explanation of her inexplicable behavior of the previous evening. To run from him had been excessively rude. Later last night she realized she had not only been running from John, but from the painful memories the sound of the water rushing onto the riverbank had brought to mind. How long would it take before those demons within her dissolved?

Once everyone had crowded onto the hard wooden pews, men seated to one side of the building, women on the other, Reverend Martin led the congregation in a short prayer. After that Governor Yeardley stepped to the podium, a wad of papers in his hand. He delivered a welcoming comment to the young ladies, then launched into the business at hand. After briefly relaying the news of the runaway children that had now been found, and the punishment meted out, he turned to reviewing the mandates passed by the first House of Burgesses, which met the previous summer. He placed special emphasis on the laws prohibiting excessive drinking and public drunkenness, which in the summer heat, he said, was always an ongoing problem. The use of profane language, he reminded the colonists, was strictly forbidden, and added that profane language was most especially forbidden on the Sabbath.

"Furthermore, any settler having no lawful excuse to be absent from Sabbath services will be fined fifty pounds of tobacco."

"But what of those of us who live beyond the sound of the church bell?" a planter shouted from the back of the building.

"In dead of winter, governor, it's demmed impossible to know when to leave for services in order to arrive before Pastor has said the last amen."

"Crawl outta' yer bed the minute ye hears yer rooster crow," retorted another colonist.

"Well said, Thomas," the governor exclaimed above the laughter elicited by the man's remark.

When everyone had settled back down, Yeardley declared it was imperative they continue the custom of publishing the marriage banns according to the guidelines set down in the Anglican Book of Common Prayer; and that all marriages, births, deaths and new land grants be officially recorded with the town clerk, whose office was now located in a building adjacent to the meetinghouse.

"And," he added, "if and when a man decides to parcel out his land to his son, or to anyone, a new land title must be recorded." He wagged a finger to emphasize the point. "Which is the only way I know to avoid future boundary disputes or disputes in ownership. Now then, another very important mandate that many of you planters have flagrantly disregarded is the law that says every planter amongst ye must plant and tend at least two acres of corn, in addition to however many acres of tobacco ye're growing."

"Not all of us has the time or the help to tend corn," shouted a disgruntled colonist.

"Then send yer wives into the field to plant yer corn," the governor responded angrily. "It only takes fifty days a year to raise an adequate corn crop."

"I only jes got m' trees girdled," one man called out.

"Then hoe around the stumps," Yardley replied impatiently. "And remember to pick yer corn before the maize thieves migrate."

"What are maize thieves?" Diana whispered into Sallie Mae's ear.

"What is maize?" Sallie Mae replied.

Diana giggled.

"I know it is difficult to believe now," the governor went on, "but cold weather will soon be upon us. Ye must put up enough corn and meat to feed yerselves through the bleak winter months. Pork from four hogs will last a man and wife throughout the winter. Hog Island is overrun with hogs, so don't think ye can't find a hog to slaughter," he bellowed.

When he began to rail against the use of manure to fertilize a tobacco crop, declaring that it made the leaves taste of manure and consequently lowered the price a man could expect to receive in exchange for a year's worth of hard labor, Sallie Mae ceased to listen. Instead, she turned to a more pleasant occupation, that of scanning the profiles of the gentlemen colonists in search of the young man she'd seen on two separate occasions, both times as she walked back to the Larsen home after visiting with Goody Weston.

He was a man of moderate height with jet-black hair and a ruddy complexion. He was not lanky and rail-thin like John Fuller, or tall and broad-shouldered like Noah; instead, he had a stocky, muscular build. To Sallie Mae, it looked as if he might be accustomed to hard work. She had seen men of similar stature on-board ship, men with barrel chests and legs like tree trunks.

In a way, she found it odd that any man would attract her notice, considering what she'd suffered at the hands of the ruffians back home. After that horrible experience, it had occurred to her that she might never allow a man to touch her again, let alone share her bed. But this man . . . her long gaze searched the crowd . . . this man somehow seemed . . . different.

Eventually the governor wound down, and one of his councilmen strode to the podium. The second man's name escaped Sallie Mae, but she began to listen when he declared that he wished to introduce several new settlers to their community; men who had recently arrived on a small ship that limped into the bay, its sails tattered and mast torn asunder.

"You may have spotted the bark from shore. She was in sad shape when she arrived, but several industrious passengers have worked diligently day and night to render the vessel seaworthy again. Unfortunately, she'll soon be heading out for an island located east and south of here, the inhabitants of which we are indebted to for supplying us with the fine tobacco seeds we now plant.

"As I was saying, several of these men have elected not to continue their journey but rather to remain here in Jamestown. Firstly, I'd like to present Jeremy Erickson, a sawyer by trade. Erickson and his brother, Henry, who has been with us some time now, have plans to build and operate Jamestown's first sawmill."

Both the Erickson brothers stood and nodded at the congregation who, with a hearty round of applause, welcomed the news of a sawmill in their township.

"Next, I'd like to introduce a man whose services all we planters sorely need. As you well know, planters are in constant need of hogsheads. Without 'em, a man has no hope of getting his leaves bundled onto a ship and exported back home to England."

Before the councilman concluded his speech, rowdy cheers from the colonists drowned out his words.

"Please welcome Jamestown's first cooper, Samuel Wingate!"

Amidst thunderous applause, a stockily built man rose to his feet. On the ladies' side of the room, Sallie Mae cried, "That's him!"

"Who?" Diana queried.

"The man I'm gonna marry!"

Diana craned her neck to see around the heads of other colonists. "He is very good looking," she replied, not bothering to whisper as the settlers were still loudly cheering.

"Samuel Wingate is the most handsome man I have ever seen!" Sallie Mae declared. That he had been living aboard the ship in the bay explained why she had not spotted him in the same place twice. Always she'd seen him scurryin' down the road as if he was in a great hurry. Now she knew why. He'd been busy workin', or rather *toiling,* at the task of mending a ship.

Diana could not help smiling to herself over this new turn of events. If Sallie Mae had indeed chosen the man she meant to marry, then perhaps Diana could leave off worrying about what additional havoc Noah Colton might wreak. For surely he would not attempt to do away with both Sallie Mae and her new husband. Moreover, it would be interesting to see how Noah handled rejection once he discovered his latest prey had set her cap for another man.

CHAPTER 21

As everyone filed from the meetinghouse that night, Diana glanced about for John, but never caught sight of him. Perhaps she would see him at Sabbath services and if he asked, try to explain away her odd behavior. Until then, she decided to turn her thoughts elsewhere.

On the walk home, talk of Jamestown's new cooper dominated the girls' conversation.

"Samuel Wingate is indeed a fine-looking man," Diana said later as she and Sallie Mae prepared for bed.

Sallie Mae turned back the coverlet. "Sallie Mae Wingate sounds quite nice. But"—her brows drew together—"how shall I meet him? I've no need for a hogshead. Therefore I've no reason to seek out his shop."

"Do you know where his workshop is located?" Diana asked, crossing the room to hang her skirt on a peg.

"Perhaps we might search for it tomorrow." Sallie Mae's expression brightened.

"Very well. We've not taken a ride on Bug-A-Boo in quite a spell."

Although the girls' search the following afternoon proved fruitless, they did enjoy the outing. "Perhaps Mister Wingate has not yet set up his workshop," Diana suggested. She brushed Bug-a-Boo's flank whilst Sallie Mae spread fresh hay on the shed floor.

Sallie Mae did not look up from her task. "Tomorrow, I shall walk up and down every street in Jamestown. I am determined to meet the man."

During the following fortnight, John Fuller renewed his efforts to win Diana, and Noah Colton returned to Jamestown and called twice at the Larsen home to see Sallie Mae. Despite her longing to spend her evenings with another man, Sallie Mae did enjoy listening to Noah's talk about the Indian tribes he visited. One evening he called to see her still attired in his deerskin clothing.

"Do all the traders dress in that fashion?" she asked as they headed up the street away from the Larsen home.

"We have only begun of late to dress in this manner. It seems to please the naturals when we wear clothing similar to theirs. Although in warmer months, they are . . . how shall I put it?" He grinned. "They are considerably *less* covered than we are."

"Oh." Sallie Mae peeked up from the corner of her eye at the tall man. She had long ceased to think there was anything to fear from Noah, or from anyone, for all that. Apparently whoever had mistook her for Hester B had long since given up on the notion to do away with her. "Other than Mistress Larsen's Indian woman, and a few other Indians I've seen walkin' around the colony, I have only seen one other. And I dinna' see him up close. He was ridin' horseback, and the horse was going so fast, I couldna' tell what the Indian was wearin'."

Her remark seemed to interest Noah. "Where did you see this Indian?"

"In the woods. Diana and I rode Bug-A-Boo into the forest on my birthday."

"Was the Indian riding a huge white horse?"

Sallie Mae's eyes widened. "You have also seen him? Mistress Larsen said the forest was playin' tricks on us."

Noah did not reply for a moment, then he solemnly said,

"Mistress Larsen told you aright."

They walked in silence for a spell. The evening seemed full of peaceful sounds, an owl hooting from the treetops, children laughing as they played in the street, a dog barking. When they came upon other couples out for a stroll, Noah seemed acquainted with every last one of them, at least the men, with whom he always exchanged a few words. Sallie Mae noticed that all the young ladies who were introduced to Noah appeared charmed by him. It was difficult to fathom that the most sought-after man in Jamestown had chosen her.

Sallie Mae plied him with a good many questions regarding his trading expeditions. "When you visit the Indian villages, do ye speak with the naturals, I mean, in their language?"

Noah nodded, his easy grin softening the angles of his handsome face. "It is not so very difficult to learn Indian words. When we traders do not understand what the naturals are saying, we do a good bit of gesturing until we all know what the other is attempting to convey. Can become quite comical at times. Were anyone watching, I'm certain our antics would appear amusing."

"Do most all the Indians live in bark houses?" A sweeping gesture indicated the row of several they were walking past. "They look like giant loaves of bread."

Noah grinned. "Some Indians live in bark houses; the tribal leaders, those with great wealth. In that sense, their society is not so very different from ours. Wealth sets a man apart from those who merely wish for it."

"What sorts of houses do those Indians who merely wish for wealth live in?"

He grinned down at her. "You are a curious little thing, Sallie Mae Brown. I think you must thirst for knowledge the same as I did when I first came to this strange new land."

She smiled up at him. "I do like learnin' new things. Diana

has been teaching me to speak proper like."

"Oh?" A hand touched her back to guide her around a corner. "I thought I would show you my home."

Both Sallie Mae and Diana had wondered what sort of house the trader lived in. Diana had said that Faith was certain he must have a very fine house, perhaps even finer than the Evans' home.

Although it was not easy to clearly see in the dim light, he pointed across an expanse of greensward to a snug little wattle-and-daub structure that sat at the end of a long street. A cleared field lay between the house and the dense forest beyond.

"My house here in town is small," he said. "Only three rooms and a loft. My home on the plantation is far larger and finer. I store much of what I trade with the Indians in an enclosed shed at the rear of this house."

"Oh." Of a sudden, Sallie Mae's ears perked up. Did he perhaps store muskets and gunpowder in that shed? If he wanted to take her inside, should she let him? "Your home appears quite nice to me," she murmured politely, then when a sudden surge of fear overtook her, she cast about for another topic of conversation. "Have ye planted corn in yer field? To satisfy the governor's mandate."

"Not this year. Though I have had corn in that field in years past."

"Perhaps it is time I returned home," she said a bit anxiously.

Without hesitation, he turned around.

"I expect you've plenty of corn and tobacco growing on yer plantation," Sallie Mae said.

"Indeed." He nodded. "However, to be truthful, the plantation is not entirely mine at the moment. It will be mine once my mother-in-law is gone. As things now stand, my trading expeditions keep me far too busy to tend corn. Servants on the plantation look after things. Once I give up trading and remove to the country, I will, of course, oversee the planting and whatnot. I'll sell the property I own here in town." After a pause, he said, "I would like to ask you something, Sallie Mae."

She gazed warily up at him. "W-what would ye like to know?"

"A bit about your life in England."

"Oh. Well, I come from a large family. There was eight of us at home."

"Do you have brothers?"

"Hmmm. And sisters."

"I expect you learned a great many things from your brothers. Such as . . . how to care for goats and chickens and . . . certain outdoor pursuits, hunting, fishing, swimming, the like."

Sallie Mae blanched. "What makes you think I know how to swim?"

"You seem to be a clever girl." A moment later, he said, "I'd like to ask you something else, Sallie Mae."

Her breath in her throat, she waited.

"If you were to marry a man such as I, one who traveled a great deal, would you be able to get on alone? That is, would ye mind not having your man around for lengthy spells?"

Sallie Mae was at a loss as to how to answer that question. In the end she merely shrugged and said she had not given much thought to what sort of man she would marry. She was quite relieved when he said no more on the subject. Later that night when she was telling Diana about it, she was still pondering why he had asked such a thing.

"I feel I must tell you that he asked the selfsame thing of Faith." Diana paused, uncertain how to proceed. She did not wish Sallie Mae to think that in the event she was wrong in her suspicions regarding Noah Colton that she was trying to dissuade her altogether from seeing him. No doubt the pretty little blond felt flattered that out of all the young ladies in Jamestown, the handsome man was now expressing an interest in her. On the other hand, she could not put aside the feeling that Noah was not being entirely truthful. "I own he is quite charming, but he appears to be a fickle sort. He only just tossed Faith aside, and now he is calling upon you. He did not tell Faith about either of his wives, and John said he treated another woman unkindly."

"I have been alone with Noah more than once and he has never been unkind toward me. We were quite near the forest tonight and he did not attempt to lure me away. When I wished to return home, he obliged at once."

"But do you not think it odd that, given the fact someone tried to kill you by throwing you into the river, that of a sudden, he asked if you could swim? No man has ever asked such a thing of me."

"Perhaps he merely wished to learn a bit about me."

"And now he is thinking of marrying you."

Sallie Mae digested that. "I own that does seem a trifle hasty."

"Noah Colton is not to be trusted, Sallie Mae."

"He is a trader, but that don't make him guilty of doin' anythin' unlawful," Sallie Mae insisted.

"No," Diana agreed, "but with One-Eye gone, that means someone here in Jamestown or hereabouts believed that what you saw was a threat to them, and that to protect their nefarious deeds, they must rid themselves of you. Who might One-Eye be bringing muskets and gunpowder to? Not to the governor. Who would stand to profit from selling . . . or trading . . . those particular items? Who in the colony appears to be very wealthy, yet is not a planter?"

Sallie Mae worried her lower lip.

"I am persuaded Noah learned from Faith that you and Hester B are one and the same. You are now living with a councilman. Noah cannot risk that you would say anything to Mister Larsen. So, suddenly Noah shows up here, attempting to charm you, to gain your confidence . . . perhaps even to marry you. Noah would not have sullied his hands in an attempt to kill you, but he could have dispatched a pair of unsavory sorts, perhaps the other two traders, to do the dirty deed for him. But the men failed. If Noah were to marry you, he could easily rid himself of you with no one the wiser. Both of his other wives are dead. Perhaps they, too, learned of his misdeeds and threatened to expose him."

"Well, I've no intention of marryin' the man; unless . . ."

"Unless, what?"

"Unless, I fall in love with him. One cannot choose whom one loves . . . can one?"

Diana had no answer for that. She did not recall actually choosing to fall in love with Hamilton Prescott.

"On the other hand," Sallie Mae said, "I truly wish to make Samuel Wingate's acquaintance. I am certain he is trustworthy." After a pause, she added, "I am persuaded, Diana, if Noah *is* the culprit, he is coming after the wrong girl. I am not nearly so clever as you. I would never have sorted the puzzle out so swiftly as you. Noah should be frightened of you, not me."

"I simply wish no harm to come to you, Sallie Mae. And to that end, I refuse to let down my guard."

The following day Diana decided to pay a call on her friend Faith to see how she was bearing up. When she entered her friend's bedchamber, it dismayed her to find Faith unchanged. The heartsick girl, still moping over the loss of Noah Colton's affections, was inconsolable.

"I rarely venture from my room," Faith mumbled from where she sat on the bed, her back leaning against the wall.

Diana was glad to see that at least her friend was fully clothed and not lounging about in her night shift as she had been. And it had also pleased her when Mistress Evans said that Faith was coming below stairs for at least one meal a day.

Diana took a seat on the floor beneath the window and drew her long skirt up to her knees. “I daresay we would find it much cooler if we were sitting in the meadow beneath a shade tree as we used to do.”

“No!” Faith exclaimed of a sudden. “I refuse to go into the meadow ever again.”

Diana looked puzzled. “But I thought you loved being out-of-doors. Have you left off tending Mistress Evans’s garden? And what of Sunshine? Do you no longer see your little orange cat?”

Faith’s lips thinned. “On occasion, Mistress Evans brings him up here to see me.”

“I am certain Sunshine misses you.”

“And I miss Noah.”

Diana sighed. “You’d best accept the fact that your former beau has now set his sights on Sallie Mae.”

“I am well aware of that.”

“Do you also know that Sallie Mae is the image of his first wife? Did you know that he *had* a first wife? And that they had a little daughter? His mother-in-law now cares for the child.” When she saw fresh tears well up in Faith’s eyes, she regretted asking the hurtful questions.

Sniffing, Faith murmured, “May we speak on another topic, please?”

“Forgive me. I did not reveal those things to you in order to be cruel. My hope is that you will come to see the truth about Noah: that he has deliberately withheld things of import from you.”

“I no longer wish to speak of it.”

Diana cast about for another topic. “I noticed this past Sunday that Robin and her young man had published their banns.”

In a barely audible tone Faith muttered, "Which means I will soon have the bedchamber to myself. As well as my bed," she added glumly.

"Faith, you will never catch another man's eye if you remain sequestered here in your bedchamber every day."

Twisting a loose tread on the coverlet, Faith made no reply.

"Well, perhaps this bit of information will please you. Sallie Mae does not care for Noah," Diana announced. "She has her eye on Jamestown's new cooper, Samuel Wingate."

Faith's green eyes cut 'round. "Sallie Mae does not wish to wed Noah?"

"No." Diana shook her head. "She enjoys listening to him speak of his adventures, but I expect that once she meets her cooper, she will quickly toss Noah aside."

Faith slipped off the bed and moved to the looking glass above the washstand. Picking up her hairbrush, she began to drag it through her tangled locks. "Perhaps I shall resume attending Sabbath services after all."

"I am surprised Governor Yeardley has not fined you fifty pounds of tobacco for the services you have already missed."

Diana was pleased when her small jest elicited the hint of a smile from her friend. It was the first she'd seen on Faith's pretty face in quite a spell. She rose to her feet. "So, I shall see you on the Sabbath?"

Faith nodded. "Indeed, you shall."

On her way home that afternoon, Diana was pleased that she had at least accomplished one thing. Faith had climbed out of bed and declared her intention to resume attending Sabbath services. Faith was such a pretty girl. Diana hoped she would soon gain the notice of another colonist. Otherwise, if Faith persisted in her quest to wed Noah, Diana would have no choice but to also concern herself with Faith's well-being. For one reason or another, Noah's wives did not seem to fare very well.

A conversation initiated by Mister Larsen over supper that night drew a bright smile to Sallie Mae's face.

Scooping a serving of succotash onto his trencher, Larsen casually remarked to his wife, "The crew began cutting tobacco leaves today." He passed the earthenware bowl to Diana. "Won't be long before the entire crop is hung in the sheds to dry."

"How long are the leaves left to dry?" Diana asked, taking a portion from the bowl and passing it to Sallie Mae, who was staring intently at Mister Larsen. "Sallie Mae, would you like some succotash?" Diana asked, still holding the bowl.

The rosy-cheeked blond absently took the bowl, though her intent gaze never left Larsen's face.

"If we've plenty of breezy days," he began by way of answering Diana's question, "it generally takes six or seven weeks for the leaves to dry."

"And then what do ye do with the leaves, sir?" Sallie Mae inquired breathlessly.

Larsen smiled at each of the girls. "Both you young ladies will make fine wives to some lucky planters. Not every young lady takes such a lively interest in a man's tobacco crop."

"What do ye do with the leaves once they've dried up, sir?" Sallie Mae asked again.

Larsen laughed. "The leaves do not dry *completely* up, Sallie Mae. They will be taken down in about six weeks; and since this is August, that means that long about October the leaves should be sufficiently dry to be stripped from the stalks and pressed into hogsheads, which we load onto a ship and send home to England."

Sallie Mae brightened. "Have ye plenty of hogsheads on hand, sir?"

"Now that you mention it, Sallie Mae, I expect I shall be

needing a few more, perhaps a half dozen more."

"Perhaps ye'd best get yer order in right away, sir. We've a new cooper in Jamestown, y'know. I expect he will soon be quite busy."

A slow grin appeared on Larsen's face. "That is a very good idea, Sallie Mae."

Diana noticed that sitting across from them Mary Larsen's lips were twitching.

"Perhaps I should visit our new cooper's workshop on the morrow." Larsen's brow furrowed. "Now, what was the man's name?"

"Samuel Wingate," both girls replied in unison.

Larsen and his wife laughed. "And would one or both of you young ladies care to accompany me? Since you seem quite eager to learn about tobacco and . . . uh, hogsheads."

Later that night, when the girls were alone in their bedchamber, Diana asked Sallie Mae if she'd prefer going alone with Mister Larsen to visit the cooper's workshop.

Sallie Mae considered before thoughtfully replying, "I believe I'd like ye to come along as well, Diana. In the event I become tongue-tied as I did the first time Noah called. If you are there and I cannot speak, you could ask Samuel a question or two whilst I cast about for me voice."

"Very well. But I shall endeavor to say as little as possible." After a pause, she said, "Perhaps we'd best think up several questions in advance that you might ask Mister Wingate."

"That would be splendid!"

Diana was inordinately pleased over this turn of events. The girls passed the remainder of that evening—except for the time they spent washing Sallie Mae's hair and rinsing it in sweet-smelling rose water—thinking up questions she could ask the new cooper.

Chapter 22

The next afternoon, Mister Larsen took the lead as the three set out to walk to Samuel Wingate's workshop. When they neared the outer edge of the settlement, Sallie Mae inquired how he knew where the cooper's workshop was located.

"According to the New Virginia Company Land Ordinance, a colonist who chooses to set up shop and practice a trade is granted four acres of land *and* a house. The council decided that since Wingate would need to begin work at once, he should be granted a parcel of land that was already cleared and had a house and outbuildings in place."

"So a previous settler had already built a house upon the cooper's plot of land?" Diana inquired.

"Quite a fine one." Larsen nodded. "Made of brick. The poor fellow had only just got it built last winter when of a sudden he contracted lung fever and never again left his bed. Alive, that is."

"How dreadful!" Sallie Mae cried. "He never got to enjoy his new house."

"You have a tender heart, Sallie Mae. I daresay you shall make some fellow a fine wife."

Before they drew near the cooper's workshop, located in one of the outbuildings on his land, they could hear the sound of his mallet as he diligently worked. Sallie Mae's eyes grew round with excitement as the threesome approached the open area of the sturdy log building. Once she'd caught sight of Samuel

Wingate, her heart began to pound wildly in her breast. Gazing at the dark-haired man, she attempted to memorize everything about him at once.

He wore a pair of black serge britches topped by a white muslin shirt with the sleeves rolled up. Though his coal-black hair was untidy, his ruddy good looks were evident to both girls. Apparently unaware that anyone had approached his workshop, the ringing of the blade against the metal truss he was forcing down the side of the barrel he was constructing rang in everyone's ears. The ripple of the cooper's muscled forearm as he worked mesmerized Sallie Mae.

Larsen and the women stood and patiently waited until the cooper glanced up and noticed that he had an audience.

"Sorry, sir. I did not hear ye come in." Wingate wiped the back of his forearm across his moist brow before casting a curious gaze at the two young ladies accompanying the finely dressed gentleman. "Afternoon, ladies."

Smiling prettily, both Sallie Mae and Diana murmured a pleasant greeting.

Larsen said, "These lovely young ladies currently reside with my wife and myself. This is Miss Diana Wakefield and this is Miss Sallie Mae Brown. The ladies mentioned earlier today that they'd never seen a cooper at work, so I invited them to join me. I am William Larsen. If you recall, we met at the council meeting a fortnight ago when we sorted out the details of your land grant."

"Indeed, I do recall." The cooper nodded. "A pleasure to meet you, ladies, and to see you again, sir."

"You appear to be doing a brisk business, Wingate."

"Jamestown planters wasted no time in ordering hogsheads for this year's crop."

"Which is why I am here. Make no mistake, I speak for all of us when I say we are mighty glad you decided to set up shop, Wingate."

The men fell to discussing Virginia's booming tobacco business, which afforded Diana and Sallie Mae the opportunity to gaze curiously about the workshop. The floor was littered with piles of staves already cut to the correct size to fashion a hogshead. Assorted metal trussing rings and bits and scraps of other wood and metal also lay scattered about the floor. A wide array of tools, a broad ax, a short-handled ax and additional trussing rings hung on pegs on the wall.

Sallie Mae pointed to an odd-shaped instrument hanging on the back wall. Made of metal, the contraption had two long legs that ended in sharp points. Both legs were connected at the top by a hinge. "What do ye suppose that thing is?" she whispered.

She hadn't noticed that Samuel Wingate was experiencing some difficulty concentrating on his conversation with Larsen. That Larsen's lips were twitching said that he had noticed. "I expect your workshop is not often visited by beautiful young ladies."

"Indeed not, sir. These are my first . . . female customers."

"Oh, we did not come to purchase anything, Mr. Wingate," Diana rushed to say. "We were merely curious about . . . about what you do. I believe Sallie Mae has a few questions she would like to ask, do you not Sallie Mae?"

As feared, full use of Sallie Mae's tongue promptly fled. Ducking her head, she blushed to the roots of her hair.

At length Mister Larsen broke the awkward silence. "Well, I expect we should let you return to your work, young man. When my hogsheads are ready, I shall send my foreman to retrieve them. Thank you for pausing to chat with us, Wingate. I daresay we have kept you from your work long enough. Come along, ladies." He ushered the girls ahead of him and out of the low-ceilinged building.

When they once again heard the ring of the copper's mallet striking metal, Larsen said, "Was the visit all you expected, Sallie Mae?"

Her blue eyes rolled skyward. "If only I hadn't lost me tongue!"

Larsen grinned. "Something tells me you'll get another chance to ask Mr. Wingate the questions you prepared."

Both girls stared up at him. "You heard us?" Diana sputtered.

"Unfortunately the walls of our home are not sufficiently thick to muffle the sound of two young ladies excitedly discussing a handsome man."

"Oh-h-h," Sallie Mae wailed.

A few days later, Noah called again to see Sallie Mae. His appearance at the door in the early afternoon as opposed to later in the day surprised everyone.

"Since you professed a keen interest in the Indians," Noah said to Sallie Mae once Mary Larsen had summoned her, "I thought you might like to accompany me this afternoon. I'm to meet with a pair of Indian braves to conduct a bit of business in a clearing not far from here."

"Oh-h, my!" Sallie Mae's blue eyes grew round. She turned to Diana. "Do ye think I should go?"

Diana most certainly did not. "Perhaps you would like me to accompany you." If there were two of them, Noah might be less likely to attempt anything of a questionable nature. For her part, she'd like the opportunity to study Noah Colton a good deal more closely.

"You are most welcome to come, Miss Wakefield. I had no idea both you young ladies were so very curious about the Indians."

At that moment, he surprised the women by glancing toward

the Larsens' Indian servant, silently working near the hearth. Noah greeted her in her native tongue. Cheiwoga smiled shyly and murmured a few words in response. Grinning, Noah turned back to the ladies clustered inside the door.

"Why, I daresay I have never heard Cheiwoga say a single word in her language," Mary Larsen exclaimed. "She is virtually silent the entire day, every day."

"Make no mistake," he said softly to Mary, "she may not say much, but she understands plenty. As do a good many of the naturals."

"They understand our language?" Diana asked.

"Far more than they let on." He stood holding his hat in his hand. "So, have ye decided? Do ye both wish to come along? We shan't be gone long," he told Mary.

Her smile was pleasant. "To be sure, you'll find the woods far cooler than it is here in town."

The three set out on foot walking toward the forest. On the way, Noah paused at his little wattle-and-daub home at the edge of the township. "I'll just be a minute." He left the girls standing on the dusty road whilst he headed around behind the house.

"He told me he stores the things he trades with the Indians in his shed," Sallie Mae explained.

Moments later, the trader returned carrying a leather pouch.

"What do ye have there?" Sallie Mae posed the very question burning in Diana's mind.

"*Wampumpeak.*" He grinned. "Indian money." Following along a well-worn path, he led them deep into the woods.

"Might we see what Indian money looks like?" Sallie Mae asked.

"Indeed." He pulled apart the leather strings of the pouch and, reaching inside, pulled out a handful of blue and purple glass beads. He handed a few to Sallie Mae.

She gazed closely at the beads, then passed them to Diana. After examining them, Diana handed them back to Noah, who dropped them into his pouch.

"There appears to be nothing remarkable about them," Diana said. Her tone sounded a trifle disappointed. "What else do you trade with the Indians?"

"They covet a good many things that we English use. Pipkins, cloth. They especially like pieces of copper . . . and, of course, knives and ax blades."

The mention of weapons sent a chill down Diana's spine. "W-where did you obtain the items that you trade?" she asked, looking past Sallie Mae to the handsome trader, who this afternoon was again dressed in buckskin breeches, although today he had on a loose-fitting white muslin shirt. She could not help noticing the strings that should have been tied at the V-neck had instead been left dangling, leaving the shirt open a good way down his chest. Having never before beheld a man's bare chest, she inhaled a sharp breath and promptly lowered her gaze. Because she had been preoccupied studying the handsome man's chest, she did not note the answer he provided to her question. By the time she regained her composure, he and Sallie Mae had already turned to a fresh topic, Noah explaining the meanings of a few Indian words.

"*Isquotersuash* is the naturals' word for gourd types of plants. Early settlers shortened the convoluted word simply to 'squash.' We eat the flesh, then the scooped-out gourd makes a handy drinking mug. *Pawschoicora* is another Indian word that we light-skins adopted, but quickly shortened to hickory."

In no time the threesome veered off the beaten path and began to pick their way through an area of thick underbrush. When Noah produced a hatchet and began to whack at the vines obscuring the path, Diana's brow furrowed. Had she and Sallie Mae naively agreed to a fool's errand? She reached to catch Sallie Mae's arm and with a speaking look, attempted to warn her. Both girls, holding their long skirts a bit above their ankles in order to avoid snagging them on a bramble, were surprised when quite soon they emerged into an open clearing surrounded by a thick grove of tall trees.

"These are pecan trees," Noah said. "In a few weeks, this whole area"—a hand indicated the forest floor—"will be covered with nuts, ripe for picking."

"Cheiwoga calls these small brown nuts *pakawns,*" Sallie Mae said, pleased that she knew one Indian word. "She uses them to make a delicious sugary pie."

Suddenly, Noah's demeanor turned solemn. "The Indian braves are here," he said in a low tone. "They will stare, especially at you, Sallie Mae, but do not be offended. They are merely curious."

"Why will they stare at me?" Sallie Mae whispered.

"The naturals are fascinated by flaxen hair and blue eyes."

His remark caused icy fingers of fear to snake down Diana's spine. She should never have agreed to this mission. Fighting a strong urge to turn tail and run, she instead moved closer to Sallie Mae and tightly clasped her hand. "We must remain close together," she whispered.

The next instant, both girls flinched when two very tall, dark-skinned Indian braves attired only in scraps of leather stretched across their loins and with soft moccasins upon their feet stepped from behind the trunk of a tree and moved silently toward them. Around both braves' necks hung several leather thongs strung with what appeared to be the teeth of wild animals. Tied into their long black hair was a wad of black-tipped white feathers, the soft ends of which fluttered upward when they walked. The sight of two nearly naked males caused both girls to suck in their breaths. Diana's free hand flew to cover her gaping mouth.

"Yellow-haired *crenepo,* take," the taller Indian said, nodding. With an appraising look, he stared at Sallie Mae.

"White women *netab!*" Noah replied, one balled-up fist pressed to the center of his chest.

The angry-looking Indian took a step forward, his hand outstretched, as if reaching for the pouch that Noah carried. "*Wampumpeak* take!"

Noah snatched the leather pouch away. "Where are the furs?"

Without hesitation, the tall Indian turned around and motioned to the second one, who stepped from the clearing and an instant later returned carrying an armload of shiny, rich beaver pelts.

Their eyes wide and their hearts in their throats, Diana and Sallie Mae breathlessly watched the exchange, which suddenly took a nasty turn.

The taller Indian raised an arm to halt the progress of the second one. With all five fingers splayed, he cried. *"Paranske!"*

Noah's tone hardened. Again he held up the single pouch. *"Nekut!"*

"Pah!" The fierce Indian spat on the ground.

When the second one followed suit, Diana and Sallie Mae edged backward a step, although Noah bravely, or foolishly, took a step forward. Both girls watched as he withdrew a second pouch from inside his voluminous shirt.

Shaking his head as if defeated, Noah offered the Indian two pouches. *"Ninge."*

"*Yough! Winnatue! Yough!*"

Noah shook his head firmly and again held up both pouches. *"Ninge."*

Again, the Indian spat. *"Nus!"*

With a shrug, Noah stuffed both pouches back into his shirt and turned to leave. An outstretched arm ushered the girls ahead of him. Diana was certainly ready to leave. But when the

Indian grunted, Noah halted and winked at the girls before he turned back to face his adversaries.

The tall Indian's face was now a thundercloud. "Take *crenepo!*"

Noah balked. "No trade woman." He pulled the hatchet from his belt. "*Wampumpeak* . . . and hatchet."

Her hazel eyes round, Diana watched with horror as Noah handed two pouches of beads and the hatchet to the disgruntled Indian. Then he hurriedly scooped up the armload of furs and, with a nod of his blond head, urged the girls ahead of him.

His blue eyes twinkling merrily, he murmured, "Let's get out of here before they realize they've been cheated."

Once they had scurried from the clearing, Diana leaned across Sallie Mae to speak to Noah. "Did you truly . . . cheat them?"

He shrugged. "This many furs are well worth what they asked: five pouches of beads. He wanted Sallie Mae."

Both girls gasped.

"You watched the proceedings. I held out for two pouches of beads and threw in the hatchet." He chuckled. "What they didn't know is that I had three more pouches tucked inside my shirt."

"I am glad we left when we did," Diana said. "They were quite angry, and you gave them a weapon. Were you not afraid they might . . . hurt you? Or us?" she asked pointedly.

"I would not have brought you ladies along if there was any danger."

"But did you not fear what they could have done, that is, if they realized you were cheating them?" Diana was unprepared for the sudden change in Noah's demeanor. His eyes became narrow slits and his nostrils flared.

"I did *not* cheat the Indians, Miss Wakefield," he ground out. "I merely negotiated a trade. They mistakenly believe I am *win-*

naytue—a rich man. But they are wrong." Of a sudden, his easy grin returned. "However, once I sell these pelts, I will be far richer than I am now."

"I thought you already were a rich man," Sallie Mae blurted out.

Diana had seen more than enough to convince her that Noah was either uncommonly trusting, or uncommonly stupid. Clearly he had put the girls and himself in danger by cheating a pair of potentially savage Indians. Perhaps her coming along had merely altered his plan. If the Indians had insisted upon it, she believed, he would have indeed turned Sallie Mae over to them in exchange for the pelts. He had said that the Indians found a blue-eyed, flaxen-haired woman fascinating. As it was, she was immensely grateful she had been there and the tense negotiations had ended peacefully.

Over supper that night, after the girls had relayed something of their adventure to little Edward, who was especially curious about the tall Indians who wore feathers in their hair, Diana decided to simply ask Councilman Larsen how Noah came by the glass beads and other items that he used to trade with the Indians.

Larsen set his pewter cup down on the table. "The colored beads are sent to the colony expressly for the traders to use in their negotiations with the Indians. We, the governor and council members, trust Noah to use his own discretion in trading for whatever he can get that is of value. The profits from his trades are used to bring down the debt we settlers owe the investors who are still purchasing shares in the New Virginia Company to finance our settlement."

Diana cast a quizzical look at Sallie Mae. "But did not Noah say *he* would be richer after he sold the pelts?"

Looking confused, Sallie Mae said she did not clearly recall what Noah said.

"I am certain he was not referring to himself, personally," Mary Larsen put in as she reached to the center of the table for a wedge of warm rye bread.

Unconvinced, Diana harkened back to conversations she had had with Faith. She clearly recalled Faith saying that Noah had told her he had a trapping business and that he sold the fox and beaver pelts he trapped for a tidy profit. He certainly did not trap these pelts. Could it be that Noah was involved in more than one misdeed? Was it possible that he was using the glass beads given to him by the New Virginia Company to conduct private trades for his own gain? She decided now that they were openly discussing the infamous trader, she'd press for more information.

"Does the Virginia Company ever send muskets and gunpowder for Noah to trade with the Indians?"

Beside her, she felt rather than saw Sallie Mae's blue eyes spring open following her bold question.

"Indeed, not!" Larsen exclaimed. "We are aware that in years past the traders gave Indians knives and ax blades, but never muskets. To do so would be quite foolhardy."

"Any muskets sent to the colony are intended exclusively for the colonists' use," Mary said, "to protect us *from* the Indians."

For the nonce, Diana chose not to mention that this very afternoon, Noah had given a hatchet to the Indians.

"Noah Colton's work with the Indians has brought a great deal of good to Jamestown," Larsen added. "He has negotiated with many an unfriendly tribe, such as the Chickahominy and the Apamatuks, and always come away the victor. Make no mistake, Noah Colton is a trader of unparalleled success."

"He seemed quite sure of himself this afternoon," Sallie Mae said. "I own I was near frightened out of my wits when those savages showed up, weren't you, Diana?"

She cleared her throat.

"The Indians trust Colton as they've trusted no one since Captain John Smith," Larsen went on. "To us colonists, he and the other two traders provide an invaluable service."

"You would not go wrong in marrying Noah Colton, Sallie Mae."

Mary Larsen's comment brought the conversation to an abrupt end, for Sallie Mae was too embarrassed to reply, and Diana was preoccupied with her own private thoughts regarding the wily trader. That the angry Indian had wanted Sallie Mae as part of the trade convinced her that Noah felt threatened by what he believed Sallie Mae saw, or knew, and that he intended to harm her. Had Diana not been along this afternoon, she feared that Noah would have blithely turned Sallie Mae over to the Indians as payment for a half-dozen beaver pelts, then rushed back to town feigning alarm that a band of Indians had taken him by surprise and made off with the girl. What's worse, everyone would believe him. Not wanting to unduly alarm Sallie Mae, she kept her thoughts regarding this afternoon's potentially deadly excursion to herself. But she vowed to do all in her power never to let Sallie Mae be alone again with the deceptive trader.

Following dinner, Mister Larsen went outdoors, as he did every evening, to bring in a few logs so Cheiwoga could build up the fire the next morning. Mary went to tuck in the children, and Diana and Sallie Mae retired to their bedchamber. Diana entered the room first and crossed in the darkness to slide open the window covering. Hearing men's voices coming from outdoors, she paused. Then, flinging a glance over her shoulder at Sallie Mae, who was entering the room carrying a lit candle, she put a finger to her lips and motioned for her to snuff out the light and join her by the opened window.

Both girls listened intently to what the men were saying.

". . . young ladies entertained us tonight with tales of their adventure in the woods today, Colton."

"Mister Larsen is speakin' with Noah?" Sallie Mae whispered.

Diana nodded.

". . . our boy hung on to their every word regarding the tall Indians with feathers in their hair."

Noah chuckled. "To be sure, the Indians are quite colorful. What . . . else did the ladies say?"

"Glass beads must have caught their fancy for they asked where you came by them. Miss Wakefield asked if you traded muskets and gunpowder with the Indians." When Larsen chuckled, Noah laughed aloud.

"One wonders where a young lady would get such a foolish notion," Larsen said, mirth still evident in his tone.

"No saying," Noah replied. "Did the girls say anything more?"

"Nothing of import. I daresay Sallie Mae is quite keen on you, young man."

The girls heard the sound of logs tumbling. Then Larsen said, "I'd best go inside. Mary will wonder where I've got off to."

"Might I help you with that, sir?"

"I am not such an old man that I cannot carry in a few sticks of firewood, Colton." He chuckled. "I expect Sallie Mae will be sorry she did not offer to help me."

The sound of both men's laughter faded away on the cool night air.

The girls moved away from the window. While Sallie Mae went to the common room to relight the candle, Diana prepared for bed. That Noah had only just "happened" to be walking past the house when Larsen went outdoors seemed odd, especially considering it was far too late for him to be paying a call on Sallie Mae. The only thing she could surmise from the incident, and from Noah's questions, was that he feared the girls might have told Councilman Larsen that he had given the

Indians a hatchet that day.

She thought nothing more of it until the following morning when she and Sallie Mae went into the shed to tend to Bug-a-Boo. Diana had just tied on the mare's feedbag when Sallie Mae walked over to tell her there was something scratched in the dirt beyond the stall. "Words and a drawin' what looks like a skull."

Curious, Diana abandoned her task to follow her friend.

"Just there," Sallie Mae pointed to a place near the hay pile. "I didn't see it right off, and I sure enough can't make out them words."

Although it was apparent Sallie Mae's footsteps had somewhat blurred the message, Diana recognized the words . . . and grasped the meaning. "Those are Latin words."

Sallie Mae's brow puckered. "What do they say?"

Diana repeated the three words. *"Plagam extremam infligere.* They refer to . . . killing someone violently. I suppose the drawing of a skull is meant to illustrate the ominous message."

Sallie Mae appeared confused. "But who would . . . ?"

Diana's lips thinned. "Apparently, either Noah had only just scratched the words in the dirt last evening and was hurrying away when he very nearly collided with Mister Larsen, who unexpectedly appeared at the woodpile. Or, because Larsen mentioned that I had asked if Noah had ever traded muskets and gunpowder with the Indians, Noah circled around, came back, and then scratched the words in the sand. Either way, this message is meant for me, Sallie Mae."

"To be sure, I wouldn't be able to read those words," Sallie Mae exclaimed. "However, his picture of a skull is quite good, wouldn't ye say?"

"You know what this means, don't you, Sallie Mae?" Not waiting for an answer, Diana went on. "It means Noah is frightened of both of us. Apparently we are the first women, other than his wives, who are now both dead, who have ever asked questions regarding his misdeeds. Because neither you nor I are married to the man, the only way he knows to silence us is . . . to kill us. Violently."

Sallie Mae shuddered.

As did Diana. That Noah's menacing message this time was in Latin told her he was especially targeting her. Until yesterday, she'd never spent time in Noah's company. From past association with Sallie Mae, he had obviously ascertained that she was not an educated lass and would not understand Latin. But apparently he suspected that she possessed an education far beyond the rudiments and more than likely would. The crude drawing of a skull was put there in the event they neither one could decipher a message delivered in a foreign language.

The following evening when Samuel Wingate knocked on the door and asked to see Miss Brown, Diana was as pleased to see him as Sallie Mae was.

"He has come!" Sallie Mae rushed to her bedchamber where Diana was seated on the bed reading her Bible. "Samuel has come! Shall I put on my pretty purple frock?"

Diana looked up. "Perhaps you might want to save it for the day you and Samuel repeat your vows."

"But I should also like to look nice for him now."

"Something tells me you've nothing to fear on that head, Sallie Mae."

Because the late summer days were still long and the cooper had called fairly early, the setting sun was only just then casting a golden glow over the landscape. Sallie Mae and Samuel strolled about the Larsen grounds, pausing to stroke Bug-a-Boo's nose, then they ambled into the orchard where apples grew thick on the trees. A few ripe ones had already fallen to the ground.

"Will soon be time for fresh apple pie," Sallie Mae said. She picked up an apple she intended to give to Bug-a-Boo when they headed back up the slope to the house. She did not feel the least bit shy around the handsome cooper now that he had come to see her.

"Apple pie sounds mighty tasty to me." Samuel smiled. "Good food is one reason I decided to live again on land."

"How long did ye live aboard ship?" Sallie Mae asked. She knew from her experience on the *King's Embassy* that every ship that set sail was required by the king to carry at least one master cooper, whose sole occupation was to maintain and repair the ship's casks, which held the passengers' and crews' drinking water and all their provisions.

"Far too long."

"Would ye like me to make ye a nice apple pie, Samuel?"

"Would ye do that for me, Miss Brown?" Samuel's black eyes twinkled merrily.

"I would if ye'd take to callin' me Sallie Mae. Miss Brown is far too formal for me."

The two grinned at one another. "Ye're a takin' little thing, Sallie Mae Brown. Yer skin is as fresh as cream from a cow's udder, and yer eyes are as blue as English cornflowers."

"I like yer looks, too, Samuel."

Sallie Mae found it difficult to sleep that night. Thoughts of Samuel Wingate kept her awake until the wee hours of the mornin'. The next time the handsome man called, he brought her a gift.

"Why, it's a little bucket!" Sallie Mae exclaimed. She hugged the small wooden bucket trussed with strips of smooth leather to her chest. "I shall treasure it always."

Samuel beamed with pride. "It pleases me that ye like m' handiwork, Sallie Mae."

"Look, Diana, Samuel made me a little bucket!" Sallie Mae showed off her treasure to her friend, who had come into the room when she heard the knock at the door, thinking perhaps the caller might be John Fuller.

"It is very fine." Diana smiled at the lovebirds, who had eyes only for one another.

Later that evening, when Sallie Mae returned home from her evening stroll with Samuel, she told Diana that he had planned a picnic for the following Saturday afternoon.

"He said he'd like you to come. He asked if ye had a suitor. I said ye did, but that I dinna' believe ye meant to marry him. Was I wrong to say that?"

"No." Diana shook her head. "You were quite right."

"Samuel said he would bring along a friend, a planter from Henricus named Luca Sheridan. Will ye come? The four of us will have a jolly time."

Diana agreed. Especially intriguing was the fact that she was at last to meet a man who lived in Henricus, which was where she thought her long-lost half-brother resided. She harbored no illusion of ever finding her kinsman, however, for her mother had never revealed her first-born child's name.

Chapter 23

On the following Saturday, an especially warm day for the month of September, both Diana and Sallie Mae excitedly awaited the arrival of Samuel Wingate and his friend Luca Sheridan. Samuel arrived carrying a basket, while his companion carried a jug of ale.

Mary Larsen answered the rap at the door and invited the men inside. "The girls are expecting you."

As Samuel and Sallie Mae greeted one another Diana mentally appraised Wingate's companion, a tall man with wavy brown hair and blue eyes. Apart from his fine looks, his equally fine clothing impressed her. Sheridan's burgundy puffed breeches exactly matched a sleeveless jerkin worn over an impeccably clean white linen shirt. A flat black beret completed his costume. Samuel was attired in his customary black serge britches and white linen shirt with the sleeves rolled up.

Samuel introduced both girls to his friend.

"I am pleased to meet you, Miss Wakefield," Sheridan said. "Samuel's description of your beauty was quite wide of the mark."

Feeling color rise to her cheeks, Diana felt as flustered as Sallie Mae very often appeared. "Thank you, sir," she murmured.

"You gentleman appear to have brought all ye'll need for a hearty repast," Mary said.

"Repast? I thought we was goin' on a picnic."

"We are going on a picnic, Sallie Mae."

"Once we've trekked deep into the woods," Samuel said, "we shall all want for sustenance."

The foursome set out on foot, Samuel and Sallie Mae in the lead, Diana and Luca trailing a few feet behind.

They entered the forest in a place the girls had never been before. "I thought we'd see where the old rolling road takes us," Samuel said.

"Rolling road?" Diana voiced the question that also sprang to Sallie Mae's mind. "What is a rolling road?"

Luca explained. "It's a road made by planters who used it to roll their hogsheads of tobacco leaves through the woods in order to transport the barrels into Jamestown to be loaded on a ship bound for England."

"Do planters not still use the rolling road?" Diana gazed with interest at her companion. "How do they get their hogsheads to Jamestown if they no longer use this road?"

Sheridan grinned. "The more successful planters—"

"He is speaking for himself now," Samuel interjected, a twinkle in his black eyes.

Luca went on. "Serious planters, those whose land fronts the river, have their own piers. They roll their hogsheads straight from the drying sheds to the ship."

"How very clever of them!" Diana exclaimed.

Just then, Sallie Mae pointed across the road. "Is that a pecan grove? Just there, beyond the hedgerows."

"Appears to be," Samuel said, gazing that direction.

"I wish I'd brought along my little bucket. We could have gathered nuts."

"Perhaps you and Diana can come back another day and gather nuts."

Sallie Mae laughed. "To be sure, I would have a difficult time getting Diana back into the woods."

"Why is that, Miss Wakefield?" came Luca's deep voice beside Diana.

"I feel . . . uncomfortable in the woods," she returned quietly.

"If I may be so bold, Miss Wakefield, perhaps you might consider the notion of facing your fears, otherwise fear becomes your master."

Diana did not wish the tall man to think her a coward. "I will take your well-meant advice into consideration, Mister Sheridan."

Minutes later, when Samuel declared they had gone quite far enough, they left the well-marked road and entered a grassy meadow, from whence they could clearly see the blue-green water of the James River. Samuel spread out the cloth that had covered the picnic basket for the girls to sit upon, whilst he and Luca seated themselves upon the thick carpet of green grass.

A cool breeze blew inland off the water, ruffling the leaves on the trees and Diana's long brown hair that hung loose beneath her tidy white cap. In no time, the four had eaten their fill of the fried halibut that Samuel had prepared, along with peppered cheese and ragged pieces of flatbread. They washed the tasty food down with Luca's spiced apple cider.

"Did you brew the ale?" Diana asked the gentleman.

"I have an Indian woman who cooks and cleans for me. In addition to putting up dozens of jugs of apple cider, she and a pair of helpers are now busy salting fish and hogs and venison, to see me and my entire crew through the winter. Winters in the New World are brutal, at best."

"Sheridan runs quite an efficient plantation."

"No more so than any other planter," Luca countered.

"I beg to differ. An advantage to working as closely as I do with planters is that I am privy to their secrets. Sheridan is quite organized, which, in my estimation, is why he is so successful."

"Speaking of success, Wingate, I wonder that you would take a day away from your own operation to fritter away on a picnic in the woods."

Samuel winked at Sallie Mae. "Some things warrant frittering away a day of work. Besides I, too, now have a helper. When I set out this morning, Jack was hard at work constructing another barrel."

"You might soon become even busier," Sheridan said. "Rumor has it a ship called the *Mayflower,* chock full of Pilgrim Separatists, is headed toward Virginia."

"The way I heard it," Samuel put in, "two ships carrying Separatists, the *Mayflower* and the *Speedwell,* are set to head this way."

When Sheridan said, "Let us hope they have a competent cooper aboard," everyone laughed.

Diana vastly enjoyed listening to the men talk. Brushing crumbs of bread from her skirt, she posed another question to Samuel. "As a cooper, do you favor a particular sort of wood for the barrels you make?"

"The wood I choose depends on what the cask will carry. White oak and hickory are best for hogsheads meant to hold liquids, such as water or ale. Wood is strong, which means the liquid will not seep through. For churns and small household buckets, like the one I made for Sallie Mae, I prefer cedar or pine. Both are soft woods and easy to shape."

"Is he not clever?" marveled Sallie Mae, which made everyone laugh.

"What sort of wood is best for hogsheads meant to carry tobacco leaves?" Diana persisted.

"I use ash for its strength. When green, it's flexible enough to bend. With tobacco harvest looming, I am obliged to build hogsheads fairly quickly now, so I expect to be using a good deal of ash."

"When we visited your workshop," Sallie Mae said, "we saw a strange-looking tool hanging on the wall."

Samuel chuckled. "I saw you girls pointing at my long-legged calipers."

"Calipers?" Sallie Mae's blue eyes were a question.

Luca explained. "Calipers are used to determine the specific width of an item that is circular in shape."

"My," Sallie Mae exclaimed, "both our gentlemen are quite clever, are they not, Diana?"

The foursome shared another laugh.

"They are also quite brave," Diana said with admiration. "You both came to this uncharted land and quickly became successful at your chosen endeavors."

"We men are no braver than you ladies," Sheridan replied. "You left family and friends behind in the hope of making a home for yourselves here in the New World. Your decision to do so must have required a great deal of courage."

As that was not particularly true in Diana's case, or in Sallie Mae's, for all that, they both merely shrugged. Sallie Mae fidgeted with a stem of greenery growing nearby.

Later that afternoon, as the foursome slowly walked back toward Jamestown, Luca asked Diana if she was finding life in the New World to her liking.

"Actually I am finding it more tolerable than I expected." She smiled up at him.

"Ah."

"My answer surprises you?"

"You seem to be a cultured young lady, Miss Wakefield. I would think perhaps the . . . ah . . . primitiveness of life here might offend your sensitivity."

"I confess I find certain aspects of life here offensive, but on the whole, I am bearing up. I daresay the woeful conditions aboard ship adequately prepared me for what lay ahead."

"At least you did not make the crossing chained down in the hold," he stated matter-of-factly.

His answer startled her. "Are you suggesting, sir, that . . . you—"

He gazed into her upturned face. "I am suggesting nothing, Miss Wakefield. I am saying that I left England in chains, that I began my sojourn to the New World as a criminal. Not to put too fine a point on it, if I had chosen to remain in England, I would have been hanged for the crime I was accused of committing."

A shudder passed through Diana. Luca Sheridan's story sounded hauntingly familiar, as much like the one she'd heard from her mother about her half-brother as to be . . . one and the same. But . . . surely, this fine gentleman could not be . . .

"Forgive me, Miss Wakefield. It appears I have offended your sensitivity."

"On the contrary, sir, although I cannot help but wonder why you felt it necessary to divulge the . . . particulars of your past to me . . . so quickly."

"Because I would rather you hear the truth from my own lips than from the wagging tongue of another. As would most assuredly happen once you reveal to almost anyone that you . . . stepped out with me." He paused. "Actually, my tale of woe is not so very unusual here. Many a colonist began his life in the New World enslaved to another."

She clung to every word.

"When I stepped off the boat, my indenture was purchased by John Rolfe, who, I expect you know, had the distinction of marrying the Indian chieftain Powhatan's favorite daughter Pocahontas. Perhaps you have heard of the beautiful Indian princess who frequently visited the Jamestown colony as a girl. Unfortunately, the lovely young woman passed away some years back whilst on a visit to England with her husband."

Diana had heard nothing of the enchanting tale. "I recall hearing Governor Yeardley speak of John Rolfe in regard to his contribution to planting tobacco."

Luca nodded. "Rolfe was indeed instrumental in bringing seeds of the sweeter-tasting tobacco that nearly all of the planters now use. When Rolfe released me from my indenture, he bestowed upon me a generous parcel of land. With the profits I realized from my first tobacco crop, I purchased additional land, and now . . . five years later, I own nearly as much land as he. I am greatly indebted to him. Rolfe is a generous man; he was quite fair with me."

"You are very industrious, Mr. Sheridan."

"Thank you, Miss Wakefield."

They reached the end of the rolling road and entering Jamestown, they headed back toward the Larsen home. Somewhere along the way, Samuel and Sallie Mae fell behind, so Diana and Luca Sheridan reached the Larsen doorstep ahead of their companions.

"I would be honored if you would agree to see me again, Miss Wakefield, although I'll not press for an answer today. I hope my past will not influence you unfavorably."

Diana longed to ask what sort of crime the man had been accused of committing, and whether or not he was actually guilty, but she refrained. To ask Mister Sheridan to divulge every detail of his past would oblige her to do the same. And for the nonce, she did not wish to tell him, or anyone, how she came to be in Jamestown or why she had abandoned her true surname. If by some happenstance, Luca Sheridan proved to be her kinsman . . . well, she did not wish to bring that unsavory business into the open either. "I appreciate your candidness, Mister Sheridan."

"I would consider it an honor if you would address me as Luca."

She smiled. "Very well, then; you may call me Diana."

"Thank you, Diana. Please understand that for the most part I have put the memory of the intolerable conditions I endured, both here and abroad, behind me. I choose now to live each day as it comes. I feel both humbled and grateful to God for the opportunities He has provided me. To be sure, it was He who showed me how to turn adversity to good advantage."

Diana smiled up into eyes that, despite his brave words, still betrayed signs of the hardships he'd borne. "You are a remarkable man, Luca Sheridan."

"Thank you for a lovely afternoon, Diana. I hope to see you again one day."

She bade the tall gentleman farewell and let herself into the house, knowing that Sallie Mae would soon follow. The hours spent with Luca Sheridan this afternoon had proven far more interesting than she could have imagined and served to push aside for a moment her gnawing fears for Sallie Mae and her persistent fear of the forest.

"Luca Sheridan is a fine-looking man," Mary Larsen said when she caught sight of Diana crossing the common room.

"He is that," Diana agreed, not pausing to elaborate on the pleasurable time spent with her friends. Although Luca Sheridan's story sounded similar to the one regarding her half-brother, his elegant manner of speaking and strong belief in God had convinced her that he could not possibly be her kinsman. She clearly recalled her mother referring to her wayward son as an untamed ruffian and a sad disappointment to both his parents and kin. Luca Sheridan's revelations of his sordid past made Diana believe that nearly everyone in the New World harbored some sort of secret.

She had only just entered her bedchamber when Sallie Mae

burst into the room, tears of joy streaming down her flushed cheeks.

"Samuel asked me to marry him!"

Chapter 24

Diana rushed to embrace her friend. "Samuel is a wonderful man, and he clearly adores you."

Sallie Mae brushed aside joyful tears. "I knew I loved him the minute I saw him. He said he felt the same about me."

"Have you decided when to exchange your vows?"

Sallie Mae grinned from ear to ear. "He gave me a choice. He said we could be married at once, or we could wait until tobacco season has passed, which he says is sometime in November. He says planters' work tapers off then; that they turn to mendin' fences or choppin' wood or other odd jobs 'round the plantation."

"Which did you choose?"

"Now!" Sallie Mae cried. "I canna' wait a minute longer to become Goodwife Wingate!"

"I see." Diana's thoughts became a tangle. Should Sallie Mae divulge to Samuel the threats that had plagued her since her arrival in Jamestown? Once wed, would the problem grow to include Samuel, or would the guilty party leave off badgering her altogether? That Sallie Mae had said nothing thus far about what she saw on the ship should serve to put the criminal's mind at ease. Or would the man not give up till she was dead? "I am happy for you, Sallie Mae, but it saddens me that we shall no longer have our days to ourselves. We shall no longer be able to ride about Jamestown on Bug-a-Boo, or sit beneath a tree in the orchard, or pick apples. You will have a husband to care for and a home to look after. You will have to cook and clean and . . . make soap."

"I will miss our time together as well, Diana. I've never had such a jolly time in all me life as I've had here with you. But, every day that I spend toiling to make my home with Samuel comfortable, I will be a'doin' it because I love him."

A smile wavered across Diana's face. "Forgive me. I am being selfish . . . and, truth to say, I cannot help but still feel fearful for your safety. Do promise me you will continue to be watchful. I shouldn't wish any harm to befall you or Samuel."

"Samuel will protect me from anyone who wishes me ill." Sallie Mae began to dance about the room. "My dream has come true! I am to become Goodwife Wingate!"

On the very eve of the day that Sallie Mae and Samuel were to repeat their vows, Noah Colton returned from a lengthy expedition and paid a call at the Larsen home. Unaware of what had transpired in his absence, he extended both hands to greet Sallie Mae when Mary Larsen summoned her to the common room.

"Ye look prettier every time I see you, my pet," he declared in his customary winsome way.

"I've something to tell ye, Noah."

"I am home for a spell now. We shall have plenty of time to talk." He turned to Mary, who wore a furrow of concern on her brow. "We shan't be gone long, ma'am."

Though Sallie Mae had no intention of walking with Noah tonight, she did step outside the house so they might speak privately. Once the door closed behind them, Sallie Mae said, "Noah, I canna' walk with ye tonight, or any night, for all that. Whilst ye were away, I met another man and I have agreed to become his wife."

Shock and anger turned Noah's face beet red. "How dare ye

make me look the fool?"

"Noah, please calm yerself."

"Calm myself? You pledge yer love to another man and ye expect me to accept the news as if ye're telling me it's a lovely night? Are ye daft, girl?"

Sallie Mae's tone was gentle. "I have fallen in love with him, Noah, and we are to be married. Our banns were posted a fortnight ago."

The veins in Noah's neck resembled taut hemp. "I meant to make ye *my* wife, Sallie Mae." His eyes became narrow slits. "You are a stupid lass. Make no mistake, you will regret betraying me!" With that, he turned and stalked away.

Her chin atremble, Sallie Mae rushed to her bedchamber where Diana awaited. "Noah called me a stupid lass."

Diana looked aghast. "I feared he would be angry, but to berate you is unconscionable."

"He said I would regret betrayin' him."

Diana's eyes widened. "He *threatened* you, Sallie Mae?"

The overset girl nodded.

Diana sprang to her feet. "There is no mistaking Noah's intentions now. He means to harm you. To declare aloud that you will regret betraying him is not a veiled threat. We have no choice now but to go to the governor, or at the very least, Mister Larsen."

Sallie Mae wrung her hands. "Please, Diana, not tonight. Tomorrow's me weddin' day, I don't wish to spoil it."

"But this is an outrage! Do you not see, you have thwarted Noah's every plan? You survived the toss into the river. Now you refuse to fall in with his plan to marry you. Had you agreed, I am convinced you would have soon turned up dead, the same as his other two wives." She began to pace. "I believe he meant to take you into the woods alone that day and either let the Indians abduct you, or help them kill you. I said nothing later because I did not wish to alarm you. He brought along a hatchet, Sallie Mae. Perhaps he meant to deliberately anger the Indians, then in defeat, hand you over. Instead, *I* was there, so he merely gave them the hatchet."

Sallie Mae's hand flew to her mouth. "I hadn't a clue he meant to kill me that day," she murmured.

"His sudden anger tonight caused him to grow careless. He delivered the threat to your face."

Sallie Mae's chin trembled. "Please, say nothing, Diana. Perhaps he is simply angry that I spurned him. He ain't done nothin' since I come to live here except draw a skull in the sand. He'll not harm me tonight. And, once I've wed Samuel, he'll protect me."

Diana continued to pace. "Why cannot anyone in Jamestown save myself see Noah Colton for the scoundrel he is?"

Early the next morning, Sallie Mae put on her new violet gown with the slashed sleeves and tried to sit calmly whilst Diana brushed her golden curls.

"Do ye mean also to wear your purple gown today?"

Standing behind Sallie Mae, Diana shook her head. "I've decided to save it for my own wedding day."

"Have ye decided which of yer suitors ye'll marry? John or Luca?" Sallie Mae grinned at her friend in the looking glass.

In the previous fortnight, John had called several times, and since the picnic, Diana had also seen Luca. That he lived in Henricus meant he did not often get to Jamestown, most especially now that tobacco harvest was in full swing.

"To say truth—" Diana sighed. "Neither of them sets my heart aflutter. Perhaps I have not yet met the man I am to marry."

"To be sure, ye will soon. There are so many unmarried men in Jamestown and more to come, Samuel says. Two girls who made the crossing with us are also to be wed today."

"Hannah Summerville is very pretty, and Debra Greene has a sweet disposition."

"It is difficult to fathom that we have been in Jamestown a full half year. I am glad we both found our way to the Bride Ship that day in London."

Diana nodded. "Had I not looked into Sara's traveling bag, I would never have found her Letter of Acceptance from the Virginia Company. It was a stroke of luck that I happened to be so near the dock when I found it. Otherwise, I am persuaded I would have never made it on board ship in time."

Sallie Mae grinned shyly. "I'm a'wearin' me new petticoat, the one ye gave me on the ship. Perhaps I should also wear my lambskin gloves, this being such a formal occasion and all."

Diana smiled. "Lambskin gloves or no, Sallie Mae, you make a lovely bride."

In minutes, both girls heard the knock at the door and knew it was Samuel, come to walk with the Larsen family to services that morning.

Her cheeks rosy, Sallie Mae beamed. "Samuel's come. Before too very long, I shall no longer be Sallie Mae Brown. I shall be Goodwife Wingate."

When the girls advanced into the common room, they found Samuel speaking in an agitated tone with Mister Larsen. It was Larsen who turned and said, "During the night, Wingate's workshop burned to the ground."

Chapter 25

"Oh!" Sallie Mae cried. "Are ye hurt, Samuel? Are we still to marry today or must we—"

He clasped her hands. "We shall still be wed today, love." He pulled her to him in a quick embrace.

"I am so sorry for your loss, Samuel," Diana said. "Do you know how the blaze . . . began?"

"Wingate's helper Jack was asleep in the workshop," Larsen said. "Young man said he saw two Indians running from the clearing. I was just telling Samuel we never know what sets the Indians off. Perhaps he and Jack unknowingly cut down a tree on a parcel of land the Indians consider sacred. One never knows."

"Was Jack hurt?" Sallie Mae asked.

"Not at all. And he managed to save a good many hogsheads we'd just completed." Grinning, Samuel turned to Larsen. "Jack grabbed m'long-handled ax and chopped a hole in the wall big enough to push the barrels clean outta' the building. When I spotted the blaze and come runnin' down the hill, first thing I saw was barrels rollin' in all directions. Not a one of 'em even scorched."

Larsen and the girls laughed, as did Mary, who had just joined them with little Edward in tow. Baby Ellen would, of course, be left behind in Cheiwoga's care that morning. "I am glad you managed to save a good many hogsheads, Samuel, but it is still a frightful shame," she said.

"You are fortunate to have other buildings on your land," Diana remarked.

"Indeed." Samuel nodded. "Fact is, I was planning to move the workshop into another of my outbuildings. Already outgrowed the smaller one."

"Did all yer tools burn up?" Sallie Mae cried. "What of yer long-legged calipers?" Her genuine concern over the special tool provided everyone another laugh.

"I have another pair of calipers up at the house, love. And m'other tools will be easy to replace. The mishap will merely cause a delay in filling some of m'orders. Jack and I will be obliged to work twice as long and hard."

"Depend upon it, Wingate, the planters will understand. Yours is not the first structure in Jamestown the Indians have set fire to."

"More's the pity," Mary murmured.

Samuel turned a gaze on his bride-to-be. "Ye look prettier than ever I've seen ye, Sallie Mae. I expect it is time we set out for the meetinghouse."

Walking toward the fort, they soon met dozens of other worshipers also headed to the meetinghouse that crisp October morn. Once there, the minister delivered his sermon before he summoned the three couples who were to be wed that day to the altar.

Diana gazed about the congregation in search of Noah Colton. Regardless of what Mister Larsen or Samuel Wingate said regarding the Indians, she firmly believed that Noah Colton was responsible for the cooper's fire and nothing could sway her from that belief.

Following the wedding ceremonies, the colonists gathered on the greensward, where a huge feast had been laid out to mark the occasion. Once everyone had filled a trencher with food—venison, beefsteak, fish and pork; squash, corn, peppers and greens; fruit pies and pumpkin tarts—Diana was pleased when Faith Plumleigh came to stand beside her.

"Sallie Mae made a lovely bride," Faith began in a congenial tone.

"Indeed, she did," Diana returned, "and you look lovely today in your blue worsted."

"Why are you not wearing your new frock?"

"I have decided to save it for my own wedding day."

"Ah, so you have settled on a suitor then."

Diana shook her head. "Not as yet." She hoped Faith did not begin to speak of Noah for she feared she could not refrain from making a disparaging remark about the man.

Faith cast a bemused gaze in the direction of Samuel and Sallie Mae, who were happily receiving good wishes from the colonists clustered around them. "Sallie Mae did very well for herself. I understand Samuel Wingate has a fine house. One of only two in the colony made of brick."

"I take it you have not learned of Samuel's misfortune?"

Faith's auburn head jerked around, her green eyes questioning. "What has happened?"

"Samuel's workshop burned to the ground last night." Diana paused. "It happened soon after Noah called on Sallie Mae and learned that she and Samuel were to be wed today."

Faith's surprised look turned to one of outrage. "You are not suggesting that—"

"I am suggesting nothing. I am merely telling you what transpired . . . and when."

Faith glanced about. "I wonder why Noah is not here today."

Her chin at a tilt, Diana said. "I am wondering the selfsame thing."

About sundown that evening, Faith decided to pay a call upon her former beau. Having learned from Diana some weeks ago where in Jamestown Noah's snug little wattle-and-daub home was located, she had taken several solitary walks and nearly always found herself standing on the dusty road in front of Noah's house imagining herself living there with him as his wife. One evening, she had ventured close to the house and begun to pull the weeds that filled the window box. She noted now that weeds were again overtaking the box. If she lived in the house, it would always be full of flowers with nary a weed in sight.

When she reached his home this evening, she was pleased to see a curl of smoke rising from the chimney. A faint light flickered in the lone window. Inhaling a deep breath of courage, she boldly walked up the path and rapped at the door.

"Who's there?" came a gruff voice from within.

"It is I, Faith. Please let me in, Noah."

In a moment the door swung open, creaking as it did so on rusty hinges. At the sight of her, Noah scowled. "What do ye want?"

Faith's green eyes drank in the sight of her beloved. It took all the restraint she could muster not to fling herself into his arms.

"Why are you here, Faith?" he growled again.

"Might I come inside, please?"

Although she noted his jaws grinding together, he edged backward a step. "Suit yerself."

Drawing in a deep breath of courage, Faith stepped into the dimly lit room. To her right a pine-knot candle flickered on the planked wooden table that sat beneath the window fronting the house. A low fire burned in the hearth. Before it sat a pair of ladder-backed chairs. Noah walked toward the one where he had been seated. Though he did not invite her to join him, Faith followed suit and settled herself in the second chair. When she again looked full at him, his face now illuminated by the bright firelight, she saw an ugly red mark that ran all the way down the side of his face.

"Noah, you are injured!" She leaned forward, one hand reaching to stroke the angry red streak.

He grasped her wrist to prevent her from touching him. " 'Tis nothing. A wayward spark from the fire."

"A mere spark could not cause such an injury. You have clearly been burned."

"I said it was nothing." He scowled. "The fire here is always out when I return home. Was too dark last night to properly see what I was about."

"If you had a wife waiting for you when you return home, the fire would never go out."

He rose and angrily snatched up the poker that leaned against the hearth. "Why are ye here, Faith?" He stabbed at the red-hot embers.

She ignored his question. "Have you had your supper tonight? If you had a wife, you'd be enjoying a hot meal about now, along with that ale you've been drinking." She gestured toward the empty jug that lay overturned at his feet. "I could prepare something for you now, if you like," she offered sweetly.

He scowled. "What I'd like is for you to leave. I am in no frame to listen to your silly notions of marital bliss."

"You professed to love me once, Noah. I do not believe your feelings have altered on that head. I also do not believe a wayward spark from the fire burned your face." Her tone was firm though not accusing. "What I believe is that you deliberately set fire to Samuel Wingate's workshop last night and a spark from that blaze burned your cheek, which is why you chose not to show your injured face at services this morning."

His eyes narrowed.

When he offered nothing by way of explanation or defense, she hurried on. "That and the fact that you did not wish to see

Sallie Mae Brown pledge her troth to Samuel Wingate."

His eyes cut 'round. "So, they exchanged their vows after all?"

"So, you *did* set fire to the cooper's workshop." She folded her arms across her chest. "Perhaps it would interest you to know that the governor intends to investigate the mishap."

"Then I shall tell them I know nothing, that Indians set that fire, the same as they've set countless others in Jamestown."

"But this time you were on hand to help them, am I not correct?"

He jabbed at the orange flames with the poker. "That I was on Wingate's land last night cannot be proven."

"The mark on your face is sufficient proof!"

When his lips thinned, Faith studied the handsome man. Despite the ugly burn mark, his features still looked inordinately handsome. It irked her to realize how deeply he cared for Sallie Mae . . . especially when she was far and away the finer choice. "She is a simple wench with nothing to recommend her, Noah."

"And you are a common trollop with even less to recommend you!"

His angry words stung. She worked to push down unbidden tears that sprang to her eyes. "I am not a trollop, Noah." Her voice quaked with emotion. "I-I gave myself to you because I . . . I loved you. I still love you."

He shrugged as he continued to absently poke at the fire. "Your love means nothing to me."

Faith's chin trembled. "You know very well that I came to you pure and unsullied." She rose to her feet and reached for him, her green eyes pleading. "You recall how we laid together in the moonlight, caressing one another. It can be that way again, Noah."

With one hand, he flung down the poker and with the other shoved Faith aside.

"Noah, please. You need a woman to come home to, a woman to keep the fire going and to cook and clean for you."

"I need no one, least of all you." He spun toward her again. "You remind me of another red-haired wench I . . . also didn't need."

"I have been told I resemble your second wife," she said quietly. "I am certain she loved you as much as I do."

"What would you know?" He snorted. "I am well rid of that one, and now it's time for you to go." He kicked over the chair where she'd been sitting. "Go! Leave me be!"

Faith stood her ground. Inhaling a ragged breath, she gazed defiantly up at the man she loved. At length, she said, "As I said, Noah, the governor means to investigate the Wingate fire. Once they see the burn on your face—"

He made a lunge for her and grasping both arms backed her against the fireplace wall. "How do you know what the council is planning to do?"

"Noah, you are hurting me."

Without a word, he flung her from him.

Regaining her balance, Faith stood rubbing the place on her arm where his hands had tightly grasped her. "The men spoke of it after services this morning. And just now," she lied, "I walked part of the way here with Councilman Evans. He was on his way to Governor Yeardley's home. I expect the men are even now discussing the matter."

When he said nothing, Faith realized she was making headway. Smiling to herself, she cast a pointed gaze toward the door of the house. "Wouldn't surprise me if they came bursting in here any moment."

His eyes became mere slits in his face. "Why would they suspect *me* of setting the fire?"

Faith's tone hardened. "Has it slipped your mind that Sallie Mae has been living at Councilman Larsen's home? Diana told me this morning that you called on Sallie Mae last evening, which is when she told you she intended to marry Samuel Wingate. That you grew angry and took revenge by burning down his workshop would not be a stretch. And you must agree that the fresh burn on your face is rather the nail in the coffin." She edged closer to him.

A guttural sound escaped his throat. "What do you want, Faith?"

She met his icy stare. "It appears to me that you need someone to vouch for your whereabouts of last evening. And what *I* want . . . is for the babe in my belly, *your* babe, to have a proper name."

A slow grin split his face. "Well, it appears I have vastly misjudged you." He reached to set upright the chair he'd earlier overturned. "You and I appear to be cut from the same cloth. I admire a wench who would lie to protect her man. Do sit down, my clever little trollop."

Later that evening, Faith persuaded Noah to escort her home. "If people see us together tonight," she reasoned, "they will likely believe that you and I were together last evening; that you returned to my arms mere seconds after Sallie Mae spurned you."

He grinned slyly. "Indeed, I have misjudged you. I daresay it will be a pleasure to be wed to a clever woman."

"So"—she cocked her head to one side—"we are to be wed, then?"

He nodded slowly. "However, little Miss Trollop, once we are married, do not expect me to remain true to my vows. I am not a man who can remain leg-shackled to any one woman, babe or no."

Faith did not care. She had won the man she wanted, the most handsome and charming man in Jamestown, the man every other girl in the colony thought they wanted. Following a quick visit with Reverend Martin the following morning, Faith and Noah's banns were duly published on the meetinghouse door, ironically on the same nail where Sallie Mae and Samuel's notice had hung the day before.

Diana thought it odd that no questions were asked of the colonists in regard to the Wingate fire. Were she and Sallie Mae the only ones who suspected Noah Colton was guilty of the crime? She was glad when Mister Larsen broached the matter one evening later in the week when he announced that the governor declared the following Sunday Muster Day.

"The council believes the colony has fallen lax in maintaining our militia," he said over supper. "Governor Yeardley proclaimed that henceforth, one Sunday afternoon per month shall be designated for drill practice."

"I think it is quite a good idea to reinstate Muster Day, William," Mary agreed.

"Can I come?" young Edward piped up. "I've a musket!"

"Your musket is only a toy, sweetheart," the child's mother said. "Now eat your cabbage."

"Of course you can come, Edward."

"William!"

"He will be a man soon."

"Sir," Diana began, "am I correct in assuming that drill practices are being resumed as a result of the cooper's fire of last week's end?"

"You are indeed correct in that assumption, Diana."

"But, sir, I cannot help but wonder why they did not question Noah Colton about the fire. He was overset with Samuel for courting Sallie Mae. I am persuaded that whatever excuse Noah might put forth regarding his whereabouts that night would prove wobbly, at best."

Larsen blinked. "You are leveling a serious charge against an upstanding member of the colony, Diana. I realize you are not well disposed toward Colton, but unfortunately, being a woman, your opinion is of . . . ahem, no account. Governor Yeardley and the council members have drawn the unanimous conclusion that since Wingate's boy saw an Indian, or Indians, flee the scene that they are the responsible parties. Given that, the council further agrees that we must be ready to wage war on the savages at a moment's notice. A hue and cry on Saturday evening last would have summoned a virtual army to aid in the pursuit of the culprits, as well as aid Wingate in extinguishing the fire. But that did not happen. This unfortunate incident is serving to unite the community in a common cause. Every man will be required to bring his musket, or some sort of weapon, to services this coming Sabbath."

Diana said nothing further. But when she called upon Faith the following afternoon, she was stunned by the news her friend imparted.

CHAPTER 26

"You are to wed Noah Colton?" Diana exclaimed.

"I am, indeed." Faith preened before the looking glass in her bedchamber. "He asked me on Sunday evening last." After a pause, she added, "We were together the evening before, as well."

Diana looked skeptical. "He called on Sallie Mae the previous evening. The night the cooper's workshop burned to the ground. You did not mention on Sunday morning that you had been with Noah the night before."

"Did I not?" She shrugged. "It must have slipped my mind. I declare, since Noah resumed calling on me, I have lost all track of time. At any rate, we are to be married and I could not be happier. We have already met with Reverend Martin and our banns are posted."

"I see." Diana drew in a breath. "Well, I wish you and Noah . . . every happiness." She paused, then said, "I wanted to ask if you would like to ride into the woods with me today and . . . gather nuts." She smiled, a trifle shakily. "I have decided it is time to conquer my fear of the forest . . . lest fear become my master."

Faith looked amused. "Sounds as if someone has been filling your head with nonsense."

"It is a known fact that I harbor trepidation about the forest."

Faith pinched her cheeks till they were pink. "Well, you must conquer your fear alone today, Diana, for I have no interest in trekking through the woods. Not today, or any day, for that matter. If Noah should call, I intend to be right here waiting for him."

"Since Noah is a trapper," Diana persisted, "do you not think it possible that he might wish you to accompany him into the woods one day to see if any animals have fallen prey to his traps perchance?"

"I will accompany Noah anywhere," Faith replied. "I did not say I feared the woods."

"I do not fear the woods either," Diana declared a bit irritably. She bade her friend "Good day," and departed.

Atop Bug-a-Boo, Diana fought back tears of loneliness. She'd felt at loose ends all week with Sallie Mae gone, but she did not wish to intrude on her friend so soon after she was wed. No matter how much Sallie Mae loved Samuel, to settle into a new routine as a married woman would no doubt prove trying at best. Which is why she decided to ask Faith if she'd like to accompany her into the woods to gather nuts.

It was a beautiful day for late October. Mary Larsen had declared it Indian Summer, which Diana hoped did not mean that Indians would be out and about. Winter was fast looming, and many days this month had already felt downright cold. Today, however, the sky was a brilliant blue and the air felt warm, even balmy. Most of the trees sported bright red and gold leaves, which made Jamestown seem especially pretty.

Determined not to let fear rule her today, Diana headed Bug-a-Boo straight for the old rolling road where she and Luca and Samuel and Sallie Mae had entered the forest the day they picnicked. Sallie Mae had pointed out a pecan grove not far into the forest, to the right of the rolling road.

That she found the pecan grove with ease pleased Diana and served to bolster her confidence. From the perimeter of the clearing she could still see the rolling road. Feeling quite proud of herself, she hopped to the ground and draped Bug-a-Boo's reins over a low bush—for ease in snatching them up quickly, if need be. Carrying one of the two baskets she'd brought with her, she began to shuffle through the fallen leaves in search of the small brown nuts. At the outset, she glanced back every few minutes toward where the chestnut mare stood. Once, upon hearing a twig snap, her head jerked up, and with no hesitation whatever, she bolted back toward Bug-a-Boo. But, hearing nothing further, and spying nothing untoward, she again moved tentatively into the grove.

At length, the tight knot of fear in her stomach began to lessen. She fell into a pattern of nudging leaves aside with the toe of her boot and reaching down to gather the exposed nuts. Growing less anxious as she proceeded in that fashion, her mind turned to ruminating upon other things—Faith and her sudden decision to marry Noah; and Sallie Mae, who she hoped was getting on well this first week of her married life.

When the basket she carried was completely full, she turned back toward Bug-a-Boo to retrieve the second one. But, after walking several feet and not spotting Bug-a-Boo, or the rolling road, her heart began to pound. Suddenly, every direction she turned looked exactly the same. In an attempt to gauge where in the sky the sun was, she gazed up, up, up through the colorful leaves, but all she could clearly see were tiny patches of blue peeking here and there in the treetops. The whisper of wind rustling the leaves and a squirrel or two scolding her were the only sounds she heard.

"Bug-a-Boo!" she called. "Where are you?" Whirling another direction, she called, *"Bug-a-Boo!"*

Because the mare did know her name, Diana fully expected to hear a soft neigh in response to her call. When she did not, wave after wave of panic surged through her.

"Bug-a-Boo! *Bug-a-Boo!*" she called louder. "Where are you?"

Fingers of cold, stark terror clutched Diana.

Flinging her basket of nuts to the ground, she raced through the dry leaves in the direction she thought the rolling road lay. Perhaps Bug-a-Boo had pulled loose her tether and wandered down the road.

But . . . after running a few yards, Diana came to a standstill. Where was the road? Dear God in Heaven! Her worst nightmare had come true. She was hopelessly lost in the woods!

"Help!" she screamed. "Help me, please!"

When choking sobs overcame her, she sank to the ground, scalding hot tears blinding her eyes. Suddenly, a shuffling sound coming from nearby startled her. "Bug-a-Boo?"

She sprang to her feet, but when she spotted what was coming toward her she very nearly fainted dead away.

Indians!

Racing for the nearest tree, Diana ran behind it and flattened her body against the back side, her breath coming in fits and starts. What should she do now? What could she do? At length, she did the only thing she could do.

Pray.

Dear God, help me; please, help me!

As the crunching footfalls in the leaves drew nearer and nearer, Diana began to recant Bible verses.

"I will lift up mine eyes unto the hills from whence cometh my help. My help cometh from the Lord, which made heaven and earth. The Lord shall preserve thee from all evil. Thou shall not be afraid for the terror by night . . . nor for the arrow that flieth by day . . ."

Arrows! Oh, dear God. Indians!

When the crunch of footfalls failed to cease, Diana spun around and shakily peered from her hiding place. She had not noticed before but . . . now she noticed that the Indian moving toward her was . . . not a tall . . . menacing-looking savage. This Indian was no bigger than she and . . . it was female.

"Go away!" Diana stuck one hand out and made a shooing motion. "Go along with you!"

The Indian kept coming. As the tawny-skinned girl drew nearer, Diana could clearly see that she was not carrying a weapon; nor did it appear that she had companions. The teensiest bit of Diana's fear abated. Perhaps she could manage to stave off . . . one . . . small . . . girl.

Suddenly, the Indian girl spoke. "Hello."

Diana's eyes widened. Still, she shrank back with alarm, then cautiously peeked out again. The girl was close enough now that Diana noted the impish grin on her face. "H-hel-lo?" The quake in Diana's voice turned the word into a question.

The Indian girl halted a few feet from where Diana stood still cowering behind the tree. "My name Lanneika. You name what?"

Diana's brow furrowed. How singularly odd! This young Indian girl spoke English!

"No me fear." The young girl's black eyes twinkled merrily. "I *netab.* That mean friend." The girl pressed a balled-up fist to her chest the way Diana had seen Noah do the day they met the Indian braves in the forest. "Me friend."

Suddenly, the sound of another female voice rang in the clearing. "Lanneika, where are you?"

An Englishwoman was here? Dear God in Heaven, thank you, thank you, thank you! Her hazel eyes round, Diana took a few steps from behind the tree trunk. Coming toward her now was a tall, elegant woman with long auburn hair hanging loose to her waist. Though she had the look of an Englishwoman, she was dressed in the same fashion as the petite Indian girl: a deerskin garment with fringe at the hem that fluttered softly about her bare legs as she walked. The only difference in the two women's clothing was that the bodice of the fair-skinned woman's dress was decorated with brightly colored beads. When the woman spotted Diana peering from behind the tree, she smiled warmly.

"Do not be frightened; neither Lanneika nor I mean any harm. My name is Catherine."

Diana relaxed the white-knuckled grip she had on the tree truck. "A-are you real?"

The English woman laughed. "As real as you are. Lanneika and I are both real."

"I-I once saw an Indian riding a huge white horse in the woods. Mistress Larsen said the forest was playing tricks on me, that the Indian was not real."

Again the English woman smiled. "My name is Catherine. What is your name?"

"D-Diana Wakefield. I came to the New World on the Bride Ship. Although I-I have not yet"—she swallowed the sudden lump of sadness that rose in her throat—"found a man I wish to marry. I . . . I fear I am hopelessly lost."

The pretty young woman's emerald-green gaze softened. "I will help you find your way back to Jamestown."

"I cannot find my horse."

"Lanneika, go and fetch the mare we saw by the stream."

"You found Bug-a-Boo?" Diana watched the Indian girl scamper from the clearing, her shiny black hair fluttering as she ran.

"Your horse wandered to the stream where Lanneika and I were gathering fish."

"G-gathering fish?"

"There is a stream near here where it is possible to simply put one's hand into the water and snatch them up. I will show you, if you like."

"No, thank you." Diana shook her head. "I came to gather nuts."

"Perhaps another time, then."

Lanneika soon returned to the clearing riding the chestnut mare. As Diana rushed to nuzzle her horse, the Indian girl slipped off its back. Diana gathered up the reins and took a step in the direction she thought the rolling road lay.

Catherine shook her head. "The colony is much closer this way." A finger pointed the opposite direction.

The three women set out walking, Bug-a-Boo trailing behind them, Diana keeping a tight grip on the mare's reins.

"I must have wandered farther afield than I thought."

"That is quite easy to do in the woods."

They walked a few paces in silence before Diana asked. "Do forgive me for being forward, but how did you . . . I mean . . . it seems most unusual to find an Englishwoman . . . do forgive me. I do not mean to pry."

Catherine smiled serenely. "I realize it must seem strange to discover a white woman in the woods, and one dressed in such an odd fashion and with an Indian girl as a companion."

Diana nodded. "I expect Mistress Larsen will insist the forest has played another trick upon me."

The sound of Catherine's gentle laughter did a great deal toward putting Diana's mind at ease. "The forest does not play tricks. The Indian you saw on the white horse that day is my husband. His name is Phyrahawque. He is the *werowance* of our tribe. Lanneika is his sister. Phyrahawque and I have two children together; a handsome little boy who will soon be two winters, and a fortnight ago, I gave birth to an adorable baby girl. Who has hair the color of mine," she added proudly.

Enchanted, Diana listened to the beautiful young woman's tale. Her voice sounded as soothing as gentle rain on summer leaves. She was so very lovely, Diana could not stop looking at her. "Your children must be very beautiful," she breathed.

"They are." Tears welled up in Catherine's shining eyes. "I

am far happier with Phyrahawque than I ever thought I could be."

"So, you do not regret your decision to live amongst the Indians?"

When Catherine shook her head, her long auburn hair swayed. "I can see where that might seem odd to you, but I have never once regretted my decision to wed an Indian brave."

"I am very happy for you." Diana smiled. "And I am very happy that you found me. I confess I was quite frightened."

"I have seen you in the woods before, you and the pretty little blond with the dancing blue eyes, the one who just wed the new cooper."

Before she could stop the words from flying from her mouth, Diana blurted out, "Did Indians set fire to the cooper's workshop?"

Catherine appeared shocked. "No, indeed. That fire was set by one of your own."

"I knew it!"

Suddenly, as if Catherine and Lanneika were responding to a signal Diana could not hear, both women stopped dead still.

"I will go no further," Catherine said solemnly.

A fresh surge of fear shot through Diana. "But where—?"

"Just there." Catherine pointed through a thick stand of tall trees. "You will soon come upon a cleared field, now lying fallow, and a small house beyond." Her tone hardened. "It is the house where I lived when I was married to a white man."

Diana knew exactly where she was now. Not on the rolling road, but farther inland. At this juncture, she would emerge from the forest only a few paces from Noah Colton's house. "You are referring to the house where the trader lives?"

A shadow fell across the lovely woman's face and the light in her eyes dimmed. Lanneika's gaze also grew shuttered. "I was once married to the trader man," Catherine said quietly.

Diana's eyes widened. "But, I thought his wife . . . I thought you were dead."

"That woman *is* dead." Catherine's chin shot up, and the fire returned to her eyes. "I am a new woman. I am now an Indian. I am very pleased to have met you, Diana. Thank you for walking with me. After I left Jamestown, there were only two white women who would deign to address me. One was the dear friend who made the crossing with me from England." A touch of wistfulness crept into her tone. "Nancy's husband purchased land a good distance from here, and now I seldom see her. The other one, my brother's wife, perished many moons ago from the sickness."

"I am so sorry," Diana murmured. "There has been a great deal of sickness in the colony."

"Many Indians have also perished. Thank you for your kindness, Diana." With that, the beautiful young woman turned to go, but before she and Lanneika walked away, she turned again toward Diana. "You must warn your red-haired friend that despite his charm and swagger, Noah Colton is not a man to be trusted. He will surely harm her." She paused. "And your gentleman caller, John Fuller, is a good man. He is quite trustworthy. In time of trouble, you can always turn to John. I hope you do not think I am speaking out of turn."

"Not at all," Diana murmured, again amazed over all that the young woman knew regarding the colony's doings.

She watched both women disappear into the deepest part of the woods. Scrambling upon Bug-a-Boo's back, she shook her head as if to clear it. No one would believe the adventure she'd had today. With a nudge of her heel, she urged Bug-a-Boo forward. The only good thing that had come from her outing was that she had, indeed, managed to put aside a good deal of her fear of the forest.

It was not until she reached home that she realized she hadn't properly thanked the beautiful English woman for her help, and that she was arriving home without her basket full of nuts. Actually she was arriving home without the basket. The other one was still dangling from Bug-a-Boo's harness. Empty.

The following morning when she went out to tend Bug-a-Boo, she was astonished to find the basket she'd dropped in the forest sitting just inside the shed door, chock full of plump round nuts.

Chapter 27

At week's end, on the Sabbath designated Muster Day, the sky dawned dark and cloudy and a blustery wind blew. The cold cast a pall over the colonists, who had hoped the temperature would be tolerable and the colony-wide event would provide them with a pleasant diversion before winter set in and every day dawned gray and cold.

Pulling their long cloaks tighter about their bodies following services, Diana and Faith ducked their heads against the icy wind as they headed, along with scores of other women, toward the far corner of the fort where the men were already assembled. Beneath the parapet where one of the colony's iron cannons maintained a constant vigil over the fort, the colonist designated Captain of the Militia barked orders.

"March! Left, right! Lunge . . . fire!"

The men, most carrying muskets, pistols, or fowling pieces, swung their weapons into position but did not fire, as that would waste precious ammunition. Still, a cheer of approval arose from the crowd of onlookers before the men were ordered to return their weapons to an upright position and commence again to march.

Diana had hoped to have a private word with Faith today. Though she did not wish to divulge that Noah's former wife was still alive and living in the woods, a fact that had immensely surprised her, she did feel compelled to deliver Catherine's dire warning to her friend. She also realized that if Faith did marry

Noah, she'd have no choice but to widen her ongoing concern for Sallie Mae to include Faith. Standing a bit apart from the clusters of other women huddled together against the cold, Diana hastened to tell Faith a bit about what transpired that day in the woods, although she left out a good many details and altered a good many more.

"You met an Indian woman in the woods who told you that I must not marry Noah because he would harm me?" Faith repeated incredulously.

"Yes. The woman said that despite his charm and swagger, Noah was not a man to be trusted and that he would surely harm you."

Faith's eyes rolled skyward. "Noah will do nothing of the sort! He loves me. You . . . and the old Indian woman . . . clearly have windmills in your head."

"The woman was . . . not old." Diana paused. "Do promise me you will be watchful of him, Faith."

Faith's lips thinned. "Noah and I intend to pledge our troth on Sunday next." She paused and in a gentler tone added, "Prudence is my guardian angel now, and she is very happy for me."

"You . . . speak to your sister?" It was the first mention in a long while of the sister who'd lost her life during the terrible storm on-board ship.

"Prudence understands more than anyone how very much Noah and I love one another."

Diana listened intently. She had often wished she could hear her mother's voice, or Sara's. She missed her loved ones terribly and knew she always would. Before Faith said anything further, Sallie Mae, also bundled up in a long woolen cloak, joined them.

"Shall we move a bit closer to the column? Samuel says there is no danger. The men will not fire their weapons as it would be a waste."

"In my estimation," Faith muttered, "the entire exercise is a waste." She cast a look of disdain at the marching men.

"Ye may be right," Sallie Mae agreed. "There are so few men present today. Apparently a good many were unable to attend due to the dreadful illness that's struck the colony."

"Mary Larsen fears her baby may be ill," Diana said. "She considered staying home today but feared her husband would not properly look after little Edward, who refused to miss the muster."

Sallie Mae laughed. "Did he bring his toy musket?"

"Indeed." Diana grinned.

Sallie Mae glanced toward the men. "Perhaps I should speak a comforting word to Goodman Weston."

"Whatever for?" Diana cried.

"Goody Weston and her newborn babe recently passed away from the sickness."

"I am so sorry for his loss, Sallie Mae, but all things considered, I do not believe Samuel would wish you to speak with him."

Faith's eyes cut around. "Your new husband is so jealous he begrudges you offering sympathy to a man who just lost his wife and child?" She cast a speaking look at Diana. "Now there's a man to fear."

Sallie Mae looked confused, but dismissing the odd remark, addressed Diana. "I spotted John Fuller amongst the men. He looks quite dashin' in his shiny breastplate and brass helmet."

"I think they look to be a rather rag-tag militia," Faith huffed. "Only a few men carrying weapons, others brandishing hoes and pitchforks." She pulled up the hood of her cloak and hurried away.

Diana reached to clasp Sallie Mae's hand, warmed, as was hers, by their lambskin gloves. "Come, let us go and stand near Mary Larsen. She will be glad to see you."

On the way, Diana told Sallie Mae that John Fuller had approached her after services and asked if he might call upon her one night next week. "I agreed to it," she said, "but I mean to tell him I can no longer see him."

"To be sure, he will be sorely disappointed."

"Perhaps not. Faith rather gleefully told me a minute ago that John has been calling upon Elisabeth Townsend."

"I doubt he cares for her half as much as he cares for you."

"Still, I should release him."

The girls soon found Mary, who in seconds declared she was far too cold to remain outdoors a minute longer. Clutching little Edward's hand, she glanced up at the dark clouds looming overhead. "To be sure, a winter storm is brewing. I do hope the men will disperse soon."

In minutes, Sallie Mae departed to go in search of her husband, saying she would have Samuel tell Mister Larsen that his family had gone on ahead without him.

Diana and Mary Larsen had only been home a few seconds before a bloodcurdling scream from Mary brought Diana running from her bedchamber.

"My baby is gone!" Mary screamed. "Ellen is gone! Cheiwoga has taken my poor sick baby!"

It was then Diana realized that the Indian woman was, indeed, nowhere in the house. With wide eyes, she beseeched Mary to tell her what to do.

At precisely that instant, both women heard Mister Larsen enter the house. Diana raced to the common room to meet him. "Baby Ellen is gone! Mary thinks Cheiwoga has taken her."

"Good God!" Larsen's brows pulled together as he brushed past Diana. "I assume you searched the house."

"Where could they be?" Mary demanded. "They are not here,

and they are not in Diana's room! My baby is gone! Ellen is dead! Oh-h-h, I should have remained at home today!" Sobbing, she flung herself onto the bed.

"I will summon the militia. Do try to calm my wife, Diana." With that, Larsen stormed from the house, the door slamming shut behind him.

Diana hurried back to the bedchamber. "The men will find Ellen and bring her home safely. Cheiwoga could not have gotten far. The afternoon was cut short." She did not know what that had to say to anything, but for the nonce, it was all she could think to say. She sat on the bed next to Mary and reached to stroke her shoulder, shuddering as she wept.

When little Edward moved shyly toward the bed, Diana reached for him. "You mustn't cry Edward. Your baby sister will be home soon, I promise."

"Oh-h-h," Mary wailed. "My precious baby is dead! How shall I bear it . . . I *cannot* bear it!"

Amidst the woman's wails, suddenly the sharp sound of someone rapping at the door reached Diana's ears. Putting Edward aside, she hurried to answer the summons. Dear God, had the men already found the infant and were returning it now to its mother?

Diana anxiously swung open the door, but was taken aback by the sight that greeted her.

"I have brought Mistress Larsen's baby home."

Blinking through the heavy mist that had begun to fall, Diana's brow furrowed. "Catherine?" Beyond the tall young woman, who was covered head to toe in a warm animal fur, Diana could see the shadowy form of an Indian sitting astride a huge white horse. Over his deerskin shirt and breeches, a plush white fur lay draped across his shoulders.

Catherine thrust a small bundle snugly wrapped in animal skin toward Diana. "Cheiwoga meant no harm. She brought the babe back to her village only to administer a healing ointment. Since tomorrow is her day away, she feared if she waited until the following day to administer the ointment, it would be too late. She wished only to help."

Exhaling an immense breath of relief, Diana reached to gingerly take the babe and hugged it close. "Please, Catherine, do come in out of the cold."

"No." Catherine shook her head. "My husband is waiting. We are not safe in Jamestown. We must go."

"Mister Larsen has summoned the militia," Diana felt compelled to say.

"Ask the child's parents not to be harsh with Cheiwoga. I have told her she must never, ever take a white woman's child, even if she means only to help. Cheiwoga did not expect the family to return so quickly from drill practice. She fully intended to have the child safely back home in its crib before its parents returned."

Nestling the sleeping infant against her shoulder, a smile flitted across Diana's face. "I am amazed that you seem to know all that transpires in our little colony."

Catherine grinned. "That used to amaze me too. But, you forget, an Indian woman is present in nearly every home in Jamestown. I must go now."

Diana watched the beautiful young woman hurry away. "Thank you!" she called. She continued to watch as the mighty Indian brave reached to encircle Catherine's body with one arm, and as if she weighted no more than one of the feathers dangling from his hair, lifted her up and settled her in front of him on his magnificent white stallion. In a swirl of white mane and tail, the huge steed whirled around and like a speeding comet disappeared into the mist.

Closing the door, Diana hurried in to Mary.

"I heard voices," Mary said anxiously.

"An . . . Indian woman . . . who speaks English, returned Ellen." She gently placed the child into its anxious mother's outstretched arms.

"Oh, dear God, my baby is alive!"

"The woman said that Cheiwoga meant no harm, but that she only wished to administer a healing ointment."

"What is that horrible smell?" Mary's brows pulled together. She furiously snatched away the tight swaddling that bound the infant. "What is smeared all over her chest?" she cried.

The unpleasant odor had also reached Diana's nostrils. She leaned forward to see what was causing the foul stench. "Perhaps it is . . . I do not know what it could be. I will get a cloth."

"No." Mary stretched forth a hand. "Let it be. Cheiwoga has before brought odd herbs into the house. Her strange ointment once saved Edward's life. Soon after he was born, I feared I was losing him to lung fever. Whatever it was Cheiwoga brought cleared his lungs at once." She looked up. "You must get word to William that Ellen is safe."

Just then, the baby opened its eyes and, spotting its mother, began to coo.

"Yes, yes, my precious darling, you are home! You are safe!"

Diana hurried to her bedchamber for her cloak, wondering all the while how she would find Mister Larsen when she had no clue where the men were mustering.

"Diana!" Mary called to her. "Go to the neighboring home and tell Goody Burton that all is well. Her boy Eric will know where to find the men."

Only moments after Diana returned home, Councilman Larsen charged into the house, demanding to see his baby daughter.

"If my child perishes, there will be nothing for it but to wage war on the savages!"

Diana followed the overset father into his bedchamber where Mary lay on the bed, cuddling her baby close. Curled up next to her, little Edward lay sound asleep.

"Lower your voice, William," Mary chided gently, "the children are sleeping."

He drew near the bed. "What is that horrible smell?"

Smiling to herself, Diana stole from the room. If not the pleasant diversion everyone in the colony had wished for, Muster Day had certainly proven far more interesting than Diana expected.

CHAPTER 28

As promised, John Fuller called on Diana one evening the following week. When the rap sounded at the door, the Larsen family was still gathered around the table enjoying warm slices of the *pakawn* and treacle pie that Cheiwoga had baked that afternoon.

"Evening, John," Larsen said.

"Do have a piece of pie," Mary Larsen said, greeting the young man. "Cheiwoga made it with the nuts Diana gathered last week."

John slid onto the backless bench beside Diana. "You gathered the nuts yourself? In the woods?" he asked incredulously.

"Indeed." Diana grinned, realizing that in truth she hadn't gathered these *particular* nuts, but she had gathered a basketful of ones just like them. "And I went alone." She popped a bite of pie into her mouth. "I daresay I have very nearly conquered my fear of the forest."

"Well done!" John exclaimed. "Now, if I can just get her to conquer her fear of marriage."

They all laughed, including Diana.

Later, when she and John were alone in the common room, their chairs drawn up before the hearth, Diana picked up the mending she'd been working on earlier that day. Before Sallie Mae married, both girls had asked Mary to show them how to sew a fine stitch, and Diana discovered she quite enjoyed the solitary work as it seemed to help soothe her fretful thoughts.

John sat quietly watching her a few minutes. “Perhaps you noticed that my cousin Beth and Robert Steele posted their banns.”

“Indeed,” Diana said, not looking up from her work. “I did see their notice. Along with Faith and Noah’s.”

John grimaced. “My sister Ann is also soon to be wed.”

Diana smiled tightly. She knew very well where the conversation was headed and prayed that her persistent refusal to wed John would not unduly anger him.

Leaning forward in his chair, he propped both elbows on his knees while the toe of one boot tapped nervously on the planked wooden floor.

Hoping to steer the conversation to a fresh topic, Diana asked, “Are your tobacco leaves ready to be shipped?”

He nodded. “We planters are now anxiously awaiting the arrival of the next ship, or ships, so that we might figure the profit we’ve earned from a year’s worth of hard labor.”

“I am sure you will do very well, John.” Diana smiled. “Mister Larsen says that when the ship comes, another hundred or so settlers will likely descend upon us.”

“Quite likely, indeed. Although winter is the worst time of year for new settlers to arrive.”

“Why is that?” Diana glanced up.

“To build a house is arduous enough during the hot summer months. Harsh weather makes building one a good deal more difficult.”

“But everyone will help the new colonists. No doubt the same kindness was shown to them when they first arrived.”

John turned a warm smile on her. “You have a kind heart, Diana. Still, with winter arriving early this year, most settlers are scrambling to get mud banks built up around their own homes and the chinks filled in. Then there's the matter of provisions."

"Will not the ship bring fresh provisions? Mary has compiled a list of things she wishes to purchase from the ship's merchant." She reached for scissors to snip a thread. "For one thing, we are very nearly out of thread. She wishes to purchase fabric to make Edward a new suit of clothes. For a certainty, the boy has grown an inch or more since I came. His coat sleeves no longer reach his wrists."

John smiled.

"Perhaps additional young ladies will also be arriving," Diana added, "which will give you young men fresh faces to choose from."

Despite the look of concern that flitted across his face, he pressed on. "Do you not agree that the pair of us conversing here before the fire, you with your mending and whatnot, rather makes us seem like . . . a married couple?" When she said nothing, he rushed on. "In the past months, Diana, my feelings for you have not changed. Rather, they have grown stronger. I was hoping that you would now be ready to—"

Diana set aside her mending. "You are a good man, John, but my feelings for you have also not changed. I . . . cannot marry you."

He looked down, perhaps wishing to conceal from her the hurt in his eyes. "What am I not doing, or . . . what might I do that would . . ." his voice trailed off.

"I wish I had an answer that would serve, John, but . . . I do not."

"Very well, then." With a resigned sigh, he rose to his feet. "I will cease troubling you with my proclamations of . . . I will cease troubling you, Diana."

Long strides carried him to the door, and without a backward glance John Fuller disappeared into the cold November night.

Indeed sorry that she had hurt such a good, kind man, Diana sighed. Some moments later, a rush of emotion welled up within her. If her mother were here, she would say something comforting . . . after she'd declared Diana a fool for refusing an offer from a successful tobacco planter. She reached to brush away the stray tear that sprang to her eye. Sara would understand how she felt and why she had refused John. Sara would understand that this was a new world; that here, a young lady was not obliged to accept the first man who offered for her.

Indeed, this *was* a new world, Diana realized. The rules from the old world did not apply. To be sure, she must eventually marry; after all, she could not reside indefinitely with the Larsens. Although, of late, Diana had begun to make herself more useful to Mary, and been glad to do so. She helped with the mending. She helped with the children. Although little Edward listened only sporadically, Diana made an effort to read Bible stories to him. On occasion, she even helped Cheiwoga prepare a meal, something that in her former life she would never have done. Even in their reduced circumstances, her family had still kept a housekeeper and cook.

Suddenly, Diana realized that in these past months she had made great inroads in adapting to this strange New World. And despite the harsh life here, she quite liked the simplicity of it. A woman had plenty with which to occupy herself. To be sure, Diana missed the fine books and lovely garments she left behind, and of course, she sorely missed her parents and Sara and Falstaff Manor . . . and Hamilton, but she was no longer the same person she had been when she stepped off the boat those many months ago. The world felt wider now, filled with more interesting things and activities than she could ever have imagined. She was learning about a new race of people who lived close to the earth. The Indians and their way of life now rather fascinated her, as did the colonists. These brave souls were carving rich new lives out of an untamed wilderness.

Somehow, living here in Jamestown made Diana feel as if she were part of something that would grow and become more than any of them ever thought possible. Life here felt as if it were moving forward, whereas life in England felt static, as if nothing would ever change, that all that lay ahead for a young woman was to do as she was told, marry well, and bring up her children to marry well, and on and on. Here, the world seemed full of possibilities. And because of that, Diana knew she was not obliged to do the safe thing: accept John Fuller's proposal of marriage out of fear that she might never receive another. She knew that, despite Mrs. Douglass's warnings against falling in love, she could hold out for the possibility that she might, indeed, meet a man she truly cared for and loved and admired. Together, they could make a home and bring up their children to become greater and more successful than they themselves had been.

Of a sudden, Diana realized that she had already fallen in love . . . with the New World and with Jamestown. And somewhere a voice inside her head—her mother's voice, perhaps?—told her that she would meet another man soon; and that it was his proposal of marriage she would accept. That is, just as soon as she was certain that both of her friends, Sallie Mae and Faith, were safe from any threat of harm.

For now, Diana turned back to her mending.

On the following Sabbath an unprecedented five couples were married inside the church on the green, which was no longer green, since the day before a blinding snow had fallen. No feast followed the wedding ceremonies today, as it was far too cold and wet outdoors. Instead, family members and friends held small receptions inside their homes to honor the newlywed couples.

The Larsens, as well as Governor Yeardley and all the other councilmen, attended the reception held for Noah Colton and his new bride Faith at Councilman Evans's home. Their large common room was packed with Noah's friends, as well as a few young ladies Faith had invited. Although Diana fully expected it, she was dismayed that Samuel and Sallie Mae were not on Faith's guest list.

After congratulating Faith, whose pretty face was flushed with happiness, Diana moved to stand near Mary Larsen. Sipping from a mug of warm apple cider, Diana quietly watched the proceedings. The bridegroom was finely turned out today in a pair of burgundy velvet galligaskins and a matching doublet with gold buttons. Froths of lace fell from the cuffs of his coat and cascaded down his chest. White silk stockings and black leather pumps with gold buckles completed the costly costume. The only thing Diana could see to mar Noah Colton's perfection today was an odd red streak snaking down the side of his cheek. It looked as if he might have been wounded and the wound had not yet completely healed. Or perhaps . . . he had been burned whilst setting a certain fire. The unsettling thought caused Diana's stomach muscles to tighten.

That Noah Colton was freely mingling amongst the leaders of the colony wearing proof of his crime in plain sight upon his face was so bold as to be unbelievable. Even if a halo were to suddenly appear and illuminate his golden head, she would not believe him innocent of every single charge she had mentally leveled against him, except perhaps that of killing his second wife, who was obviously alive and well and living in the forest. Otherwise, as ever, Noah Colton was the finest-looking man in the room.

By contrast, Faith, wearing a simple blue worsted gown with a white eyelet collar, appeared rather plain, although her rich auburn hair, brushed to a shine, looked lovely falling in soft waves down her back. To Diana it looked as if Faith had at last been eating a bit more, as her figure seemed slightly fuller. Ruminating further, she wondered if, because Noah's former wife, Catherine, was not dead as everyone thought, was he actually free to marry again? How many colonists, apart from the brother Catherine had mentioned, knew that his second wife was still alive and had taken an Indian husband? Diana shook off the tangle. It was too confusing for her to sort out. She only hoped that in Noah's care, Faith would remain safe and happy for the rest of her days. And that Sallie Mae would also remain safe from the deceptive man.

One afternoon the following week, Diana decided that despite the snowy weather, she would ride to the outskirts of Jamestown and pay a call on Sallie Mae. She had not yet been inside her fine brick home and had sorely missed chatting with her friend following Sabbath services on Sunday last.

Approaching the path that led to the cooper's house, she noted the burned-out ruin where Samuel's workshop had stood. A curl of smoke rising from the chimney of another of the outbuildings told her it was now the location of the cooper's workshop. Reaching the two-storey home, she noticed another horse already tethered to the rail outside. Slipping from Bug-a-Boo's back, she looped her mare's rein over the same rail, then tramped up the snow-covered steps to the house.

Once indoors, she and Sallie Mae embraced and were gaily exchanging pleasantries when Samuel and another gentleman emerged from an anteroom into the hallway that split the house in two. In warmer weather, the doors at either end of the long corridor would no doubt be thrown wide open, allowing a cool breeze to drift through the center of the house.

"Good afternoon, Diana," Samuel said with a smile. "To be sure, Sallie Mae has missed you." He turned to his guest. "This young lady is Miss Diana Wakefield. She made the crossing on the Bride Ship along with my lovely wife."

The tall gentleman nodded cordially. "A pleasure to meet you, Miss Wakefield. I am Adam Parke."

Diana nodded a bit shyly, then she hurried after Sallie Mae, who was gesturing for her to follow her up the stairs. As the ladies gained the interior of the house, Diana could hear the deep timbre of the men's voices as they resumed their discussion.

A beaming Sallie Mae proudly showed Diana into every room of her home, which, by Jamestown's standards, was quite grand. It featured wooden floors and walls that had actually been painted.

"I daresay your home must be finer than Governor Yeardley's," Diana declared with awe.

"Samuel said the councilmen told him it is one of the finest in Jamestown."

She showed Diana into both bedchambers on the upper floor, then led the way to a smaller parlor also above stairs. The cozy room featured its own fireplace but was nearly bare of furniture. Instead there was a window seat and a single chair positioned before the fire. Leaning against the walls and spread out on the floor were nigh on a dozen bolts of multicolored fabric.

"I am makin' curtains for all my windows," Sallie Mae exclaimed. "Mine will be even prettier than Mary Larsen's. As you can see, the former owner left behind a great deal of fabric."

Sallie Mae knelt to move aside several pieces of cloth in order that the girls might sit on the floor. "I wish to give you a length of fabric for a new frock, Diana. I know you've a birthday soon, and I wish to give ye something special."

Diana laughed. "The day marking my birth will not be here for another month."

"Then your new gown will be ready and waitin' for ye the

day ye turn eighteen."

The girls spent a pleasant hour sorting through the fabric. When Diana had selected her favorite, they did their best to calculate how much might be necessary to fashion a new gown. Sallie Mae reached for her scissors to cut the cloth.

"I have learned how to sew a stitch," Diana remarked, "but I confess I will be obliged to call on Beth Fuller to help me cut out the proper pieces for my new gown."

"I understand Beth is soon to be wed."

"Indeed. John mentioned as much when he called last week and . . . and asked me to marry him . . . again."

Busy cutting the fabric whilst Diana held it taut, Sallie Mae did not look up. "Adam Parke is unmarried."

"Who?"

Sallie Mae laughed. "The gentleman Samuel just presented to ye. Below stairs when ye arrived. He is a planter and he hasn't a wife."

Diana blushed to the roots of her hair. She had noticed the ruggedly handsome man. In fact, that she had noticed him accounted for her lapse in recalling his name. He was, indeed, fine looking, with auburn hair and even features. Though she could not say why, something about him seemed familiar. "W-what do you know of him?" she asked quietly.

Grinning, Sallie Mae sat back on her heels. "So, you *did* notice."

On her way home, Diana thought about her pleasant visit with Sallie Mae and her lovely new home. Sallie Mae was indeed fortunate, and her marriage to a tradesman clearly illustrated Diana's theory that here in the New World, class distinctions no longer held as fast and strong as they did in England. In the old world, very few to no girls of Sallie Mae's station could aspire to better herself by marrying a tradesman. And Diana, being the daughter of a country squire proud of his connections, however distant they might be, to the aristocracy, would never have befriended a peasant's daughter. Which would have been a dreadful shame, for Diana felt exceedingly blessed by her friendship with Sallie Mae. The girl had brought untold joy and laughter into her life, and Diana would step up and do anything in her power to keep her friend safe.

Even Faith, by old world standards, the daughter of a yeoman farmer, had bettered herself by marrying Noah Colton, by all accounts a successful trader held in high esteem by his fellow man.

At length, Diana's thoughts fixed on Adam Parke, the man to whom she had just been introduced. What had been his circumstances in the old world, she wondered, and what had brought him to the new? Sallie Mae had said he was a widower with a small son and that nearly a twelvemonth ago his wife had perished. Adam Parke was a prosperous planter; in fact, his tobacco crop had been so large this year that he had used every available hogshead on his plantation to pack his tobacco leaves and now needed a half dozen more in order to store winter provisions. She found herself wondering, a bit wistfully, if she would ever see that handsome planter again.

Chapter 29

Near week's end a pair of ships sailed up the James River. News that two barks had arrived during the night caused a stir amongst the colonists. However, a torrential rain that morning kept many settlers from crowding onto the riverbank. On the second morning, a cheerful sky drew hoards of anxious men, women and children to the muddy shore where they anxiously awaited to see what goods and luxury items the ships had brought.

Diana walked to the riverbank with Mary Larsen. The two stood side-by-side on shore taking in the colorful sights. Diana noted that nearly every young lady who'd arrived on the Bride Ships was there, most carrying missives to send home to family and friends telling of their safe arrival in the New World, or perhaps even their good fortune in finding husbands. Diana had considered writing a letter to Sara's parents, but could not decide if she should divulge the whole truth about the accident and Sara's death, or if she should attempt to mimic Sara's handwriting and forward the notion that she was Sara Wakefield, alive and well and getting on nicely in the New World. Because she never reached a decision, she never wrote the letter.

She saw both Beth and Ann Fuller, along with Ann's brother John and Beth's betrothed Robert Steele. No doubt, most of the girls who had married or were about to be married hoped to purchase household items from the ship's merchant, as there was no place in Jamestown from which to purchase things they needed. Mary Larsen carried letters in the pocket of her cloak. In another pocket, coins William had given her to spend on whatever she wished from the ship's merchant jingled when she walked.

The colonists patiently watched and waited as longboat after longboat of new settlers were rowed ashore, some coming to join family members, others arriving in the New World, as had the Bride-Ship ladies, with the hope of carving out bright futures for themselves. The final shallop to be dragged ashore carried a motley assortment of men and women who, Mary told Diana, had made the ocean voyage chained down in the hold. It tore at Diana's heart when she caught sight of the weary faces of those poor young women, their wrists tied behind their backs, their hair unkempt, their bodies skeletal beneath their ragged clothing. Their blank stares brought memories of her own shipboard journey to mind, most of which she'd as soon never think of again. She had no idea where in the colony the prisoners would be housed until their indentures were purchased, but she hoped they would all be given something nourishing to eat and a blanket to warm their emaciated bodies.

As it turned out, many of the indentures were sold on the spot. Samuel Wingate stepped forward to purchase two, that of a young woman to help Sallie Mae with the household chores, and a sturdy man to help him in his workshop. Whilst her husband took care of business, Sallie Mae moved to speak Diana.

"I only just mentioned to Samuel a few evenin's ago that it would be nice to have help in the house. He promised at once to seek someone out."

"You are fortunate to have such a thoughtful husband," Diana replied. "I had wondered how you were managing all alone."

"Some days, my chores seem endless, but all things considered, it has not been terribly difficult. Many of Samuel's customers paid for their hogsheads with preserved foodstuffs or firewood so our winter storehouse is very nearly chock full, and we've enough firewood to last out the winter."

"That is wonderful!" Diana enthused, her hazel eyes still following the activity on shore. Mary had migrated toward other women of her acquaintance as they all anxiously waited for the ship's merchant to set up his store.

"Come spring," Sallie Mae went on, "I shall be obliged to plant and tend the required field of corn. Governor's orders, ye know." She grinned.

"Good afternoon, ladies," came a male voice from behind them.

When both girls turned around, Diana was surprised to see Mister Adam Parke touching the brim of his black felt hat. Dropping her gaze, she murmured a polite greeting whilst Sallie Mae boldly spoke up. "I see ye made it downriver today, Mister Parke."

"Indeed, I did. Need to make arrangements with the ship's captain to pick up my hogsheads."

Diana looked up into his sea-green eyes. "You do not roll them into town on the rolling road?"

His lips twitched. "Now, how would a cultured young lady like you know about the rolling road?"

Both girls laughed. "Samuel showed it to us," Sallie Mae said.

"I've no need for Jamestown's rolling road," Parke declared. "Harvest Hill has its own pier."

"Harvest Hill is the name of Mister Parke's plantation," Sallie Mae told Diana.

"What a lovely name." She smiled into his eyes. "It brings all manner of pleasant images to mind."

Gazing down upon her, he eventually said, "Perhaps you

would allow me to show you my plantation someday, Miss Wakefield."

"I would like that very much, Mister Parke."

With a polite nod, he bade the ladies a pleasant day and strode toward one of the long boats.

"Methinks ye have an admirer." Sallie Mae beamed.

Diana's eyes followed the tall gentleman's progress. Again, she had the oddest feeling that she was already acquainted with the man. Moreover, her heart had warmed to him at once.

Diana did not see Adam Parke again that day, but both she and Sallie Mae spotted Faith and her new husband when the newlywed pair approached the riverbank seated atop a cart pulled by a single ox. Diana assumed he'd borrowed the ox and cart from Ed Henley since his was the only one in the colony. In the bed of it lay a stack of shiny beaver pelts as well as other fine furs.

Diana watched with interest as Noah approached the ship's merchant, who had only just begun to spread out his wares in the bottom of a longboat. From their gestures, it became apparent that both men were haggling over what would be a fair price to pay, and receive, for the rich pelts. When Noah appeared to be growing impatient, the ship's captain was consulted, and at length a price was decided upon, for Diana noted that pouch after pouch of coins were given to a now smiling Noah. She marveled that he was bold enough to conduct his business in plain sight of the entire colony, but then he knew that everyone trusted him. Nothing Noah Colton did seemed to arouse suspicion. Apparently, so long as the Indians did not openly attack the settlers, they all believed that Noah and the other traders were above reproach and dispatching their duties as instructed.

Diana and Sallie Mae noticed that he handed several pouches of coins to Faith, who had hopped down from the cart and approached her husband as the negotiations concluded.

"I haven't any money of my own to spend"—Diana turned to Sallie Mae—"but shall we go and see what the ship's merchant has to offer?"

They fell in with the hoard of other women hurrying that direction. "When I told Samuel we was in desperate need of a pipkin," Sallie Mae said, "he gave me a few cents to purchase one."

It appeared their friend Faith had more than a few cents to spend, for by the time Diana and Sallie Mae managed to elbow their way through the crowd of woman squeezed around the small boat, Faith had already snatched up a number of items and was paying the asking price, no matter how dear.

"Five shillings is a great deal to pay for a pipkin," Diana exclaimed, standing beside Sallie Mae as she examined a small pot with a wide handle arched across the top.

"If you don't want it, I'll take it!" Faith declared, reaching past Diana and actually grasping the handle.

"I intend to purchase it," Sallie Mae said, jerking the pot beyond Faith's reach.

"And if she don't want it, I'll take it," cried another woman squeezed in beside them. "Five shillings or no, I've nothing to boil me water in. Fire burns up a gourd afore I gits m'mush made of a mornin'."

"Ladies, ladies!" The merchant laughed. "I've plenty more pipkins in my crate. Ye may all have one."

Faith bought two. She also purchased a length of fine worsted for a new gown, a white cap, a pair of leather boots, several pairs of woolen stockings and a number of other household items.

"My," Sallie Mae muttered, "Noah's furs musta' earned him a fine profit."

"Indeed. It appears trapping is quite lucrative," Diana said with no small amount of sarcasm. Her gaze followed Faith as she carried her armload of purchases toward Noah, who was telling a man where in the cart to toss several heavy bags of grain.

On the way home that afternoon, Diana could not resist telling Mary Larsen, who had managed to purchase the items she coveted, about watching Noah sell his pelts on shore that day, then turn around and hand a number of the pouches of coins he'd just received to Faith.

Mary's lips pressed together. "I realize that for whatever reason, you do not think as highly of Noah Colton as the rest of us do, Diana, but I am quite certain he is being fair in his dealings with the Virginia Company. Were his activities the least bit nefarious, surely someone on the council would have noticed by now."

"Indeed," Diana murmured contritely. "I am speaking out of turn. For a certainty, Noah would never withhold monies that do not belong to him."

"No," Mary said firmly. "He would not."

Diana vowed to refrain from mentioning her mistrust of Noah Colton again, at least to the Larsens. Perhaps she would speak of it to John Fuller, who seemed to share her dislike of the trader. Although, she reminded herself, it was not likely she'd ever have occasion to speak with John again, as it was widely known he was now pursuing Elisabeth Townsend.

One day during the following week, Diana decided to pay a call upon Faith to assure herself that she was indeed getting on well now that she had become Noah's wife.

"Oh, it is you," Faith said in a somewhat irritable tone when she found Diana standing on the doorstep of her small home.

"May I come in?"

Faith had already spun around and was headed back to the

hearth where she'd been stirring the contents of a pot suspended over the flames. "I scarcely have time to chat. Noah demands a hot meal awaiting him when he comes home, and I've a long way to go."

Removing her cape and hanging it on an empty peg near the door, Diana was struck by the marked difference in her friend's appearance. Even when Faith had taken to her bed, languishing over Noah's lack of attention, she had not looked as unkempt as she did now. Her thick auburn hair had obviously not been brushed in days; the front of her gown was soiled, and the bottom half of her skirt appeared to have been dragged through the mud. Although the winter days were now downright cold, perspiration stains were clearly visible beneath her arms. Gathers were torn from the waistband of her skirt, revealing a dingy petticoat beneath.

"You . . . look as if you have been hard at work," Diana remarked, although glancing about the room told her Faith's work had not included cleaning the house.

Faith's lips thinned as she brushed back an errant lock of auburn hair from her brow. "I am a married woman now, Diana. All of my days are filled with . . . drudgery of one sort or another."

Diana's glance fell to the heavy wooden yoke that lay haphazardly to the side of the hearth. One of the buckets had tipped over, and what water it had contained had spilled onto the earthen floor, creating a mud puddle right there inside the house . . . and perhaps explaining the caked-on dirt soiling the hem of Faith's gown. Or perhaps she herself had walked to the well and whilst balancing the heavy yoke on her shoulders had been unable to keep from dragging her skirt through Jamestown's muddy streets.

"Might I do something to help?" Diana offered, casting another curious gaze about the common room. A planked table with a pair of backless benches stood beneath one of two windows in the room. The tabletop, she noticed, was littered with soiled trenchers and utensils. An ale jug lay overturned, the amber puddle it lay in telling its own tale. Although Diana now stood quite near the blazing fire, she edged closer and rubbed her hands up and down her arms in an attempt to ward off the cool air eddying about the room.

"We've no glass in the windows," Faith said matter-of-factly. "Oiled cloth doesn't do a great deal toward keeping out ice cold air." After a pause, she added, "Noah is home so infrequently, he seems unaware how cold the house stays."

"I expect everyone's home is cold these days. Perhaps when Noah fills in the chinks in the walls, the house will be warmer."

Faith's disheveled head wagged. "Despite the vast number of years my husband has been in Jamestown, he appears blithely unaware that—" She exhaled a weary sigh. "There is no use complaining. I have brought up the matter of the chinks in the walls again and again. There is also a hole in the roof. When it rains, in the rain pours!"

Diana glanced up. Sure enough, there was a ragged hole in the thatched roof wide enough for a bird or even a squirrel to come through. "Why does he not patch the hole, or at least add another layer of thatch to the roof?"

"When I asked the selfsame thing, he grew angry and called me a nag." Another weary sigh escaped her. "Nothing can be done for it. Noah says the day his mother-in-law dies, we will remove to the plantation, so he sees no reason to patch up this house."

"I should think that keeping you warm and comfortable would be reason enough."

Faith said no more on the subject, so Diana also abandoned it. "Well, it feels quite toasty here by the fire," she said, "although the air seems a bit thick with smoke." She waved a hand past her nose in an attempt to brush it aside. "I take it Noah has not yet cleaned the chimney this winter?"

Faith snorted. "That, too, would involve hard labor."

"There is a man in the colony who charges only a few cents to drop a chicken down the flue. Mistress Larsen gladly let the man clean our chimney in that fashion. The chicken makes quite a squawk as it falls, but on the way down, its feathers collect a good deal of soot."

"No doubt in this chimney, the chicken would catch fire and drop dead upon the hearth," Faith replied dryly.

"Well, then," Diana retorted, "for only a few cents more, you and Noah could have a nice chicken stew for dinner."

She was pleased when the veriest hint of a smile lifted the corners of Faith's lips.

"Might I do something to help you?" Diana asked again.

Faith's small smile dissolved. "I could use a scoop of dried peas and corn if . . . if there is any left in the loft."

"Of course." Diana headed toward the ladder, quite a nice one actually, with a handy railing along one side. Yet, as she stepped onto the loose floorboards of the loft, she was nearly overcome by the filth and debris that greeted her there. Spider webs crisscrossed a room filled with a mélange of dusty items—half a dozen barrels that she assumed contained foodstuffs, the rumpled remnants of someone's sleeping pallet, piles of old clothing and worn boots. Batting at the cobwebs, Diana turned this way and that until she located the barrel containing hard kernels of dried green peas. Using the scooped-out gourd she found lying on the floor, she reached deeply into the barrel to fill it with the green kernels, then, righting the barrel and herself, she glanced about for another gourd with which to fetch the corn, but paused when she heard Faith call up to her.

"We've only one gourd."

"Oh."

As Diana headed back down the stairs, she heard Faith mutter beneath her breath, "In a fit of rage, Noah threw the other one into the fire."

Diana waited while Faith dumped the peas into her pot then hand the empty gourd back to her. Gaining the loft a second time, Diana couldn't help casting a quick glance about in search of . . . what? The night Noah had openly threatened Sallie Mae had convinced Diana beyond a doubt that he was guilty of setting Samuel's workshop on fire; now here she was in the man's loft. Where, she wondered, did he store the contraband she knew he had? Here, perhaps? Her lips thinned when the only incriminating evidence she spotted was the pile of beaver pelts, which she already knew Noah had not trapped himself, for she'd watched the Indians hand them over to him, already caught, cured and ready to sell. She brushed past the skins on her way to the barrel containing corn and . . . something else. Upon closer inspection, she pulled a face. In amongst the hard yellow kernels were small black pellets that could only be . . . rodent droppings. Rather than overset Faith, she took the time to pick out the offensive specks before taking the gourd full of corn back down to Faith to add to the pot.

"Here you are," she said cheerfully. "I see where Noah has been busy trapping beaver again."

Faith's eyes rolled skyward. "Despite my husband's grandiose claims, he is not a trapper. To trap and cure pelts would require far too much work. Noah merely trades . . . *things* . . . with the Indians. Then he sells the pelts to the ship's merchant and pockets the profit. He thinks he is being quite clever."

Diana listened intently. Here was proof positive of Noah Colton's deception! "He . . . told you this himself?"

"He did not have to tell me." Faith stirred the mixture boiling in the pot. "I have learned a great deal about my husband in the past few weeks."

Diana's mind churned. A moment later, she noticed moisture pooling in Faith's eyes.

"Oh, Faith. Perhaps something can be done. If the governor or any one of the council members were to learn of Noah's—"

Faith shook her head. "You must say nothing against him, Diana! He . . . when I threatened to . . . expose him, he vowed to . . . please, Diana, you must say nothing." She turned an imploring gaze upon her friend. "Promise me you will say nothing against him."

Though Diana was loath to do so, she agreed to Faith's heartfelt request. "I promise."

"I am persuaded my husband's secrets and lies will come to light one day."

"But what does he do with his ill-gotten gain? I saw him give several pouches of coins to you the day we all gathered on shore. And you purchased a good many things, new boots and a length of fabric."

Faith's lips pressed together. "Which I will never have time to stitch into a new gown. I scarcely have time to wash the clothing I now own. To wash my frocks seems a waste of what little water I am able to cart home from the well."

"How did Noah keep his clothes clean without a wife to wash them for him?"

Faith huffed. "Noah's clothing is very fine. I expect when a doublet became soiled, he simply purchased a fresh one when the next ship docked. The spare bedchamber is full of costly clothing, doublets and galligaskins of every color, plumed hats, top boots, leather pumps with silver buckles." The derision rose in her tone. "He gives a good bit of money to Ed Henley. Noah is quite fond of Ed's stout brew. My husband consumes a great deal of the stuff when he is home."

"I see." Diana cast a glance toward the overturned jug on the table. Again edging closer to the fire, she held her hands up before her to warm them. "Perhaps he would agree to purchase panes of glass for the windows. I understand there is a glass manufactory plant on the peninsula. Perhaps one of the new settlers would be glad to earn a few coins to fit them into the windows, or to fill in the chinks in the walls, or build up a mud bank around the perimeter of the house. Or patch the roof," she added. "Mister Larsen says a mud bank is quite good for holding in the warmth."

"As I said, Noah appears not to notice the chill. He finds . . . other ways to keep himself warm. He spends many nights in the Indian villages he visits. Inhabitants of the Indians' bark houses are warmed by plush animal furs and . . . women."

"Oh!" Diana sucked in a breath. "Oh, my." Of a sudden, Diana wondered if John Fuller had somehow also uncovered the ugly truth about Noah. She thought again about the beautiful woman she'd met in the woods who said she had once been married to the trader man. Perhaps she had grown weary of concealing Noah's deceptions and had simply left him. Perhaps . . . Faith could do the same. "Perhaps you could . . . leave him, Faith. If Noah has deceived you—"

"Leaving Noah is not an option. There is something you do not know." In an emotionless tone, she announced, "I am with child."

Diana was about to offer congratulations before she realized that Faith had only married the man a few weeks ago, meaning sufficient time had not yet elapsed for her to know whether or not she was . . .

"I became pregnant before we married," Faith confessed flatly. "I know I have sinned against God and that . . . my transgression will soon be evident to everyone in Jamestown."

"Many a babe is born before the proper time has elapsed," Diana rushed to say. "Oh, Faith. I am so sorry."

Faith's fire returned. "Do not pity me! Despite everything I still love Noah. Unfortunately, I do not believe my feelings for him will ever change. I just . . . expected our married life to be . . . different." She swiped at the tears that again welled in her eyes. "I am hopeful that once the babe comes, things will change. Surely, he will care for his own child. And surely he will see that to set a good example, he must put aside his . . . lying and cheating. It will all work out for the best in the end. I am certain of it."

"Perhaps you are right," Diana replied, although even to herself her tone sounded dubious.

"Please go now. Noah will be home soon . . . no doubt, with another armload of pelts. It would not do for him to find you here." She smiled crookedly. "Strangely enough, he is suspicious of others. I expect he fears that someday, someone will uncover his many deceptions."

Diana hurried to fetch her cloak from the peg where she'd hung it. "You may come to see me anytime, Faith. By comparison, you'll find the Larsen home quite warm."

Faith's head shook. "I've no time to pay social calls. I stay busy from sun up to sun down." She exhaled another weary sigh. "Enjoy your freedom, Diana. Once you are wed, your life will also drastically change."

On the following Sabbath, when Diana spotted Faith on Noah's arm, she could not help noticing yet another dramatic change in her friend's demeanor. Noah was being his usual charming self, smiling at the ladies, greeting the gentlemen, but he was also lovingly patting his wife's gloved hand where it lay over the crook of his arm, even bringing it to his lips for a quick kiss. A time or two, he reached to tug her cloak tighter about her shoulders as if solicitous of her comfort. Her cheeks flushed, Faith appeared quite happy. In fact, she seemed as much in love with her husband as the day they wed. Clearly Faith believed that despite Noah's wayward bent, he loved her dearly and that all would be well once their child was born.

Suddenly, Diana wondered if Noah's quick decision to marry Faith had come as a result of learning that she was carrying his child. Which he must have got on her before he suddenly transferred his affections to Sallie Mae. Still, she had to concede that to do right by Faith did point to a certain honor in his character. Once again, she tried to tamp down her worries regarding Faith. Perhaps her friend was right. Perhaps becoming a father would persuade Noah to abandon his wicked ways.

Chapter 30

The long, dull days of winter dragged on, each blurring into the other with only slight changes in the weather marking one day different from another. One morning the colonists awoke to rain mixed with snow, the next day brought sleet, and the James River iced over. A week of bitter cold days followed with everything hidden beneath a thick blanket of snow. Diana was dismayed to learn that the holy days observed in England in the autumn and winter months—Michaelmas in September, All Saints' Day and St. Martin's Day in November—passed unnoticed here in the New World. The traditional feasts and festivals, entertainments and dancing, and even a bit of the revelry held in every English hamlet and village would certainly make these bleak winter months easier to bear. She wondered if the holy day of Christmas would be observed, or if that special day, too, would come and go unnoticed as did every other day in Jamestown. To be sure, she did not expect masques or play-acting at Christmastide, and possibly no wassailing, but she hoped there would at least be a special service with singing at the meetinghouse and perhaps a Christmas pudding served at dinner.

She tried not to think about how her life used to be with her family and Sara in England. Those days, and the life she had thought to live there, were gone forever. And although she had embraced her new life here, a prickling nostalgia plagued her during these gray winter days.

Making an effort to fill her mind with more pleasant thoughts, she spent a great deal of time helping Mary and playing with the children. Little Edward, who had recently celebrated a birthday and at five, now considered himself quite grown up, enjoyed playing Cat's Cradle, a simple game played by wrapping string in and around and through one's fingers.

Several afternoons, groups of men in the colony, who also had less to occupy themselves with in the dead of winter, got up excursions to search out the wild horses that roamed in herds beyond the forest. When Edward wanted to tag along with his father, Mary, of course, put her foot down, but she did allow the boy to stand inside the fence, Diana close by, to watch for the men as they returned to town. To Edward's delight, the men returned leading, or rather tugging, a recalcitrant animal along behind them.

"Next winter," Edward cried, "I shall be big enough to go and get my own pony!"

"I am certain you shall," Diana agreed. "But this year, I'll wager you are big enough to play roll the hoop."

Edward's eyes lit up. "Do we have a hoop I might roll in the street?"

"I shall ask the cooper if he can spare one the very next time I see Sallie Mae."

"You won't forget?"

Diana grinned. "I promise I shall not."

Diana and Mary passed many long cold afternoons stitching a new suit of clothing for Edward and also small garments for baby Ellen, whose life-threatening illness had long since passed, thanks to Cheiwoga's foul-smelling remedy.

Because Beth Fuller had not yet married and still lived with her cousin John, who had, indeed, wed Elisabeth Townsend, Diana decided against calling on Beth to help her fashion her new gown from the fabric Sallie Mae had given her. Therefore, she and Mary began the daunting task of cutting out the pieces and stitching up Diana's new gown. Made from dark green damask, Diana thought it turned out rather plain, as there was nothing on hand with which to decorate the bodice or hem. With no contrasting colored fabric to use as insets for slashed sleeves, the long sleeves were also devoid of trim. Still, because the gown was new and it was green, Diana decided to wear it to the Christmas service, which she was pleased to learn had indeed been planned to mark that special day.

Although the colony was larger now by the one hundred or so new settlers who had recently arrived, the colonists had been hard hit, by both bad weather and sickness. Without fail, every Sabbath morning for the past several weeks, Reverend Martin had read off the names of those settlers who had succumbed to lung fever, dysentery or influenza. At times, he read off as many as ten names. Funeral services in the colony were now as plentiful as weddings.

On a brighter note, the colonists had also celebrated a number of births, although only a scant few of the infants had survived. With no doctor thereabouts, the only medicinal aids came from herbal ointments contributed by the Indians or prepared by those women who possessed knowledge of the healing arts and who cultivated the powerful herbs in their kitchen gardens.

Since the day the ships arrived, Diana had looked long and hard each Sabbath for the handsome planter Adam Parke, but thus far, had not seen him. Sallie Mae told her that Mister Parke generally made the five-mile journey into Jamestown via the river, although Diana recalled that he had reached the cooper's home the day she met him on horseback.

Despite the heavy snow that fell on the eve of Christmas, Christmas Day dawned clear and bright. Bundled up warmly in their boots and heavy woolens, the Jamestown colonists trudged through the snow, calling cheery greetings to one another as they made their way to the meetinghouse for the special service. That she was wearing her new green gown for the first time helped lift Diana's spirits. She also thought the colorful sparkleberries created by the dazzling sun on the snow lent a festive air to the day.

But she could scarcely believe her eyes when the very moment she and Mary Larsen entered the meetinghouse and moved away from William Larsen, the sexes being obliged to sit apart from one another, she caught a glimpse of the man whose handsome face she had diligently searched for the entire past month. Throughout the lengthy service, she could hardly keep her mind on the reverend's words as she cast about for a way in which to put herself in Adam Parke's path once the service concluded.

When no viable plan sprang to mind and the three of them, Diana, Mary and William Larsen, set out for home, Diana's spirits dissolved, becoming as bitter as the icy wind that swirled about them on that cold winter day. However, she pasted a smile on her face as the family sat down to partake of the fine dinner of roasted turkey, steamed corn and tasty bread pudding that Cheiwoga had prepared in their absence. Afterward, Diana spent the remainder of that long day playing games and reading Bible stories to the children.

One week later, on the eve of the new year, Governor Yeardley's aid rapped at the Larsens' door bearing a message. After reading the handwritten note, William approached his wife and Diana, both sitting quietly before the crackling fire, their heads bent over their sewing.

"Governor Yeardley has invited us to join him and the other council members at his home this evening. No doubt to usher in the new year with a mug of ale, since he requested that we bring our own mugs," he added with a laugh. "You are invited, as well, Diana."

A *soiree?* Diana could scarcely believe her ears. She and Mary set aside their work at once and excitedly began planning what to wear. Diana again put on her new green gown and brushed her long brown hair till it shone.

In the fading daylight, they approached the governor's home on foot. Diana noted that already candlelight flickered from every window of the clapboard house. From the street, the sound of mingled voices and merry laughter further lifted Diana's spirits. This was the first festive gathering, other than the rather subdued one celebrating Faith and Noah's wedding she had attended, since coming to the New World. Anticipating what lay ahead, she did not notice that several horses stood tethered to the gatepost in front.

"Do join us!" bellowed the governor. "Fill yer mugs and raise a toast to the new year!"

"He means raise *another* toast," a fellow colonist explained, one who'd obviously been toasting the new year for some time that afternoon.

"Thank you, Governor," William Larsen said, whereupon he and Mary and Diana blended into the noisy crowd.

Already the spacious great room was filled to capacity with merrymakers. Diana recognized the faces of many of the colonists. After all, she'd beheld them at services nearly every Sabbath for months. However, at the meetinghouse their demeanors were always quite solemn and pious. Not even at the picnics and numerous wedding feasts held on the greensward did they appear as lively and raucous as they were tonight.

Nearly everyone, she noted, most especially the women, were clothed in their finest garments, although some of the men looked as if they'd come straight from hunting or fishing. In only seconds, Diana caught a glimpse of Noah Colton's handsome face. The trader was finely turned out as always, tonight in a green velvet doublet and matching galligaskins. Wondering if Faith was also here, she gazed about for the pretty auburn-haired girl. She never caught sight of her, but just beyond Noah's blond head, in a far corner, she did see Samuel and Sallie Mae. She headed that direction, but on the way, caught sight of another tall handsome gentleman, this one with rich auburn hair. Her stomach did a funny flip-flop.

Would Adam Parke remember her?

Should she approach him . . . or should she wait for him to—?

At that very second, Mister Parke glanced up from the conversation he was engaged in . . . and their gazes locked.

Diana froze. Would he . . . should she . . . ?

She had not long to wonder. An instant later, she saw him nod to the gentleman with whom he was speaking and begin to wend his way through the throng . . . toward her.

Be the time Adam reached Diana, the smile on his lips had reached his eyes. "Miss Wakefield, what a pleasure to see you." When he noticed that the gourd mug she carried was still empty, he said, "Appears we need to fill your mug with some of Sir Yeardley's fine ale."

Diana hadn't yet said a word when he reached for her elbow to steer her toward one of the wooden casks sitting atop a pair of planked tables shoved up against the wall. The jangle of loud voices and merry laughter in the room precluded intelligible conversation between them, but once Adam had filled her mug and topped off his own, he steered her to one of the smaller chambers in the house, where fewer merrymakers were gathered.

"Now then," he said, taking up a position near an opened window, "perhaps we shall be able to hear one another speak."

"The lesser noise in here is far more conducive to conversation," Diana agreed. Her bright eyes not leaving his face, she took a sip from the gourd mug she carried. "Oh, my," she swallowed the stout brew. "I shan't be able to drink a great deal of this."

He chuckled. "I see you are not a tippler." He lifted his mug to his mouth and took a long draught.

"And I see you are." Diana grinned.

"Touché." His eyes twinkling, he set his pewter mug down on the windowsill.

Feeling a bit ill at ease now that she was actually in the presence of the very man she'd wished for so many long weeks to see, Diana cast a nervous gaze about. "It appears the governor has invited nearly everyone in the colony to toast in the new year."

"Everyone of consequence."

Diana's lashes fluttered downward. "Then he should not have invited me," she said softly.

He boldly reached to tilt up her chin. "I do not believe that."

She was growing more flustered by the minute. She hadn't the least notion how to persuade a man to like her. In truth, her experience with men was middling to none. She had managed well enough with John Fuller, but somehow, he didn't count. From the beginning, John had felt like a friend, not a . . . lover. Before John, there had only been Hamilton. But he was her cousin and they had grown up together, playing as children and romping in the meadow. True, they had often spoken of setting up a home together one day after they both grew up, but now, here, her feelings for Hamilton Prescott suddenly seemed like exactly what they were: child's play. What she had always thought of as her "great love" for Hamilton was in truth nothing in comparison to what she felt for Adam Parke. Never in all her life had she felt so drawn to a man.

"I-I meant I am not a member of the governor's council, nor am I married to a councilman. I am not a successful planter. I have accomplished nothing of import since I came to

Jamestown."

His tone turned solemn. "But, you *came,* Miss Wakefield. That alone is of consequence. You were brave enough to leave your home and family and friends behind and you survived the treacherous crossing. You are *here,* an adventurer in a New World; one that is sometimes savage and always . . . dangerous."

It felt dangerous now. "I-I had not thought of it in that manner, Mister Parke."

Holding her gaze, he reached again for his mug and took a small sip from it.

"Diana!" came a feminine voice from behind her.

Diana turned. "Sallie Mae, how delightful to see you! Good evening, Samuel."

"Diana. Evening, Parke." The men shook hands.

"Your new frock is beautiful!" Sallie Mae cried. "I looked for you at Christmastide service, but I never saw you. I knew you would be wearin' it." She turned a smile on Adam Parke. "For Diana's birthday, I gave her a length of fabric for a new gown. Does she not look lovely?"

Diana blushed.

"You have read my mind, Goodwife Wingate. Miss Wakefield does indeed look lovely tonight."

"Thank you, sir," Diana murmured, feeling so flustered now she wished she might slip through one of the cracks in the floorboards beneath her feet.

"This is quite a to-do, ain't it?" Sallie Mae exclaimed, a bright smile on her face, her cheeks rosy. "Have you met the governor's wife, Lady Temperance?"

Diana's hazel eyes widened. "I was unaware the governor had a wife."

"Oh, indeed, he does. And his proper title is Governor *Sir* George Yeardley. He was recently knighted, you know," she said primly.

"I-I did know that."

"Were you also aware that he has three children?"

"No, I confess not. One wonders where he has been hiding them. And his wife."

Sallie Mae giggled. "Lady Temperance only just gave birth to their third child. She named the boy Francis. I understand she and the children live on their plantation, Flowerdew. I confess I only just learned the governor has a plantation. He ordered half a dozen hogsheads from Samuel. Seems the man who has been making his casks recently passed away from the bloody flux."

"Oh, my."

Because the men were engaged in conversation, Diana continued to speak exclusively with Sallie Mae. She leaned closer. "A moment ago, when Mister Parke and I crossed through the great room, I caught sight of Noah. Have you seen Faith this evening?"

"She is not here," Sallie Mae replied. "I heard Noah telling someone that she is ill."

Diana's brow furrowed. "Oh, dear." She worried her lower lip, considering whether or not to reveal to Sallie Mae that Faith was now with child. "You do know that she is . . . increasing."

Sallie Mae nodded. "I suspected that might be the case."

"Perhaps we should call on her. To see how she is getting on." Diana quickly told Sallie Mae about her recent visit with Faith and how frazzled the bride appeared beneath her load of new responsibilities. "She will surely require help soon, if she does not now."

Sallie Mae glanced past Diana's shoulder. "I see Noah now. Just there, standing inside the doorway. I do hope he does not come this way."

Diana gazed that direction. But upon hearing Adam clearing his throat, she glanced back toward him. And was startled by the sudden change in his demeanor. He, too, was looking straight at Noah Colton, who was now engaged in conversation with two other men standing only a few feet from them. His jaws ground together, and Adam's eyes had narrowed to mere slits. To Diana, he looked angry enough to kill. To be sure, there was something vastly amiss between Adam Parke and Noah Colton. She glanced back at Noah in time to catch the look of animosity he directed at Adam before he turned to exit the room.

"I understand the New Virginia Company will be appointing a new governor soon," Samuel said, apparently oblivious to the unspoken exchange between Adam Parke and the finely turned-out trader. "D'ye suppose it will be the esteemed Noah Colton?"

Adam's sea-green eyes cut round. "If it is, I shall be on the next boat back to England."

Samuel laughed. "Bad blood between you, eh?" He glanced toward where Noah's hasty retreat had been halted by another beaming colonist. "Seems folks around here either love him or hate him."

"I make no bones about being a member of the hate-him party."

Samuel grinned before downing a long draught from his mug. "I confess I am unacquainted with the man, but I understand I am not someone he favors. Seems I married his sweetheart, didn't I, Sallie Mae?" He slipped an arm around his pretty wife's waist. Tonight she'd left off her tidy white cap and instead tied a blue ribbon around her thick blond curls, now long enough to reach her shoulders. "I expect we'd best be headin' home, Goodwife Wingate."

"If you say so, Mister Wingate." Sallie Mae snuggled close to her husband's strong chest.

Watching the couple, who quite obviously loved one another more now than the day they wed, warmed Diana's heart. After the friends had wished one another a prosperous new year, Adam Parke addressed Diana.

"So you have celebrated a birthday since you arrived in Jamestown. How many years do you have in your dish, if I may be so bold?"

Diana smiled self-consciously, her lashes again fluttering against her flushed cheeks. "I am now eighteen, sir."

"Ah." Adam nodded. "The same age my sister was when she arrived in Jamestown."

Diana looked up. "You have a sister? Perhaps I am acquainted with her."

He shook his head. "She is . . . no longer with us."

"Oh, I am so sorry. I . . . know how it feels to lose a loved one."

A small silence followed, during which Diana cast about for something to say. She did not yet wish to tell him of the tragedy she had suffered, although that door had been opened. So, she took a small step inside. "I recently lost my parents," she murmured, then, looking up at him, hastened to add, "so perhaps that means I am not quite as brave as you think, sir. I did not leave my family behind in England . . . they left me."

"I am indeed sorry for your loss, Diana. May I call you Diana?"

His question pleased her, as it indicated that he, too, wished them to be on a more familiar footing. She smiled. "If I may address you as Adam."

"Indeed, you may."

The twinkle in his eyes brought a smile to her lips. Adam Parke was a wonderful man. Now that they'd begun to speak intimately, she wished to stay by his side forever. On the other hand, not wishing him to think her forward, she bit back the many questions she longed to ask. When did he come to the New World? And why? Was he still mourning his late wife? How old was his little son? Was he ready now to . . . love again? Instead, she said, "I fear I am monopolizing your time this evening, sir."

"You just agreed to address me as Adam. And you are not monopolizing my time, Diana. I am choosing to speak with you of my own accord. Besides, I can think of no one I would rather have monopo—"

"So here you are, Diana," came a woman's voice. "I have looked everywhere for you!"

"Good evening, Mistress Larsen," said Adam. "You are looking well."

Mary laughed. "Thank you, young man, but ye'd best save your compliments for the unmarried ladies. I am, as ye well know, already taken."

Everyone laughed gaily, and at that moment Luca Sheridan, accompanied by another gentleman, stepped up.

"You look lovely tonight, Diana," Luca said by way of greeting. He introduced both ladies to the gentleman at his side and Diana did the same for Adam, who, as it turned out, was unacquainted with either of the men.

"As you and Adam are both successful planters," Diana remarked, "I would have thought you would be acquainted with one another."

Suddenly, their conversation was interrupted by a joyous whoop, and almost everyone in the smaller chamber began to surge toward the great room beyond.

"Where is everyone going?" Diana asked.

"There is to be dancing!" Mary Larsen exclaimed. "That is why I came in search of you. I knew you would enjoy it." She turned to Luca. "Diana has been so glum of late, I am persuaded she greatly misses her fine life in England."

"Oh, not at all!" Diana cried.

"Since we've no masques or fancy dress balls here in

Jamestown," Mary went on, "I knew you would not wish to miss the dancing."

"I trust you will allow me to claim the first dance, Diana." Luca smiled down at her.

Completely flustered by the attention she was receiving from, not one, but two men, Diana replied politely, "Indeed, Mister Sheridan. It would be my pleasure."

To her chagrin, Luca reached to clasp her hand to lead her away. Diana flung a quick glance over her shoulder at Adam. His tight-lipped nod felt like a shard of ice piercing her heart.

Chapter 31

Since the great room of Governor Yeardley's home was not nearly great enough to accommodate the revelers, let alone dancing, it was decided that that activity would take place out of doors.

"Who shall provide the music?" Diana asked of no one in particular as her party fell in with the throng of colonists spilling from the house.

"Some of the militiamen have gone for their fifes and drums," Mary Larsen replied.

In minutes, three or four men carrying reed-thin fifes and two others toting small round drums did their best to produce a tune the revelers could hop or match dance steps to. No one seemed to mind the crisp, cold air as the men and women stamped their feet and merrily twirled arm-in-arm. Diana had danced many times before, but never out of doors in the middle of a dusty road on a cold winter's night, and never wearing a pair of thick-soled brogues on her feet. As she and Luca attempted to match their steps to the music, she noted that rather than the delicate patterns one carefully learned to perform on a polished ballroom floor in England, dancing here more closely resembled galloping to whatever rhythm one could detect from the raucous noise the musicians produced.

Still, she joined in the laughter and enjoyed the carefree abandon. Even William and Mary Larsen joined the couples whirling in the street. She saw John Fuller with his new bride.

Once, as she and Luca stood on the sidelines clapping their hands, she glanced up to find John Fuller looking straight at her. When she smiled, he quickly turned back to his new wife. Diana's lips thinned at the sight of Noah Colton whirling one after another of the pretty young girls, as if the man hadn't a care in the world or a pregnant wife at home. To Diana's surprise, William Larsen even caught her about the waist for a quick turn on the street. Watching them from the sidelines, a smiling Mary stood next to Luca, Mary clapping her hands, her cheeks rosy from her exertion.

Several other gentlemen stepped up to claim a dance with Diana. Luca danced with Mary and a few other unmarried girls. Colonists who lived nearby but who had not been invited to the governor's party, had, upon hearing the commotion in the street, quickly joined the merrymakers. If Governor Yeardley had been in a frame that night to level fines for public drunkenness and, in some cases, even lewdness, the town's coffers would have been full on the first day of the new year, and there'd be a waiting line for the pillory. But since it was all in good fun, the law-breakers' antics were duly forgiven.

Sometime later, a fatigued, although still smiling, Mary Larsen declared that she was ready to leave. Diana, who'd spent the past hour hoping Adam Parke would seek her out for a dance, conceded that apparently it was not meant to be. Only moments before she and the Larsens set out for the return walk home, did she catch a glimpse of Mister Parke climbing atop his horse and, without a backward glance, ride off into the dark winter night.

Halfway home, William remembered he'd forgotten the three mugs they had carried with them. When he said he'd go back for the gourds, Mary balked.

"To be sure, there will be a slew of forgotten mugs. Temperance and George will never know to whom any of them belong. I shall have Cheiwoga scoop out fresh gourds."

"Oh," Diana said, "might I take one to Faith?"

"Of course you may, dear. Do come along, William. I am fagged to death."

Diana lay awake a long time that night, thinking over the evening and attempting to sort out the thoughts swirling through her mind. More and more she was coming to realize that she hadn't a clue what love was all about. She had always thought she loved Hamilton, but perhaps she had merely clung to him out of habit. Back home in England she knew very few men. Her father, as a member of the landed gentry, enjoyed a certain elevated status; therefore, she could not look for a husband beneath her father's stature, but due to their reduced circumstances, she could hardly aspire to acquire a husband of greater consequence, even if it was what her parents had pinned their hopes upon. So to Diana's way of thinking, then, that meant her only choice was to . . . cling to her cousin. Hamilton had kissed her once when she was a girl of fourteen and he sixteen. It had not been a romantical occurrence, but more an experimental one. He had asked if he might kiss her and she had agreed. Truth was, she could scarcely recall the encounter now. It seemed a very long time ago.

She could not imagine Hamilton here in Jamestown. He was a young man of twenty years now; here, he would be a bewildered boy, unsure how to go on and completely at a loss as to how to survive in this uncharted New World. Hamilton would never be able to build a house, plant tobacco, or even split logs for the fire.

Would she love Hamilton now if he were one of the men courting her in Jamestown? Would she choose to marry him if he were here?

Sadly, she had to admit that she would not. Despite his age, Hamilton was still a boy, and would likely always be, his only concerns similar to those of Noah Colton: which costly garments to don that day and how to charm the ladies. Diana would never be drawn to a man like Noah Colton. However, she might be drawn to a man like Samuel Wingate. He was kind and loving and strong and clever. He was perfect for Sallie Mae. They were both good, honest sorts, and their love for one another palpable. She sighed. Since coming to the New World, she'd become so caught up in sorting out the mystery she'd become embroiled in, she'd made little to no headway finding a family to replace the one she'd so tragically lost. Other than Sallie Mae, whom she now thought of as a sister, she had no family.

But how to go about choosing the right man to marry?

She did not want to make a foolish choice, as she firmly believed Faith had done. Mulling the matter over further, Diana drew the conclusion that she truly did not know what love was, but she had a notion what it was not. It was not possession, or pity. It was not simply smiling into one another's eyes, but instead, looking ahead together in the same direction. It was traveling through life side-by-side, helping one another, buoying up the other when the need arose, caring how the other felt and being willing to do whatever it took to help make one's partner feel better.

Something told her that both Luca Sheridan and Adam Parke would make fine husbands. They were both strong, capable and dependable men, men to whom a woman could turn when she did not know which way to turn. To have such a man by her side would indeed make her feel safe in this wild, new land. To lie beside such a man at night would be comforting. And to bear such a man's children would be the grandest thing Diana could imagine.

Further comparing Luca and Adam, she admitted that Luca seemed the more refined of the two, but there was something about Adam that drew her, a magnetism that seemed to pull her to him. And there was that nagging feeling that she already knew him. Of course, that was preposterous. In the end, though she was hard-pressed to explain why, she knew that of all the men she'd met since coming to Jamestown, the one she would choose above all others to become her husband would indeed be Adam Parke. But how, how—when she had no idea how to accomplish such a feat—was she to go about winning the heart of the man she wished to marry?

CHAPTER 32

A few days later Diana climbed atop Bug-a-Boo's back and rode to the Wingate property to collect Sallie Mae. Together, they set out for Faith's home to see how she was feeling, or to determine if she needed anything. It was a bitter cold January day, but the blue sky and sunshine overhead made it seem more like autumn than the dead of winter.

"What if Noah is home?" Sallie Mae asked from her perch behind Diana on the mare's back. Both girls wore long woolen capes over their clothing, and their lambskin gloves.

"Then we shall simply deliver the gift I am bringing to Faith and take our leave."

"I have no gift," Sallie Mae exclaimed. "I should also like to take Faith a gift. What shall I bring?" When Diana did not offer a suggestion, Sallie Mae said, "I shall take her a length of fabric! I have plenty left from the draperies I made. Faith can have a nice warm skirt or a blanket for the baby. And she'll also need cloth for baby garments. Let us turn around. I shall gather up scraps of cloth for the baby and fabric for Faith."

"That is very thoughtful of you, Sallie Mae." Diana tugged the reins to halt Bug-a-Boo and back they went to the Wingate home.

Before they arrived, Sallie Mae asked, "What are you bringin' Faith?"

"Compared to your gift, nothing." Diana laughed. "I am simply taking her a pair of gourd mugs. When I was there last,

Faith said Noah had thrown one of theirs into the fire."

"Why would he do such a thing?"

"You and I both know Noah is a volatile man. Apparently something set him off."

A half hour later, both girls stood on the doorstep of Faith and Noah's small house on the edge of Jamestown. Diana glanced toward the cleared plot of ground that fronted the forest. She recalled the day she'd parted ways with the beautiful young woman she'd met in the woods, the day she'd gone alone to gather nuts. She could scarcely imagine that lovely young woman wed to Noah Colton, or living here. She had not had an opportunity to tell Sallie Mae the tale; perhaps she would tell her today.

When Faith answered their rap at the door, Sallie Mae was vastly surprised by the change in Faith's appearance. Whereas before she had been a pretty girl with creamy skin and shiny auburn hair, her skin was now blotchy, her hair straw-like, and her hands, rough and work-reddened. The blouse above the tight confines of her soiled bodice was tattered and the waistband of her skirt torn.

"Oh, it is you, Diana. And Sallie Mae." A dirt-encrusted hand swiped at the wisp of hair that tumbled across the girl's furrowed brow. "I am frightfully busy today. As ever."

"We shall not linger. Might we step inside for a moment, please?"

Faith opened the door a jot wider. "Very well. But only for a moment."

Sallie Mae followed Diana inside the small house. The cluttered interior and foul smells inside repelled her. The house was cold, and the air was smoke-filled due to an ill-drawing chimney, Sallie Mae surmised. But the air also reeked with the stench of unwashed clothing and a chamber pot beggin' to be emptied. Did the poor girl not know how to empty a slop bucket, wash linens, or scrub a trencher?

"I brought you and Noah a pair of gourds," Diana was saying, "and Sallie Mae also brought you a gift."

"W-why are you bringing me gifts?" Faith muttered.

"Look at what I brought ye, Faith," Sallie Mae said brightly. She cast a glance about the disorderly room in search of a place to spread out the fabric. The floor was strewn with sour-smelling straw, and the planked wooden table littered with food-encrusted trenchers and a couple of overturned ale jugs. "Well." She unfurled the length of blue damask over one arm. "There is sufficient cloth here to fashion a new skirt. Diana tol' me ye was carryin' a babe, so I thought ye might be needin' a new skirt."

"Show her the rest of the fabric, Sallie Mae." Diana reached for the length of damask while Sallie Mae dug into the pouch she'd slung over one shoulder.

"I've five or six squares of cloth here plenty big enough for baby clothes!"

"Oh. My. I-I don't know what to say." Faith fingered the damask draped over Diana's arm. "It's lovely. Thank you." The hint of a smile flitted across her face. "I haven't had anything new to wear in a . . . long while."

"Might we sit here on the bench and talk a bit?" Diana asked.

"I . . . well, I suppose . . . but just for a moment. Noah should be . . . he is . . . he should be returning in a bit." She scooped up a filthy jerkin draped over the backless bench that fronted the table and kicked a pair of muddy boots to one side. "You may sit here, Sallie Mae."

All three girls sat down, Diana and Sallie Mae side by side on the bench, Faith on a tree stump that sat at the top of the table.

"We looked for you at Governor Yeardley's party on the eve of the new year," Sallie Mae said. "It was a lovely party."

"You would have enjoyed the dancing," Diana put in.

"There was *dancin'?*" cried Sallie Mae.

"Indeed. It was got up soon after you and Samuel departed."

"Well, I surely would have enjoyed that," Sallie Mae exclaimed. "Did you dance with Adam?" Before Diana could reply, she turned to Faith. "Our Diana has two fine gentlemen suitors now, Mister Adam Parke and Mister Luca Sheridan."

"Hmmm," Faith murmured.

"I did not see you at Christmastide services either," Diana said. "Are you feeling unwell, Faith, what with the . . . the babe and all," she faltered.

Faith bit her lip.

An awkward silence followed. At length, Faith drew in a breath. "Noah does not wish me to . . . to attend services any longer. At least, not until after the baby comes."

Diana leaned forward. "Are you feeling terribly unwell, Faith? Sallie Mae said she overheard Noah telling someone at the party that you were ill."

"Well, he . . ." Faith swiped at her nose, which did seem a trifle runny. "Oh, what can it matter? Noah does not wish anyone to know that I . . . that I am as far gone as I am. He does not wish anyone to think ill of him, or of me. He believes that if it is bandied about that we . . . laid together before we married that it will harm his chances to be named governor."

"A new governor has already been selected," Sallie Mae said matter-of-factly. "A peddler from New England popped into Samuel's workshop some days back and delivered the news; said it came straight from England. Official papers are on a ship headed this way even now."

"Oh-h." Faith let out a breath. "I-I . . . wonder what Noah will say to that?"

"Perhaps he will agree to let you attend services again," Diana said. "I cannot think it is healthy for you to stay cooped up here every day, Faith. You need to see other people on occasion."

"Oh, I see other folks. A neighbor from across the way stops in to check on me. Goody Smithfield. Actually, I've purchased food from her a time or two." She worried her lower lip. "I-I shudder to think what Noah will do once he learns I paid for it with . . . with two of his fine beaver pelts. But, I-I don't know where he hides his money, so I saw nothing for it but to give her the pelts. Truly I didn't." She appeared to be appealing to them for approval of her actions. "We . . . have so little food . . ." She appeared flustered. "I-I shouldn't be carrying on so." She pushed up from the table. "I really should get back to my work now. Noah expects a hot meal when he . . ."

"Perhaps we might help," Sallie Mae offered cheerfully. "I'll wager you could use another bucket of water to . . . wash the linens and . . . what not." She glanced at the wooden yoke and empty buckets propped against the wall, then glanced back at Faith, and for the first time, noticed how very large, indeed, her middle had become. "Oh, my. Ye do need help, Faith. Plain as a pikestaff, ye do."

"When will Noah be returning home?" Diana asked quietly.

Faith nervously ran her hands up and down her arms. One hand reached to rub at a smudge of dirt on her cheek. "I-I cannot say for certain. He . . . rarely stays home for any length. He has such a great deal to take care of, what with the tradin' and . . . trappin'."

"Faith, you told me Noah doesn't do the actual trapping."

Of a sudden, Faith's eyes filled with tears and her shoulders sagged. Diana reached to help her sit back down on the tree stump.

"Tell us what the trouble is, sweetie. Perhaps Sallie Mae and I can think of an answer."

Faith sobbed into her hands. "Nothing can be done for me

now. I have nowhere to go."

Sallie Mae and Diana exchanged worried frowns.

"Sallie Mae, go and see if there is anything left to eat in the loft," Diana said softly.

"No!" Faith looked up, her eyes wild. "You mustn't go up there, *please!*"

"But, why, Faith? If you need corn, or peas . . ."

"Please, go now. You shouldn't have come. Noah is taking good care of me. Truly he is. Everything will be all right once the baby comes."

Diana and Sallie Mae exchanged fretful looks.

Sallie Mae thought Faith seemed not to be makin' much sense. "Did you and Noah wed because you was carryin' his child?" she boldly asked.

Faith's demeanor suddenly turned to that of a child. "He married me because I asked him to," she declared. "Because I-I knew he had done something wrong, and . . . and I told him that if he did not marry me, I would tell everyone what I knew. He did the right thing by me. He married me." She turned a wide-eyed gaze on her visitors. "Noah is a good man. He will love our babe, the same as he loves me." Again, she stood up, albeit a trifle shakily. "Please go now so that I might prepare a nice supper for my husband. Thank you for the lovely gifts, ladies. Good day to ye now."

Diana and Sallie Mae watched as their friend waddled across the room and disappeared into the adjoining chamber.

"What should we do now?" Sallie Mae asked.

A concerned expression on her face, Diana crossed the room in the direction Faith had gone. When she peeked in and saw that the girl had lain down upon the rumpled bed, she turned back to Sallie Mae. "She appears to have fallen asleep."

"She is worn to a frazzle, poor thing. Shall we see if there is any food in the loft?"

Diana thought a moment. "I think not. Our footfalls might awaken her. Let us do as she asked. Perhaps on our way back home, we can think of a way to help her."

Once outdoors, Sallie Mae said, "Perhaps we might bring in a few logs for the fire 'afore we go. House seemed frightful cold to me."

Both girls tramped to the side of the house in search of the woodpile. Diana cast a gaze at the enclosed shed. For a farthing, she'd go inside and nose around. Something told her she'd find incriminating sacks of gunpowder and a couple of casks full of muskets.

"There is scarcely any wood here a'tall," Sallie Mae lamented as the girls headed toward a smattering of spindly logs. "No wonder the house is cold. It's as if Noah has left Faith to fend for herself."

Between them, they managed to cart in all that was left of the logs. Indoors, Sallie Mae, who'd had more experience than Diana at that sort of thing, located a somewhat rusty iron poker, and by the time the pair quitted the house, bright orange flames again danced in the grate.

Seconds after they climbed atop Bug-a-Boo's back, Diana said, "Perhaps we should make inquiries of Faith's neighbor, Goodwife Smithfield. The one whom Faith said she purchased food from."

Sallie Mae's long gaze traveled across the brown field that lay beyond the dusty road here and the one running down the opposite side. "Faith said 'my neighbor across the way,' so perhaps the woman's home is over there." She pointed toward a row of thatched-roofed cottages some yards away.

"Hold tight." With a nudge of her heel, Diana urged the mare forward and in seconds the horse had galloped pell-mell across the way.

"What a splendid ride that was!" Sallie Mae laughed merrily

as she slid off the horse's back to the ground.

"Bug-a-Boo needs a good run from time to time," Diana replied as the two walked toward a small house. "We could let her gallop all the way back home if you're not afraid of slipping off. Without a proper saddle, hanging on can sometimes prove difficult."

No one answered their rap at the first door. At the second, a woman directed them to a third hovel where she said Goodwife Smithfield and her husband lived.

Once inside the tidy Smithfield house, which felt quite warm and filled with the delicious aroma of freshly baked bread, Goodwife Smithfield seemed delighted to have two pretty young ladies call upon her.

"How about a nice mug of apple cider and some warm yeast bread?"

"Oh, no thank you, ma'am. We do not mean to trouble you. We merely wished to—"

"Rubbish! I insist!" The rosy-cheeked woman hurried to the hearth, filled two scooped-out gourds with spiced apple cider, set the mugs before the girls, bustled off and returned carrying a trencher with two generous wedges of fluffy brown bread upon it. "Now, then," she sat down opposite the girls, an expectant smile on her face, "tell me yer names and why ye have come."

"I am Diana Wakefield and this is Goodwife Wingate. We—"

"Why ye're the new cooper's little wife! My, we was glad to see him a'comin'. How are ye a'farin', dear? I'll wager yer husband stays real busy, now don't he? And ye've a fine new house, too, ain't ye? But . . . ye was sayin'?"

Diana swallowed the delicious bread in her mouth. "We wished to consult with you about our friend, Goodwife Colton, who lives across the way."

Already the older woman was shaking her graying head.

"Dreadful shame, that. Poor gel's too weak now to manage a thing. M'husband and I feel frightful sorry for 'er. Not her man, though, make no mistake."

"Does she ever leave the house, ma'am?" Sallie Mae asked.

The woman's head wagged. "Not since he tol' her he don't want her a'showin' her face anywheres. He don't fool me none. He jes don't want folks a'knowin' about the babe, it comin' so early and all. I look in on her most days. And I've sent m'Indian woman to fetch water for 'er. I mean to take 'er some o' this bread 'afore long. Poor gel ain't eatin' enough for two, and there it is."

"What of Noah? Faith says he is rarely at home."

"Oh, he stops in, changes 'is clothes, then off he goes. M'husband, we can hear 'em quarrelin' all the way over here. Little spit-fire, she can hold her own w' 'im, all right, but not when he's a'drinkin'; which 'e does most nights when 'es home. Don't mind sayin' I fear for 'er, but what's a body to do? I can't jerk her outta' there, though many's the day I wish I could, make no mistake."

Sallie Mae exhaled a breath. "Faith said she has purchased food from ye on occasion."

"Indeed. Nigh on a fortnight ago was the last. Paid for it w'two of 'er husband's fine beaver pelts. Not that he done the actual trappin', mind ya. More like some savage give 'em to him, if ye ask me. He knows how to do the pretty for the ladies all right; but that wastrel has more'n one face, make no mistake."

"Sallie Mae and I wish to help our friend. Perhaps we could bring some corn or peas here to you and you could take them to Faith when you are certain Noah is not at home. It would put our minds at ease."

"Would please me to help. 'Deed it would. Be glad to see you young ladies again, too. Rarely 'ave callers, don't ye know. You are both welcome to call any time."

That night over supper, Sallie Mae told Samuel about their visit with Faith and her neighbor, Goodwife Smithfield.

"Faith's shabby little hovel smells like a pig sty, Sam. She's nigh on as big as a cow. I 'spect that's why she can't do much in the way of cleanin'." She ladled a spoonful of scrapple and green beans onto her husband's trencher and scraped the remainder onto her own, then she slid onto the fine ladder-backed chair drawn up before their planked wooden table. "I want to help her, Sam."

"Ye've a big heart, Sallie Mae. But the girl has a husband to do for her. Wouldn't want him to think we're a'meddlin'."

"We ain't meddlin'. Noah clearly ain't doin' what he ought. Thank heaven I had the good sense not to marry the man."

"I do thank heaven for that, Sallie Mae." Sam paused to tear off a piece of flatbread and mopped up what was left of the scrapple on his plate. "What would ye like to do?"

"She needs firewood. I thought that tomorrow evening, when you and Jack finish yer work, ye could take a load of kindlin' over there. Faith is not strong enough to carry logs of a size into the house, but she could cart in sticks and twigs. They'll burn good."

"We've kindlin' to spare, all right," Samuel agreed. "Sticks and twigs are no use to me. Just been burning 'em off anyways."

"Somethin' terrible's gonna happen to that poor girl, Sam. I can feel it. You and I have plenty o' food to spare. I want 'ye to take a bushel of corn when 'ye takes the firewood. Fact is, we could take the corn over tonight and some of this nice scrapple. There's a good bit left in the pot. You don't want any more, do ye, Sam?"

"I've had more'n my share, love. We'll take some to your

friend if that'll make ye happy."

Sallie Mae grinned. "You make me happy, Sam."

On Sabbath next, Sallie Mae scooted onto the polished wooden pew beside Diana. "Samuel took some kindlin' and a bushel of corn to Faith the other evenin'," she whispered. "Said there wasn't a light burnin' in the house, but he rapped at the door anyways."

"Did Faith come to the door?"

Sallie Mae nodded. "He set the bushel o' corn inside the door, then handed her the trencher of scrapple and green beans I sent. Said she appeared a bit dazed, but took it all the same. She thanked him and closed the door."

Diana shook her head. "Something's amiss, Sallie Mae. I wonder why she didn't want us to go into the loft?"

Sallie Mae shrugged. "Ye s'pose Noah's hiding' somethin' up there?"

The minister stepping up to the podium precluded further conversation between the girls. When he solemnly bowed his head, the girls did likewise. Both prayed for Faith.

CHAPTER 33

One evening the following week, Councilman Larsen arrived home from a meeting with the governor accompanied by a friend, whom he told his wife he had invited home for dinner.

Hearing the men's voices from her bedchamber, and recognizing one of them, Diana's heart began to pound in her chest. When Mary rapped at her door to tell her they had a guest, Diana had already changed into her favorite plaid woolen gown and was hurriedly brushing her hair.

Initially, the talk over the tasty meal of fried venison, buttered squash and spoon bread was primarily between the men and centered around Adam Parke's recent purchase of additional indentures, and the fact that he was now entitled to additional land grants.

"You will soon have one of the largest plantations in the settlement," Larsen said. "Rivaling the size of Rolfe's or even Yeardley's."

"I did not realize Governor Yeardley had such a large plantation." Diana, who thus far had said little during the meal, seized the moment.

"Yeardley has two working spreads," Larsen replied. "Flowerdew Hundred, and the Mulberry Island plantation he calls the Stanley Hundred."

"Flowerdew seems an unusual name," Diana mused.

"Both Stanley and Flowerdew are family names," Mary told her. "Governor Yeardley's wife was the former Temperance

Flowerdew. She has been in Jamestown a good long while. I understand she was one of the few women to survive the starvin' time." She turned to Adam. "As did your late wife," she said softly.

Adam nodded tightly.

"You have suffered a great many losses since coming to the New World, young man. Your father, your wife."

"And his sister," Diana put in, before realizing she was thoughtlessly bringing up yet another painful memory for Adam. The undue length of the awkward silence that followed her careless remark caused her to fling a puzzled gaze from one to the other. What had she said wrong?

"Indeed," Mary murmured, "your sister." The smile on her lips was tight. "How is your little son faring?"

Drawing another breath, this time perhaps one of relief, Adam smiled. "Eli is doing very well, thank you, ma'am. He is a strong, healthy boy."

Again, Diana seized the moment. Surely to ask their guest about his child, whom they were already discussing, would not render her further guilty of ill judgment. "How old is your little boy, Mister Parke?"

"Just over three years now."

"I assume one of the women at Harvest Hill looks after him," Mary remarked.

Again Adam nodded. "Margaret Morgan kindly offered to care for him when I am unable to do so and, of course, there are other goodwives on the plantation and five or six Indian women."

"With those carrot-red curls—" Mary smiled. "Eli is an adorable child."

"My concern is that with so many women doting on him, he will grow up spoilt rotten and be of no use to anyone."

Everyone laughed.

"I am certain you have nothing to fear on that score," Mary assured him.

"I only just learned that Governor Yeardley has three small children." Diana tried again to enter the conversation.

"Indeed," Mary said. "Temperance recently gave birth to a second son."

"When is the new governor expected to take office?" Diana asked, feeling a good deal more comfortable now.

Until Adam's head whirled around. "You are aware a new governor has been elected?" He turned to address Larsen. "I did not realize the official proclamation had been made public."

Larsen's lips twitched. "Our Diana listens well."

"I heard the news from Sallie Mae, who said a peddler brought word straight from New England."

"Ah, well, so there it is," Adam declared. "A simple rumor."

"With fact at its base," Larsen stated firmly. "As you know, a good many of us expected Noah Colton to be named Virginia's next governor."

Diana's heart plunged to her feet. Once again she had inadvertently brought up a subject that could prove disastrous all around. So far as she knew, she was the only person present who knew where both men stood on the matter of Noah Colton. Larsen believed strongly in his trustworthiness. Adam hated the man. This past week, Diana had purposely said nothing to the Larsens regarding Noah's ill-treatment of his new wife. To pit the two men against one another at this juncture could very well dash whatever small in-roads she stood to gain from Adam Parke's appearance here tonight.

"Who has been named to take Governor Yeardley's place?" Mary asked innocently.

"Sir Francis Wyatt," her husband replied. "A kinsman of Sir Edwin Sandys's by virtue of having married his niece."

"I suspect Colton will be outraged at that," Adam muttered.

Again Diana held her breath. With no help from her, Adam himself had brought his disdain of Noah Colton to light. She noted his jaws grind together with suppressed anger. And again she wondered why he felt as he did. She was glad when the talk turned to other things.

Larsen confirmed the rumor that a group of Pilgrim Separatists, who had been living in exile in the Netherlands for nigh on a decade, had set sail for Virginia in the fall, but a few months back, had instead landed off course in New England.

"One wonders how the Separatists are faring now that winter has set in," Mary mused.

"It is said they were met on land by an Indian who spoke perfect English," her husband remarked.

"The way I heard it," Adam spoke up, "several explorers have met up with an Indian who can perfectly mimic the words of any man who speaks to him, whatever the language."

"Ah. Well, at any rate, had an English-speaking Indian met Captain John Smith when he came to these shores, I daresay things would have been vastly different at the outset," Larsen declared.

"Will likely be a twelvemonth before the truth regarding the Separatists filters down to us," Adam concluded.

Everyone nodded agreement.

"Unfortunately, rumors are rampant," Larsen went on. "Our king could fall ill and die and we'd know nothing of it for nigh on a decade."

"Oh William, it is not half so bad as all that!" Mary said.

Diana cast about for what she hoped would be an innocuous remark. "When did you first arrive in Jamestown, Mister Parke?"

"Nearly a decade ago," he replied quietly.

"Oh, my," Mary said, "that indeed makes you one of Jamestown's founding fathers."

"And that makes me sound like an old man."

Everyone's burst of laughter relieved a whit more of the tension that had caused Diana's stomach to churn.

Until Larsen said, "I'll wager there was very little to sing and dance about in those early days. I say, Parke, did you enjoy the dancing at Governor Yeardley's home the other evening?"

Once again, Diana's heart plunged to her feet.

Adam set down his mug of ale and raised the napkin in his lap to his lips. "I confess I did not dance, sir."

"Why ever not? Our Diana danced nearly every set." He paused, as if realizing he might be treading on someone's toes. "Mary and I danced until she begged for mercy. Said she was fagged to death."

"Oh, William, I said no such thing!"

"You did, indeed, my dear."

"Well, in my estimation," Mary declared, "the bulk of the cavorting about in the street that night hardly resembled dancing, wouldn't you agree, Diana?"

Her heart still drumming in her ears, Diana merely smiled self-consciously.

"Diana is an accomplished dancer," Larsen told Adam. "I expect back home in England she received excellent instruction in all the feminine arts, did you not, Diana?"

Her smile was tight.

At long last, the uncomfortable meal drew to an end and Mary and her husband rather pointedly bade Mister Parke a good evening and retreated to their own bedchamber, leaving their guest and Diana seated alone in the great room before the fire.

"I hope, sir, that you do not feel as if you have been thrown at my head," Diana said, a small smile on her lips as she gazed up at the handsome man. Adam had initially suggested they take a short walk that evening, but before they'd had time to don outer clothing, the threatening sounds of a storm brewing caused them to abandon the plan.

"On the contrary. I confess it was I who hinted to Larsen this afternoon that I was staying the night in town but had nowhere to dine."

Diana grinned. "Well, then, I am pleased he took you up on your offer to dine with us."

Adam chuckled. "Perhaps in future, I will not be obliged to invite myself to dinner."

Now that they were alone, Diana felt a good deal less ill at ease in his company. "I recall you once asked to show me Harvest Hill." Her chin sat at a coquettish tilt. "I wonder if I shall be obliged to invite myself to see your plantation."

He laughed. "I can think of nothing I would rather do than show Harvest Hill to you, Miss Wakefield. You have only to—" The rumble of thunder drowned out his subsequent words.

As Diana had not clearly heard what he said above the noise of the storm and the sputtering fire, she merely murmured, "Thank you, sir."

After a pause, they both began to speak again at the selfsame moment.

"Forgive me. Please go on," Adam urged.

Diana smiled demurely. "I wished you to tell me more about what your life was like when you first came to Jamestown. What did you do then? I mean, before you established your plantation?"

"Well." He cleared his throat and settled back on the straight-backed chair, one long leg crossed over the other. "As I said, I came over nearly a decade ago with my father and a . . . friend, another young man of my own age. The three of us put up a bark house outside the fort. Back then, land grants did not yet exist. Every man was expected to work for the good of the colony, clearing land and whatnot, so that we might plant corn, which we deposited in Jamestown's storehouse. The earliest settlers, it seems, had made the mistake of depending on the Indians to supply their food."

"How singularly odd," Diana exclaimed. "If the Indians were supplying food to the settlers, then why did they not supply it during the starving time?"

"The Indians starved then, as well. I was not here then, but it was my understanding that that year was bleak for everyone. Game was not plentiful, everyone went hungry."

"How terribly sad." Diana paused. "And yet the Indians survived, as did enough of the colonists to eventually make a go of it."

"True, although far more of the Indians survived than did we colonists. Make no mistake; the Indians are far more adept at taking things in stride than we are. They move their villages from place to place. They know when to let the land lie fallow and when to plant again. The Indians have excellent hunting and trapping skills."

His mention of trapping again brought thoughts of Noah Colton to mind. But how was she to broach *that* topic without appearing to pry?

After a pause, Adam said. "I am boring you."

Her head jerked up. "On the contrary. I find all that you are saying quite fascinating."

His gaze held hers. "I find *you* fascinating, Diana."

At his unexpected admission, a smile of pleasure wavered across her face. "Thank you, sir."

"However, I . . . could not help noticing that you . . . seemed to enjoy Mister Sheridan's company a great deal."

"Mister Sheridan and I became acquainted some time ago."

"I do not mean to pry, but . . . do you see him a great deal?"

Diana smiled. "I rarely see him at all. That he resides in Henricus means he does not often find his way to Jamestown."

"Ah."

Another long pause ensued in which Diana, realizing she might again be treading on thin ice, again cast about for something safe to say. Before she could fix on a topic, Adam began to speak in a rather emotionless tone.

"I was little more than a boy when I first came to Jamestown. The only thing on my mind in those early days was survival; clearing the land, putting food on the table, praying for a decent harvest so there might be food come winter. I did not marry at once, and when I did, my efforts turned to caring for my wife and making a home for us. Then, when I was granted my own share of land and following my father's death, also his shares, I became consumed with the notion of becoming a successful planter. What I am trying to say is that . . . I know little of courtship."

Diana was listening intently to his every word, but the conclusion he reached rather startled her. Truth was, she also knew precious little about courtship, which might account for why she feared she'd been making such a muddle of simply trying to talk to him tonight.

Adam drew in another breath. "When I saw you dancing with Sheridan the other evening, laughing and appearing to have such a gay time, I felt awkward and ungainly. I did not claim a dance with you, Diana, for the simple reason that I do not know how to dance. I never had occasion to learn."

"I see." His admission quite relieved her. She feared he had not asked for a dance because Luca had so boldly drawn her away from his side and she had felt helpless to stop him. "I do not believe, sir, that the ability or inability to dance is so very important."

"Sheridan is a refined man, an educated man. He is as refined as you are. I confess I find you quite to my liking, Diana, but it is plainly evident that you and Sheridan are far better suited to one another than . . . you and I are."

Diana's brow puckered. She might not know a great deal about courtship, but she did know that it was not a lady's place to declare herself to a gentleman before he declared himself to her. Therefore, how was she to dissuade Adam from his erroneous viewpoint without it appearing that she was throwing herself at his head? In a quandary, she directed a thoughtful gaze into the flickering flames of the fire. "I-I do not know what to say." Further complicating matters was that Adam's sentiments were . . . square on the mark. Luca was indeed all that Adam had said and more. She and Luca were an excellent match. "If it matters to you at all, sir, Mister Sheridan has . . . not yet declared himself, nor has he offered for me."

Adam leaned forward. "Are you saying that you might . . . that *I* might . . . ?"

She looked up. "Indeed, sir. That is precisely what I am saying. I have only just met you, Mister Parke, but I . . . I find you quite to my liking."

"I understand you rejected John Fuller's suit."

Her eyes widened. "I am astonished at how one's private conversations so quickly become public knowledge."

"Forgive me. I have overstepped the bounds." He drew in an uneven breath. "You are, indeed, too refined for me, Miss Wakefield." He inhaled another breath before beginning to speak, again in a flat, unemotional tone. "I hailed from a small village in England where my father was a tenant farmer. I learned to read and write as a boy sitting on the floor at the feet of a Dame Teacher in our small village. Both my father and I came here without a farthing to our names."

"But you paid your own passage over. Otherwise you would not have received a land grant. And now you have become one of Jamestown's most successful planters."

"A man's present does not obliterate his past."

Diana said nothing for a long moment, then she declared, "If what you say is true, Mr. Parke, then *I* have erred in coming to the New World, for I have placed all my hopes on carving out a future that will completely erase my past."

His lips pursed. "I cannot believe there is anything in your past that would require erasing."

"I take it you also know nothing of Luca Sheridan's past."

His gaze turned quizzical. "Having only just met the man, I confess I know nothing of him at all."

"I refuse to carry tales, but suffice to say that Mister Sheridan's past is far more checkered than anything you have revealed to me of yours. However, he and I are of the same mind. We both believe that an unblemished future can indeed obliterate a . . . distasteful past. If what you profess to believe is true, sir, then you make a mockery of our Christian beliefs."

His gaze turned quizzical. "How is that?"

"It is my understanding that all that is required to obliterate a man, or a woman's, checkered past is God's forgiveness of it."

His lips twitched. "Once again you hint at some sordidness in your past that will require forgiving."

She smiled tightly. "We all harbor secrets that are better left hidden, Mister Parke."

He grinned. "You remind me of my sister."

"How is that?" Her head sat at a tilt.

"You are not afraid to speak your mind, or to cross a man when you disagree with him."

"I did not say I disagreed with you, merely that our viewpoints differ."

"I daresay there is far more to you, Miss Wakefield, than meets the eye."

That he had again addressed her as Miss Wakefield seemed to suggest that he was retreating further and further away, as opposed to coming nearer. Diana feared once again she had said too much. Instead of gaining ground with him, she had merely widened the gap between them. Of a sudden, she blurted out, "Perhaps I could teach you how to dance, Mister Parke."

He laughed. "Once again, your candidness catches me off guard." He rose to his feet.

Which made Diana believe that perhaps he was ready now for his first dance lesson. She also stood.

He seemed to know the meaning she had read into his action. "I believe we have done enough cavorting for one evening."

"Perhaps another time, then?" Even to her ears, her tone sounded a trifle too anxious.

He smiled. "Perhaps."

They both moved toward the door. Outside, the storm sounded quite fierce. As Adam was shrugging into his cloak, Mister Larsen walked briskly into the chamber.

"You are welcome to stay the night here, Parke. Weather seems to be cutting up nasty."

"Thank you, Larsen, but Yeardley has offered me shelter for the night. I should be off."

"Very well, then. Good evening." Larsen left Adam and Diana standing together before the door.

Adam gazed down upon Diana's sweet face. "I quite enjoyed our discussion . . . Diana." His tone was now quite warm.

She smiled. Perhaps not all was lost. "Thank you, sir. I, as well, quite enjoyed your company."

Shutting the door behind him, Diana hoped she had not made a complete muddle of things and that she would indeed see the handsome man again one day.

Chapter 34

One snowy afternoon, Diana had a surprise visit from Sallie Mae. Bundled up in a long woolen cape, a snow-speckled hood covered her blond curls while lambskin gloves and boots kept her hands and feet warm.

Diana answered the rap at the door. Noting her friend's wind-reddened cheeks and nose, Diana exclaimed, "Do come in out of the cold, Sallie Mae! Oh, my—" Glancing past her friend, she spotted a black horse tethered to the gatepost. "Is that your pony?"

Removing her cape and gloves, Sallie Mae nodded. "Samuel and Jack caught two wild horses in the clearin' beyond our house. When I told Sam I wanted one, he let me have m'pick. I call him Chestnut. Ain't he a beauty?"

"Indeed. Nonetheless, you must be near frozen. I shall have Cheiwoga fetch you a mug of hot apple cider."

"Thank you. That would be splendid. I have a great deal to tell you, Diana. I've been to see Faith and came straightaway to see you."

"Has something untoward happened? I hope she has not taken ill."

"Her pregnancy ain't progressin' as it should," Sallie Mae declared. "I found her lying abed."

The girls drew chairs up before the warm fire. When Cheiwoga appeared carrying mugs of hot cider, they smilingly accepted them.

"Does Goody Smithfield continue to check on her each day?"

Nodding, Sallie Mae paused to take a sip of cider. "Her Indian woman brought a bucket of fresh water whilst I was there. I think that Indian understood ever' word I said."

"Some do, you know. They may not let on that they understand our language, but they do."

"Faith said the Indian woman brung her a salve to rub on her belly for the stabbin' pains she's been a'sufferin'."

"Oh, my."

"Poor Faith ain't eatin' enough to keep herself alive, let alone the babe growin' inside her."

Diana sighed. "I do wish Faith could come here. I am certain Mary would welcome her."

"Samuel and I would, as well, although Noah would never allow it."

"Faith's condition is a dreadful shame. Truth to tell, she has essentially become another of Noah Colton's well-kept secrets."

"Faith said he was frightful angry when he discovered a good many of his beaver pelts missin'." Sallie Mae's tone turned conspiratorial. "And, I found out why Faith didn't want us goin' up to the loft that day."

Diana leaned forward. "*Why?*"

"Muskets." Sallie Mae whispered.

Diana's eyes widened. "You *saw* them?"

"Faith told me straight out that Noah is tradin' muskets with the Indians. She said he'd done it afore, that he'd been storin' the ones he only jes got in the shed, but now the roof is leakin', so one by one, in the dead o' the night, he brung 'em inside the house and hid 'em in the loft. She said he put the gunpowder up there, too. Which is why Faith didn't want us goin' to the loft and seein' what was hid there. She said Noah told her if anyone found out about it, he'd kill *her!*"

"Oh, my." Diana glanced over her shoulder lest Mary be near

enough to overhear their conversation. "Why do you suppose Faith told you? Does she not believe Noah would make good on his threat? Apparently she does not know that she is placing herself in grave danger by exposing his secrets. What else did Faith tell you?"

Sallie Mae's eyes narrowed. "That Noah killed a colonist."

Diana's mouth fell open. "Did she say why? Or, more importantly, who?"

"He killed his wife's first husband so she could marry him. He was jealous and spiteful, so he killed the man."

"Oh, Sallie Mae, this is so very dreadful, I can scarcely believe it."

"I believe it. Why else would Faith be a'tellin' it? What's more," she added, "he killed the man with a bow and arrow so as to lay blame on the Indians. She also told me it was Noah who burned Samuel's workshop to the ground."

"This is frightful, Sallie Mae. He also let everyone believe the Indians committed that crime. You were brave to run the risk of seeing him today."

Sallie Mae sighed. "Poor Faith is beside herself. She don't know what to do. She's convinced Noah wishes he'd never married her. Said she should've paid more heed to Mrs. Douglass's words, somethin' about once a man has his way with a woman, he'll abhor and despise her." She paused. "Faith seems to have growed bitter toward her man. Said she's weary of lying to protect his secrets, and don't really care what happens to herself."

"Oh, my." Diana sighed. "Apparently Noah has pushed her beyond the edge of her forbearance. So do you know if he continues his trading now, during the dead of winter?"

"Faith said he does, that he has been gone quite a spell this time. In fact, despite her claim to the contrary, she seemed a trifle worried. Poor girl looked so weary and downtrodden, I could hardly bear it. I took her a kettle of rabbit stew and sat beside the bed to see she ate a good portion of it."

"You have a kind heart, Sallie Mae."

"Perhaps. Only now I wish I didn't know quite so much. Makes me fearful for Sam." She paused. "Should I tell him what Faith told me, or keep it to m'self?"

Diana tried to think what was best to do. "I cannot say for certain. Mister Larsen has made it plain that he and the governor and the councilmen all believe Noah to be above reproach. I do not know what we should do at this juncture." For now, her fears for Sallie Mae shifted entirely to Faith, but what could she do to ensure her safety? "Being married to Noah now places Faith beyond our reach," she murmured. "I cannot think how we, or anyone, can help her now. Goody Smithfield declared she and her man have wanted many a time to take her away from Noah. I cannot think what we can do, Sallie Mae. Perhaps Faith's well-being is in God's hands now."

Eventually the girls turned to speaking of other things. Diana told her friend about her unexpected visit with Adam Parke. "I wish I knew the cause of his grievance with Noah. It is apparent he harbors a great deal of anger toward him, yet he does not expound upon it."

Sallie Mae's brow puckered. "Ex . . . pound?"

Diana grinned. "Speak of it. Adam does not speak of his anger, or explain the cause behind it."

"I see." Sallie Mae's blue eyes sparkled with mischief. "I daresay I shall confound Samuel tonight with that word. I 'spect he don't know the meanin' of it neither. In the meantime, you and me must think of somethin' to do to help poor Faith."

Diana heartily agreed. That night as she lay abed, she thought again and again over all that Sallie Mae had told her. A part of her wondered why Faith had opened up to Sallie Mae when before, she seemed so disdainful of her. More perplexing, why had Noah freely confessed his crimes to his wife?

In the end, she decided that even if she or Sallie Mae betrayed Faith's confidence, they ran the risk that the governor would conclude that once again the young ladies were spreading slanderous lies about one another. Or he might think that Sallie Mae regretted her decision to marry Samuel and wished she had instead married Noah and was now fabricating falsehoods in an attempt to slander Faith and perhaps draw Noah back to her. Or that perhaps he'd think Faith regretted her decision to marry Noah . . . although not a woman in Jamestown would believe that . . . and *she* was spreading malicious lies about her husband. When all was said and done, it would come down to one girl's word against another's since no one, Diana was firmly convinced, would ever believe anything said against Noah Colton.

On the following Sabbath when Diana spotted Adam Parke near Mister Larsen in the meetinghouse, she hurried that direction the second services concluded. Perhaps she could get a moment alone with the planter and question him privately about his thoughts regarding Noah Colton. Perhaps he would be able to think of a way to help Faith without Noah's knowledge.

"Good afternoon, Mister Parke," she began, smiling up at him prettily.

"How are you, Miss Wakefield? As the weather is quite fine today, I had intended to seek you out and ask if you'd care to accompany me to Harvest Hill this afternoon. I will, of course, see you safely home this evening."

Diana's smile brightened. "I would be delighted, sir."

They apprised the Larsens of their plan and, accompanied by another couple named Morgan, who also lived on Adam's plantation, the foursome set out for the river where Adam's shallop was moored. When Diana realized they were to travel by water, apprehension surged through her, but with sheer force of determination, she pushed down her fear and willed herself to focus on the pleasant conversation between Adam and the likable pair traveling with them. She learned that Robert Morgan, his wife and son had been in Jamestown only a few years and that Morgan was a carpenter. The couple's son Ethan, who as it turned out was close on Diana's age, had recently married, and his new little wife was expecting their first child. Both Morgan and his son had worked for Adam on the plantation since arriving here.

The short row up the James River brought them straight to Harvest Hill's private pier, which jutted out over the water.

"I recall you telling me you had your own pier," Diana remarked to Adam.

"Indeed." He jumped out to tie up the boat before returning to assist her onto the wide-planked pier. After exchanging a few parting words, the Morgans headed toward their home, which was located elsewhere on the plantation, while Diana and Adam trudged up the hill toward the painted clapboard house surrounded on three sides by tall trees. The two-storey house faced the river.

"The aspect from here is beautiful," Diana marveled, looking about.

"We are privy to lovely sunsets when the weather is fine."

Diana could scarcely believe that only a short distance upriver from Jamestown, she felt as if she'd entered a different world. Though the air today was cold and crisp, here it smelled sweet and pure. Without realizing it, she must have become inured to the various malodors—cooking, slop bucket contents, the ever-present smoke wafting from chimneys—associated with dozens of families living on top of one another in Jamestown.

Drawing nearer the house, delicious smells of roasting meat and freshly baked bread drifted toward them.

"I smell our dinner," Adam said, smiling down at her.

"As do I." Diana nodded. "Am I to meet your little son today?"

Although his expression was agreeable, Diana detected a slight reticence in his manner. "You are . . . the first young lady I have brought home since . . . since his mother passed."

"If you would rather I not meet him, I—"

"Oh, no. I wish you to . . . know him."

They crossed the wide veranda that led to the entrance of the house. Indoors felt delightfully warm and cozy. Diana noted the planked wooden floors were covered with colorful knotted rag rugs. An Indian woman silently appeared to take their wraps. She and Adam exchanged a few words, partly in English, partly in the woman's native tongue.

"You are fluent in their language?" Diana asked as Adam led her into the front parlor.

"Sometimes there's nothing for it but to learn their words if one wishes to communicate with them." His tone bespoke a whit of exasperation. "One of the Indian women, one my wife used to call Mary, as we could not pronounce her name, was quite adept at understanding nearly every word we said, whilst the woman herself rarely spoke."

"Is Mary still with you?"

"One day she simply did not show up. We . . . later learned that she was needed in her village. To care for . . . a high-ranking warrior's newborn."

Again, Diana felt Adam was not revealing all that was on his mind. What was he withholding? And why? Perhaps over their meal, she could draw him out. The Indian woman appeared again in the doorway, this time carrying Adam's little son in her arms. Upon seeing his father, the boy squealed with delight and fairly flung himself into his father's arms.

"Pa-pa, home!"

"He is adorable!" Diana exclaimed.

Adam did his best to convey to the three-year-old his lady friend's name, but in the end, gave up with a shrug.

"My, what pretty red hair you have, Eli!" she said.

Little Eli squirmed to get down from his father's arms and on chubby legs ran to a chair upon which lay one of his toys. Snatching it up, he returned to show it to Diana. "Onck-onck."

She knelt and, turning the carved wooden toy over in her hands, gazed up at Adam. "Did you carve this for him?"

His guarded look became a self-conscious grin. "Indeed, though I am not an artist."

"On the contrary." Diana handed the toy back to Eli. "What a lovely pig you have."

Moments later, the Indian woman again scooped up Eli and his pig and retreated from the parlor. Soon another Indian woman appeared in the opposite doorway.

"Food ready for eat now."

"Thank you, Hespatakie." Adam turned to Diana. "Shall we?"

Together they entered a second chamber that contained a polished wooden table and six high-backed chairs. A square cupboard stood along one wall, the shelves holding pewter plates, mugs, long-handled knives and forks. On the opposite wall, a cheery fire burned in the grate, noteworthy by the absence of a pot suspended over the flames.

"This is the dining chamber," Adam said. "The kitchen where the cooking is done is in the rear of the house."

Diana shook her head in wonder. Only in Sallie Mae and Samuel's home had she beheld a dining chamber separate from the kitchen. "This is a lovely room," she murmured as Adam pulled out a chair for her to sit.

An earthen bowl on the table held steaming succotash, another, corn pudding. A mountain of pork sizzled on the pewter platter. Steam rose from a scooped-out gourd bowl containing hot greens and bacon bits while another platter held squares of Injun bread, which Diana knew was made by combining rye flour with cornmeal.

After Adam spoke a heartfelt blessing, conversation between them was thin as they began to eat. Although Adam was being the perfect host, Diana still had the gnawing feeling that he was withholding something of import from her. Which meant, once again, she was unable to feel completely at ease with him. Suddenly, the sound of a female voice coming from the front of the house caused her host to leap to his feet.

Diana glanced up in time to see Adam's face turn ashen, as if he'd seen, or heard, a ghost.

"Adam!" came the female voice again. "Where are you? I've brought the baby."

Adam fairly bolted from the room and in his haste only partially closed the door behind him. With it standing ajar, Diana could hear the low rumble of his voice, although she could not clearly distinguish his words, yet the replies from the woman were quite distinct.

"But Adam, I would love to meet your lady friend."

". . . not a good idea," Diana heard Adam reply, then she made out a few more words. "Haven't yet told her about yo— oh, very well."

An instant later, both Adam and his guest burst into the dining chamber. Diana looked up . . . and gasped.

"Catherine!"

"Diana!" the pretty auburn-haired girl exclaimed.

Shock registered on Adam's face. "You . . . are acquainted with one another? How? When? *How?*" he repeated, his tone incredulous.

Both girls laughed.

"May I sit down, Adam?"

"I-Indeed." He pulled out the chair opposite Diana. Retrieving another pewter plate from the cupboard, he set it before her. "Help yourself, Catherine. After your long ride through the woods, I expect you are famished."

"Adam is my brother," Catherine told Diana, a bright smile on her pretty face.

The news astonished Diana, but did explain why since meeting Adam she'd felt as if she already knew him. Brother and sister were very much alike. They both had the same coloring and pleasant, forthright manner.

Today Catherine was once more dressed as a natural, in a long-sleeved doeskin garment and soft boots to her knees. Helping her plate with the tasty offerings, she turned to Adam. "I told Hespatakie to take the baby into Eli's room. The children's things are on the verandah. One of your stable hands took our horses."

Adam still appeared dazed. "Very well."

"I would love to meet your children," Diana said.

"And *I* would like to know how you two became acquainted," Adam demanded, his auburn head jerking from one to the other. The bewildered look on his face again caused both girls to laugh.

"We met quite by accident one day in the forest," Catherine began, her lips twitching. "Lanneika tramped into the clearing where Diana was gathering nuts. Gave her quite a start," she added, scooping a generous portion of corn pudding onto her plate.

"A start is putting it mildly," Diana exclaimed. "When I saw an Indian coming toward me, I was scared out of my wits."

Catherine laughed merrily. "I recall Lanneika never slowed her step."

"And I wasted no time in scampering behind a tree." Diana looked at Adam. "Then I noticed that this Indian was no bigger than me and she was not brandishing a weapon. Instead, she was grinning."

Adam still appeared flummoxed.

"Lanneika has taken to wearing a single feather pointing straight up from the top of her head. She thinks it will make her appear taller and more imposing."

"Hardly likely," Adam muttered. "Is Lanneika with you today?"

Catherine nodded and stopped talking long enough to swallow a few bites of pork and succotash. "I daresay she will also be famished." The fringe on the sleeve of her doeskin garment fluttered as she lifted the mug of ale to her mouth. "Anyhow, on the way here, Silverhawque, my little boy," she clarified to Diana, "saw a deer in the woods, a fawn near its mother, and wished for a closer look, so he and Lanneika trotted off that direction—"

"And you are not afraid for his safety?" Diana cried.

"They'll be along shortly. Although Silver is but two winters, he is very brave. He will one day become *werowance* of our tribe," she added proudly.

Diana heard Adam's audible intake of breath.

"I have also met Catherine's husband," Diana told her host.

"You met . . . Phyrahawque?" Adam directed another astonished gaze at the girls.

Catherine nodded. "The day we returned Mary Larsen's baby to her."

"Without Mary's knowledge," Diana explained, "Cheiwoga took little Ellen, who was ill, to her village to . . ."

"Did the child recover?" Catherine interrupted.

"Indeed. She is right as rain now. The ointment smelled quite foul, but Mary Larsen insisted we leave it be, said another of Cheiwoga's remedies had once healed little Edward."

"I'll be demmed," Adam muttered. "Here I was worried that

once I told you about my sister and her Indian husband . . . I'll be demmed."

All three dissolved into merry laughter.

Before they'd concluded the meal, Lanneika appeared with the toddler in tow. Catherine insisted that the petite Indian girl sit down at the table and eat her fill while she took her little son onto her lap and coaxed small bites of food into his mouth. Diana found the child, who had nut-brown skin, silky black hair and alert black eyes, enchanting. She also enjoyed listening to Lanneika, whose amusing manner of speaking quite delighted her. Still, she could not help but find it a trifle odd to hear Catherine, an English woman, refer to the Indians as "her people" and "her tribe."

Later, as they all sat in the parlor, Catherine told Diana a good deal more about her mixed family. She explained that her husband and Lanneika were blood-related, that they both had the same mother but different fathers. Catherine's husband Phyrahawque was the son of the late, great Powhatan leader Wahunsunacocke, called by the English simply Powhatan; therefore, their son Silverhawque was considered very high ranking. "Similar to the grandson of an English king, a royal prince," she explained. "Which is why he will one day become the leader of our tribe."

"How did your son come by his name?" Diana asked.

Catherine's green eyes softened with fond remembrance. "On the night our son was born and my husband came to spirit me away, our trail through the woods was lit by the most glorious silvery moon I had ever seen. I began to call the baby my silver-child. When I explained to my husband why I did so, he declared our son would be called Silverhawque."

"That is a lovely story," Diana exclaimed.

When she asked if she might see Catherine's baby daughter, the two of them and Lanneika, carrying a now drowsing Silverhawque, tiptoed into the nursery where the sleeping little girl lay.

"Phyrahawque allowed me to choose our daughter's name, so I chose Charlotte after my grandmother." She grinned. "Not nearly so exotic as Silverhawque, I admit. We call her Lottie."

Diana noted the little girl's skin was a lovely mocha color, a good bit lighter than her brother's, and the soft down on her head was pale russet. To Diana, she looked no different from any other English baby. "Does she also have black eyes like her brother?" Diana asked softly.

"Her eyes are green, like mine," Catherine replied proudly. "The Indians are fascinated by her coloring. I am known as Phyrahawque's flame-haired woman. I expect Lottie will become known as his flame-haired daughter."

They quietly returned to the parlor, and Catherine told her brother why she had arrived so unexpectedly. Because Lanneika had remained with the children, Catherine spoke freely regarding Indian affairs. She told Adam that the spirit of Lanneika and Phyrahawque's mother, who had long been the matriarchal *weroansqua* of their tribe, had recently left her body.

"I am sorry to hear of your mother-in-law's death," Adam said.

"I loved her dearly," Catherine murmured. "Although the Indians do not often speak of departed ones, I believe it is due to her passing that dozens of tribal *werowances* chose suddenly to convene. For some reason unbeknownst to me, Phyrahawque thought it best that I not remain at home." Catherine's lighthearted manner turned solemn. "I confess I fear something is afoot, Adam, and I cannot think what it might be."

A fretful sigh escaped him. "I pray it is nothing that will affect our peaceful relations with the Indians. Unfortunately, since Powhatan's brother Opechancanough assumed leadership, our footing with the Indians has been tenuous, at best."

"Whatever it turns out to be"—Catherine's beautiful smile again appeared—"I can always count on my beloved husband's protection. Unlike my former husband, Phyrahawque will let nothing harm me, or our children, or our tribe," she added.

Rowing back downriver to Jamestown that evening, Adam voiced his relief that Diana was so very accepting of Catherine. "Not every citizen in Jamestown so blithely overlooks the fact that she took a second husband whilst her first one still lives. That she did so does put her outside the church, and the law," he admitted. "But Catherine is my sister. I forgive her everything."

Diana recalled the awkward silence at the Larsens' dinner table that night when she brought up the fact that Adam's sister was gone. Now she understood why nothing further was said on the subject. "Perhaps many colonists do, indeed, believe your sister to be dead."

"Quite possibly." Adam nodded. "Most especially the newcomers." He went on to tell her that following Catherine's disappearance, Noah put out the story that he had fought with the Indian warrior who barged into their home and abducted his wife and newborn babe. Because Noah was found wounded and unconscious on the floor of his home, a spent musket at his side, it was speculated that Noah had mortally wounded the Indian, who stumbled into the forest and later died. Noah's injuries, Adam said, were little more than a knife wound to his shoulder. And a blow to his pride.

"Catherine later told me the whole truth," Adam went on, "that Phyrahawque could have easily killed Noah that night, but instead he merely snatched his musket from him and fired a hole into the roof."

"That hole is still there!" Diana cried. "Noah has not repaired it, and now the roof leaks dreadfully."

"You have been in Colton's home?"

Relief flooded Diana. Now that the door had finally been opened on the subject she had so longed to discuss with Adam, she told him all about her friend Faith, and Noah's reprehensible treatment of his wife. She also told him a few of the things Sallie Mae had said following her recent visit with Faith, although she mentioned nothing about the muskets or gunpowder or any of the threats made on Sallie Mae's life. "Faith said that Noah once killed a man, a colonist."

Already, Adam was nodding. "I confess I always believed Noah killed Victor, Catherine's first husband. Even Catherine believed that Noah killed him. But nothing could be proven. Catherine knew no one would believe her suspicions regarding Noah, and that it would come down to her word against his, so she remained silent. At the time, she feared for her own life and that of her unborn child."

"Then, you would advise Sallie Mae and me to do the same? Say nothing?"

He nodded. "It happened a long time ago. There would be no way to prove anything now. No doubt, you young ladies would also be disbelieved."

"But apparently Noah actually confessed to committing the crime," Diana pointed out.

"Had he been drinking when he told Faith he killed a colonist? Sober, Noah can charm anyone into believing anything. For him to voluntarily confess to committing the crime would be expecting a great deal of him. Asking Noah to be truthful about anything is, in my estimation, asking too much. Mark my words, when the governor's laughter died away, any charges against Noah Colton would be summarily dropped. And then, poor misguided Faith, or you—if you were the one who brought the matter before the governor—would be slapped with a charge of slander. To say something at this juncture would serve only to call down trouble upon your own head, Diana." He leveled a solemn look at her. "I do not wish to see that happen to you, or to Sallie Mae. Best to stay silent on the subject. You've nothing to fear from Noah. Pray, let us keep it that way."

Although she wasn't entirely convinced that Sallie Mae had nothing to fear from Noah, Diana was grateful for Adam's wise counsel. She toyed with the notion of telling Adam all she knew, but in the end, decided against it. Adam's advice would, no doubt, be the same. There truly was no way to prove that Noah Colton was guilty of anything. On the other matter, that of helping Faith, he also didn't have a clue what could be done to remedy the woeful situation.

"Noah hasn't a scruple to his name. To him, a wife is a possession, and although he may treat her shabbily, he is jealous of anyone who might attempt to lure her away from him. No doubt he would view your plan to help Faith by removing her from his home as meddling and take offense." He exhaled another sigh. "Again, I believe the wise course is to let it lie. Faith will give birth and thereafter have no time for anything beyond caring for her husband and her child."

Diana digested everything Adam said. "I can easily see now why you so heartily dislike Noah."

"I have known him the bulk of my life."

The admission surprised Diana.

"Noah is the friend who came to Jamestown along with my father and me."

"You were chums as boys?"

Adam nodded. "My father loved him like a son. Catherine was sweet on him. Noah's father was the clergyman in our small village."

Suddenly one more piece of the puzzle fit. Noah being the son of a clergyman explained his knowledge of Latin. Diana shook her head. She had learned a great deal today. "If Noah put out the story that he killed Phyrahawque, that also explains why the mighty Indian warrior who flies through the forest on a huge white stallion is now a legend in Jamestown."

Adam nodded, his strong arms rowing the small boat, the oars causing lazy ripples to float away on the water. "Phyrahawque is a mighty warrior and a wise leader. I expect the story Noah forwarded about him has greatly enhanced his image, not only amongst us light-skins, but also amongst his own people. Many Indians also fear Phyrahawque."

"Do you not fear for your sister's safety, living in the forest with the Indians?"

"I confess at the outset Catherine's choice was difficult to accept, but she is far happier now than she has ever been in her life. I cannot begrudge her that, nor would I attempt to take her or her children from their father. Phyrahawque is, indeed, a mighty warrior, but he has a gentle nature. The loving kindness that shines from his eyes when he looks at Catherine and their children is . . . something to behold."

"I do hope Noah was not terribly cruel to Catherine. When I met her she told me to warn my friend Faith about him. I knew you heartily disliked him," she added. "I detected anger in your tone every time his name was mentioned."

Adam ceased rowing to gaze intently at Diana. "You detected nuances in the tone of my voice?"

A smile softened her expression. The only sound now was the gentle lapping of the water against the side of the shallop. It occurred to Diana that snug inside the little boat with Adam, she felt no fear of being on the water. "Indeed. I have noticed that when you are amused the corners of your eyes crinkle. Or your lips twitch." She paused. "When you are angry, your jaws clench, and when you are agitated, your left thumb drums on the table."

He resumed rowing. "You astonish me, Miss Wakefield."

She looked down, one hand fingering the thumb of her soft lambskin glove. "I wonder why you sometimes address me as Miss Wakefield and other times, you use my given name."

"I had not realized my manner of addressing you varied."

"I quite like it when you use my given name, Adam."

"And I quite like *you,* Diana."

By the time they reached Jamestown, darkness enveloped them, yet even as Diana stepped across the rippling water to the shore, she felt no fear. In her heart, she knew she had fallen even deeper in love with Adam today, and also with his beautiful family, but still she had no notion how to convey her true feelings to him.

As they commenced to walk through the shadowy streets of Jamestown, she toyed with the notion of simply telling him. But what if he merely laughed at her? Or what if her feelings for him were unreciprocated?

"You are unusually quiet," he observed.

She looked up at him in the dim light. Beyond his tall form, she could see flecks of light flickering through the windows of houses they walked past. The night air felt so cold and crisp, she wished to snuggle closer to him, but didn't dare. "I was thinking about the day we met, at the cooper's home. I had called on Sallie Mae that afternoon. Your horse was tied to the railing in front."

He grinned down at her. "I recall. I thought you were quite lovely, although terribly shy. You refused to meet my gaze."

"I had the oddest feeling that we had met before. Now I realize it was because you are so very like your sister. Her loveliness mesmerized me the moment I saw her."

"Catherine has that effect on everyone."

"How sad that so many have turned their backs on her now that she is . . . with an Indian."

"According to society's reckoning, Catherine is completely

beyond the pale." He paused. "It pleases me, Diana, that you accept her as you do."

When they reached the Larsen doorstep, he turned to gaze deeply into her eyes. "What I behold in your heart, Diana, is even more beautiful than your lovely face."

The longing to throw her arms about his neck nearly overwhelmed her; instead, she felt color rush to her cheeks and her lashes fluttered downward. Gazing shyly back up at him, she silently watched him turn to go.

"Adam?" She found her tongue.

He looked back.

"Will I see you again?"

His lips twitched. "Indeed, you will, my dear. You will see me again and again."

Smiling her delight, Diana let herself into the house. Perhaps her dream of finding love and happiness and a new family here in the New World was at long last, about to come true.

Two mornings later, Diana sat alone in her bedchamber still dreamily thinking about the pleasant afternoon she'd spent with Adam and his sister and the three adorable children. Though it was a cold winter day, there was not a cloud in the sky. The sun shone brilliantly. Diana heard winter birds trilling in the bare treetops and the sounds of children calling and shouting to one another as they played in the street. Suddenly, a whoosh of cold air swept into the room, telling her the front door of the house had been flung open. When she distinctly heard William Larsen exclaim, "Mary, gather the children, something terrible has happened!" Diana froze.

Chapter 35

Diana ran from her bedchamber into the great room just as Mary also appeared, both women's eyes wide with fear.

"What is it, William, what has happened?"

Agitated, Larsen paced before the blazing fire. Running a hand through his hair, he demanded to know if Cheiwoga was with the children.

"William, what is it? You are frightening me!"

Larsen's nostrils flared. "Indians are on a rampage. Only minutes ago, a band of shrieking, howling savages dumped the bodies of all three traders inside the fort. The men were obviously killed in a frenzy, arrows sticking in all directions from their bodies."

Both women gasped.

Larsen strode to the front door and threw the bolt. "Are the windows secured?" he demanded.

"The Indians are pillaging homes in Jamestown?" Mary cried.

After testing the front window, Larsen flung the draperies together, shutting out the bright sunlight. "We are uncertain where the Indians are now. Or what they will do next."

When he turned around, Cheiwoga and the children had silently appeared in the room, the Indian woman's expression also a question.

"Get out!" Larsen bellowed. "Leave the children and get out!"

The frightened woman dropped the hands of both children

and scampered to a small door near the hearth where she generally entered and exited the house. Larsen followed her and bolted the latch behind her. "In future, we will manage on our own!" he told his wife.

"But the traders, William, are all three of them . . . dead?"

"Sharpe was still alive, but just barely. Unfortunately, his tongue had also been cut out so he was unable to tell us what happened."

"What of . . . Noah?" Diana asked in a small voice.

Larsen directed a dark gaze her way. "Colton is the only one of the three who, in addition to being scalped, had also been bludgeoned beyond recognition; his arms and legs broken, a dozen or more arrows sticking from his chest."

"Oh-h!" Both women gasped afresh.

A hand to her breast, Diana fell onto the backless bench fronting the table.

"You were recently at Parke's plantation," Larsen accused. "Was that treasonous sister of his also present?"

Diana gulped. She had not breathed a word about Catherine to the Larsens and certainly had not mentioned that Catherine was also at the plantation when she visited there. Should she lie now to protect both sister and brother? In an instant, she made her choice. "I thought Adam's sister was dead."

Apparently mollified, the irate man seemed to dismiss Diana altogether when his wife asked, "Has anyone told Noah's little wife that her husband is—?"

"The girl will be told eventually. For now, we've more pressing matters to deal with. Colonists must be alerted, militia summoned, settlement secured. There is no saying where or when the savages will strike again."

"Poor dear child," Mary murmured, "I understand she is having a difficult pregnancy."

Diana bravely stood. "I will tell Faith that Noah is dead."

"Neither you nor Mary will leave the house!" Larsen bellowed as he stalked toward the door. "I am off to meet with Yeardley and the council. We will, no doubt, declare war on the Indians."

"On *all* of them?" Mary's eyes widened. "We will surely lose, William. We are vastly outnumbered."

But her plea went unheeded as her overset husband charged from the house. "Throw the bolt and let no one in . . . or out!"

The morning seemed to drag on interminably. Mary did her best to keep the children quiet. Although Diana read a Bible story to Edward, she could not concentrate on the words. Her mind continued to hark back to Catherine telling Adam that she feared something was afoot. Her words made sense now. Apparently Phyrahawque knew of the attack that would soon be made on the traders and did not want the band of angry Indians to come after his wife simply because she had once been married to the trader-man. Apparently the Indians had had enough of Noah's deceptions and thievery. Though Diana would never admit it aloud, a part of her believed that Noah's death was for the best. With him gone, it would be far easier to help Faith, to remove her from that filthy hovel and take her . . . where? To Sallie Mae's home? Or perhaps to Harvest Hill. Adam would surely provide her sanctuary.

Diana looked up from her reading. At her feet, Edward had curled up on the braided rug before the fire and drifted off to sleep. Seated beside Diana, Mary, staring into the flickering flames, snuggled the baby close to her breast.

"I can no longer read," Diana whispered. "I am far too frightened for Faith."

At that instant, a light rap sounded at the door. The women exchanged alarmed gazes. "I will see who it is," Diana said.

"Do be careful!"

Diana crept to the window near the door and peeked out. Relief washed over her when she saw who was standing on the doorstep. As quietly as possible, she unlatched the door and let a wide-eyed Sallie Mae into the house.

"I came the minute I heard the terrible news."

"No one has yet told Faith. We must go to her. I'll fetch my cloak." Diana sailed past Mary on her way to get her cloak and gloves.

"Oh, Diana. Must you?" From her chair before the fire, Mary's tone was alarmed. "William will be . . . oh, my dear, do be careful. And do hurry back."

Both girls climbed atop Sallie Mae's black horse. Diana wrapped her arms tightly around Sallie Mae's middle as she spurred the spirited animal into a gallop. As they flew though the deserted streets of the settlement, fear instead of smoke seemed to rise from every chimney of every rooftop. Now and again the pungent whiff of lye stung the girls' eyes as they sped past the home of a colonist where some goodwife had been busily washing the family linen. But the task abandoned, the colonist's yard now lay deserted. Diana's gaze darted here and there. The savages could be lurking anywhere, behind that tree, beyond that shed. They galloped past the occasional settler, the man's gaze anxious, his eyes also alert as he scurried toward the fort on foot. Some carried muskets, a few clutched other weapons: an ax, a hatchet, one even carried a scythe; but Diana never once spotted a single Indian.

At length, they reached the last house on the dusty road that gave onto the woods. Both girls fairly flung themselves to the ground and raced into the house. In their haste, they did not notice the stench of sour ale and spoiled refuse inside. Hurrying through the great room to the darkened bedchamber, they found their friend Faith lying abed, her eyes closed.

"Faith," Sallie Mae said as the girls drew near the rumpled

bed. "We have come."

Faith's eyelids fluttered open. The look of dull defeat in her gaze caused Diana's breath to catch in her throat.

"Ye have come to . . . tell me . . . he is dead."

"How did you know, sweetie?" Diana murmured. She reached to brush a stray wisp of auburn hair from the girl's fevered brow.

Faith swallowed. "I heard . . . hue and cry . . . in the street. All three traders are . . . dead?"

"We are so very sorry, Faith. Sallie Mae and I came to fetch you." It was clearly evident their friend was frightfully weak. "Goodman Smithfield can carry you—"

"No." Faith weakly lifted a hand. "No."

"But, Faith," Sallie Mae protested. "We must take you—"

"No." One arm resting on her distended belly, the other hand reached to shove aside the bedclothes, which at once released the coppery scent of blood into the air. When Diana and Sallie Mae saw the girl's blood-soaked garments and the drenched bed upon which she lay, they both gasped aloud.

"Faith, what have ye done?" Sallie Mae cried.

A hand flew to cover Diana's mouth as she stared aghast at the bloody bed.

"God is . . . punishing me . . . for my sins."

"God does not punish us for our sins," Diana said, "He forgives us."

"My sins . . . too terrible."

"No-o!" Sallie Mae cried.

"There is no sin so great that God cannot forgive!"

"Vengeance . . . is mine . . . sayeth the Lord."

Sallie Mae fell to her knees beside the blood-soaked bed. "Tell me what ye have done to yerself, Faith! Perhaps it is not too late!"

Several seconds passed before Faith had gulped in enough air to proceed. "I told . . . Goody Smithfield's Indian woman . . . everything. I was angry. I . . . betrayed Noah. I am guilty of . . . vengeance."

"Sallie Mae, fetch Goody Smithfield. She will know what to do!" Sallie Mae scrambled to her feet and ran from the room. Diana turned to Faith. "Noah was not killed because of you, Faith. The Indians have long known of Noah's treachery."

Faith's tongue moistened her parched lips. "But they did nothing . . . until I . . . spoke the truth. I never meant for . . . the others to die." She coughed and a drool of blood oozed from her mouth. "God is . . . punishing me." Her eyelids fluttered shut.

Her own heart pounding with fear, Diana tightly grasped her friend's hand. "Stay strong, Faith. Goody Smithfield is on her way."

Faith attempted to shake her head in protest. "I now know how Prudence felt. Life is . . . too wretched to be borne."

"Life will seem brighter once your baby comes."

"I wish to see . . . Prudence." Her ragged breath grew shallow. "To tell her . . . how sorry I am for . . . not helping her."

"Prudence's death was also not your fault." Diana tried to console her distressed friend.

"We should never . . . have come. I . . . *am* to blame. Noah's death *is* . . . my fault."

"You are wrong, Faith. Please, listen to me—"

"Noah believed Ann Fuller."

"Are you saying that Noah believed you were a witch? That you possess . . . *powers?*"

Faith nodded weakly. "He feared that my power would . . . cause others to see . . . the truth. About him. He drank. The more he drank . . . the more he talked."

Which, Diana realized now, was why Faith had revealed so very much of what Noah said to Sallie Mae.

"But you are not a witch, Faith. I know you are not."

The flicker of a smile twitched at the corners of Faith's parched lips. "I managed . . . to kill Noah. Now, God is . . . killing me."

"Noah also killed a man. Perhaps Noah's death is God's way of punishing *him*. You are not a witch."

Faith seemed unable to draw sufficient air into her lungs to form a reply, then Diana heard her faintly murmur, "Perhaps, you are wrong . . . about m—" She seemed to make one last fruitless gasp for air, then Diana watched her friend's head fall limply to one side.

"No-o. Dear God, *no!*"

But Diana knew her friend was gone. Tears filled her eyes as she sank to the floor and began dully to repeat the Lord's Prayer. When Sallie Mae returned—without Goody Smithfield or her husband in tow—Diana looked up and simply said, "Faith is gone."

"They was afraid to come, they said the Indians—"

"We must pray for her soul. For both of their souls."

"Fret no more, Diana," Mary Larsen said after Diana told her what had happened, although not the part about Faith declaring it was she who had betrayed her husband, or that at the end, Faith had alluded to being a witch. True or not, Diana vowed, that was one secret she would never reveal. "Faith and Noah and their unborn child are now safe in our Heavenly Father's arms," Mary added.

Diana nodded sadly. She deeply regretted spending so much time attempting to sort out the mystery regarding the muskets and gunpowder. "I should have insisted upon helping her."

"You mustn't blame yourself, dear."

"I feel I am partly to blame for her death."

"That is not true, dear. None of us knows why God chooses

to call his children home."

Diana bit back a sob. Knowing what she did now about Noah, she knew she could no longer stay with the Larsens. Mister Larsen would never believe the truth about the trader, nor countenance a word said against him. "I wish now to go with Sallie Mae. We must console one another."

"I understand, dear. Truly, I do." Mary followed Diana into her bedchamber. "William will send for Reverend Martin. The men will take care of things. They will lay poor Faith next to her husband, more's the pity."

Diana hurriedly tossed her few belongings into Sara's oiled valise, the one Diana had pulled from the muddy shores of the River Thames nearly a twelvemonth ago, the night Sallie Mae, parading as a stable lad, had come to her rescue. She also lost her dear friend Sara that night. Now Faith was gone. Of her beloved friends, only Sallie Mae remained.

"Tell Mister Larsen I am indebted to him for sheltering me since I came to Jamestown." Grasping the handle of the valise, Diana glanced about the room. "Sallie Mae is in the shed harnessing Bug-a-Boo."

"I will miss you, dear. As will the children."

"I will never forget your kindness."

Mary followed Diana back through the house. "Go swiftly and beware the Indians. You recall they burned Samuel's workshop to the ground."

Diana bit back an angry retort. No one now save she and Sallie Mae knew that Noah had committed that crime. With him gone, all of his lies and deceptions would be put to rest along with his battered body in a grave that would soon be overgrown with weeds and forgotten.

Reaching the door, Diana quickly embraced Mary. "Tell the children I will come for a visit."

"I pray we will all live to see another day, and that my children will grow up to have children of their own. Go now, before William returns and forbids you to leave."

Diana smiled tightly. "I am convinced the danger has passed and life in Jamestown will return again to normal."

"Godspeed." Mary unbolted the door and Diana slipped out.

On the way to the Wingate home, Diana told Sallie Mae a bit about what Faith had said before she drew her final breath. "I do not believe Faith was a witch," Diana added sorrowfully. "But apparently Noah thought she was. Apparently his fear of her 'powers' drove him to excessive drink, and whilst in a drunken fit, he confessed to her his many transgressions."

"It does make sense."

"I pray God will forgive them both for their secrets and lies."

Sallie Mae nodded. "The three of us, you, me and Faith, came to Jamestown carryin' secrets."

"And we have each been guilty of telling lies in order to protect them."

"It's a bit hard to hate Noah now, ain't it?"

"Indeed," Diana murmured. "I find now I simply feel sorry for him. It is true he killed a man. But in the end, he grew fearful, just like the rest of us." Diana exhaled a sigh. "It all seems such a waste now."

"I believe it is best if we cease to think on it," Sallie Mae replied solemnly.

Diana nodded her agreement. "Perhaps in His infinite wisdom, God will show mercy upon Noah and forgive his soul." She thought a moment. "Still, I cannot help but wonder why Noah did not simply kill Faith himself. Since he'd made it clear that he'd not let anyone stand in his way."

"Perhaps he truly loved her."

"Or perhaps he truly did fear her powers and believed, as many do, that the only way to be certain a witch is really dead is to burn her alive at the stake."

"I thought witches was hanged."

"Some are. But many folks believe that a truly powerful witch can change her shape and at the last minute, easily escape the noose."

"Well," Sallie Mae said wryly, "whichever method Noah'd choose would likely draw undue attention. Someone surely woulda' noticed if he tied his wife to a stake and set fire to her."

"Most especially since the governor did not believe Faith had the evil eye and had already dismissed all charges of witchcraft against her." Noah, Diana concluded, had simply met his match. "I, too, am guilty of fabricating lies and of meddling," she confessed. "I pray God will forgive my sins."

"I am certain you have nothing to fear on that head, Diana."

Although the puzzle was now solved, the answer changed nothing. Faith was dead and so was Noah, and other than Sallie Mae, Diana now had no one to turn to. Unless . . .

"Sallie Mae," she asked anxiously, "does Samuel know the way to Adam Parke's plantation?"

Sallie Mae grinned. "I expect he does."

CHAPTER 36

Given the circumstances, Samuel Wingate did not think it wise to take Diana into the forest that day.

The following day, despite the fact that fear and anxiety still ran rampant in Jamestown, the grieving colonists all emerged from their homes to attend the funeral service held for the three traders and Faith. Although she did not really expect to see him, Diana strained for a glimpse of Adam, but he was not there. It irked her to sit quietly between Mary Larsen and Sallie Mae whilst the governor and other esteemed members of his council, including William Larsen, eulogized Noah Colton.

What, the governor demanded of no one in particular, could have caused such a blatant betrayal of the trust the brilliant trader had cultivated with the Indians? Why? Why? Why had God allowed such an atrocity to happen? And how, how, how would Jamestown, or more aptly, the entire New World, get along now that this valuable and highly respected giant of a man had been cut down by the very ones he trusted? Where would the settlement turn now for help in dealing with the naturals?

That little was said about Faith except that she had come over on the Bride Ship and was Noah Colton's wife deeply saddened Diana. But it reminded her of a comment Faith had made following her sister Prudence's drowning: that no sweet words had been said over her. No sweet words had been said over Diana's parents or her dear friend Sara either. Life, Diana concluded sadly, was not always just.

Still, the entire colony of Jamestown, it seemed, could not lament long enough or loud enough for Noah Colton. Diana began to fear that if the men did not soon leave off lamenting his death, they would declare the man a saint, leaving her no choice but to spew forth the bile that rose in her throat following every word of praise they heaped upon his head.

A few days into the following week when it appeared that all danger from the warring savages had passed, Samuel at last agreed to take Diana on horseback to Adam Parke's plantation.

So anxious was she now to see Adam, Diana scarcely slept the night before. By the time she spotted Harvest Hill through the trees, daylight was nearly gone. Diana thanked Samuel and bravely rode the rest of the way alone. Nearing the house, she spotted Adam outdoors, his shirtsleeves rolled up as he labored to split fresh logs for the fire.

"Adam!" she called.

He turned. "Diana?"

Flinging herself from Bug-a-Boo's back, she ran toward the man she loved with all her heart. By the time she reached him, tears of emotion filled her eyes.

"I had to come!"

"What is it, love?" He laid aside his ax and gathered her into his arms. When she began to shiver from the cold, he led her into the house. In the parlor they sat side-by-side before the blazing fire.

"Tell me what is amiss."

Now that she was finally here, Diana wasn't at all certain how to begin . . . or where to begin. "I . . . assume you know Noah is dead."

He nodded. "Phyrahawque came for Catherine and the children only today. Phyrahawque told us what happened.

But . . . surely that is not why you came."

Diana looked down. Why could she not simply tell him how she felt? That she loved him? That she wished to spend the rest of her days with him? "I . . . came because I . . . I wish to tell you the whole truth about myself."

"Ah. The sordidness that will require my forgiveness, eh?"

His small jest relieved a bit of her anxiety. "My truth is not so sordid as all that." The hint of a smile flitted across her face. "I simply wish you to know . . . how I came to be here, in Jamestown."

Now the floodgates were open, she found it easy to pour out everything—about her friend Sara who was set to come to the New World, about their journey into London, the carriage accident, her parents' and Sara's drowning, how she felt helpless to save them, and that it was Sallie Mae who pulled her from the River Thames.

She smiled wanly. "Sallie Mae also has secrets in her past. I know not if she has revealed the whole truth to Samuel. I pray you will hold what I am revealing to you in strictest confidence."

"All of your secrets are safe with me, my dear. Yours and Sallie Mae's."

Diana inhaled a long breath before telling him how distraught and alone she felt after the tragic carriage accident, about how in the flick of an eye she decided to take her friend Sara's surname in order to board the Bride Ship.

"I daresay you chose wisely," he said quietly. "I am certain it must have appeared to you that you had no other choice."

"I could have endeavored to find my kinsmen in London, but I hadn't a clue where to look."

She told him about Prudence's death on the crossing and how helpless she felt not being able to save her either. "Once again, it was Sallie Mae who flung herself into the raging ocean in an attempt to save Prudence. And Faith never knew of it. She scorned Sallie Mae. Yet Sallie Mae continued to help her. I . . . still feel terrible about what happened to Faith, and also . . . about the children—"

Adam leaned forward. "The children?"

Tears of sadness welled up in Diana's eyes. "I feel so sorry for the children of Jamestown who must wear iron collars. I wish I could adopt them all!"

Adam reached to grasp her hand. "You are one small girl, Diana." His tone was sympathetic, "You cannot heal everyone's hurts."

"But, I feel so useless. Sallie Mae is brave. She saved my life. She took firewood and food to Faith." Sad hazel eyes appealed to Adam. "Tell me what I can do to make myself useful, Adam. I have changed so very much since I came to Jamestown. In England, I was expected only to marry and provide my husband with an heir. Had I stayed in England, I would never feel as I do now. I knew so little then of pain, of sorrow or injustice. I knew about nothing that truly matters."

"And what do you believe now that truly matters?"

"Loving people; caring for one another."

He smiled. "And is there a . . . particular person you care for?"

With tears streaming down her cheeks, Diana nodded.

Adam drew breath. "Might I ask who that person is?"

She looked down. By all that was right, Adam should declare himself first.

"I am a good deal older than you, Diana. I have outlived one wife. I have also known the sorrow of losing one's parents. But since meeting you, I . . . feel alive again. You are helping me, Diana. You have vastly helped me."

"Truly?" Her innocent gaze was trusting.

"You have awakened my heart. I think of you constantly. I look forward to week's end for the opportunity to see your smiling face at services. Until now, I have said nothing because I feared you were not ready to . . . take me on."

"Oh, Adam," she sighed. "I want nothing more than to become your wife and mother to little Eli." Her chin trembled with pent-up emotion. "There is no man on earth I would rather spend my life with than you. I love you with all my heart."

The smile on his face broadened. Rising to his feet, he scooped her into his arms. "And I love you, Diana." He hugged her to his chest, then, gazing deeply into her shining eyes, he lowered his head and gently pressed his lips to hers.

Her heart pounding, Diana returned the kiss. And several more.

Because it was far too late for her to return to Jamestown that night, Adam instructed Hespatakie to prepare the guest bedchamber for her. The Indian woman placed a heated stone at the foot of the bed to warm it.

The next morning Diana broke her fast sitting across the table from Adam, who held his little son Eli on his knee. Together they laughed at the child's unintelligible babbling.

"The boy knows as many Powhatan words as he does English ones."

"Perhaps Eli will one day become Jamestown's premier trader. Growing up with his little cousin Silverhawque, he will undoubtedly know a great deal about the Indians."

"True." Adam nodded. "Now they are simply two little boys who like to play together. Neither Eli nor Silverhawque are aware of any difference between them, such as the color of their skin."

"Which is perhaps the way God intended for all of us to be," Diana said. Love shone from her eyes for the man sitting across from her, and for the dear little boy on his knee.

"You will make a wonderful mother to my son," he breathed.

"To *our* son," he modified.

Afterward, she and Adam set out on horseback for the Wingate home. On the way, Adam told her more about life at Harvest Hill.

"Come spring I will spend every day working alongside my men in the fields. Growing tobacco and harvesting it is a daunting task, but in the end, all one's hard work pays off. You will be alone a great deal," he warned.

"I will have your little son to care for."

"*Our* son," he reminded her.

She smiled. "Our son."

He told her Hespatakie did the bulk of the cooking, but she'd be expected to lend a hand when they put up winter provisions.

"A good many of the plantation women perform tasks together," he said. "Sewing, making soap, the like."

"I once helped Sallie Mae and Goody Weston make soap."

He smiled warmly. "You will get on very well as my wife, Diana."

She had never been so happy. After telling Sallie Mae and Samuel the news, they paid a call on Reverend Martin that very day, and that very day, he posted their banns.

A fortnight later, on a cool bright Sabbath morning, Mister Adam Parke and Miss Diana Wakefield were united in holy matrimony. A smiling Sallie Mae Wingate, wearing a fashionable purple frock, stood beside the bride, who was dressed in a similar gown of a deeper shade of lavender than her bridesmaid's. Sallie Mae's husband Samuel Wingate stood beside the groom.

Her sweet face shining with love, Diana solemnly repeated her marriage vows, then lifted her chin to receive the customary kiss from her new husband. In her heart, she praised the dear Lord for bringing her to Jamestown and for helping her find exactly what she had hoped to find here: a loving husband and a new family to replace the one she had so tragically left behind in England.

After the ceremony concluded and everyone had eaten their fill of the sumptuous wedding feast, Sallie Mae, her blue eyes twinkling merrily, sauntered up to Diana and whispered into her ear. "I've a secret to tell ye."

A look of horror marred Diana's lovely face. "I never wish to hear another secret in all my life!"

"Then I have no choice but to tell ye a lie." Sallie Mae's eyes danced.

"A lie? Oh, Sallie Mae, must you?"

Her tone turned saucy. "I am *not* to be a mother, and Samuel will *not* be a father."

Diana began to laugh. "That is wonderful news, Sallie Mae! Have you told Samuel?"

"What are you young ladies giggling about?" Adam asked as he and Samuel joined their merry wives.

"Nothing," Sallie Mae replied quickly. She cast a speaking look at Diana, whose smiling eyes rolled skyward.

Sallie Mae locked her arm through her husband's and gazed coyly up at him. "I've something to tell ye, Sam."

Diana gazed lovingly up at her new husband. All things considered, this wild, untamed wilderness called the New World was, indeed, a safe and wonderful place to be.

AUTHOR'S NOTE

Many of the girls who traveled to the New World in the early 1600s to become colonist's wives were, in fact, as young as thirteen. When my story began, the three main characters were still in their teens. Four hundred years ago, unmarried girls were taught to live according to rules: their parents' rules and those dictated by the church. They did not have access to self-help books and guidance counselors, as do young girls of today. They did not listen to Oprah or Dr. Phil. Their preparation for marriage came from the Bible, and from published works of the time known as Conduct Books.

In 1564, Thomas Becon wrote *The Booke of Matrimony,* passages from which were quoted well into the 1600s. Becon inspired many of Mrs. Douglass's teachings, as did those of Henry Smith, whose book, *A Preparation to Marriage,* was published in 1591. To prepare them for marriage, young people attended Marriage Sermons. Henry Smith was a popular Marriage Sermon speaker whose lectures were very well attended. In 1619, William Whately gave a Marriage Sermon titled *A Bride-Bush* in which he called marriage "a happiness beyond all other earthly blessings." Popular speaker and author Jeremy Taylor wrote *The Mysteriousness & Duties of Marriage,* in which he referred to marriage as "God's first blessing" and declared that the married person's body was "ministered to by angels." William Gouge wrote *Of Domesticall Duties* in 1622.

From the Bible, young girls were taught that the man was the head of the household and that they must submit to their husbands in all ways. A marriage lecturer named Vives warned unwed girls by declaring "if she was disobedient to her husband, she was an offence to her own father and mother and kin." Vives declared that a wife must "bear with her husband even if he was evil. If he struck her or even beat her, she must try to understand his mood and to accord herself with him as long as she could feel she obeyed God's will." Vives assured girls that if they "could live peaceably with their husbands in adversity that they would inherit eternal glory."

For a young wife to question whether or not she was happy after marriage, or whether or not her marriage was "what she wanted," was simply not done. For her to speak aloud of her discontent would have been considered self-indulgent and against the church. Young people who entered into marriage knew that the married state was for life. After 1602 there was no legal escape from marriage except by the death of one's spouse. In the event of desertion, remarriage was not allowed if both parties were still alive. Divorce was not only expensive and time-consuming, but it took an Act of Parliament to grant one.

During this time period, girls knew nothing about examining their feelings, or questioning why they loved a particular man, or if their husband's "ways" were wrong or harmful or detrimental to their own health and well-being. If a young woman found herself in a loveless or abusive (by today's definition) marriage, her only option was to suffer in silence, to ask God to forgive her for *her* sins and to help her make it through another day. I expect many young wives and mothers were not only confused but also overwhelmed by the challenges they faced. But to whom could a young bride turn? Older, supposedly wiser, women were trapped in the same situation. Yes, by 1620, Jamestown and other settlements in the New World were considered to be thriving, but figuring out how to create a happy fulfilled life, while also dealing with the many daily inconveniences facing the colonists, was still hundreds of years into the future.

Regarding my reference in *Secrets and Lies* to rape, it was quite common in those days for men to be sexually abusive to young women in their employ, even as it later became common for plantation owners to sexually abuse their black female slaves. In his book, *Everyday Life in Colonial America,* Dale Taylor states on page 128: "Rape was a crime against married or engaged women, or girls under ten. In *all other cases,* the woman was considered to have given in to her inherent lustfulness and consented, reducing the crime to mere fornication. Witnesses were essential to prove rape for if she did *not* cry out for help, she consented by not resisting." From this, it is apparent that men in the early 1600s who sexually molested their female servants did not believe that (1) they were doing anything wrong beyond committing fornication, or adultery if they were married, and that (2) there was little to no chance they could ever be proven guilty of rape.

My allusion to witchcraft in the Jamestown colony is supported by historical fact. Fear of witches and witchcraft was prevalent for centuries in Europe before the Salem witchcraft trials took place in this country in 1692. In England in 1563 Parliament passed *The Witchcraft Act,* which imposed the death penalty on those guilty of "invocations or conjurations of . . . evil spirits." In 1584, Englishman Reginald Scott authored a book titled *Discoverie of Witchcraft.* During his reign, King James I republished a book he had written in 1597 called *Daemonologie,* warning his English subjects against the dangers of witches and demons. In 1612, in Lancashire County, England, eight women and two men were hanged for the crime of witchcraft. The accused were believed to have sold their souls to the devil or to evil spirits in return for the power to kill or lame whomever they pleased. The Pendle Witches, as they came to be known, were believed to have murdered a minimum of seventeen people in and around the Forest of Pendle.

Before that, King Henry VIII accused his wife Anne Boleyn of practicing witchcraft after she consulted with sorcerers in an attempt to conceive a son. Henry and Anne's daughter, Queen Elizabeth I, also believed in sorcerers and as a young woman, avidly studied the art of alchemy. She later gave Essex a magic ring said to protect him from highway robbers while traveling.

Early records show that witches were persecuted, tried and put to death not only in England, but also in France, Germany and Italy. Settlers from these countries who came to the New World brought with them strong superstitions and beliefs in witchcraft: Witches could cause strange diseases to manifest in children, they could change men into horses, put spells on muskets and other weapons, and cause cattle to choke on hair balls. Swedish immigrants believed that when one sold a healthy cow, the owner must snip and keep a hank of its hair if he wished good luck to remain on his own farm. Another Swedish superstition also involved cattle: on Christmas Eve every cow briefly acquired the ability to speak. Because this miracle was never witnessed, it understandably remained unproven. Swedes also believed that saying the Lord's Prayer backward would prevent rain during a harvest. German immigrants believed that anyone unfortunate enough to be born during the first three days of a new year was doomed to an unhappy life. Germans also declared that a newly purchased pig must be backed into its pen if it was to remain healthy; that is, of course, until the day it was slaughtered. In Virginia, if a man happened to stumble over a grave in a field, everyone knew that he had better jump backward over it; otherwise, one of his own kinsmen would soon die.

Many scholars believe that the Salem witchcraft trials ended the hunt for, and persecution of, witches in America. Records show, however, that a witch trial was held in Virginia as late as 1706, and another in North Carolina in 1712. Doubtless there were other such trials elsewhere in the early American colonies. In later years, witches were no longer put to death in England or in America; however, belief in witches and their antics and other superstitious beliefs continued to flourish in this country well into the eighteenth century.

BIBLIOGRAPHY

Brown, Ralph A., and Marian R. Brown. *Impressions of America.* New York: Harcourt, Brace & World, 1966.

Cantacuzino, Marina. *A London Christmas.* Gloucester, UK: Alan Sutton Publishing, 1989.

Cheney, Glenn Alan. *Thanksgiving.* New London, CT: New London Librarium, 2007.

Coddon, Karin, ed. *Colonial America.* Farmington Hills, MI: Greenhaven Press, 2003.

Collier, Christopher, and James Lincoln Collier. *The Paradox of Jamestown, 1585—1700.* New York: Benchmark Books, 1998.

Dow, George Francis. *Everyday Life in the Massachusetts Bay Colony.* New York: Benjamin Blom, 1967.

Earle, Alice Morse. *Home Life in Colonial Days.* New York: Grosset & Dunlap, 1898.

Emerson, Kathy Lynn. *The Writer's Guide to Everyday Life in Renaissance England.* Cincinnati, OH: Writer's Digest Books, 1996.

Gunn, Giles, ed. *Early American Writing.* New York: Penguin Books, 1994.

Hakim, Joy. *The First Americans.* New York: Oxford University Press, 1993.

Hall-Quest, Olga Wilbourne. *Jamestown Adventure.* New York: E. P. Dutton, 1950.

Hawke, David Freeman, ed. *Captain John Smith's History of Virginia.* New York: Bobbs-Merrill, 1970.

______. *Everyday Life in Early America.* New York: Harper & Row, 1988.

Hoffer, Peter Charles. *Law & People in Colonial America.* Baltimore: John Hopkins University Press, 1992.

Holler, Anne. *Pocahontas: Powhatan Peacemaker.* New York: Chelsea House Publications, 1993.

Hoobler, Dorothy, and Thomas Hoobler. *Captain John Smith: Jamestown and the Birth of the American Dream.* Hoboken, NJ: Wiley, 2006.

Horn, James. *A Land As God Made It, Jamestown and the Birth of America.* New York: Basic Books, 2005.

Kupperman, Karen Ordahl. *The Jamestown Project.* Cambridge, MA: Belknap Press of Harvard University Press, 2007.

Lange, Karen E. *1607: A New Look at Jamestown.* Washington, DC: National Geographic Society, 2007.

Lizon, Karen Helene. *Colonial American Holidays and Entertainment.* New York: Franklin Watts, 1993.

Middleton, Richard. *Colonial America: A History 1565—1776.* Malden, MA: Blackwell Publishing, 1992.

Moulton, Candy. *Everyday Life Among the American Indians.* Cincinnati, OH: Writers Digest Books, 2001.

Pearson, Lu Emily. *Elizabethans At Home.* Stanford, CA: Stanford University Press, 1957.

Picard, Liza. *Elizabeth's London: Everyday Life in Elizabethan London.* New York: St. Martin's Press, 2003.

Philbrick, Nathaniel. *Mayflower.* New York: Viking, 2006.

Pobst, Sandy. *Life in the Thirteen Colonies: Virginia.* New York: Scholastic Library Publishers, 2004.

Price, David A. *Love & Hate in Jamestown: John Smith, Pocahontas, and the Start of a New Nation.* New York: Vintage Books, 2003.

Sakurai, Gail. *The Jamestown Colony.* Danbury, CT: Grolier Publishing, 1997.

Stevens, Bernadine S. *Colonial American Craftspeople.* New York: Franklin Watts, 1993.

Taylor, Dale. *Everyday Life in Colonial America from 1607–1783.* Cincinnati, OH: F&W Publications, 1997.

Terkel, Susan Neiburg. *Colonial American Medicine.* New York: Franklin Watts, 1993.

Thompson, John, ed. *The Journals of Captain John Smith: A Jamestown Biography.* Washington, DC: National Geographic, 2007.

Townsend, Camilla. *Pocahontas and the Powhatan Dilemma.* New York: Hill and Wang, 2004.

Vaughan, Alden T., ed. *America Before the Revolution, 1725–1775.* New York: Prentice Hall, 1967.

Warner, John F. *Colonial American Home Life.* New York: Franklin Watts, 1993.

Web Sites

Powhatan Language & the Powhatan Indian Tribe. www.native-languages.org/powhatan.htm.

Smith, Captain John. Generall Historie of Virginia: 1624. Glasgow, 1907. www.historyisfun.org.

Rediscovering Jamestown. www.apva.org, www.preservationvirginia.org.

Historic Jamestown. www.historicjamestowne.org.

Essays, maps, and engravings. www.virtualJamestown.org.

Werowocomoco Research Project. http://powhatan.wm.edu/.

ABOUT THE AUTHOR

Marilyn J. Clay grew up drawing pictures, reading voraciously, and writing stories. After graduating from college with degrees in Art and English, she illustrated children's textbooks, owned a graphics design studio in Dallas, became a fashion illustrator and a creative director for a fashion magazine, and served as University Editor for The University of Texas at Dallas. For sixteen years, she published *The Regency Plume,* an international newsletter focused on the English Regency. She has had six Regency romance novels published, three translated to foreign languages, and designed the Romance Writers of America's RITA award statuette. *Secrets and Lies* follows *Deceptions* in Marilyn J. Clay's colonial American Jamestown series. Her Regencies and nonfiction works are available on Kindle. For information about Marilyn's novels and artwork, visit http://theregencyplume.tripod.com/.